THE
DEVIL'S
HEART

STAR TREK ®

THE NEXT GENERATION™

THE
DEVIL'S
HEART

Carmen Carter

POCKET BOOKS

New York London Toronto Sydney Tokyo Singapore

POCKET BOOKS, a division of Simon & Schuster Inc.
1230 Avenue of the Americas, New York, NY 10020

STAR TREK is a Registered Trademark of Paramount Pictures.

This book is published by Pocket Books, a division of Simon & Schuster Inc., under exclusive license from Paramount Pictures.

Library of Congress Catalog Card Number: 92-51109

ISBN: 0-671-79325-X

First Pocket Books hardcover printing April 1993

10 9 8 7 6 5 4 3 2 1

POCKET and colophon are registered trademarks of Simon & Schuster Inc.

Printed in the U.S.A.

*Dedicated to Kate,
who read my books
even before she knew me.*

Acknowledgments

Dave Stern believed in this story from the very beginning and fought for two years to provide me with the opportunity to write it. If not for him, you would be holding some other *Star Trek* book in your hands right now. I owe him a debt beyond measure. Thanks, Dave!

Many of my friends have followed the progress of this book since its inception, some page by page. Their wealth of comments and reactions helped me to structure the book and then to polish it. My special thanks go to:

Kate Maynard, who casually said, "Why don't you make the archaeologists Vulcans?" T'Sara was born as a result of that suggestion, and my path into the story began to unfurl.

Cary Dier, who wanted to read this book years before the first words were written and never lost hope that the Heart's story would eventually see print. Her keen eye and relentlessly linear mind made her an invaluable editor.

Delia Turner, who steadfastly wielded her blue pencil over the manuscript pages when she would rather have just enjoyed a good read.

Jessica Ross, for letting me use the idea behind the Borg sequence.

ACKNOWLEDGMENTS

The Star Trek universe has become increasingly complex, so there were times when I needed to delve into technical details beyond my own understanding. Several people provided me with timely assistance.

Betsy Ramsey and Cary Dier provided me with computer terminology that wouldn't make hackers scream in agony or die laughing, and thus saved me from public humiliation.

"Doc" Audrey Gassman cast her professional eye over Beverly Crusher's medical scenes. I confess that I decided to let dramatic license overrule authenticity in a few instances, so don't blame Audrey for the results.

I also relied heavily upon the *ST:TNG Technical Manual* by Rick Sternbach and Michael Okuda for information about the construction and operation of the *Enterprise*. Any errors in that area are due entirely to my misunderstanding of their exceptional reference work.

Great Minds Think Alike Department: In the two years between the submission of my first proposal of *The Devil's Heart* and the final acceptance of the storyline by Paramount, Peter David wrote *Imzadi* and saw it published. By sheer coincidence, both of us made use of the Guardian of Forever, although it plays only a minor role in my story. For the record, neither of us was aware of the duplication.

THE
DEVIL'S
HEART

Prologue

Iconia was dead.

The planet itself would remain intact until its sun went nova, but the world he had known, the soft tissue of life rooted on the fragile mantle, had already been destroyed. Constant weapons bombardment had vaporized its shallow seas, incinerated its verdant plains, and eradicated all who had once inhabited its surface.

Barbarians.

Kanda Jiak swayed on his feet as yet another tremor rocked the Gateway chamber. The station was shielded against detection and proof against even a direct photon blow, but the land itself was shifting under the impact of ceaseless explosions. Could there be anything left worth attacking on Iconia, any city that had not been razed by the firestorms? Or was their hatred so fierce that they prolonged this holocaust out of sheer bloodlust? After First Contact, the philosopher Senega had warned that a disparity in technologies could unsettle other races; she predicted that knowledge of Iconian superiority would foster fear and distrust; and as a final legacy before her death, she prophesied the final fatal connec-

1

tion between fear and the rage to destroy what could not be understood.

Demons of air and darkness, that is what they call us.

Ironically, after the diplomats failed to turn back the space-faring hordes gnawing at the edges of the Empire, the Gateways that inspired such superstitions had provided the ultimate salvation for the surviving Iconians. Over the last few days, ten thousand of his people had slipped through narrow rips in the fabric of space; they and their descendants would build new homes on the remote outposts of Ikkabar, DiWahn, and Dynasia. Iconian language and culture would survive even if this world was pummeled into dust.

Now it was Jiak's turn to cross the threshold.

He settled the weight of the Gem into the crook of his arm. In a room of gleaming metal panels, humming consoles, and the crackling blue energy of the Gatekey, this rough rock seemed strangely out of place, yet it had built this structure just as surely as the legions of architects, engineers, and technicians. The secrets of the entire universe were locked inside this ancient relic, and three generations of Iconians had only begun to coax out that knowledge.

Blue. Red. Blue. Jiak tapped out a familiar sequence on triangular buttons. A jagged bolt of light shot out of the central control globe, forming a dancing umbilical cord to the narrow frame of an activated Gateway.

He scanned the cycle of shifting landscapes. Three habitable worlds were open to him, yet his final choice meant nothing to him; all were primitive compared to Iconia.

Farewell.

Jiak stepped forward, and through.

No! This is wrong!

On the other side, the blare of a red sun seared his eyes, and a gust of dry, heated air sucked the moisture from his lungs. He sank deep into the ground as shifting grains of sand gave way beneath his feet; his weight had doubled under the force of a heavier gravity.

This desert world was not of his choosing, and he could not survive in this harsh climate.

"Save me!"

For the past three decades, the Gem had been his talisman. He stroked the stone in supplication, but in the midst of this blazing oven it had turned ice cold.

Jiak collapsed onto the ground. The Gem fell from his weakened grasp, and he watched it roll out of his reach.

"Betrayed," he whispered hoarsely. "You have betrayed me. Why?"

Alone out of all the Iconians, Senega had called the Gem a curse rather than a blessing . . . the price of True Knowledge comes high . . . too high.

As he slipped toward death's embrace, Jiak dreamed that his life was nothing but a mirage shimmering in another mind . . .

She cried out her fear of dying alone in the desert until her flailing arms wrapped themselves around the stone.

Not lost after all. Not dying.

She awakened enough to separate her own thoughts from Jiak's identity, to remember that she was safe in her own bed on a planet called Atropos. Her covers were tangled about her feet, but the Gem's heat warded off the chill night air seeping into her tent. With a sigh of relief, the old woman curled on her side, tucking herself around the sphere as if afraid it could still tumble away from her.

Ko N'ya.

Yes, that was the Gem's name in her language . . . and that language was Vulcan.

I am T'Sara.

Even lying still on her cot, T'Sara's body felt limp, drained by the ordeal that had been Jiak's and her own blurred together. True sleep would help restore her strength, but she begrudged the waste of time. She wanted to explore the lives of all who had held this stone before her, and that quest could take many years to complete.

Tonight, in this dream, T'Sara had seen her homeworld through the eyes of an alien being, felt the heavy pull of its gravity on a body that was not her own. Most important of all, however, she had discovered another bridge in the meandering path of the Ko N'ya. The leap from far-distant Iconia to Vulcan would have eluded her otherwise.

Any thought of embarking on another search was suspended by the sound of movement in the compound outside. The other archaeologists had cleared the rubble from around their shared habitations, but T'Sara had no patience for such domestic touches. She could hear the scuffle of boots climbing over mounds of fallen stonework and crumbling walls. By her count, at least four Vulcans were headed toward her tent.

The visitors came to a stop just outside the domed enclosure. Someone's hands brushed lightly across the fabric wall until probing fingers found purchase on the ridged seams marking the entrance. A shaft of moonlight slipped through the widening breach.

"T'Sara?"

Because it was Sorren, she said, "Enter."

The young man slipped inside, then resealed the portal with more care than she had taken. Each day she was less and less concerned with the basic necessities of survival. If not for Sorren's prodding, she would forget even to eat.

She made no move to activate a lantern, and he did not ask for light. The darkness made it easier for him to ignore the Ko N'ya when they talked.

"T'Sara, your cries have awakened everyone in the camp . . . again."

The others who had kept him company remained huddled outside. She could hear them taking shallow breaths of the frigid air. "I was restless."

"These spells of unrest are becoming more frequent."

"I have slept away too much of my life," said the woman. "I intend to make better use of my remaining years."

"I am still young, however; and I will never reach your august age if I am robbed of my sleep now." There was a hint of wry humor in Sorren's remark, a rare self-indulgence from such an earnest young Vulcan.

"Then go back to bed, my child, and I promise not to wake

4

you again." Her position as leader of the expedition invested her words with the authority of a direct command.

"Very well," he said. She heard the rustle of the seals parting, felt a cool draft of air, then saw Sorren's willowy silhouette as he stepped through the opening. "I will bring you some tea in the morning."

He closed the entrance, plunging her back into darkness and warmth, yet T'Sara could hear him whisper to his waiting companions. "It was only a bad dream."

"That is what you said last night," said Sohle. His gruff voice merely roughened when he tried to speak quietly.

"It is no less true for having happened a second time."

"How many disturbances does it take to convince you, Sorren?" asked T'Challo. "T'Sara is ill."

"My last medical scan did not confirm any ill health."

"You are no doctor," said T'Challo. "And it is time we . . ."

The voices faded away before T'Sara could overhear any more of their discussion, but she had no interest in their bickering. Morning was still a few hours away.

She had just enough time to fall into another dream.

CHAPTER 1

Captain Jean-Luc Picard slept with the same air of authority he carried with him on the bridge of the *Enterprise*. Even in the privacy of his darkened cabin and the haven of unconsciousness, he maintained a commander's demeanor. The silken blue pajamas he wore only emphasized the hard contours of his body: he lay flat on his back, his lean frame held at attention except for one arm flung above his head; his lips were set in a firm, unyielding line.

It was not a comfortable pose, but then Picard was not a comfortable man.

A spacious cabin with generous furnishings, their smooth wash of pastel colors, a lush plant gracing the table by his bed—none of these luxuries had softened his sense of responsibility, or his conviction that danger could be held at bay only by unceasing vigilance.

As if to vindicate his subconscious wariness, the trill of a communications call marred the silence that had surrounded him. The captain was awake and alert before the second ring of the summons had sounded. Quickly rolling to a half-sitting position, he cleared his throat to erase any trace of sleep from his voice.

"Picard here."

"Incoming message from Starbase 193, Priority Two."

"Thank you, Ensign Ro. I'll take it here in my quarters." Knowing the commander of the starbase in question, Picard automatically scaled down the urgency of the call by at least one degree; Miyakawa had a tendency to overdramatize, an occupational hazard for officers mired in the mundane activities of an administrative post. He allowed himself the indulgence of a leisurely stretch before slipping out of bed to activate the transmission.

At his touch, the viewscreen on the wall flickered to life. The first part of the communiqué was brief and to the point, but then Vulcans were not given to circumlocution. Miyakawa's subsequent request for aid was brusque, even imperious, as if she suspected the captain of the *Enterprise* might balk at such an insignificant task.

Perhaps there were some captains who would resent the diversion of a galaxy-class starship on a small errand of mercy, but Picard was not one of them.

Besides, he wanted this particular mission.

A combination of natural reticence and Starfleet training stripped Picard's voice of emotion as he activated the intercom and issued orders to the bridge crew. His excitement was strictly personal and had no place in the execution of duty.

"Course change initiated."

Data's voice betrayed no reaction to the new coordinates, but Picard could swear he heard Ro Laren's muffled curse in the background.

Merde. The captain belatedly remembered the consequences of this diversion on the crew's own affairs. "Increase speed to warp six." That was faster than the assignment warranted, but a more moderate pace might tax everyone's patience.

In the time it took him to step out of his pajamas and into a clean pair of uniform pants, Picard was hailed over the intercom yet again.

"Riker to Captain Picard."

"It's a routine diversion, Number One," said Picard,

aiming his reply at the ceiling intercom. "At warp six, we'll only experience a short delay." He slipped the tunic jacket over his head, confident that the heavy cloth could not drown out his first officer's emphatic response.

"With all due respect, sir, routine missions aren't rated Priority Two. If this takes more than a few extra days . . . well, it's damn inconvenient for Geordi's maintenance agenda at spacedock."

"Ah, yes, the new magnetic constrictor coils," said Picard, careful to keep the smile on his face from seeping into his voice. Reaching for his boots, the captain did his best to allay Riker's anxiety. "In my opinion, the urgency of the situation was slightly overstated, so we should be able to make up the lost time without too much difficulty. Schedule a briefing this morning for all senior officers so we can ensure a swift completion of this mission."

"Aye, sir."

The soft hum of the open channel cut off.

Now that the immediate demands of duty had been fulfilled, Picard walked out into his living room and turned his attention to breakfast. As was his custom, he ordered a light menu for two from the food synthesizer. However, reflecting over Riker's strained reaction to the change of plans, the captain considered the probable effect on his guest's more volatile temper.

"Computer," he said quickly. "Extra butter and cream."

He had added two different fruit juices and a jar of orange marmalade to the spread on the table when his chief medical officer arrived. Some mornings, Beverly Crusher appeared with the slightly rumpled look of a doctor just coming off duty, her eyes darkened by fatigue, but the previous night must have been free of medical emergencies because her face was free of stress; the lines of her blue medical coat were sharp and crisp, and her long red hair was neatly coiled at the nape of her neck.

"What's the special occasion?" Crusher asked, surveying the offerings.

"Nothing beyond the pleasure of your company."

"Hah!" She spooned a large helping of eggs onto her plate. "If I weren't so hungry, I'd seriously question your motives."

"I'm wounded by your suspicion, Doctor."

Fortunately, her mouth was too full for her to press the issue, even in jest.

Judging from her animated spirits, Beverly seemed to have missed the news working its way through the ship's grapevine; he would be able to inform her of the diversion himself. Later. He sought safer ground by asking about the progress of her latest theatrical production. Unfortunately, his mind was too preoccupied with their new destination to actually absorb much of her answer.

Picard had started on the French toast when she turned their conversation to the ship's next port of call.

"There's a restaurant on Luxor IV," said Crusher, her blue eyes bright from the recollection, "that serves the best pancakes in the entire Federation. It would make a great place to celebrate—" she caught herself just in time, "shore leave."

"I'm afraid there will be a slight delay, just a day or two, in our arrival to Luxor IV. We've been diverted to a fringe-territory star system on a medical assistance mission." Picard assumed a look of nonchalance in the face of Beverly's sharpened attention. "In fact, the *Enterprise* was chosen specifically for this mission because of your expertise in handling Bendii's syndrome."

"What?" she stopped mid-bite into a scone lathered with butter. "I'm not an expert in Bendii's syndrome! I've only seen one case in my entire medical career."

"Yes, well, it seems that even one is one more than any other doctor outside of the Vulcan Medical Academy."

"And Ambassador Sarek wasn't even my patient," she said, shaking the scone at him for emphasis. "I didn't treat him, I just diagnosed the condition."

"Think of this as an opportunity to expand your medical experience."

"Thank you, Captain, but I prefer to do that on my own time and not at the expense of my patients."

Picard poured her a fresh cup of tea with a generous measure of cream. "We're also the only Federation starship within easy reach of the system. Under the circumstances, there is no other option for you or for your new patient."

The doctor sighed in reluctant agreement. "So just who is this Vulcan with Bendii's syndrome?" She hastily popped the last bit of bread into her mouth, then accepted the cup he offered her.

"A scientist. T'Sara."

Beverly frowned. "You say that name as if I should know her."

"Forgive me," Picard said. "Just because I've followed her work for years, I expect others to be aware of her as well." He nodded in the direction of his bookshelves. "She began her career as a preeminent folklorist renowned for her work in comparative mythology, then moved on to archaeology."

"Ah, so that's why she's out in the back of beyond."

"Yes," said the captain. "For the past ten years, T'Sara has been the expedition leader for an archaeological excavation on Atropos. Her assistant radioed for medical assistance, claiming that her erratic and irrational behavior appeared to be symptomatic of early stage Bendii's."

"She was diagnosed by an *archaeologist?*" Crusher rolled her eyes in exaggerated despair. "Save me from amateurs."

"I'm sure Sorren will welcome your professional assessment."

"I'm sure he's very welcome."

Despite her sarcasm, she seemed resigned to the necessity of the mission. Picard smiled with satisfaction as he offered the doctor another scone.

Timing is everything on a starship: from the warp drive engines that mesh matter and antimatter for a duration measured by the single pulse of an electron, to the life support systems that regulate the smooth flow of air through the vessel, even down to the measured movements of the crew who control the day-to-day operations of the ship.

First Officer William Riker was a master of timing. And the master of time aboard the *Enterprise*. His skillful juggling of the duty schedules had created a small window of opportunity, one that allotted a select group of people the same break from their respective shifts.

Five senior officers, the same ones who were due at a mission briefing later that morning, were gathered together in the close confines of Riker's cabin. Their captain, however, was conspicuously absent.

Picard's quelling influence fostered a degree of decorum that was entirely lacking at this assembly. During the early days of his posting on board the *Enterprise,* William Riker had tried to mimic the captain's imposing demeanor, only to find that he had a tendency to bluster and bully when he asserted himself. Over the years, the first officer had developed his own style, a looser and less obvious grip on the rein of command. So, for the moment, he let the meeting run its course without his participation; instead, he sat with his large frame sprawled carelessly over a chair, one leg thrown over the armrest, and watched everyone from under hooded eyes.

Geordi La Forge was the first to speak out. His metal visor might mask the expressiveness of his face, but he managed to communicate his indignation without any difficulty. "I say it's a trick! Somehow the crew of the *Telarius* managed to bribe someone to pull us out of the sector."

"Oh, honestly," said Deanna Troi. She had been the last to arrive and was perched on the edge of the sofa with her feet dangling uncomfortably off the floor. Her dark, exotic features and shapely figure usually inspired immediate gallantry from the men around her, but on this occasion not one of them had given up his seat. Riker suspected that the unintentional slight was at least partly responsible for the edge of asperity in her voice. "No one would go to that much trouble just for a—"

"You'd be surprised, Counselor," said Geordi. "Anybody who works on Starbase 193," he grimaced when he mentioned the base, "would sell his grandmother for ten credits."

"Cowards. They have no honor," said Worf. At the start of the session, before Riker could call out a warning, the lieutenant had settled his weight into a soft chair that would offend his warrior sensibilities as much as it offended his spine; Riker judged that the Klingon was as uncomfortable as Troi, but the sensible solution, an offer to trade places with her, probably reeked too much of Human courtesy. "Of course, a Klingon ship would never waste time on a *medical* call."

"Stop glaring at me," said Crusher to the security officer. "It's not as if I volunteered for this mission."

"However," said Data. "If not for your specific medical expertise, the *Enterprise* would not have been chosen for this particular assignment."

"Nonsense. Captain Picard told me we were the only starship in range of Atropos."

The android's face creased into his best approximation of a puzzled frown. If he saw Riker's frantic hand signal from across the room, he failed to fathom its meaning; Data continued inexorably. "I am afraid the captain was in error. At the time we received the distress call there were two other starships which were in greater proximity to the star system."

"Swell," muttered Geordi.

"This is not my fault!" Crusher's grim expression was a sure sign that she had just added deception to her list of grievances against Picard.

Now was the time, calculated Riker.

"I'm glad we've been diverted."

With all heads snapped around to stare at him, he followed the heretical declaration with a broad, flashing grin. "The delay gives us that much more time to hone our skills, and it gives the crew of the *Telarius* a false sense of security. They know we're their only serious competition, and if they think we won't show, we can catch them off guard."

"Yeah, but what if we don't make it to Luxor IV in time?" demanded Geordi.

"Nah," said Riker with a dismissive wave. "This is a

routine pickup. We'll be on our way back before you know it. The trick will be to make sure we don't arrive too soon. We may have to find some excuse to slow down our return trip, a way to ensure a proper entrance . . . say, five minutes before the championship begins."

His confidence was infectious, and he noted with satisfaction that Geordi had started to smile at the dramatic image Riker had conjured; Worf never smiled, but at least he had stopped snarling.

Unfortunately, Troi still looked dubious; Riker wondered if she could sense the uneasiness beneath his bluff. To his relief, she played along anyway. "Will, what about Captain Picard? Won't he suspect that something is going on?"

"Oh, I'll take care of the captain," said the first officer without blinking an eye at the ethical contortions that simple statement might involve. "All you have to worry about is improving your game."

Springing out of his chair, Riker flourished the deck of cards that he had kept nestled in the palm of his hand. Data was right on cue, as well, whipping out his dealer's visor and a stack of chips.

"We have just enough time for a practice round." Riker shuffled the deck back and forth in an arc through the air like a juggler. "Ante up, my friends, ante up. We're going to be the next poker champions of Starfleet!"

In the normal course of events, Picard resisted the temptation to read while on duty; his love of the written word was so intense and his concentration so focused that he never trusted himself to pay sufficient attention to the demands of command when he held a book in his hand. Just as a proper gentleman never shared his affections with more than one woman at a time, he confined his reading to his leisure hours.

On this mission, however, Picard had decided that a review of T'Sara's texts would help prepare him for his impending interaction with the scientist. After the briefing session with his senior officers, he had retrieved the Vulcan's books from his cabin and carried them off to his ready room. He even went so far as to sit on the sofa, rather than behind his desk, but he did so with the firm intention of only glancing at a few of the more recent forewords.

Reading her spare yet elegant prose, he was newly reminded of T'Sara's ability to present brilliant insights as if they were self-evident truths and to use logic to convince and persuade with a skill that was almost seductive. For a Vulcan, she possessed a keen understanding of her very emotional subjects.

When the door chime pulled him back to the present, Picard noticed with a start that he had been immersed in *Oral Histories from the Andorian Middle Kingdom* for over an hour. And the chime had been ringing repeatedly.

"Come."

The doors snapped apart and the ship's first officer barreled through the opening. "Captain, are you al—" Riker skidded to a sudden halt. His worried frown transformed into a knowing smile. "Oh, you've been reading."

"Guilty as charged." Picard sighed and tossed the book aside, only to automatically pick up another in its stead; this second choice had vellum pages that were thickly covered with the patterns of an alien script.

"We're within hailing distance of Atropos, but we haven't raised the campsite yet." Riker canted his head to one side in order to read the title on the spine; his lips tried to form the words, but failed. "I didn't know you could read Vulcan, Captain."

"I can't." Picard's eyes skimmed down a page. "At least, I shouldn't be able to . . . but occasionally, as I look over the text, I gather a hint of meaning in certain words and phrases."

"A legacy of your mind-meld with Ambassador Sarek?"

"Yes, I believe so." Picard set down the book on a side table with an exaggerated care that bordered on reverence. "This volume belonged to him; it was a gift to me from Perrin after his death."

One of the traits of a good first officer, as well as a good friend, was knowing when to share silence. A few minutes later they walked out of the ready room.

As he crossed the deck of the circular bridge, the captain noted which of his crew were working at the back duty stations. Deanna Troi and Beverly Crusher were already seated in the central command area behind the helm; Ensign Ro and Data were operating the forward stations. All accounted for, all as it should be, but he tried never to take that for granted.

"Still no response from the archaeological camp," said Worf from the aft deck.

"Continue hailing, Lieutenant," said Picard as he settled himself down into the captain's chair between Riker and the ship's counselor. "Status, Mr. Data?"

"Estimated arrival at Atropos in eleven minutes, thirty-two seconds."

"Steady as she goes, Helm." Picard fixed his eyes on the main viewscreen, studying a single pinpoint of starlight and the space that surrounded it. A most unremarkable sight, he concluded. At the beginning of time, when countless cosmic wonders had been sown throughout the galaxy, this area had been overlooked. In fact, to the best of his knowledge, the Federation's claim to this sector had been made solely to facilitate traffic through the territory; until T'Sara's expedition, no one had bothered to linger.

Troi spoke quietly, easing her way into his thoughts. "Beverly tells me you've followed T'Sara's scholarship for years. You must be looking forward to meeting her in person."

"Yes . . . very much so." He could never tell when the counselor used her empathic abilities to read him or simply judged his moods by subtle physical cues that he was unable to repress. Either way, Troi always caught him when he was brooding, so there was no point in trying to disguise his one misgiving about this encounter. "Yet, on the other hand, I do not relish watching another brilliant mind disintegrate from illness."

"Perhaps T'Sara will be spared Sarek's fate," said Crusher. "Medical research has advanced considerably in the last year; treatment, even a cure, may be developed in time to help her. That's assuming the diagnosis is correct; after all, I haven't confirmed anything yet."

"Well," said Riker. "If she does have Bendii's, we'd better warn Guinan to put away the breakables in Ten-Forward."

Crusher shook her head. "Psychic disturbances like the ones broadcast by Ambassador Sarek don't occur until a more advanced stage of . . ." She turned to the captain. "I only know that because I've been studying the medical literature on the syndrome. *Any* doctor in the Fleet could read a casebook file and do what I'm doing."

Just as Picard had feared, Beverly must be suffering the brunt of the crew's frustration; a speedy conclusion to this diversion would improve tempers all around. "Lieutenant Worf, have you established contact with the Vulcans yet?"

"Channels are open, but they are not answering our hail."

"You can't trust a bunch of academics to operate a simple subspace radio," said Riker with a heartiness that seemed a little forced.

"And archaeologists are the worst offenders," added Picard. He caught himself rapidly tapping one finger on his armrest and stilled the impatient motion.

"Long-range sensor scan complete, Captain." Data looked up from his console to confirm the transfer of incoming data to the main viewscreen, then nodded with satisfaction at the image of a marbled orb that appeared there. "Increasing magnification."

Picard leaned forward to study the surface features that were slowly coming into focus; gaps in the dusky-red cloud cover revealed mountains, valleys, several large canyons, scattered seas. "Data, are we close enough to scan for life-forms?"

"Accuracy may be somewhat compromised by the distance, but it is technically within range." After a few minutes of manipulating the console controls, the android turned around to face the captain. "Sensors detect no life-signs."

Riker shifted uneasily in his chair. "Try another pass, Lieutenant."

"Scanning the campsite . . . expanding the search area." At the sound of a soft beep, Data studied the console output. "Confirmed; there are no discernible life-signs on the surface."

The captain rose from his chair, taking a step forward as if to confront the planet itself, but the clouds had thickened, shrouding the surface below.

"Well, Number One," said Picard. "It seems this is not a routine mission after all."

CHAPTER 2

The United Federation of Planets was founded on a tenet of inclusion. Thus, as Starfleet charted and explored ever greater tracts of space, new worlds and their civilizations were eagerly drawn into the loose web of interstellar government. As in any rapidly growing organization, however, the Federation's reach occasionally exceeded its grasp. Inevitably, the grip of central authority weakened as it stretched out to the most recent annexations along an ever-expanding frontier.

Starbase 193 was held very lightly indeed.

From a distance, the station looked like a gleaming metal teardrop suspended in space. Its recent construction guaranteed a level of technology far superior to older, more established structures; and the sophisticated docking and maintenance services it offered were crucial for supporting commercial traffic through the sector. However, aside from the base itself, Federation presence in the sector consisted of one career officer.

Commander Miyakawa was forced to work without one of the standard benefits of a bureaucratic posting closer to home: a well-regulated support staff. Most of the day-to-day operations of the base were dependent on a shifting pool of labor: settlers who had run out of money before reaching their chosen paradise, technicians who had overslept a shore leave and lost their berth on a freighter, or confirmed drifters who would leave when the tendrils of civilization crept too close for comfort.

The permanent inhabitants of Starbase 193 were employed in business ventures of their own.

DaiMon Maarc sauntered into the murky recesses of the Due or Die with an air of confidence that marked him as an especially prosperous merchant among a race of merchants. His tailored gray business suit was cut to flatter his form; its sleeves were embellished with bands of jewel-encrusted cloth; and the broad, soft collar was studded with gold pins. For a Ferengi, it was a discreet display of solid financial success.

A DaiMon of means would usually avoid a bar as dingy and cramped as the Due or Die. Beauty was not the only quality that was missing from the establishment; cleanliness and comfort were also in short supply. However, Maarc had little interest in the quality of the decor. Tourists and the credit-poor rabble of the station might come here for cheap drinks, but he had come to see Camenae.

As he threaded his way between wobbling tables, the Ferengi calculated his current cash reserve for speculative ventures. Any purchase he made today would be expensive.

Most of Camenae's clients came to the bar with a specific question; if they could meet her price, most walked back out with an answer. Sometimes they paid with a handful of round tokens, the only currency that had any meaning inside the bar, but it was common knowledge that Camenae preferred an exchange for new information to tuck away in anticipation of future requests.

Besides forming the basis for her business, facts were also her private passion, and matching the right fact with the right customer brought Camenae a deep sense of personal satisfaction. So, on occasion she informed certain select individuals that she possessed an answer to a question they hadn't thought to ask yet.

Just such a notification had reached the Ferengi a few minutes earlier, and he had not wasted any time in responding to the call. Through experience, DaiMon Maarc had learned that Camenae did not let her goods grow stale. He would have been a much richer merchant today if he had paid more attention the first time she offered him a question.

"I'm expected," boasted Maarc to the Norsican who blocked his way. The guard nodded and stepped back to allow the Ferengi to pass through another door into an even darker room.

Maarc's steps faltered as he waited for his eyes to adjust to the dim light, but there were no unseen obstacles waiting to trip him. Shadows were the only decoration in the bare interior, and the only touch of color was in Camenae's burgundy robe.

New clients expected a greater display of security, but in time they realized that Camenae stored her most valuable capital beyond anyone's reach: her dark, round face betrayed no secrets, and a sleek cap of black hair covered the impenetrable vault of her mind. Tokens marking a financial transaction were redeemed elsewhere.

"I got your message." Maarc settled down at the small table where Camenae held court. "How much will this information cost me?"

She named a sum that made the Ferengi merchant hiss with outrage.

"A consortium of DaiMon in your guild could gather the necessary funds," she said, unruffled by his reaction. "And given the amount involved, I'm willing to extend a line of credit."

"That is very generous of you," he sniffed, "considering that *you* approached *me* with this offer. Be warned, I have no intention of assuming a ruinous debt to satisfy your greed."

"The price would be much higher if you were my first customer."

"What!" His gnomish face squinched into a mass of creases. A certain amount of theatrics was obligatory, but Maarc's irritation was only partially feigned.

Camenae shrugged an apology. "My preferred customer list has grown so large that there are, inevitably, certain conflicts of interest."

"Double insult!"

"It was never my intention to offend, DaiMon. To make amends for any ill feelings I have inadvertently created, I offer a discount."

He grunted in disdain, but his nose twitched at the whiff of a bargain. She knew him well enough to sense his renewed interest.

"Against my usual policy," said Camenae, "I will waive the charge for the question."

"You would have charged me for the question itself!" This time his outrage was completely genuine.

"Of course," she said. "Good questions are often far more valuable than the answers."

"You should have been a Ferengi." Maarc's good humor was partially restored by her audacity. "So, what is the question I should have asked?"

When he heard Camenae's reply, the DaiMon quickly reached into his vest pocket. Withdrawing his hand, he placed a token on the table. "Here is a deposit. I will raise the full sum of the answer's price within the hour."

He stacked a second token on top of the first. "I will double the amount if you also tell me the identity of your first client."

Then he added a third token to the pile. "And I will triple the amount if I am your last client to receive this information."

Camenae smiled as she gathered up the coins. "It's always a pleasure doing business with a professional, DaiMon Maarc."

CHAPTER 3

As the *Enterprise* swung into orbit around the yellow sun's lone planet, Counselor Troi had already begun her reconnaissance work for the mission. However, unlike the Away Team members who would soon transport to the ground below, her terrain was the flaring emotions of the crew.

Data's announcement had set off a tremor of tension through the bridge, and Picard sat at its epicenter. His rising anger was probably rooted in frustration at arriving too late to prevent whatever catastrophe had occurred on Atropos. Since the captain had a tendency to view this type of event as a personal failure, Troi made a mental note to monitor this reaction over the next few days. There should be no problem unless he persisted in blaming himself, but Picard usually recovered his perspective without her intervention.

Troi had exerted her empathic abilities to read the captain, but she strengthened her block against Will Riker's mind; *Imzadi* was all too easy to read, and at close quarters his emotions blared out like a siren. Each visit to a new world keyed the first officer's nerves with excitement, but this time the additional element of unknown danger let loose a surge of adrenalin that urged him to leap forward, to move, to run, to shout. Riker continued to sit quietly in place next to the captain, but she could see the younger man's cheeks flushing from the strain; still, he would be fine as soon as he had permission to lead the Away Team to the surface.

Beverly Crusher was another matter; her anticipation had soured into apprehension when she learned the results of the sensor scan.

"Beverly?"

"At least before I had a chance of helping my patient," said the doctor under her breath so only Troi could hear her. "Now . . ." She lifted the medical field kit off her lap and slung its strap over one shoulder in preparation for the Away Team's departure.

"Landing coordinates confirmed," announced Data as the flow of sensor information to the computers finally slowed. "The campsite appears intact."

Captain Picard's silent nod released a storm of movement.

Riker shot out of his chair, finger stabbing at the two helm positions. "Ro, Data, with me."

Dr. Crusher was already ahead of him, striding up the ramp to the aft turbolift.

"Energizing."

At the sound of Chief O'Brien's warning, Crusher braced herself for the frisson of the transporter beam. Seconds later, a whistling shiver rippled its way through the cells of her body, and when the shiver faded, the bright glare of sunlight stabbed her eyes. She dropped her head down, blinking furiously to clear away the dancing hot spots on her retinas. When the doctor's vision cleared, she could see her boots resting on a ground cover of orange moss.

She could also see a dead body lying at her feet.

Crusher lifted her gaze and counted three more bodies of Vulcans in the campsite: one stretched across the threshold of a field tent, two others fallen in a tangled heap onto the ground in the center of the compound. More bodies were probably hidden amidst the ancient, weathered blocks of stone that had tumbled from their foundations.

"Well, that accounts for four out of the ten," she said, pulling out her medical tricorder. She passed the instrument over a Vulcan male in his middle years, but the scan was little more than a formality since the cause of death was all too obvious: his chest and face were charred from a close-range phaser blast.

She proceeded on to the intertwined bodies. Dropping down to a crouch, she started another scan.

At Riker's direction, the rest of the Away Team kept moving, spreading out to survey the area around the landing coordinates. Their progress was slow as they skirted crumbling walls and broken columns and sought firm footing over piles of debris.

"There's someone over here," called out Ro. Crusher glanced up to watch as the ensign stepped over a moss-covered ridge to inspect her discovery. Whatever she saw on the other side sent the Bajoran stumbling backward. "Also dead."

The doctor bent back down to complete her inspection. The man and woman appeared to have been struggling over the phaser locked in the grip of the man's hand, then both had been killed by its activation.

"Some of the equipment was also damaged by phaser fire," said Commander Riker when he had circled back to the starting point. "But the wreckage is haphazard and nothing of value appears to have been taken."

Just their lives, thought Crusher, as she snapped shut the scanner.

Riker sighed as he surveyed the carnage. "We had outbreaks of violence on the *Enterprise* when Ambassador Sarek was on board; could T'Sara's illness have triggered a mass homicidal rage among these Vulcans?"

"Please, Commander," protested the doctor, as she rose to her feet. "It's far too early for me to speculate on—"

"Over here!" Data rarely raised his voice; she and Riker whirled around at the android's shout. "I detect life-signs ahead . . . extremely faint."

Crusher broke into a run to follow Data down a twisting

path, rushing past more dead bodies, ignoring everything but the call of the living.

It was a very weak call indeed.

When Crusher fell to her knees by the side of the elderly Vulcan woman, she feared that Data was mistaken or that T'Sara had loosed her hold on life only seconds before their arrival. The shadows of a looming tower had shielded the archaeologist from the full heat of the planet's sun, but the phaser wounds on her side and shoulder should have killed her long before.

"Data, I'm not getting any readings."

Then the medscanner trilled once; the life-signs were not only faint, they were also widely spaced.

"Of course," said Crusher. "She's in a Vulcan healing trance. I must get her up to the ship immediately." She hit her comm link. "Emergency transport! Two to sickbay."

T'Sara was no heavier than a child when Crusher gathered her up in her arms. The doctor whispered in the woman's ear, "You're safe, you're among friends, and you're going to live!"

As the transporter beam took hold of the doctor and her patient, Beverly Crusher hoped she could keep that last promise.

Over the many years of their service together, Picard had learned to trust his crew's observations and perceptions, to let them serve as his eyes and ears on Away missions. This rapport had helped ease the captain's sense of frustration at remaining so far removed from the reconnaissance of Atropos.

The planet loomed large in the conference room windows as two members of the landing party summarized their activities of the last few hours. Between Data's detailed recital of the essential facts and Riker's more subjective evocation of the carnage, Picard was able to recreate their experience in his own mind.

His first officer had worked his way through a list of the dead to the last archaeologist. "We finally found Skorret at the bottom of one of the excavation pits. He had been working near the edge, evidently cataloging some ceremonial weapons, when someone took the broken shard of a sword and stabbed him through the back."

"I detected blood-stained fingerprints on the hilt," said Data, "so it will be possible to determine who is responsible for Skorret's murder. Unfortunately, culpability will prove more difficult to establish in most of the other cases."

"Under the circumstances," said Riker, "the question of guilt or innocence hardly matters since the murderers are all dead, too. Assigning blame for this tragedy won't provide much comfort to their families."

In Picard's experience, Vulcans were less interested in comfort than in truth. "This is not so much a matter of justice, Number One, as it is of discovery. In order to unravel why these murders occurred, we must catalog the way in which they occurred."

"Standard forensic recovery procedures are already in effect," confessed the first officer. "Two paramedic teams have been assigned to remove the bodies from the planet surface and take them to sickbay for autopsies."

As Picard suspected, Riker's instincts were sound, even when he professed to balk at Data's dispassionate perspective. The captain smiled at the quizzical look on Data's face. The android appeared confused by the apparent contradiction between the first officer's words and his actions.

Checking a final notation on his padd, Riker then said, "Lieutenant Worf will supervise the removal of the team's personal effects from the planet surface, but what should we do about the research equipment and camp facilities?"

Unfortunately, Picard realized, this was one detail Commander Miyakawa had not thought to clarify in her briefing report. "Data, check the camp records to see who has jurisdiction over the property. We'll need instructions on whether the excavation will continue without T'Sara and the other Vulcans."

"I can't imagine it would be abandoned," said Riker.

"From what I saw, the ruins are quite extensive. There must be hundreds of artifacts to be recovered."

"How odd." The first officer's observation triggered a new avenue of curiosity for Picard. "What you describe would be considered a major research project, yet I don't believe I've ever heard of this site before."

"Falling behind on your journal reading, sir?"

"On the contrary," said Picard. Having achieved minor acclaim as an amateur archaeologist, he made a concerted effort to remain current in the field. "I used to follow T'Sara's research reports with great interest, but her last publication appeared nearly two decades ago, before the departure of the *Stargazer* on an extended deepspace mission. By the time I returned to the Federation, I had lost track of her whereabouts."

As soon as the captain turned to Data, the android nodded and said, "I will broaden my search to cover a profile of the expedition."

"Thank you, Mr. Data."

The background information would be useful, but Picard doubted it would provide any insight into the mystery of the violence on Atropos. Instead, his thoughts shifted to sickbay, where the answers to his most pressing questions lay just out of reach, locked deep in T'Sara's mind.

He would continue his investigation there.

She had a gaunt, wrinkled face and hair leached white by the passage of centuries. Curled on her side, covered by a light blanket, T'Sara appeared to be sleeping peacefully on the diagnostic bed. The only clue to her steep dive into a healing trance was the weak flutter of indicators on the medical scanner; her life-signs barely registered.

The loose sleeve of Beverly Crusher's coat brushed against Picard's arm. He couldn't tell if the doctor had moved to his side to offer silent comfort or to seek it out for herself.

"She's much frailer than I expected," whispered Picard. He knew T'Sara was unable to hear him, yet he couldn't bring himself to speak louder. "Her writing is so robust that I unconsciously imagined her to be a Vulcan Amazon, strong-limbed and tall."

"She must have an incredibly strong constitution to remain alive this long." Crusher's voice matched Picard's in softness. "Professionally speaking, there's little more that I can do for her except trust that the powers of her mind will heal the damage."

He stepped away from the bedside so that he could speak more freely. "The recovery work on Atropos is only beginning, but I will order an immediate departure if you feel her condition warrants the attention of a starbase medical facility."

"No." Crusher's answer was swift and firm. "I've already discussed that option with Dr. Selar, and we both determined that our medical assistance is equal to any provided outside of Vulcan. We could never reach one of their master healers in time to make any difference to T'Sara's recovery. The outcome will be settled within the next twenty-four hours . . . one way or another."

Her prediction measured out hope and despair in equal portions. Picard decided he must balance his expectations on the same razor-edge of uncertainty.

One of the medical staff had been hovering discreetly out of range of the conversation between the captain and his chief medical officer. She quickly took advantage of Picard's silence and stepped forward.

"Yes, Nurse D'Airo?" asked Crusher.

"The first shipment from the planet surface has arrived."

Picard could see the muscles in Beverly's neck tighten, and he realized the nurse was referring to the bodies of the Vulcan archaeologists. The doctor's voice flattened into a monotone as she issued a set of instructions concerning the preparations in the two surgical suites in sickbay.

When Nurse D'Airo had jotted the last instruction on her data padd and slipped away, Crusher turned back around to face the captain. "I hate autopsies," she said with a grimace. "When do you need these results?"

"As soon as possible. Until T'Sara awakens, the results of

the examinations are our only clues to explaining the murders. Not to mention that those results may serve to corroborate her future testimony."

"What?" said Crusher. "Captain, you make her sound like a suspect in the murders. Remember that she was one of the victims."

"Beverly, given Sorren's misgivings about T'Sara's failing mental health, I can't afford to accept her explanation of the events on Atropos without some supporting evidence."

Looking over at the huddled figure of the elderly Vulcan, Picard wondered if she would live long enough to tell her version.

The encampment on Atropos was still bathed in daylight when the *Enterprise* cycled into night. Seventeen hours after the priority distress call had pulled the starship off its course, weary crewmembers drifted into Ten-Forward or sought quiet refuge in their quarters; corridors fell silent, drained of their traffic; and lights dimmed or guttered into darkness.

Of course, there were some exceptions—a few stubborn pockets of activity—and one of these was the captain's ready room.

Picard rubbed the bridge of his nose in a futile effort to ease his aching head and blurring vision, then he scanned the text on his desk computer one more time.

"No, that's not right either," he muttered and tapped a key that would delete the paragraph he had just written.

The preliminary mission reports to Miyakawa and Starfleet command had been easy to draft, but the captain was experiencing more difficulty with his personal message to the director of the Vulcan Science Academy. On the surface, Vulcan culture was straightforward and rational, but appearances could be deceiving; logic took some unexpected twists and turns when mixed with primal issues such as murder and death. Picard had written and rewritten his description of T'Sara's injury and the death of her colleagues, but although his instincts could lead him away from certain phrases that might offend, he was less sure of what words to put in their place.

The trill of the ready room doorbell was a welcome distraction from the frustration of his task.

"Come," called out Picard, then waved his visitor to one of the chairs on the other side of the desk.

"Good evening, Captain," said Data with typical formality. "I apologize for taking so long to prepare my report. I was delayed by an unfortunate discovery: the camp's computer data files were erased by the electromagnetic pulse from a phaser blast."

Merde. Picard assumed the Vulcans were methodical enough to maintain duplicate records elsewhere, possibly at Starbase 193, but tracking them down would take more time.

"Fortunately," said Data, "I was able to reconstruct the broad outlines of the expedition's history from our own library archives. The project's formation was quite unusual."

"In what way?" asked Picard.

"Earlier Federation surveys established that most items of note were removed from Atropos several hundred years ago by the original inhabitants. Although the reasons are obscure, the colony was deliberately and methodically abandoned, thus rendering it of minimal scholastic value. As a result, T'Sara was unable to secure support from academic institutions to explore the ruins, and eventually she sold her family estate on Vulcan to fund the venture herself."

"A private expedition? That certainly bespeaks considerable dedication." T'Sara's reputation for radical departures from conventional scholarship was well-founded. "So what was the basis for her fascination with Atropos?"

"The avowed purpose was considered to be 'illogical,' even downright eccentric. T'Sara claimed that an artifact called the Ko N'ya was buried somewhere on the planet."

"The Ko N'ya?"

"Yes," said the android. "The Ko N'ya is—"

"Thank you, Data." Picard had become adept at stemming the android's excess of information. "However, an explanation won't be necessary. I'm quite familiar with the legends of the Ko N'ya, quite familiar indeed."

Ko N'ya.

Years had passed since Picard had uttered that name aloud. The emotions it evoked were rooted in childhood and threaded through the long years of his adulthood. His earliest recollections surfaced first and sent a shudder of excitement and fear up his spine and out through the tips of his fingers.

It was a delicious sensation.

CHAPTER 4

When the Iconian people fled through the Gateway to seek safe havens, Ikkabar was the most inviting of the new worlds. Its lush plains and shallow seas were familiar to homesick eyes, and a walk along the curving coastlines of the northern continent could trick the mind into thinking Iconia's destruction had been nothing more than a fading nightmare.

To this first generation of settlers, Ikkabar was a clean slate on which to reconstruct their history and culture. They raised cities filled with the same delicate architecture that had been trammeled to dust by enemy weapons, then they picked up the threads of their past lives as if nothing had changed. Many called the planet New Iconia, and this belief in a serene rebirth clouded their vision with bright colors that had been mixed under the light of a different sun.

The next generation was not so complacent.

Children born to this world saw more clearly than their elders; young eyes were not so easily fooled by the appearance of tranquillity. There were shadows on this landscape that had not been charted, subtle intimations of a darker geographic history that no one had bothered to read. The children still called themselves Iconians, but they restored the planet's name to Ikkabar as a reminder that they were strangers to this place.

Over the following centuries, vague fears of lurking danger began to harden into grim knowledge. The temperate climate that had greeted the early settlers was only a brief respite in a pendulum swing from one harsh extreme to another. The planet's orbit was irregular in the extreme, and its climate equally so; there came a time when the warm seas dried entirely in the heat of summer, leaving nothing but sucking mud flats that stretched to the far horizon; in winter, torrential rains washed away the mud and flooded the plains. Growing seasons contracted, bringing famine to a people who had never wanted for food. The foundations of their buildings began to shift and slide in the softened ground, then harden at angles with their walls cracked open and lofty spirals splintered.

Old traditions were abandoned as each succeeding generation desperately searched for new ways to grow food and to build structures that could safely house their families. Nevertheless, their offworld heritage was still treasured. When Ikkabar cycled back to a temperate climate and the halcyon days of legend returned, the Iconians rejoiced. There was talk of a cultural renaissance, and ancient tomes, carefully preserved, were opened and read by those who still retained some measure of that dying skill.

The joy was short-lived. Bitter disappointment took its place as the weather began to grow colder, and the seas turned to ice rather than mud. Much of the knowledge brought from Iconia was lost forever as precious books were burned as fuel. A few of the elders fought to save those relics; they were burned as well.

The hardy survivors of ancient Iconia now called themselves the Ikkabar. They moved from their ice-block fortresses to grass huts and back again with greater ease and fewer deaths, but even so, their numbers continued to dwindle.

Few remembered the sprawling cities that had been their first home; however, the buried remnants of these ancient settlements served as a beacon to space-faring races. The sensors of a passing Federation starship traced the record of past grandeur hidden beneath layers of ice and mud, and a discreet probe gathered data on the people who lived on this harsh planet. Little was done with the knowledge until an ethnographer at the Vulcan Academy of Science happened to read the field report. Each year after that, T'Sara petitioned the Federation for a more extensive survey of Ikkabar, and each year she was refused, but her constant pressure pushed its name higher and higher on the list of projects waiting for funding and personnel. At last, eight years after its first visit, the USS *Galeone* returned to the planet.

There were even fewer people alive on the surface now.

The census results unleashed a storm of controversy among the members of the survey team. T'Sara led a faction that favored First Contact so the Federation could provide aid to the scattered hunting tribes scrabbling for food. The Vulcan argued that these were the descendants of a people dependant on a highly developed technological culture. They were ill-matched to this primitive world and its demands; and just as one rescued the crew of a wrecked ship, these people were in dire need of assistance.

Unfortunately, her evidence for this theory was weak. Memories of Iconia and the Gateway had degenerated into a vague creation myth of a lost paradise, and the similarities to real places and events were impossible to corroborate. The opposing faction in the observation team maintained that the hunters were native to Ikkabar and that their evolutionary history had been erased by the same climatic upheavals that had toppled their ancient civilization.

That winter, more of the Ikkabar died than were born.

Despite the continuing drop in numbers, T'Sara could not convince her colleagues that this was not part of the normal fluctuations of population growth. There was ample precedent for the wisdom of leaving a preliterate culture in strict isolation, so the expedition withdrew.

As decades passed, one after another of the observation probes malfunctioned, stressed beyond tolerance by the brutal weather. Mounting tensions between the Federation and its enemies channeled Starfleet resources in other directions, so the probes remained silent for several years.

When the Federation was finally free to turn its attention back to Ikkabar, the children of Iconia had lost their battle to survive on this third world. All that remained of these long-suffering people was one hungry child found huddled by the coals of a fading fire.

The boy clung to his alien saviors with a desperation born of fear and loneliness. With what little they knew of his language the crew of the USS *Clements* learned he was called Kanda Jiak. T'Sara could have explained the importance of this name, but she had left Vulcan to continue her search for the Ko N'ya, and the news never reached her.

Fourteen years and a few months after he was rescued from Ikkabar, young Kanda Jiak took his first trembling steps toward reclaiming his lost Iconian heritage.

The decision to set off on this quest had been made on the eve of Jiak's departure from his second home on Redifer III. Perhaps it had been made even earlier, because he was one of the few students on that world who applied to an off-planet college. In either case, the trip to Terra Sol University had provided him with a convenient cover for leaving Redifer, one that would not arouse any opposition from his parents.

His resolve held firm throughout the first week of travel away from home, but when the passenger liner actually docked at Starbase 75, Jiak cowered in his cabin for the first hour of the brief shore leave. It would be so much easier, so much safer, to continue on to Earth as everyone expected him to do. His quest could wait until he was older.

Yet somehow the last survivor of Ikkabar suspected that if he failed to act now, he would never walk down this path in the future. After a few more years, Kanda Jiak would be fully assimilated into his life as a citizen of the Federation. The tattered threads of his origins were already worn too thin for memory; what little he knew of his people came from reading the ethnography reports from the crew of the *Galeone*.

So, just a few minutes before the passenger recall sounded, Jiak walked off the transport liner.

He had half-hoped someone would stop him, but the ship's first officer had smiled perfunctorily at the request to permanently disembark, and a harried crewman had ushered him to the docking gate. Evidently passengers frequently changed their itinerary midway through a trip.

Jiak faced a second trial of courage when he walked through the series of interconnecting domes that formed the main terminal. Overwhelmed by the massive complex and the jostling crowds that surged in currents around him, he felt like a small boy about to drown in a treacherous sea.

Rooted in place by fear and indecision, he automatically scanned the stream of alien faces for one that matched his own in color and shape. It was an old habit, a holdover from his early childhood when he still believed that someday his own people would miraculously appear to whisk him back to Ikkabar. Over the years he had grown to love his adopted world and his foster parents, yet the impulse to search persisted. On all of Redifer, and even here where over a dozen different races were passing by him every minute, Jiak was unique.

That would change soon.

"Hey! Are you lost?" The question was followed by a sharp jab to his arm.

"No," he said, turning to face his inquisitor.

"You look *very* lost." The woman was dressed in a rumpled blue jumpsuit, but he noticed the row of captain's pips on the collar. They weren't Starfleet design, so she was in charge of a civilian ship, possibly a freighter.

"I know where I am now," said Jiak, mustering a bravado he did not feel, "and I know where I'm going next, so I don't see how I could be lost."

Her hand darted upward to tuck a stray wisp of her hair back into place. It was a futile effort; the twisted braid she wore was bristling with errant curls. "So where are you going?"

His final destination was none of her business, yet the

young man was grateful for her concern, even if it was rather roughly expressed. Jiak compromised by revealing an intermediate stop. "Well, as it happens, I'm on my way to Davenport V."

The captain snorted derisively at his answer. "And have you already got a ticket?"

He shook his head. "I need to buy one now. I'd be in your debt if you could show me where to—"

"It's not a big tourist spot and that means top rates." Then she quoted the price of passage to that distant world.

The cost was staggeringly high. Jiak had been sure his spending allowance for the first term would cover all his travel expenses, but instead this one ticket would wipe out the entire allotment on his credit chip. He would be left with no funds for the final leg of his journey from Davenport to DiWahn.

His dismay must have been obvious, because the woman sighed heavily. "Go back home, kid."

"I'm not a kid, and I'll find another way to get there." He would have to find it soon. In another few days his mother and father would learn that he had never reached Earth and would begin to trace his steps. They had no authority to stop him now that he was of age, but Jiak wanted to escape their pleas for him to return to the comforting familiarity of Redifer.

As if she had been reading his thoughts, the woman said, "I guess you're too old to be running away from home, but you're still young enough to have stardust in your eyes. That won't last long on my ship."

"What did you say?" asked Jiak.

"The name is Captain Del," she snapped, "and I'm not offering you a glamorous job. Some kids expect a joyride through space, but you'll work damn hard for your berth."

"I don't want glamour, just free passage off this starbase."

"As long as you remember that, we'll get along fine." Del jabbed a finger at the bundle by his feet. "Is that all your freight?"

"Yes. I travel light."

"Good." She smiled her approval at this evidence of thrift. "Come on, then. Don't dally. I have a tight delivery schedule."

Still too startled to fully grasp his good fortune, Jiak hoisted the backpack into place and trotted after Del.

In truth, he hadn't had time to retrieve the rest of his luggage from the passenger liner, and those heavy cases were on their way to Earth by now. With careful tending, however, he could make do with the one change of clothing he carried with him.

His only other remaining possession, the one that weighed most heavily on his shoulders, was a copy of T'Sara's *Legends of the Iconian Diaspora.*

CHAPTER 5

Even from his position at an aft station console, Data easily followed the overlapping exchange between Captain Picard and Dr. Crusher.

"I'm sorry, Captain, but there has been no change in her—"

"What about the—"

"The autopsy reports are still being—"

"Let me know as soon as you have anything to report."

Data noted the way in which the two officers consistently anticipated the next request for information. Humans persisted in this curious behavior even though his own observations indicated that it often led to misunderstandings.

Data heard the captain's chair creak ever so softly as Picard's weight was lifted from the cushions. With his acute senses, the android easily followed the sound of Picard's distinctive tread as he moved up a side ramp to the elevated deck. He walked to a spot just behind Data's chair and stopped.

"Yes, Captain?" Data turned around, thus observing the cultural dictate of face-to-face interpersonal interaction.

"I'd like to see the team profiles again."

Data had kept the files cued for instant access. On reflection, he realized that this was an example of anticipating the captain's request.

Picard leaned over Data's shoulder and called the names out one by one. "Skorret . . . Sohle . . . Sorren . . ."

Data was careful to run the biographical profiles at a speed that would accommodate the captain's slower neural responses. The android's own positronic brain had already committed all the information on the archaeological team to memory after one scan, but he accepted the fact that Humans required this continual review process to fully assimilate new information.

"Soth . . . T'Challo . . . Tessin . . ."

The lagging pace was never boring, however, because Data could occupy himself with alternate sensory input, such as the conversations of the bridge crew passing by the science station; he could also generate simulated poker hands to calculate odds and refine his betting strategy; or he could compare various renditions of musical compositions to better understand the aesthetic impact of a conductor's style. At the moment, he was doing all three of the above.

"Run the Vulcan distress call again," said Picard.

"Yes, Captain."

Data cued the transmission to begin with the archaeology team's identification frame, written in both Vulcan and Federation Standard. This was followed by the image of a Vulcan male with the long face and high cheekbones characteristic of his species; although exact age was always difficult to determine in such a long-lived race, he appeared to be less than a half-century old. He was dressed in a dusty worksuit; the ruins of an ancient alien edifice served as his backdrop.

"I am Sorren, assistant to our expedition leader, T'Sara. It is the consensus of the archaeological team that T'Sara is in need of medical attention. Her behavior is growing increasingly erratic: she is prone to outbursts of emotion and persists in . . ." [crackle] . . .

"There," said Picard, with a jabbing motion of his hand. Data responded instantly, freezing the badly fragmented image on the screen. "That short burst of static obliterates part of Sorren's message. From the context, it appears to be an elaboration of what constitutes T'Sara's erratic behavior." The hand dropped and Data continued the review.

". . . is my belief these symptoms are characteristic of Bendii's syndrome. I request immediate transport so that T'Sara can receive appropriate medical treatment before her condition deteriorates any further."

Data stopped the recording and waited for the captain's next command.

"That missing segment was unimportant while Sorren was alive," said Picard with a thoughtful rub of his chin. "But now it may be our only clue as to what happened in the camp these last few days. Is there any way to recover the information?"

"If the team followed standard communications procedures, an intact original would be stored in the memory banks of the subspace radio transmitter. Unfortunately, the equipment damage erased all records of previous activity."

"Just as the expedition's data files were destroyed," said Picard. "If this vandalism is an example of T'Sara's 'erratic' behavior, she was also extremely methodical in its execution."

Data added two new tracks of activity to his mental processes. In one of them, he analyzed the captain's voice and identified the stress pattern as indicative of irritation, suspicion, and curiosity; of all the crew, Data found Picard's complex emotional states the most challenging to unravel. The second train of thought led to an announcement. "Captain, I have identified the static interference as a substantial burst of Hovorka radiation."

Given the captain's lack of reaction, Data belatedly realized that the conundrum was not self-evident.

"Hovorka emissions are generated during the collapse of

brown dwarf stars, but there are no such sources for this radiation anywhere in this sector or in the area stretching between this solar system and Starbase 193."

"Then how can you account for its presence?"

"I cannot." Then, anticipating the captain's next question, Data said, "Neither can I theorize a connection between the events on the planet and this anomaly; nevertheless, the radiation should not be there."

Picard was just as quick at anticipating Data's next request.

"You know how I feel about mysteries, Mr. Data; it may be inconsequential, but I still want it explained. Proceed with your investigation."

The slow, measured beat of the diagnostic scanner exploded into a flurry of sounds and flashing lights. Seconds later the chief medical officer and two nurses were clustered around T'Sara's bed. The Vulcan woman had remained limp and unresponsive when her wounds were first tended, but now her limbs twitched ever so slightly with muscular tension.

"She appears to be coming out of the healing state," said Crusher as she tracked the life function indicators. Despite the wild fluctuations, the overall pattern was of an increase in cellular and metabolic activity. "But dammit, it's too soon! The tissue damage has barely begun to regenerate. If she wakes up now, she'll die of her injuries."

At this point, Crusher knew the ideal treatment was for a Vulcan healer to forge a mind-link and guide the patient back into the trance, but not even Selar was qualified to initiate that therapy.

Fortunately, there were cruder methods available to persuade the body to resume its regenerative efforts.

"Ten cc's of Tochizine." Crusher held out her hand and felt the satisfying weight of a loaded hypospray slap into her open palm.

The doctor pressed the instrument against the base of the patient's neck and triggered a spray of the drug through the skin.

"Metabolic activity is stabilizing . . . decreasing," confirmed Nurse D'Airo. She began to read off the declining values, then paused. When she resumed the count, the numbers were climbing again.

"Fifteen cc's of D'armacol," ordered Crusher, but neither that nor an additional fifteen cc's of Hyzolidine had any lasting effect on the readouts. "It's as if her body is constantly adjusting to the injections and neutralizing the effects."

Crusher accepted a recharged hypo from D'Airo and positioned it against bare skin, but she did not trigger the blast. The Vulcan's drive to regain consciousness could not be repressed without a massive chemical assault that would do equal damage to her weakened system.

Then T'Sara snapped open her eyes; they were onyx-black and clear of any confusion.

"All right," said Crusher softly. "If this is what you want."

T'Sara extended a thin, spindly arm toward the doctor. From a Human the gesture might have appeared imploring, but there was no mistaking the imperious demand of a Vulcan. The fingers of the hand flexed, then clenched like steel clamps around a fold of Beverly's coat. Even nearing death, T'Sara had sufficient strength to pull the doctor closer until the old woman's mouth was pressed against Crusher's ear.

T'Sara's hoarse whisper was like a gust of desert air. "Ko N'ya . . . the blood never stops flowing."

Picard had managed to catch a few hours sleep since his last visit to sickbay, but he suspected his chief medical officer had not been so lucky. Standing in the close confines of her office, he could hear a rasp in Beverly's voice and see dark smudges forming beneath her eyes.

"Are you sure that's what she said?" asked Riker.

"Yes, I'm sure." Crusher had delivered her medical report with a crisp detachment, but now that it was over she shoved aside her medical padd and sagged back into her desk chair. "T'Sara spoke quite clearly . . . before she died."

Picard saw Beverly's gaze shift away to the sickbay ward

outside her office; he glanced back in time to see two nurses lift a still, covered body onto an antigrav sled. By the time he and Riker left this office, T'Sara would be gone, whisked away from the presence of the living.

Having witnessed Sarek's last days of suffering from Bendii's syndrome, Picard wondered if this was a more merciful end.

"What does that mean? Ko Ni—" Riker faltered over the delicate contraction of the syllables.

"Ko N'ya," corrected the captain with a grasp of the inflection that came naturally to him through long usage. "The name is ancient, with origins in a pre-Reform Vulcan dialect. There is no direct translation, but the cultural concept is roughly analogous to 'the Devil's Heart'."

Crusher frowned at the explanation. "What an odd choice for one's dying words."

"Not so odd for this particular Vulcan," said Picard. "For the past two decades, T'Sara has . . . *had* been obsessed with tracing an object which she believed appeared in the mythology of disparate worlds. Her theory, widely discounted by other scholars and historians, is that this talisman really did exist and that it was the factual source for all those legends. She also believed that the Ko N'ya had somehow ended up on Atropos, and she spent the last ten years trying to find it there."

"What a waste," said Riker. "Could this obsession of hers have been caused by the Bendii's?"

"Would everyone please stop speculating ahead of the evidence," snapped Crusher. "Sorren was an archaeologist, not a doctor, and he was not qualified to diagnose such an extremely rare disease. Until my lab tests confirm—"

"How soon—" began Picard.

"I'm working as fast as I can, Captain," said Crusher stiffly. "My staff is working as fast as they can. When the results are ready, I'll let—"

She stopped suddenly, took a deep breath, then began again. "And when I've gotten some sleep, I may even remember how to be civil again."

"No offense taken, Doctor," said Picard. Sleep might help, but he suspected her weariness had another, darker, source; Beverly's next task was all too obvious.

His chief medical officer rose from behind her desk. "If you'll excuse me, gentlemen, I have another autopsy to attend to."

"Captain?"

"Sorry, Number One," said Picard, when he realized that he was still standing in the corridor outside sickbay, lost in thoughts of T'Sara and her fruitless quest. He launched himself forward, setting a brisk pace. "You were saying?"

Riker fell into step beside him. "According to Worf's progress report, the research camp is almost completely dismantled. We should be able to break orbit in the next few hours."

"Not yet," said Picard. "Not until we have a clear idea of what happened down on the surface. We may need to examine the site again."

There was sufficient truth in this statement to ease Picard's conscience. An additional, unspoken reason was his need to make peace with T'Sara's murder. His grief at the scholar's death was more intellectual than emotional, yet an empty feeling of deep loss could not be dislodged no matter how fast he walked.

"I think it's time for me to see Atropos for myself." Without slowing his pace, Picard executed an abrupt turn to his right and marched through the open doors of a turbolift that had just discharged a passenger. "Deck 6."

Riker dashed into the compartment just before the doors closed. As the turbolift whined into motion, the first officer said, "Are you going down there as an archaeologist or as a detective?"

"A bit of both," admitted Picard, "but also to pay my respects."

When T'Sara's life had been cut short, her ceaseless quest for the mythic Ko N'ya had also come to an end. Atropos, with its covering of ruins, was a fitting tombstone for both of them.

The hard metallic grill of the transporter platform transmuted into spongy turf, and Picard felt his boots sink ever so slightly into the ground.

He surveyed his surroundings, from the plants crushed under his boots to the strange jumble of ruins, like the bleached bones of an ancient goliath scattered all around him.

Massive tiles had once paved the area with alternating squares of bright colors, but their pattern was disrupted now. Some tiles had settled unevenly, their surfaces tilted at wild angles; others were shattered into pieces; all were smeared with a thick layer of dust and dirt. In the center of the plaza was a jagged ring of stone, all that remained of a high tower that had crumbled down to its base. Judging from the amount of debris, the structure had dwarfed every other building within miles; even its ruins still reached high enough to block out the sun.

The air was dry and tartly scented, and he inhaled deeply, eager to flush his lungs of the odorless mixture of gases that filled the starship. Picard smiled, savoring the feel of his mind stretching to encompass an alien landscape.

The smile faded when he caught sight of a small metallic tag driven into the ground; it marked where a body had been found. Four archaeologists had died in the plaza that sprawled out before him.

Lieutenant Worf stepped out of the shadows where he had been waiting for the captain's arrival. He pointed to a marker by his feet. "T'Sara fell here."

Three other tags were arranged in a rough semicircle around the Klingon, placed where the archaeologists had gathered to face their leader. According to Riker's mission report, Soth and T'Challo were also armed, and T'Sara was caught in their cross fire.

Picard tried to reconstruct the scene in his mind, but it was difficult to place Vulcans in the midst of such violence. For ten years T'Sara and her colleagues had patiently worked their way through these ruins. What combination of actions and reactions among them could have led to this fatal tableau?

"Lieutenant, where was their last excavation site?"

"Over here." Worf retreated into the shadows.

The captain followed, picking his way through a maze of fallen blocks, wary of loose tiles that rocked underfoot.

"We removed a scanner and several sonic tools from this area," said Worf.

As his eyes adjusted to the shade, Picard could see that a patch of ground had been cleared of stones to provide access to a delicate bas relief of hieroglyphics carved on the tower wall. One section was partially restored, but if the Vulcans had managed to decipher the alien language, the message had been lost again when the expedition's data files were erased.

"I had hoped for something more momentous," said Picard with a sigh, "but I'm afraid this would only have been a footnote in her latest—"

He spied a black shadow breaking the expanse of gray wall; it was tall and narrow, like a doorway.

Curiosity demanded an explanation. Picard walked to the wall, but even up close his eyes strained to see through the opening. He stretched out an arm. His hand sank into the darkness and touched air that was several degrees cooler than where he stood.

"Another footnote?" asked Worf.

"Perhaps. Why don't we find out?"

Picard stepped through the opening.

The tunnel was narrow—he could hear the sound of Worf's shoulders brushing against the sides of polished stone—and if the light grew any dimmer he would be foolish to forge ahead. The darkness did not thicken, however. Instead, a glowing light beckoned him to continue his exploration.

They soon discovered that the illumination came from a field lamp abandoned in the corridor. Its light revealed that the end of the tunnel had once been bricked over, but the archaeologists had cut through the barrier to reach the circular chamber beyond.

"More than a footnote," said Picard when he caught sight of the interior.

A huge throne, hewn out of the same stone as the tower above, was set in the center of the bare room. The attenuated figure that sat on the throne was no statue, however. On his first breath, Picard had inhaled the musty odor of mummification. Skin and tissue had dried, shrinking against the skeleton beneath.

In life, the alien had been tall and willowy; in death, it was crouched like a spider in its web.

"It's holding something," he said, observing how its arms and hands came together as if cupping a small object in its palms. When Picard approached for a better look, his boots stirred dust motes of decay into the still air.

The object was gone.

He knew the prickle of apprehension that shuddered through him was irrational and unwarranted. Surely, the contents of this chamber must have been plundered centuries before the Vulcans had set foot on the planet.

"I've seen enough."

Worf nodded impassively, but he scrambled out the portal somewhat faster than he had entered. Picard ducked his head as he edged through the breach, then froze in place.

"Captain? Is something wrong?"

"Yes, Lieutenant, although I suppose it hardly matters now."

The signs were so clear; surely T'Sara had seen them, too? Picard reached out one hand, trailing his fingers over the crumbling bricks and mortar, wondering what fierce emotion had driven the hands that had built this wall.

"This chamber was sealed from the inside."

CHAPTER 6

Embedded discreetly along the outer shell of Starbase 193 were a series of subspace signal collectors, a small part of the vast communications network that linked one end of the Federation to another. These electronic scoops gathered up decaying transmissions from passing freighters or from settlements uneasily perched on the fringe of Federation territory, then computers sorted the compressed digital packets and directed them to the appropriate transmitter along the upper rim of the station. The newly fortified signals were flung back into the void toward their destination or to yet another of the relay boosters seeded throughout Federation territory.

The process was automatic, so the communications packet from the *Enterprise* passed through the system in a matter of seconds. It would have taken even less time, except Captain Picard's mission report had to be detached from the compressed bundle before the remaining portion of the transmission was sent on its way to Vulcan.

Suffering yet another half-second lag, the captain's report was routed through a short system subroutine. Following the program's instructions, the computer created a duplicate of the transmission and shuttled this copy to an untitled buffer file. The original proceeded to Commander Miyakawa's message terminal.

Minutes later, a technician in the communications center accessed the duplicate and perused its contents. After the first quick reading, a nervous tic began to tug one corner of his mouth askew. He read the message a second time.

This breach of security procedures would have been more difficult to implement on a starbase fully staffed by Starfleet officers, but Thomas Grede often worked unsupervised, so the subroutine had been relatively easy to install. None of the other operators knew the system well enough to discover the alteration, and few would have cared.

He was depending on this same apathy when he slipped away from his post in the middle of a shift.

No one noticed his departure, but then no one noticed Grede much of the time anyway. He was a slight, timid man who had grown accustomed to being overlooked by the people around him. Competent and reliable, his only weakness was a hunger for attention, yet this craving had persisted unfulfilled for most of his life.

On Starbase 193, one person had seen his need and used it to her advantage.

As a matter of routine, any new employee hired by the base commander was soon tempted to provide certain business interests on the station with private services. Grede had stood firm against repeated bribes, and over several years of steady if unspectacular performance, he had earned a high security clearance. During this time, however, Camenae had patiently cultivated his friendship with a few kind words and the occasional free drink at the Due or Die. This mild flattery was all it took to buy his loyalty.

Grede grew anxious to please her. Without any prompting, one day he came to her with the gift of a coded communiqué to Commander Miyakawa that he had skillfully intercepted. Camenae had paid him for the betrayal, but it was her smile of appreciation that thrilled him. Unfortunately, her gratitude did not last very long, and soon her manner toward him grew cool and distant. Desperate to regain her favor, the technician realized that the only way he could maintain his good standing was with a constant stream of tribute.

Today, as he scurried through the doors of the Due or Die, Grede belatedly admitted that the price of pleasing Camenae was climbing higher than he could afford.

"I have information." These were the magic words that had first fulfilled his desire to impress the knowledge-broker. These three words persuaded the Norsican guard to move aside and allow Grede access to the inner sanctum.

He knew the way into Camenae's shadowed office by heart, but he stumbled over the threshold anyway, his feet tangled by haste and a fear so strong it weakened his knees. She waved him to a chair, but he continued to stand, bouncing on the balls of his feet, ready to sprint away again.

"I've just seen the latest report to Miyakawa from the *Enterprise*," he said, still panting from his run to the bar. "Camenae, the Vulcans on Atropos are dead!"

"So the *Enterprise* is handling this matter. That's definitely information I can use." She reached into the folds of her robe and withdrew a token.

"No," cried Grede, his voice rising in pitch. "I didn't come here to sell you something. Camenae, this situation is getting out of hand. We're talking the death of prominent Federation citizens. That means an investigation, questions, officials prying into every corner of this starbase."

She shrugged. "I'm not responsible if you failed to consider the consequences of our last transaction."

"Dammit, I could get into serious trouble for what I've done!"

"In that case," she said, palming the coin he had rejected, "I'll put this on your account. You may have need of it in the future."

He searched her face for some sign of compassion. The corners of her mouth were turned down, but not out of concern for his misfortune. Camenae was merely impatient for him to leave.

* * *

Sendei shut his eyes.

After a century of practice, this simple act should have slipped him easily into meditation, but today that skill eluded him. The Vulcan struggled to submerge himself and failed. He could still hear the muffled exchanges between students and professors in the hall outside, and the outlines of his office remained clearly visible in his mind.

He took a deep breath. Then, like a child just learning the first steps of emotional control, he summoned the construct of two hands and imagined them cupped over each of his ears.

When all sounds had faded, Sendei passed the hands in front of his face, and his awareness of the room in which he sat receded as well. The removal of these distractions released other thoughts that were not so easily blocked.

He was haunted by memories of the dead.

Over ten years had passed since he had found T'Sara standing on the crest of a moonlit dune, gazing out across the plains to the blackened silhouette of Mount Selaya. Sendei had argued with her for hours, nearly until dawn, but logic could not deter T'Sara from selling her estate to continue her search for the Ko N'ya. He had stormed away when his emotional reserve finally shattered against her obstinacy. By the time he had recovered his composure, she had left Vulcan.

He never saw her again.

T'Sara had no close family, and the distant branches of her clan had severed all contact after she ceded her ancestral lands. As of this moment, Sendei claimed her as his own kin. He would write her name in his family's annals so that his children's children would revere her memory.

Her image faded and he was alone in the desert.

Dipping his hands into the dune, Sendei filled cupped palms with sand, then focused his attention on the grains as they streamed from between his fingers. This second construct helped him descend to another level of the meditative state.

He did not see Sohle's face, but he remembered the gruffness of the man's voice. Although Sohle had never professed belief in T'Sara's quest, he had been the first archaeologist at the Academy to announce his decision to accompany her to Atropos, and he had met the storm of criticism leveled against his participation with a short answer. "I will learn more from her folly than from the wisdom of my colleagues."

Other professors and students had been persuaded by these words, so T'Sara did not leave Vulcan alone.

Now Sendei would have to inform Sohle's children that their father was dead, just as Tessin's brothers must be told that their only sister would not return home. Skorret would never finish his dissertation on pre-Reform metalwork, and the Academy had lost forever T'Challo's insights into early Vulcan art forms.

So many names lost . . . so many lives disrupted . . . so many families wounded by this tragedy.

Drifting grains of sand could not shore up his crumbling emotional defenses. Sendei loosed a thundering earthquake across the desert. The ground trembled and shook until a jagged fissure opened beneath his feet. He dropped down into total darkness, into the very center of his despair.

Sorren is dead. My son is dead.

Sendei's reaction was Vulcan, silent but deeply felt. Offworlders often mistook that lack of outward show for indifference, but the pain of such a loss was not meant for display. Few Vulcans managed to extinguish all emotion, but most had mastered the ability to contain it. According to the philosophy that the Vulcan race had adopted, there was no reason why any emotion, no matter how intense, should influence behavior or cloud the path of logic.

Deep in meditation, Sendei searched for a final construct that would contain his unruly emotions. He chose the image of a river rushing through an underground chasm. Here his rage and grief could run freely and purely in their own channel until death brought him inner peace.

CHAPTER 7

"**T**here is no Bendii's!"

Beverly Crusher had charged through the doors of the captain's ready room after only a token ring of the chime. She was brandishing her medical padd like the head of a vanquished enemy.

Picard lowered the teacup that had been on its way to his lips and waved the CMO to a chair in front of his desk. "I take it your medical report is ready."

"Yes, by god, it is." She moved into place with the grace of a dancer, the tails of her lab coat billowing out behind her. "Tissue cultures from T'Sara's metathalamus were negative for Bendii's syndrome. In fact, during the autopsy I found no signs of any kind of pathology in her brain or nervous system: no lesions, no tumors, nothing organic that could result in violent or irrational behavior."

"Then what could have triggered such violence among the Vulcans?"

"Oh, but I'm not convinced of that either," said Crusher. Heightened spots of color on her cheeks betrayed her excitement. "I may be rusty on the finer points of forensic medicine, but it appears that several of the Vulcans were stunned before they were killed, and almost all of the bodies show obvious signs of having been moved after death."

She jabbed at her padd screen, consulted the new readout, then continued. "For instance, Soth was found lying face-down in the plaza, but blood had pooled on the back of his body; T'Challo's arms had small scrapes and bruises that occurred after death, and three of Sohle's fingers were broken after rigor mortis had set in, apparently to force his hand around a phaser grip."

Picard already had a notion of where this discussion was leading, but he sipped his tea as Beverly continued to develop her argument.

"Not to mention that Tessin's fingerprints were found on the weapon that killed Skorret, even though the rate of cellular degeneration suggests she died at least a half hour before he did." Tossing the data padd onto the captain's desk like a gauntlet thrown down in challenge, Crusher said, "Frankly, I find it highly unlikely that a group of homicidal Vulcans would concern themselves with moving their victims from one place to another; a far more likely explanation of the entire situation is—"

"—is that off-planet intruders staged a clumsy cover for the murders."

"Exactly!"

The new scenario unfolded before his mind's eye: T'Sara caught unawares, falling under the unexpected barrage of phaser fire, victim of an attack from without rather than from within. Although the forms that wielded the weapons were shadowy and undefined, their existence had the solidity of truth.

"I concur with your interpretation of the evidence," said Picard. "The question remains, who would do this and why?"

She shrugged. "Sorry, Captain, that's not my department."

"No," he sighed. "But it is mine." The answers to T'Sara's death danced just out of reach, elusive, tantalizing. What would it take to bring them into focus?

He tapped the communicator on his chest. "Picard to Data: What is the status of your current project?"

"I have not yet concluded my investigation, but there is sufficient progress to warrant your attention."

"Thank you, Data. I'm on my way to the bridge." The captain rose from behind his desk. "Doctor, I think you should hear this, too."

Riker's steps echoed loudly as he crossed the deck of Cargo Bay 12. The loading crew was gone, as was the fleet of airsleds they had driven into the spacious hold. After a brief frenzy of activity, Worf's team had left behind a tidy mountain of faceted shipping cartons.

Each carton had a number stenciled on its surface, and as Riker entered that number into his data padd, the tablet's display screen revealed the contents stored inside. The first series included tents, computers, dating scanners, thermal sensors, laser drills, and sonic picks. Every last stake and stray piece of rope had been gathered up and packed away.

Next, Riker checked through the artifacts uncovered by the excavations: shards of pottery and statuary, broken weapons, small pieces of jewelry. These were the discarded remnants of a society, not its treasures. According to the captain, it was from precisely this sort of detritus that most archaeologists teased their understanding of a culture, and T'Sara had displayed a genius for making these extrapolations.

The last two cartons were filled with items found in the archaeologists' living quarters. Vulcans were not a materialistic race, so the list Riker scanned was spare and consisted mostly of clothes and books. Even after their long tenure on the planet, the scientists had made no attempt to decorate their tents with frivolous trinkets; every personal article was utilitarian in purpose and discreetly labeled with the owner's name.

Upon a second glance, however, the first officer noticed that every member of the team possessed a pocket holo. So, at the end of a long day of excavation and research, even Vulcans wanted reminders of home and family.

Three of them had brought musical instruments as well. Riker envisioned a small group of tired men and women gathered together under the stars, listening to the soft strains of a lyre and a flute. The scene made the knowledge of their deaths more poignant, almost painful, but it helped to overshadow his memories of contorted bodies mired in blood.

With a final tap on the padd's controls, Riker transferred the confirmed manifest into the starship's main computers. Nothing of the Vulcans remained below on Atropos. Their decade-long presence had been completely erased.

"Sorren's distress call appears to have been altered in several ways," said Data. "The first modification was to the identification slate."

Picard automatically leaned closer to the science station, then shifted slightly to allow Crusher an unobstructed view of the screen. The circular seal of the United Federation of Planets—a field of stars flanked by olive branches—floated on a blue background; below the logo was a small block of text.

The two officers studied the slate and its standard display of information about Sorren's message.

Origin: UFP 567045-B12-10A (Atropos)
Destination: UFP 567045-B23-22C (Starbase 193)
Stardate: 45873.4

"I see nothing out of the ordinary," said Picard as he exchanged puzzled looks with the doctor.

"At first, neither did I," said the android. "However, when I examined the transmission envelope I discovered a discrepancy in the date stamp. Since the envelope is usually accessed only by the transceiver hardware, its information is never visible to the recipient of the message."

With quick, practiced movements, Data unzipped the coded interface and called forth a dense stream of unformatted data. Numbers flew by more quickly than Picard could follow until suddenly Data froze the image. His pointing finger highlighted the pertinent section of a line.

FM:UFP567045-B12-10A/TO:UFP567045-B23-22C/SD: 45873.3

"45873.3," read Picard. "One day earlier!"

"Correct," said the android. "The last digit designating the day has been changed on the identification slate. That alteration obscured a twenty-four-hour lag between the receipt of the original message at Starbase 193 and the transmission of a forged version to the *Enterprise.*"

"And during that time," said Crusher angrily, "the Vulcans were being slaughtered."

"That would appear to be the case."

The screen image shimmered as Data advanced the recording to the middle of Sorren's communiqué. Black and white lines lightly scored the Vulcan's face, then increased in intensity, fracturing the picture beyond recognition.

Data continued his explanation. "The second modification involves the sudden appearance of static that obscures part of the message. Any transmission interference should have been noted by the subspace receiver; however, the data verification field indicates that the Vulcan's message was received intact at Starbase 193. Neither is there any record of difficulty in the transmission from the starbase to the *Enterprise.* Thus, I surmised that the burst of Hovorka radiation is actually a graphic forgery introduced to suppress five seconds of the image."

"Can the original be restored?" asked Picard.

"Yes, I believe so. The transmission envelope contains a compressed digital duplicate of lower resolution, but this copy contains sufficient information for our purposes. By judicious cross-referencing and multiple digital sampling I can reconstruct the missing segment."

"Make it so."

A high whine ensued as the android ran the message at high speed; his fingers blurred with equal rapidity over the console as he adjusted controls, then repeated the process again and again. With each repetition the tape image became clearer. "This should be sufficient for comprehension."

Sorren's movements slowed to real time, and his voice dropped back to a deep pitch. Despite a slight blurring of image and sound, his words were intelligible.

"Her behavior is growing increasingly erratic: she is prone to outbursts of emotion and persists in irrational accounts of her communion with the Ko N'ya."

"The Ko N'ya again," exclaimed Crusher.

Picard's thoughts flashed to the memory of two gnarled hands, the hands of an alien who had walled itself up alive. What had those cupped palms been holding when T'Sara entered the chamber?

"After all these years of searching," he wondered aloud, "could she really have found it?"

Troi stirred in her cabin bed, her legs thrashing beneath the sheets until she kicked off her covers entirely. The loss of warmth and a nagging agitation prodded her up through the layers of unconsciousness.

Her eyes fluttered open for only a second. Fighting against the impulse to wake, she buried her face back into a pillow. This nap was no luxury. The last few days had been filled with emergency sessions that had pulled the counselor out of her cabin in the middle of the night. That was often the case after Away Team missions that involved violent death, and this time several members of the paramedic team had been plagued with nightmares.

Of their own accord, Troi's feet twitched as if she were pacing back and forth across a deck.

Of course. Imzadi.

Belatedly, the empath realized what was happening. Commander Will Riker was striding through the *Enterprise* with a heightened vigor and intensity of purpose, and she was unwittingly keeping him company. His forceful emotions often overrode her mental block, like rising floodwaters spilling over the edge of a dam. Stronger defenses would prevent these intrusions, but the effort would require a constant mental strain, and it would also mute the comforting knowledge of his presence.

Having identified the source of her unease, Troi damped down her emotional link with the first officer until the muscles in her legs relaxed. Then she groped for her covers and sighed contentedly at the prospect of falling back asleep.

She drifted lazily into unconsciousness.

"Data to Counselor Troi."

Troi's eyes flew open. "Yes, Data?"

"The captain has called an emergency conference for all senior officers."

Stifling a groan of exasperation, the counselor said, "I'm on my way."

According to the engineering schematics on file at the Utopia Planitia Fleet Yards, Ten-Forward was merely a spacious room designated as a crew lounge. All galaxy-class starships had a Ten-Forward with its standard-issue bar and curving transparent aluminum windows, but only the USS *Enterprise* had Guinan, which made this particular Ten-Forward uncommonly special.

Riker welcomed that difference when he pushed his way through the familiar double doors. Ever since his visit to the cargo bay, the first officer had been plagued by a vague restlessness, but now the urge to keep moving faded. No one rushed to leave Guinan's company.

Her shapeless robes and fanciful headgear were flamboyant; Guinan herself was contained. She listened more often than she spoke, yet when she had something to say, the mellow tones of her husky voice were compelling.

"You look like a man in need of a little excitement," said the hostess, setting a tall thin glass of a fizzing liquid on the counter. Riker had never seen a drink quite like it before, but then Guinan had a fondness for experimentation.

"Is it that obvious?" sighed the first officer as he swung onto a bar stool. "We've only been in orbit around Atropos for two days, but I'm ready to leave again."

"Odds are against it," came a mocking voice from behind him.

Riker took a deep breath, then turned to present a forced smile to the angular Bajoran woman who slid into place next to him. *Never turn your back on Ro Laren.* "What's that supposed to mean, Ensign?"

"Just that the ship's pool is running two to one that we won't make it to Luxor IV in time for a game of canasta, much less poker. Of course, the crew of the *Telarius* would probably win the championship again anyway."

"O ye of little faith." She was baiting him, and he knew it, but Riker still couldn't stop himself. "As it happens, our business here is almost finished, and a steady warp seven will get us back on schedule. Then the crew of the *Enterprise* is going to show the crew of the *Telarius* how real poker should be played."

"Don't waste your bluffs on me, sir," said Ro with an incredibly infuriating and condescending chuckle. "Save them for the championship match . . . sometime next year."

"I'm *not* bluffing."

"A hundred says you are."

"You're on," he snapped. "Guinan, you heard her."

"I heard both of you," said Guinan softly. "In fact, everyone in the room heard both of you. Now will you taste that drink I poured for you? The flavor is very delicate, and it won't last much longer."

Riker reached his hand out for the glass.

"Data to Commander Riker."

His hand moved up to his comm insignia instead. "Riker here."

"The captain has called an emergency conference for all senior officers."

"Understood, Mr. Data," said the first officer as he pushed away from the bar. "I'm on my way."

"A hundred credits will come in very handy on my next shore leave." The Bajoran was openly smirking.

To add insult to injury, Guinan slid his untouched drink

over to the ensign. The bartender shrugged an apology to Riker, then turned back to watch Ro's reaction to the beverage.

Heading out of Ten-Forward, Riker grudgingly admitted there was a high probability that Ro would win their bet. Unfortunately, the loss of a hundred credits would not hurt half so much as the loss of his pride.

Each of the chairs around the oval conference table would be filled soon, but for the next few minutes Picard and Crusher had the observation lounge to themselves. After the turmoil of the last few days, the captain welcomed this oasis of tranquillity. Usually he would have resented sharing it with anyone else, except Beverly was not just anyone else.

"So," asked the doctor, "when did you develop this fascination for the Ko N'ya?"

"As a child," said Picard. "My brother was the one who introduced me to the legend. Although, since Robert was a bit of a bully, his aim was to terrify little Jean-Luc."

"Did he succeed?"

"Oh, yes." Even after fifty years, Picard could recall trembling in their night-darkened bedroom and burrowing under his blankets as if they were armor against monsters. "Robert would wait until our parents were asleep and the house was completely still, then he would whisper yet another impressively embellished tale of blood and gore. He developed quite a flair for the dramatic and considered himself amply rewarded if he reduced me to tears."

"How charming," said Crusher wryly, but then she was the mother of an only child. Picard could never explain to her the complex web of love and hate that bound him to his brother.

"However, as I grew older, my fear turned to fascination, and I would beg Robert for more stories."

"Let me guess," she said with a smile. "At that point, Robert lost interest in the Ko N'ya."

"Exactly." Perhaps she understood the relationship between brothers after all. "So I began to read the original lore for myself, and when those books were exhausted, I moved on to others. That was the start of my lifelong passion for history and archaeology of all kinds."

"Jean-Luc, do you really believe T'Sara could have found this object? Has myth turned out to be history after all?"

"I hardly dare believe it." Yet he still could not shake the image of those mummified hands. "Touching the Ko N'ya would be like touching history itself. For such an opportunity, I would . . ." Picard groped for the limits of his desire but found them surprisingly difficult to define.

"Sell your soul?" said Crusher.

Her suggestion had been made in jest, so Picard answered in the same lighthearted vein. "No, not sell . . . but perhaps rent it for a while."

Once the words were uttered, however, he realized they were uncomfortably close to the truth.

CHAPTER 8

"There have been some new insights into the murders of the Vulcans on Atropos," announced Picard. Then, with a nod, he signaled Beverly Crusher to recite the results of her autopsy findings.

As the assembled officers listened first to the doctor and then to Data, Picard watched the crew's changing expressions. The revelation of each new facet of the deception on Atropos tightened the line of Riker's jaw and deepened the sorrow in Troi's eyes; Geordi La Forge grew still and silent, whereas Worf shifted in his chair as if ready to lunge at an approaching enemy.

When the reports were finished, a circle of grim faces turned toward the captain.

"Given the circumstances," said Picard, "we must proceed under the assumption that all our communications with Starbase 193 are being monitored. I've prepared a report of our investigations for Admiral Matasu at Starbase 75, but it will take hours for him to even receive the message."

"Which means we're on our own for now," said Riker, with an emphatic tug at his tunic. The gesture, one he unconsciously borrowed from the captain, was a mixture of defiance and anticipation.

Picard was more ambivalent about this prospect than his first officer. One of the most invigorating challenges of command lay in making decisions that were his alone, but autonomy from Starfleet authority was accompanied by an equal measure of responsibility for the consequences of his judgment. Nonetheless, he had already reached one firm resolution.

"Our first priority is to locate the intruders that we believe murdered the Vulcan archaeologists."

"Agreed," said Crusher. "Any delay in pursuit would give them more time to get away." A supporting chorus of murmured assent quickly rippled around the table.

"There's one thing I just don't understand," said La Forge. "Why would anyone be willing to kill for some dusty old relic?"

Picard smiled at the engineer's naive description. "Oh, but it's not just any artifact. This is a mythic icon of tremendous allure. Ko N'ya, the Devil's Heart . . . it has been called many names in many languages throughout the galaxy."

Data cocked his head, silently accessing information from a vast storehouse of knowledge. "The Belnarri call it Nota; the Andorians know it as Telev's Bane; and to the Klingons it is the Pagrashtak."

"Pagrashtak!" exclaimed Worf. "The Bloodstone!"

Picard was startled by the intensity of the Klingon's reaction.

"So you know about this, too?" asked Troi. Picard could practically hear her clinical persona click into place. Evidently the counselor sensed considerable depth in the lieutenant's agitation.

"Yes, I have heard of it," said Worf reluctantly. The captain wondered if his scowl was a product of embarrassment at the outburst or whether the warrior's reserve was still shaken by mention of the Pagrashtak. "According to Klingon legend, Lord Kessec founded the First Empire with its powers . . .

and Kessec warned that he who holds the Pagrashtak must drain his veins of blood or his next of kin will do it for him."

Riker rocked back in his chair, startled by the severity of Worf's expression. The first officer's eyebrows knitted together in genuine puzzlement. "So what exactly is this thing?"

Where to even begin? wondered Picard as he struggled to condense the work of T'Sara's lifetime into a few words. "The Heart's exact nature is unknown, and its origins are lost in antiquity; all that survives are tales of its passage through different cultures. In the mythologies T'Sara collected, the Heart has been variously described as a stone, a jewel, even an energy cell. One hypothesis is that the Heart is an artifact of some ancient and forgotten race, one highly advanced in science." His brother Robert's voice whispered another explanation in his ear. "But worlds which believe in magic consider it to be a powerful talisman of Darkness."

"A talisman of *darkness?*" snorted Riker. "With the power to do just what?"

Data was ready with the answer. "No one knows its true capabilities, but they are suspected to be vast, enabling its possessor to control men's minds, to amass wealth and power, even to change the flow of time itself."

"Data, you don't really believe that?"

"*Our* belief is not really relevant," countered Troi. "T'Sara believed, and whoever killed the Vulcan archaeologists must also have believed. Regardless of whether this Devil's Heart has any real powers, people have killed to gain possession of it."

"Devil's Heart, Bloodstone," said Riker. "I begin to see why it has such morbid names."

"Yes," said Picard. "According to many of the legends T'Sara gathered, the price of gaining the stone is death or the spilling of blood. Those who have ruled by its powers have died in combat or been betrayed by their friends."

Troi suddenly switched her scrutiny from Worf to Picard. "Captain, what do *you* believe—"

"*Bridge to Captain Picard.*" A voice brusque with controlled urgency drowned out the counselor's question. *"We're picking up an automated distress call from a Ferengi vessel in this sector."*

"I'm on my way," said Picard, already rising from his chair.

Riker was on his feet a half second later. "I have a bad feeling about this, Captain."

"Yes, Number One, it does appear this sector is becoming rather crowded."

The Ferengi Marauder-class starship floated in space, drifting listlessly; its crescent-shaped rear hull was pitted and scored, and a gash in the horned front section was charred down to the duranium frame. Lights were scattered at random through the decks, but they flickered weakly.

Picard surveyed the damaged vessel with a dispassionate eye and a suspicious nature. "Raise shields."

"They don't look ready for another fight," said Riker.

"Perhaps not," conceded the captain. After all, even Ferengi guile had its limits. "But we have yet to account for whoever attacked—"

The deck rocked beneath his command chair as the ship's deflector shields sparked and crackled. Alert sirens blared, and bridge lights dimmed momentarily as power was rechanneled to the defense systems. A less-seasoned officer might have mistaken the impact for a weapons salvo, but Picard recognized the telltale blue flash of Cerenkov radiation that resulted from a mid-flight collision.

"Helm! Go to quarter-impulse."

As the *Enterprise*'s forward motion slowed, the force of subsequent collisions was diminished to the light patter of hail on a rooftop.

"Power reserves holding steady," said Data as sensor chatter echoed noisily across the navigation consoles.

"A trap?" asked Riker.

"I don't think so, Number One." Picard studied the view of the space surrounding them and confirmed what he had expected: the *Enterprise* had plowed into the middle of a field of debris. Chunks of dark, twisted metal were scattered in all directions, their serrated edges glinting in starlight. "I suspect we've found the second player in this drama."

Flashes of blue light danced across the viewscreen as more of the fragments ricocheted off the protective envelope of the deflector shields.

"My analysis of the particles supports that theory," said Data. "The total mass of the debris appears equivalent to that of another vessel, although one somewhat less formidable then the Marauder class."

"Any speculation as to its origins?"

"That may be difficult to determine since the wreckage has been distorted by intense heat." The android magnified several different sections of the viewscreen until he located a twisted beam that still retained identifiable form. "This molded tritanium truss is characteristic of the Orion Signet series."

"An Orion ship?" Riker turned to Picard. "They usually give wide berth to the Ferengi."

"Yet this time it seems two scavengers have fallen on each other."

"To the detriment of both," said Data. "I detect no life-signs aboard the Ferengi vessel."

"And the blood is still flowing," murmured Picard.

Riker frowned at the repetition of T'Sara's dying words. "So you think this battle is related to the attack on the Vulcans?"

Worf's deep voice thundered down from the tactical station on the aft deck. "One can find the Pagrashtak by following the flight of carrion-eaters; keeping it is not so easy." The Klingon leaned over the rail and added a more subdued explanation. "That was a quote from *The Ballads of Durall.*"

Riker was struck speechless by the unexpected declamation, but Picard's composure was still intact. "Thank you, Lieutenant." He agreed with Worf: the mythic quality of this quest seemed to invite the heightened language of ancient texts.

"Well," said the first officer, "if the Orions had T'Sara's relic when their ship was destroyed, we'll be sifting through space detritus for weeks. So I suggest we search the Ferengi Marauder first."

"Agreed, Number One. Prepare an Away Team for . . ."

Touching the Ko N'ya would be like touching history itself.

"No," said Picard suddenly. "Belay that order."

"Sir?"

"Indulge me, Will. I'd like to lead this mission." The temptation was simply too strong for Picard to resist, but he would prefer to persuade Riker into agreement. A confrontation over this issue would only waste time and delay the recovery effort. "You know that I've been fascinated by the legend of the Heart for most of my life, and if it should actually exist . . ."

To his relief, Riker gave way with a broad grin. "Understood, Captain. Just don't make a habit of doing my job."

He was already out of his chair. "Worf, Data, with me."

With each step up the bridge ramp, Picard felt like he was marching his way into one of Robert's epic tales of heroic adventure. His two Away Team companions followed on his heels into the turbolift, obedient knights sworn to attend their liege lord.

By the time the three of them reached Deck 6 and mounted the transporter dais, Picard had banished the fantasy image from his mind. He was a Starfleet captain on a mission. Of all the dreams he had held as a child, this one was the most powerful.

"Ready for transport, Mr. O'Brien."

"Aye, Captain." The chief checked his console settings. "I'll set you down in the main bridge."

The transporter chamber glittered away. Then, in the space of a heartbeat, new surroundings materialized around Picard.

He coughed reflexively as swirling smoke entered his lungs. The air was cold, a sign that life support systems were failing.

At a glance, Picard could see that the command center of the Marauder was smaller than the main bridge of a starship. Everything in its interior, from the decks and walls to the computer consoles, was painted a muted gray. Everything was also broken. Shattered ceiling panels dangled from overhead, spilling out streams of wire; the deck was tilted and walls were buckled; and several cracked equipment consoles squealed softly as if in pain.

Scattered throughout this wreckage were a half-dozen bodies of the Ferengi crew.

Despite his sense of urgency, Picard realized that the task ahead of them was rather daunting. If the Heart really was here in the midst of all this rubble, how could he find it? Would he even know it when he saw it?

"Confirmed," Data said after a sweep of the tricorder. "There are no life-signs."

At a nod from the captain, Worf and the android moved forward, picking their way through the rubble. Picard chose a third path, but he had taken only a few steps when his boot heel caught on a loose deck plate, throwing him off-balance. He reached a hand out to the nearest console to steady himself, but a humming sound warned him not to touch the surface. He quickly shifted his weight and recovered his footing.

"The Signet's plasma bolts seem to have fused the electrical system," explained Data.

"And electrocuted the crew," said Worf, warily prodding aside one of the dead crewmen who lay slumped over the helm.

"Are we in any danger?" asked Picard as he stepped over a loosely coiled conduit.

"The initial charge has dissipated," said Data. "However, the short circuits in the system are capable of delivering a shock that would prove uncomfortable to the Human body."

"Thank you, Data. I'll keep that in mind." His breath was frosting now as the ship's heat continued to leach into space.

Picard continued his inspection while keeping a healthy distance from any sparking equipment panels. He scuffed the toe of one boot kicking aside loose rubble and snagged his uniform jacket on the sharp corners of twisted metal; his back began to ache as he contorted his body to peer into dark corners. From the crashing sounds off to his left, the captain could tell that Worf's search technique was even more vigorous.

It occurred to Picard that he might not be the first one to find the Heart.

"Captain," called out Data. "Is this what you are seeking?"

Casting aside all caution, Picard pushed his way through the wreckage to the front of the bridge. He found the android kneeling by the corpse of a Ferengi DaiMon. Either the electric current had contorted his face into a rictus of ecstasy, or he had been killed in the throes of rapture.

In his hands he clutched a dull, rough rock.

"The Heart," whispered Picard. "It must be."

Data carefully pried the object out of the DaiMon's grip and profferred it up to the captain.

Picard could feel his pulse racing as the weight of the stone settled into his palms.

It was warm.

CHAPTER 9

"**C**aptain's Log, Stardate 45873.6: The *Enterprise* broke orbit from Atropos to respond to an automated distress call from a Ferengi vessel . . ."

Picard had aged well, decided Miyakawa as she reviewed the captain's mission report. As a young cadet, his prominent nose and forehead had overpowered his face, but in his middle years these same strong features were compelling.

". . . encountered a Marauder-class starship . . ."

Cadets Picard, Crusher, and Keel had moved in tandem through Starfleet Academy, and the common expectation among their classmates had been that each member of the trio would garner early commissions and eventually end up back at the Academy teaching a new generation of cadets. Life had worked out a bit differently for them; Jean-Luc was the only one of the three left alive.

But then I'm not where I thought I'd be either.

". . . all crew aboard the vessel were dead. I'll provide more details when they're available."

To Miyakawa's surprise, Picard's narrative came to an abrupt end at that point.

"Wait a minute! Dead of what?" she demanded of the

blank screen on her desk viewer. Picard had omitted a wealth of vital information from his log: coordinates for the Marauder, the basis for its distress call, even the next destination of the *Enterprise.*

"Dammit, that wasn't a report," muttered the commander as she rocketed out of her chair. "I know a stall when I see one." She also knew where she might find some answers to her questions.

Unhooking her uniform jacket from the wall, Miyakawa stormed out of her office and headed for the far end of the starbase.

"How dare you call in this debt!"

Anlew-Is slammed a chit down on the table and continued to pound his fist at regular intervals while he screamed in Camenae's face.

"I've lost a Signet-class vessel, not to mention five of my best-trained mercenaries, and you expect payment for my ruin? You should pay *me* for the damages I've incurred in this odious venture!"

Camenae leaned back in her chair, trying hard not to breathe too deeply. She wondered whether it was the olive-green skin or the black fibrous hair that gave Orions their penetrating odor.

"You paid for the information, Anlew-Is, not for a favorable outcome to your schemes. If you want insurance, go do business with Aghlarren the Mote."

"But you sold me out to the Ferengi consortium! I would have the Heart in my hands if not for your greed and treachery!"

"Don't blame me for either your shortsightedness or your miserly nature," said Camenae with a stern frown. "You know my policies and my prices, yet you consistently refuse to cover the cost of exclusivity. DaiMon Maarc knew the value of a long-term investment."

"Ha!" he said, bathing her face with a blast of fetid air. "Dead men make no profit."

Camenae sighed, her only concession to the truth of that

statement. There was little use in denying the DaiMon's death; the remaining members of the consortium were still seated at the bar of the Due or Die, all loudly wailing and keening over the imminent collapse of their fortunes. True, DaiMon Bruk had been sent out on the obligatory salvage mission, but the presence of a Federation starship in the sector had shaken their faith in any recovery effort. Camenae suspected their pessimism was well-founded.

The thump of a green fist shook the table again. "I'm made of sterner stuff than mewling Ferengi merchants: I won't pay the balance!"

"Very well."

"What?" His arm stopped in midair, aborting yet another assault on the furniture.

"In accordance with my policy concerning delinquent accounts, I will be forced to liquidate certain information about your organization that I have kept out of general inventory. The sale of that information will be applied to your outstanding debt."

"That's blackmail, Camenae!"

"I call it a sound business procedure."

"Damn you!" His fist slammed down yet again, but this time he left a token in the wake of the hammer blow. "You'll get another next month and not a day before."

He turned and stomped his way across the deck with a deafening clatter.

"Anlew-Is," she called out. "Do you wish to be kept informed of the Heart's location?"

"No," he screamed from the doorway. "The Heart can go to blazes for all I care!"

The Ferengi had given much the same answer an hour before, although the whole troupe of them did not generate half the commotion made by one Orion black marketeer.

In the blessed silence that had been restored to her chamber, Camenae considered the selection of her next customer.

When Anlew-Is erupted out of the bar's back room, Miyakawa leaned farther back into the shadowed recesses of her booth. Her caution was hardly necessary since the Orion was far too preoccupied with broadcasting his indignation to pay any attention to his audience. As she listened to his loud ranting, and to the background chorus of the doleful Ferengi, the commander gleaned enough details to reconstruct their recent activity in the sector.

Anlew-Is was still fuming when her eyes tracked a robed figure gliding across the bar and into Camenae's office. Reyjadán was a permanent resident of the base, so Miyakawa knew his name and his homeworld, but the details of his personal life were a mystery. The DiWahn was an alien who kept to himself, rarely appearing in public. However, if he was one of Camenae's customers, it might be prudent to learn more of his background.

The glass in Miyakawa's hands was empty, but the commander feigned a sip of her drink so the waiter would leave her alone. Like a hunter tucked in a blind, she was in the mood to remain undetected and wait for more game to pass by.

The creature was swathed in cloth from head to toe, although Camenae was not entirely sure the figure hidden beneath the heavy robes possessed either of those features. Its voice issued forth from the folds of a drooping hood, and it spoke as if an oily, serpentine tongue formed its words.

"I am Lord Reyjadán. Your servant outside referred to me as 'the DiWahn.' You are both in need of correction. I am unDiWahn: one who is from, yet not of, that world. My people's origins are of greater eminence than that rough planet could ever generate."

"Thank you for that clarification." Camenae automatically filed away this free fact, although its value was dubious. "I have information you seek."

"The Dream Gem!" it said with a dry rattle of alarm. "What you call the Heart—the rumors of its discovery are true?"

"Yes. It has been found."

"Why was I not informed of this earlier?" hissed the cowl.

"I stated my interest in the Gem ten years ago when I first arrived on this starbase."

"I noted your demand at that time," said Camenae with a dryness that was lost on the alien. "But I have other customers who make greater use of my—"

"Kei! I do not involve myself with gossip or deal in issues of petty trade. My only concern is with the Gem. Where is it?"

"The answer to that question will cost—"

"Such insolence," said the alien. "You cannot put a price on my birthright."

"I can, and do, put a price on everything that is said in this room, Lord Reyjadán." After adding an extra ten percent exasperation tax to her previously decided on figure, Camenae firmly stated the cost of the proposed transaction. "Take it or leave it. I have other customers who would—"

"Spare me your tiresome haggling tactics. I will pay the sum in full." A jangling sound came from inside the voluminous sleeves, and a necklace crafted of refined dilithium crystals spilled out onto the table.

Camenae shook her head. "I only accept—"

"But I expect full service from you," said the alien. "There will be an additional requirement for the fulfillment of my quest, and I expect it to be provided without additional charge."

"Oh, very well," she said, impatient to end the transaction. After all, Aghlarren the Mote would offer a fair price for the crystals. "What is the additional service you require?"

To Camenae's intense regret, the demand he outlined was reasonable and easily arranged.

Half an hour after Reyjadán's departure, Commander Miyakawa had just about decided to put an end to her afternoon of hiding in the shadows of the Due or Die when Thomas Grede skulked into the bar and sidled through to the back room.

She settled back into her seat and ordered another drink.

Base personnel were not prohibited from frequenting the

Due or Die since such a regulation would have been impossible for her to enforce, but the technician's familiarity with the Norsican guard betrayed more than a casual acquaintance with the staff. The knowledge that Grede merited a solo audience with Camenae was even more intriguing.

I'm just one officer. I can't supervise all my personnel.

Miyakawa had been promised more support, but most of Starfleet viewed an assignment to Starbase 193 as a punitive measure and a blot on their record. So far, all the officers designated to serve on the station had successfully wrangled reassignments; the most recent lieutenant to be posted to the station had chosen to resign from Starfleet instead.

Until reinforcements arrived, Miyakawa would do her best to hold the fort. Today that meant having a little talk with Grede after his next duty shift.

"I have some information for you."

"For me?" said Grede. "But, Camenae, you know I haven't got enough credits to buy anything from you."

"Oh, but this information is free."

"Free?" He squirmed uneasily in his chair. She could see fear pooling in his eyes.

"According to my sources, Starbase 75 is now receiving Captain Picard's mission reports." Unfortunately, the contents of the communiqués were beyond her reach, but this fact alone was sufficient for her purpose.

Grede was a little slow to make the obvious connection, but it finally came to him. "They must know the distress call was altered." That realization drained color from his face.

"Furthermore," said Camenae. "A Tellarite freighter headed for Orion passed within hailing distance of the *Enterprise;* it appears to be on a direct heading for this base." The starship's destination would be common knowledge within the hour, but the captain of an outbound vessel loaded with contraband had gladly paid for the early warning.

"Camenae, you've got to help me!"

"Help of that magnitude is not free. It requires another investment on your part."

"Another . . . but that's how I . . ." His voice trailed off in confusion. "I'm in enough trouble already."

Camenae assumed her most reassuring smile. "I can arrange for your transport beyond the reach of the Federation authorities."

"How soon?" he croaked.

"Just as soon as you transmit a series of coded messages for one of my clients and then erase all records of the proceeding."

Grede seemed to fold in upon himself, shoulders slumping and head drooping. As she waited for the technician's answer, Camenae felt a stab of irritation at the difficulty he had making such a simple decision.

Finally, he mumbled his assent.

Commander Miyakawa tossed two tokens next to her empty glass before slipping out of the booth. There was no point in trying to pay for her bar tab—she had lost that battle long ago—but as a compromise she always left a hefty tip for the waiter.

The money was well spent. Over the last few hours, Miyakawa had surmised much of what Captain Picard had left out of his mission report. Now all she needed to know was why he had held back this information from her.

CHAPTER 10

"T'Sara."

She did not want to let loose her dream, but somewhere on the other side of consciousness there came an insistent demand for her to wake. Her name was repeated over and over again until she grew weary of resisting and opened her eyes.

"You sleep deeply these days," said the man who knelt before her. The muscles of Sorren's face were marshaled into an impassive mask, but he still lacked the necessary discipline to erase concern from his voice; she hoped he never learned to tame his dark, expressive eyes.

Despite the lingering memory of a soft cushioned bed, T'Sara realized she was sitting upright and the wall against her back was hard and unyielding.

"I was dreaming that I was a man asleep—dreaming of mad Vulcans sifting a dry dusty planet in search of lost shards of knowledge. When he wakes, my life will fade away, as will all the stone and mortar surrounding us."

"You spend too much time in this chamber." Sorren was unaware of the frown that slipped past his control; he glanced up at the enthroned figure that loomed over them. "I do not fear the dead, but neither do I seek out their company."

"The Collector was a less pleasant companion when she was alive," said T'Sara before she thought to curb her tongue.

His fierce glare was like a shout of anger. "Another dream?"

She tightened her grip on the Ko N'ya. He had tried to wrest if from her once before when she spoke of Surak on the plain of Ishaya. Logic dictated that a young male approaching his physical prime could easily overpower an old woman, yet he had failed to take it from her then.

"No, T'Sara, I did not come to argue with you over the stone." He still refused to utter its name. "The time for discussion has passed."

"Explain."

"I feel honor-bound to inform you of the action we have—"

"We?" she demanded.

"Sohle, T'Challo, the entire archaeological team. It is our unanimous decision that your thinking has become increasingly disordered and that you are in need of medical assistance. This morning I received confirmation that a Federation starship has been authorized to return you to Vulcan."

"My colleagues at the Science Academy will not thank you for that," she said. "My enemies have thought me mad for over a century, and even my supporters are embarrassed by my empathy for alien cultures. They all would rather that I confine my ravings to a small group of students as far from Vulcan as possible."

"There is a difference between unorthodox methods and insanity. I have long admired and respected your research, and I value highly what I have learned of your excavation techniques, but even I have lost patience watching you squander your abilities on this quest for the Ko N'ya. And your recent behavior . . ."

Were Vulcans always so long-winded, she wondered as Sorren prattled on, or had her patience worn as thin as her aging skin? Her wandering thoughts seized on his earlier words.

"Sorren," she said with a sharpness born of alarm. "Did you speak of the Ko N'ya in this message of yours?"

"What?" After a moment to reorient himself to her question, he said, "Only in passing."

"Child, you must not let your adherence to logic block your understanding of races who act on their emotions. News of the Ko N'ya is a beacon for the greedy who . . ."

She fell silent.

"T'Sara?"

The walls of the chamber were too thick for sound to penetrate, rather she had felt the shouts ringing in the air outside. An inchoate mental surge washed over her again.

"A Call," she said.

"Yes, I heard it, too!"

They both scrambled to their feet, but Sorren was young and supple and left her far behind as he raced through the dark tunnel toward daylight.

Pushing her bones and muscles beyond the petty annoyances of pain, she gained a new burst of speed and emerged from the ruins. The noonday sun was baking the tiles of the plaza.

"Sorren!"

He was standing just a few meters ahead of her. At her cry, he twirled to face her, and she saw that his chest had blossomed into fire. Horror thwarted her understanding, then she realized he had been shot and the force of the phaser blast had thrown his body around, because Sorren himself was already dead. His husk twitched, then collapsed.

T'Sara caught a fleeting glimpse of armored figures, tall men with dusky green skin, rushing toward her. Orions were not known for showing mercy to their victims. Before she could escape back into the shadows of the tower, she was buffeted by two hammer blows of searing heat.

As she fell to her knees, weakened by the destruction gnawing its way through her body, the desire to retaliate against her attackers raged through her mind. She could will their death and the stone would obey.

No, T'Sara, only a foolish old woman would ignore the wisdom of Surak any longer.

She let loose her grip, dropping the Ko N'ya. It hit the ground with a ringing sound, then rolled away with a curious vigor. As the intruders scrabbled in the dirt to recover it, T'Sara curled in upon herself with one last conscious thought.

I will not give it to any living being.

The desert sand faded out from under her . . .

. . . to be replaced with the smooth texture of fabric.

The man shivered in the cool air of the cabin and wrapped the covers more tightly around his body. The sensation of a burning pain in his side faded away, but the landscape of the dream itself was etched into his memory.

I am . . . Jean-Luc Picard.

He opened his eyes and saw T'Sara's stone glittering in the dark by his bedside.

CHAPTER 11

The chime trilled for a second time, then faded into silence. The door remained closed.

Beverly Crusher silently debated the wisdom of pressing the call button a third time. She was beginning to feel oddly conspicuous standing in the corridor outside Picard's cabin at such an early hour of the morning. Not that their breakfast routine was a secret, but she was wary of drawing too much attention to any intimacy between the captain and his chief medical officer. This balancing act between duty and friendship was hard enough to sustain without an audience.

Before she had taken more than two steps away, Crusher heard the door whooshing open behind her.

"Beverly."

The slurred quality of Picard's voice prepared her for the sight of his rumpled pajamas.

"Good morning, Jean-Luc."

He squinted in the bright light of the corridor. "Sorry, I was up late writing reports for Admiral Matasu, not to mention the Vulcan Science Academy. Then I had the strangest dream . . ."

"I'll take a rain check on breakfast."

"No, please come in." Picard moved aside to let her pass through the doorway. "I want to tell you about my dream."

She set about ordering tea and biscuits from the replicator while Picard changed into his uniform in the bedroom. By the time the coffee table was set, he had emerged a transformed man, dapper and alert.

"That's the Heart?" asked Crusher when she saw the object the captain carried with him. She had heard a secondhand recounting of the discovery from Worf late last night when she tended a gash in his hand.

"Yes, this is T'Sara's Ko N'ya." Picard settled down on the sofa beside the doctor. "They were both in my dream."

"Tell me." Crusher sipped her tea and listened to Picard recount his version of the Vulcan's death. As he talked he rolled the stone over and over in his hands as if searching for a chink in its rough surface, a key to the interior.

"So, Detective Hill," she said when he had reached the end of the tale, "your subconscious thinks a band of Orions killed T'Sara?"

He glanced up from his study of the Heart. "I realize it's not such a startling conclusion given the evidence."

"Well, you've got a fifty-fifty chance of being right," said Crusher. From here, the gem that had built empires looked like an ordinary rock. "But whether it was the Orions or the Ferengi, there aren't any criminals left alive to bring to justice."

"Yet there's at least one accessory lurking on Starbase 193. We're due to arrive there soon, and I hope the element of surprise will give us an advantage in—"

"How could so many people die fighting each other for that thing!"

His eyebrows shot upward at her outburst.

"It's just so . . . drab," said Crusher. "I expected something more dramatic."

"A faceted ruby the size of a watermelon?"

"Something like that," she admitted with a laugh.

"If this is the Heart, I'm afraid its only value lies in its historic significance."

She leaned over the table and dropped her voice to a whisper. "But what about its powers over Darkness?"

Picard smiled somewhat sheepishly. "Oh, I grant the legends are grandly melodramatic . . . still, it is a rather curious object."

"In what way?"

He started to speak, then hesitated, then began again. "Perhaps its my overactive imagination at work, but I can feel a heightened quality about it. Nothing I can put into words." He shrugged away his inability to explain. "Perhaps Data will be able to quantify its properties."

"This should provide material for an impressive article for the next archaeological symposium. Not bad for an amateur." But she could tell from his lack of reaction that Picard wasn't listening to her anymore.

Propelled by an inner train of thought, the captain suddenly bolted from the table and was halfway across the cabin before he remembered he had company. "Oh, my apologies, Beverly. It's just that Data is expecting me to bring the Heart to his laboratory."

"But, Jean-Luc, you haven't eaten a thing." Even his teacup had gone untouched.

"I'm not hungry. No, really, I'm not."

"Well, I am. Do you mind if I stay here long enough to finish my biscuit?"

He had the good grace to flush. "Please make yourself at home." Stopping in the doorway, Picard called back, "I'll make it up to you. Why don't we have dinner tomorrow night?"

"Yes, I'd like—"

Then he was gone.

"This may take some time," said Data as he carefully placed the stone in the center of a small metallic stage.

"Actually," said Picard, craning his neck to follow Data's movements, "I'd like to stay and watch."

"As you wish, sir." The weight of the specimen triggered a ripple of electronic chirps across a control console; Data quickly tapped a series of minor adjustments to the estimated calibration figures he had entered earlier.

After he positioned the first equipment array over the stage, Data provided a running commentary of the laboratory procedure in specimen analysis. To his gratification, the captain appeared to welcome the information; unfortunately, this was not always the case.

"By combining the three different techniques," the android continued, as he concluded the final step of the third measurement, "I should be able to determine the age of the stone to a value of plus or minus one hundred years."

The results of the calculation were not what he had expected.

"Is something wrong, Data?" asked the captain, stepping closer to the equipment. "What have you found?"

"Preliminary dating analysis indicates the object is remarkably young, falling in a range between eight hundred and one thousand years old. This would fall far short of the reputed age of the Ko N'ya."

Picard was silent for a moment, then said, "I suggest you run the dating analysis again."

"Certainly, Captain. As you wish."

Data reached out to reconfigure the equipment for a repetition of the dating scans.

"What else did you find?" asked Picard.

"Meir-Delaplace analysis indicates the rock was formed from a mixture of a common crystalline form of silicon dioxide and a metamorphic sandstone—"

"Data!" Evidently this answer did not please the captain either. "T'Sara did not spend over a hundred years of her life looking for a rock. It may look like rock, but it is . . . well, more than that. According to her theory this relic possesses unusual and puzzling features. For instance, what about the warmth?"

Data assumed a slightly puzzled frown as a visual adjunct to his reply. "I record no difference between the temperature of the object and that of the ship's interior."

"But when I held it before I could feel the warmth." Picard

shoved aside the equipment array to seize the rock. "I can feel it now."

"Indeed?" Data double-checked his instrument readout, but there was no indication of a scientific basis for the captain's perception. "Perhaps you could hold the stone while the analysis is in progress?"

"Certainly, if that's what it takes to prove my point."

Before Data could activate the appropriate equipment, they were interrupted by an intercom call.

"Riker to Captain Picard."

"Picard here."

"We're being hailed by Starbase 193. Commander Miyakawa requests a conference with you concerning your mission progress."

"I'll conduct it in my ready room, Number One." With a sigh of exasperation, Picard sketched a parting wave to Data. "You'll have to carry on without me."

"Captain?"

"Yes?"

"I would like to continue my analysis of the . . . object." Data pointed to the stone still cradled in the crook of Picard's arm.

Picard stopped in mid-stride. "Oh, yes, of course."

Data retrieved the specimen from the captain, then stood in place holding the stone in his hands.

It never warmed to his touch.

"Qué pasa, Picard?" Estrella Miyakawa still rolled the *r* in his name, but her Mexican accent had been muted over the years. He studied her image on the desk monitor and noted a few streaks of white in her straight black hair; otherwise, time had touched her very lightly.

"Estoy bien," answered Picard. She had taught him what little Spanish he knew in exchange for tutoring her in calculus; he never mastered the language, and she failed the Academy course.

"So why have you been sending me mission reports that could be written on the head of a pin?"

Age had not softened her blunt manner. "Perhaps I erred on the side of succinctness," said Picard, displaying his most genial, diplomatic smile.

She laughed in his face. "Captain, you've cut me out of the information loop since your departure from Atropos, and I want to know why."

"Commander, my last report on the Ferengi distress—"

"Did not contain one word about the destruction of the Orion ship *Dark Runner.*"

"How did you hear of that?" asked Picard.

"News travels fast in this sector. Although, as a Federation official, I was probably the last person on the starbase to find out. Any idea why they were fighting, or are you going to keep that to yourself as well?"

He sighed at the increasing tone of bitterness in her voice. Any further attempt at secrecy would only alienate his one ally on the base, not to mention cost him the goodwill of an old friend. "Estrella, I have reason to believe that the security of your communications system has been breached. Until the source of the leak is found, I prefer not to discuss the details of the mission."

"Oh, I have a pretty good idea of who's responsible already," she said grimly. "One of my communications operators—Thomas Grede. Unfortunately, Mr. Grede met with an accident last night. It seems that when he came off shift, he took a wrong turn and walked out an airlock."

"He was murdered."

"Thank you, Jean-Luc, but that thought had occurred to me already. I'll fill you in on the details when you arrive."

There went his advantage. "How the devil did you know the *Enterprise* was headed for Starbase 193?"

"The usual base channels," said Miyakawa with a wry smile. "I overheard it in a bar."

"Of course, it's not just any bar," explained the commander later that day as she and Picard walked through the doorway of the Due or Die. "This is Camenae's bar, and that makes all the difference."

The dimly lit room was crowded, with no empty tables, but one of the waiters waved them over to a booth. Two Tellarites and an Andorian scrambled off the benches with half-filled drinks still clutched in their hands.

Picard heard their muttered curses as he and Miyakawa settled into the hastily vacated booth. Another waiter swept by and left two glasses of synthehol in his wake. "Are these the perks of base command?"

"Some of the very few," sighed Miyakawa. "Camenae, for reasons I haven't yet fathomed, likes to maintain the fiction that I'm a power to be reckoned with on this station. Perhaps the tourists find the illusion of law and order comforting."

"You weren't this cynical at the Academy."

She shrugged and gestured toward the patrons of the densely packed bar. A group of Ferengi merchants were huddled at one end of the room; Orions were at the other end; in between, Picard counted at least ten other alien races, none of them known for their pacifism or a highly developed sense of ethics.

"I'm one Starfleet officer working alone in a den of smugglers, thieves, and cutthroats. If I ever manage to get my hands on any hard evidence of criminal activity, I'll probably end up walking out an airlock just like Grede." She downed her drink in one gulp, then said, "Which hasn't stopped me from trying, mind you. However, Camenae is fond of me, so she works very hard to keep compromising materials out of my reach."

"Just who is this Camenae?" asked Picard.

"Officially, she's merely one of the inhabitants of the starbase, but unofficially, I'd have to say that Camenae is the real administrator of this place. I may supervise the base's technical services and facilities, but Camenae runs its affairs. She always knows what's going on in every corner of this sector, so if someone wants information, she sells it to them; when something needs to be done, she arranges it."

"Does that include murder?"

"I'm sure it does." Miyakawa frowned, then shook her

head. "But I don't think she ordered Grede's death. It was a sloppy job, and Camenae would never allow one of her informants to be killed in such an obvious way."

"But you think she knows who did?"

"Yes. Not that I'll ever be able to get that information out of her; and unless she gives the signal, there's not a single being on the starbase who will talk to me about Grede's death."

"So you're telling me that the murderer will go free?" said Picard angrily.

"Without any evidence, or any witnesses, my hands are—"

Miyakawa was cut off by the crash of heavy furniture and a stream of curses uttered in a mixture of Ferengi and Federation Standard.

"Nothing!" continued the Ferengi who had overturned a chair as he staggered to his feet; he was weaving back and forth in place. "Bruk says he found nothing in the wreckage but my brother's corpse!"

One of his companions plucked at the sleeve of his gray jacket, but the Ferengi swatted away the restraining hand.

"The salvage effort alone will bankrupt me. All it brings me is the trouble of selling Maarc's ship for scrap metal and the exorbitant expense of the crew's funeral."

"I think I've met his brother," said Picard softly. "Perhaps we should leave before—"

"Ah ha!" The Ferengi was staring directly at them. "The captain of the *Enterprise* has come to laugh at my defeat."

"Too late, Jean-Luc," said Miyakawa, as the bantam-weight Ferengi bore down upon them as fast as his unsteady legs could carry him. His domed head and flaring ears had flushed a deep red from too much drink and an excess of rage.

"You were there, thief!" His finger jabbed repeatedly at Picard's chest. "Return what is rightfully mine, what you stole from my brother!"

Before Picard could form a reply, a dark hand settled on the Ferengi's shoulder. The woman's grip was firm enough to choke off any further accusations.

"DaiMon Tork," she said in a low voice. "I prefer my customers to conduct their private business with greater discretion and decorum."

So this was Camenae.

Then the bar owner turned her attention to Picard, and he was struck by the intensity of her gaze. There was a familiar quality to her face that he couldn't quite place.

"Welcome to the Due or Die, Captain Picard. My apologies for the disturbance."

The Ferengi uttered a strangled squeak of protest.

"DaiMon Tork," said Picard in a voice loud enough to carry to all corners of the bar. "You have my word that we took nothing that belonged to the Ferengi off that ship."

Camenae's lips curved into a smile, and she released her hold on Tork.

"Just as I thought," the DaiMon groaned, collapsing onto the floor. He rubbed gingerly at his sore shoulder. "Scrap metal and funeral expenses."

With a snap of her fingers, Camenae signaled Tork's companions to carry him away, and they scurried forward to do her bidding.

The sense of familiarity deepened. "Have we met before?"

"I'm disappointed, Captain Picard. I expected a more original opening line from you."

En garde.

Perhaps she would respond to a direct approach. "Commander Miyakawa tells me you're in the information business. I'd like to become one of your customers."

"That's a much better tactic," she said. "Unfortunately, Starfleet doesn't have an account with me, and I'm not accepting new clients at the moment. If you like, I'll put you on my waiting list."

Lunge and parry.

"At the very least," said Picard, "I'd like the opportunity to talk to you in private . . . about Thomas Grede."

Camenae shook her head gently. "I have nothing to say to you that can't be discussed right here in the middle of the Due or Die. Private meetings with Starfleet officers are bad for my business reputation." *Touché.* "Now, if you'll excuse me, Captain, I must get back to work."

She glided away.

The memory of Camenae's smoky eyes haunted Picard all the way back to the *Enterprise.* However, standing in his brightly illuminated ready room, Picard realized that his impressions of the Due or Die and its elusive owner would be impossible to convey in words. He restricted himself to relating the bare bones of his experience to his first officer.

"That's it?" Riker rocked back in his chair so he could look Picard in the eye. "Grede was the victim of an accidental death under unknown circumstances?"

Picard's hands gripped the back of his desk chair. He could not bring himself to sit down since at any moment he should receive a call that would pull him away. "I'm not comfortable with Miyakawa's preliminary ruling either. However, I have a better appreciation for the difficulties of her situation now that I've actually visited Starbase 193. The Federation's control of this area is relatively recent and definitely precarious."

Riker held up one hand and ticked off the points of contention across his fingertips. "So the Orions can't be brought to justice because they were killed by the Ferengi, and the communications officer who leaked the information about the Heart has conveniently died so *he* can't be charged, and the case of the murder of ten Vulcans is now closed."

"Yes, it is suspiciously neat and tidy," said the captain. The call still had not come, and he began to admit that the delay worried him.

"So what do we do now?" asked Riker.

Picard appreciated the effort it must have taken for his first officer to maintain a neutral tone to ask this question. At warp eight the *Enterprise* could still reach Luxor IV in time for the poker tournament. "I've assured Commander Miyakawa that we'll remain in the area another twenty-four hours to provide at least a token show of strength in the sector."

"I'm glad to hear that, sir." Despite the personal sacrifice involved, Riker's reaction seemed sincere. Picard knew the first officer disliked letting bullies go unchallenged. "Will you consider allowing shore leave privileges—"

"Let's continue this discussion later, Number One," said the captain. He moved out from behind the desk at a brisk pace. "I should have received Data's report on the Heart by now."

Picard bolted out the door before his first officer could trail after him.

Data accepted as an axiom of his construction that he did not possess emotions; therefore, he could initiate yet another repetition of his laboratory procedures without an accompanying sense of frustration or anger. However, based on his experience with the crew of the *Enterprise,* the android greatly suspected that these were precisely the set of emotions that he *should* be feeling at this time.

Moving the equipment array into position over the specimen, he closely monitored his actions so that he might detect any departure from his previous routines. No difference. He had followed the same pattern of movement with the same precision each of the four times before.

Data repeated the dating measurement a fifth time.

A new result appeared on his viewscreen. Entirely new. Over the course of hours, he had not been able to obtain the same age for the specimen twice in a row.

Since there was no reason to believe that a sixth attempt would reveal any new insights, Data concluded that another approach was required. Unfortunately, the formulation of such an approach eluded him.

The android was pondering the nature of scientific inspiration when the doors of the laboratory parted to admit a swiftly moving Captain Picard. Judging from the somewhat grim set of the captain's facial features, Data surmised there was no need for an exchange of pleasantries and launched into an immediate explanation of the project's difficulties.

Picard's expression hardened even more as he listened.

"The largest given value was twenty million years old,"

continued Data. "Which would be consistent with the theory of the Heart's involvement with ancient history. Unfortunately, the extreme variations raise considerable doubt as to the validity of any of the results I have obtained."

"Obviously your equipment is malfunctioning, Mr. Data," said Picard. He plucked the stone off the scan stage and carefully examined its surface for signs of damage.

"I ran extensive diagnostic tests subsequent to each of the anomalous findings. There is no sign of malfunction. Furthermore, my measurement of all other test objects has been consistent and predictable. There appears to be some substance in the specimen itself which interferes with the scan."

"Earlier, you claimed it was nothing more than a rock."

Data attempted a shrug. "Apparently the composition analysis was in error. I shall repeat that procedure as well."

He extended one arm, reaching for the stone, but Picard took a step backward as if to evade him. "I think we should suspend any further analysis until you've straightened out the technical difficulties in the laboratory equipment."

"Captain, the specimen would be useful in determining—"

Picard stepped away again. "Until you can establish the nature of the malfunction, I won't risk inflicting any damage to the Heart." Cradling the stone in the crook of his arm, he said, "I'll keep it in my cabin for now."

Data searched for the emotion that might best suit this situation. The answer came to him just after the captain's departure: exasperation.

He wondered what it felt like.

CHAPTER 12

For one hour every night, the Due or Die was closed for a perfunctory cleaning. Grumbling patrons were pushed off the premises or carried out into the corridor if they lacked the ability to walk by themselves; it was an open secret on the starbase that the synthehol served at the bar had an unusually potent effect on anyone who slipped a hefty tip to the bartender.

Other branches of Camenae's business, however, were open at all times. So while Orlev wiped stains off the pitted countertop, Camenae perched on a barstool, waiting patiently for the arrival of one of her operatives.

"We've been very busy lately," said the bartender as he gathered up an armful of dirty glasses.

His breathy, sibilant complaint reflected her own train of thought. She sighed in agreement. "For ten years we laughed at that old Vulcan woman and her quest for a mythical treasure. But now, it seems the joke is on us. She found that damn Heart—and disrupted this entire sector."

Of course, the greedy scramble after the relic had also fattened Camenae's coffers, but she distrusted these windfall profits. They were short-lived and unpredictable, not to mention that her overhead had also risen sharply.

For instance, there was the matter of Thomas Grede.

She had promised to transport him to safety, and she was in the habit of keeping her word. After all, broken contracts were bad for business.

A warning whistle from Kajima announced the arrival of someone at the threshold of the bar. "It's the Squib," announced the guard after he checked the image coming from the security camera.

Camenae nodded and slipped off the barstool. The Norsican knew to wait for her retreat into the back office before he released the lock on the entrance.

She was seated in her customary place when she heard the clicking sound of chitonous legs on the metallic deck. Krtakk scurried forward to greet her with a customary wave of its eye stalks. As a longtime operative, it knew not to waste any more time on extraneous civilities.

"As you suspected, Camenae," it said in a chittering voice. "Lord Reyjadán stole the transport papers from Grede and obtained free passage on the *Villareal* all the way to Smelter's Hold."

"After that?"

To her disgust, Krtakk bobbed its hard-shelled body up and down, a submissive gesture that signaled failure. "I could find no trace of the unDiWahn after leaving the *Villareal.* He has gone into hiding somewhere on the Hold, but it will take time and money to determine who is sheltering him."

"Continue the trace, whatever the cost."

The Squib chirped its acceptance of the task. "There is one item more: Grede was supposed to erase all traces of the alien's transmissions, but the new tech in communications was able to recover a scrap that escaped overwrite." Krtakk executed a rapid series of nervous bobs. "Unfortunately, the price for commissioning the effort was exorbitant and the result disappointing."

"Let me hear it anyway," said Camenae with a sigh of resignation at the escalating cost of her revenge.

A tentacle looped up over the table edge and dropped a small vocoder into the palm of her hand. Camenae pressed a control switch and sound issued forth from its speaker.

"*. . . seeking has ended. The Gem has been uncovered, and it is again . . .*"

That was all. Such a small scrap and yet so very revealing.

"Thank you, Krtakk. You have done well."

The Squib squeaked, surprised by her praise, then scuttled away with a churring prattle of self-congratulations.

Camenae played the short recording over several times, listening carefully to the quality of the voice instead of the words. The content was indeed unrewarding, but there was an unexpected value in hearing Reyjadán speak in private: his crisp enunciation of Federation Standard was devoid of the thick oily accent and hissing sound he had used with her.

Evidently she had underestimated the unDiWahn. And poor Grede had paid the price of her miscalculation.

Some men turned to fat in their old age, but First Prefect Lorris had added no weight to his lean, muscular frame as decade piled on decade. By his ninetieth year, his eyesight had not dimmed, the peaked scrollwork of his ears missed no whisper of gossip or slander, and his dry laughter had developed a blade-sharp edge that could cut his victims to the quick. If his reflexes had slowed any since his youth, Lorris had hidden that change beneath an imposing dignity of bearing.

His one concession to the passage of time was a diminished patience for disruption and disorder. So, as his family size swelled with succeeding generations of offspring, Lorris retreated more and more often to the sheltered confines of his library.

Only on this morning, when the prefect entered his sanctuary he found it already occupied. His irritation at the violation of his privacy was mollified once he recognized the uniformed intruder. Subcommander Vedoc was rooted in place by one of the tallest bookshelves, head bent over an open book; he was so immersed in his study that he had not heard the door of the room open.

"For a soldier, you read a great deal of history, Nephew."

The young man twirled around. Then, with a smile of greeting, he ducked his head in an informal gesture of respect that acknowledged close family ties yet did not forget the distance between their ranks. "Your library is impossible to resist, Uncle. I have spent many of my ship leaves in this room."

"Hah! If you value your career, you should be out whoring and drinking with your shipmates." Settling into a broad chair in the middle of the room, the old man beckoned his sister's son to come closer. "There was a time, in the early days of the Empire, when an officer was despised as a common throat-slitter if he did not also cultivate a knowledge of art, music, and literature. Those days are gone. Most of my fellow prefects are either mercenaries or bureaucrats, and I suspect that they consider me to be a peevish eccentric."

"Then I appear to take after you."

"You could do worse," said Lorris with a sniff. Vedoc had always been a favorite of his, more so than any of his own spawn. The prefect was struck with a sudden inspiration, and he forged his attack strategy with the same rapidity that he had used as a commander in battle. "That book you are holding is contraband."

The young man looked down in surprise at the volume in his hands. "But if that is so, however did you obtain it, Uncle?"

Lorris chuckled at the boy's naïveté. "One of the advantages of a military career is the chance to make contacts with unsavory characters; the Ferengi, for instance. A loathsome race, but they do have their uses."

"They smuggled Federation books to you for payment?"

"For payment, yes," said the old man. "But also for trade. There are those in the Federation who are equally curious about the Romulans. In fact, as a centurion I provided the author of that very book," he pointed once again to the tome in his nephew's hands, "with a copy of the early history of the Romulan people."

"I've read several of her works here in the library," said Vedoc eagerly. "She's a fine scholar."

"*Was* a fine scholar. According to my contacts, T'Sara died just a few days ago."

"Of old age?"

"Perhaps," said Lorris with a shrug. "She must have been close to three centuries old. Yet the report is that she died along with a group of other Vulcans, which implies the death was not natural."

"Her loss will be a blow to Federation science."

"I agree, but the Vulcans do not value her scholarship as highly as we do. Evidently T'Sara's uncanny understanding of alien emotion offends their delicate sensibilities."

The young man frowned. "There is much I do not understand about the Vulcans."

"They are a dull race, Vedoc. Their philosophy of logic leaves no room for the vices that make life worthwhile." It was time to test the waters; with a deep sigh, Lorris added, "Yet the only vice I have carried into my old age is curiosity . . . and I am curious to learn how T'Sara died and what has come of her research into our legends. The answers I seek may do nothing more than satisfy my meddlesome nature, but then again . . . well, they may do far more."

Vedoc's eyebrows angled upward; this turn in the discussion had definitely piqued his interest.

"I have the ear of the Praetor," continued the first prefect, "and in payment for some long-standing debts born of my attention to his private affairs, he has agreed to send a warbird beyond the Neutral Zone to investigate the matter."

His nephew's interest heightened into alarm. Eyes wide with disbelief, he said, "He would violate the Neutral Zone treaty for this venture?"

"For a chance to possess the Ko N'ya, the Praetor would do anything." Lorris chortled softly. "Or at least, order someone else to do anything."

"The Ko N'ya," whispered the young man. The library was

warm, yet he shivered as if a cold draft had chilled his bones. "A myth risen from the Vaults of the Dead."

"You have a vivid imagination, Vedoc, but then so did I at your age. Military service will teach you how to channel that faculty into more sensible pursuits."

His nephew stiffened to attention, a tactful response that did not commit him to agreement.

Enough dallying, thought the prefect. There was not much time to implement this revision to his plans. "It would please me to have these proceedings supervised by someone who is personally concerned with our family interests."

Vedoc caught his meaning without difficulty. "Can you arrange for my transfer to the warbird?"

"Oh, yes," said Lorris with a wry smile. "I have nearly as many favors to call in as I have books on these shelves."

"Then I am yours to command, Uncle."

"Excellent. Prepare to leave this house within the hour." Lorris was impressed by the young soldier's courage. His sister's son would make a fine prefect some day and bring new honors to the family name.

If he survived this mission, of course.

Those called to the Gathering began to assemble when the first moon of DiWahn started its climb up through the twilight sky. Out of houses and inns, through darkening streets, the robed figures streamed toward the Gateway Temple. Heavy cowls hid the faces of those who called themselves the unDiWahn. Some walked singly, others in pairs or small groups, but by the time they reached the tiled plaza surrounding the high tower, their swelling numbers had merged into one mass of the Faithful.

Townspeople not sworn to the Faith cowered in their homes, for within memory there had never been a Gathering as large as this one. Every Guardian on the face of the planet must have journeyed to the walled city of Iconiadán, but no one outside the order had envisioned there were so many to answer the call; the sound of their swishing robes seeped like flood waters through barred doors and shuttered windows.

Those men and women who had settled into a complacent acceptance of their adopted world were reminded once again of half-forgotten legends of ancient Iconia and its lost grandeur. In fearful whispers, they wondered what cabalistic cataclysm had roused the Guardians. The Faithful kept alive the memories of their race before the Passage through the Gate, and they possessed knowledge beyond the understanding of farmers and merchants; therefore, whatever alarmed the Guardians might well terrify a commoner.

When the moon reached its zenith, tolling bells chased a few stragglers through the massive archways at the base of the tower, and thick doors hewn from the strongest wood swung back into place to seal all entrances against any uninitiated intruders.

Body pressed tightly against body inside the domed chamber that barely contained the assembly; but in the very center of the densely packed crowd there was a clearing just large enough for one hooded figure to sit cross-legged on the floor. The abstract mosaic design beneath this Guardian marked the spot where the first Iconian had stepped through the Gateway; only a handful of the Faithful had the right to occupy this place of honor.

After the last knell faded into silence, the Master rose from the floor and pushed back the heavy folds of the hood to reveal a man in the middle years of his life. The scalloped ridges of his forehead were plainly patterned, devoid of beauty yet not quite ugly; his skin was the pale shade of violet that marked him as a native of the southern hemisphere of the planet.

One by one, the members of the Gathering followed his example. When all of the Guardians had bared their heads, Kieradán spoke in a deep, melodious voice that could reach every straining ear and fill it with honey. The only sound from the listening host was their soft breathing.

"Here is the story, as my grandfather told it to me . . ."

When I was a young man, newly initiated into our order, an offworlder came to my village to live. She was a tall woman with delicate, sweeping features and hair the color of ash; her dark eyes burned with the desire to learn the language and ways of our people. I had never seen her like before, and she said that she was the first of her race to set foot upon DiWahn; however, my elders among the Faithful knew her already.

At that time, I was still too young to have learned more than a half dozen Dreams, but Ikajadán assured me that T'Sara was part of the Gem's lore and that she was destined to become one facet of the Dreaming.

For weeks I listened as the Guardians debated their part in the Gem's plan and how to fulfill it. Some among them said it would be sacrilege to even contemplate action, that such direct interference would actually disrupt the course of the Dreaming; others denounced this passivity, believing instead that the unDiWahn had been chosen to set T'Sara on the proper path.

In the end, the way was simple.

Ikajadán invited her to attend the Tellings. There was no precedent for allowing one unsworn to the Faith to hear the Dreams, and T'Sara quickly sensed that she had been greatly honored. So night after night she joined me as we took our place in the circle of Guardians; and each night someone recited one of the Dreams recorded by our Iconian ancestors, although never one in which she had a part.

She listened patiently at first, then with a growing hunger that carried her through the entire winter. On the first day of spring, Ikajadán recounted the death of Iconia, and thus reached the end of the ancient lore. By this time, T'Sara yearned to discover what had become of Kanda Jiak's Gem and to fully understand its powers.

Her restlessness drove her away from our world, but she was not lost to us. Always I knew where to find her, and those Dreams were the ones I never tired of hearing.

Kieradán paused for breath, then said, "That is the end of my grandfather's Telling, but the story does not end there.

"For many years, T'Sara sent word of her search to several of the unDiWahn who had tutored her. Then, one by one these Guardians grew old and died, until there was no one left among the Faithful who was known to her, and her letters stopped.

"My father took part in the Gathering that chose one of its number to leave DiWahn and seek her out. Jaradadán spent the rest of his life on this mission, wandering from one planet to another in T'Sara's wake, always careful to keep out of her sight. His son was born offworld and continues the work of his father."

Raising his hands high into the air, Kieradán proclaimed, "Reyjadán has this to say to us: T'Sara's seeking has ended; the Gem has been uncovered; and it is again time for the Faithful to take a part in the Dreaming."

His words unleashed a storm of emotion from the Guardians. Shouts of joy mixed with the sobs of those moved to tears by the arrival of a day foretold in myth. Young and old, men and women, strangers and friends, all embraced each other as kin.

Kieradán waited for the throes of their fervor to calm, then he drew a scroll from the folds of his robe. The parchment was yellow with age, and it was tied with leather laces.

"We have prepared for this day in many ways. There are those among you who were chosen to pave the path we must follow, others to walk its length." He scanned the multitude of eager faces that had turned back toward him. "Daramadán!"

A large, heavyset man pushed his way through the assembly to the center of the chamber. Few of the Guardians had ever met this man, but everyone knew of him by another name; his inclusion in the order had never been revealed before.

"Are you with us?" asked Kieradán. It was a ritual question, but the answer had never carried so much weight as it did tonight.

"I am with you," said the one that most of DiWahn knew as Admiral Jakat. "As are my forces."

"Hai!" A chorus of voices scattered throughout the crowd attested to the loyalty of the senior officers Daramadán had brought into the order.

Bowing his head in a gesture of subservience, the admiral

of the DiWahn space fleet asked, "Where are we to go, Master?"

"To the Appointed Place," said Kieradán. At his touch, the brittle leather ties circling the scroll crumbled into dust. He unfurled the sheet and held it high so all could see what was drawn on its surface.

It was a map filled with stars and a single blazing comet.

CHAPTER 13

The sighing winds carried aloft the moans and cries of the dying as if beseeching the heavens for pity, but the red sun was merciless. Blazing in noonday splendor, it dried the throats and tongues of men too weak to crawl toward shelter, and beat down upon bodies that had no warmth of their own. Small fires smoldered in the blood-sodden ground, then guttered out in trails of dark, foul smoke. Here and there across the littered field were flutters of movement: the trembling of limbs as death finally took hold of an eviscerated warrior, the lazy flap of wings as a carrion-eater feasted on the carnage, the rippling of a clan banner whose broken staff was driven through the chest of the standard-bearer.

As the sun tipped over on its westward descent toward the jagged peaks of Mt. Selaya, and the dry desert breezes gathered strength, one lone figure broke the taut line of the horizon. He picked his way carefully, stepping over the fallen warriors if possible, skirting around them when the mounds of intertwined bodies grew too deep. His tunic was clean, unspotted, untorn, but his legs and sandal laces were streaked with the olive color of drying gore.

The boy stopped for a moment, winded by his long run

from the mountain village and his tortured progress through the battlefield of Ishaya; closed eyes gave respite to his mind. His mother and the healers had demanded that he stay in isk'Kahr, but he had twisted out of T'Leia's grasp and raced away.

"Wait!" they had cried after him. "You are too young," they had Called into his mind when he passed beyond hearing.

He was much older now.

In the last hour he had learned that the colorful scenes of clashing armies intricately embroidered in tapestries and the lilting melody of the War Ballads were all treats for children, just like the tales of wise old sehlats who talked to lost hunters. Emerald-green thread shimmered in lamplight, but the blood that covered his own legs was not so pretty, and armor had no luster when it was splattered with gore. Five Vulcan clans had emptied their veins into this sandy plain, sullying its air with the stink of putrefaction; few survived to sing tales of bravery, or even of treachery. Where was the glory in this silence?

Come.

The need to continue pressed against his mind again. He had mistaken the desire for his own curiosity, for his own willfulness, but now he recognized that the summons was from without, a Call from someone alive and adrift in this sea of corpses. He opened his eyes and scanned the torn landscape.

"Father?"

He was answered by a visceral tug toward the north, as if a hand plucked weakly at his sleeve when lips could no longer form words.

His pace quickened now that he had been given a path to follow and a sense of purpose. Even the horrors of the killing field were less shocking than before. The endless variations of mutilation—charred limbs, split skulls, sunken chests—all played out the basic theme of death. The weapons also varied in configuration, yet all had drawn sufficient blood to silence their enemies. Some of the slain were unmarked, showing no open wounds, but their faces were clenched and contorted in the grotesque physical manifestation of the Calls that had expertly twisted their minds.

The tattered remnants of a bright red flag caught his eye. He approached it with dread, torn between the urgency of his father's Call and fear of where it drew him. Yes, his family had fought here. By a freak accident of the wind, the cloth was draped like a shroud across the body of one of his clansmen, mimicking the act of a healer acknowledging the limits of her art. His search was almost over.

My son.

The Call was weaker than before, yet still he could sense that his father lay nearby.

He took one step forward, then faltered when he saw the face of the body lying in his path. Surrell lay crumpled on the ground where a shard of metal had pinned him down; he had died in agony, thrashing to free himself. To lose any brother was a cause for grief, but this brother had been a favorite, and his death brought more pain than all the other horrors the boy had witnessed. A second step revealed another slain brother. Then a third.

All the dead before him had names; he had seen each of these still, pale faces laughing in the radiant moonlight during the last Festival of Moons. Brothers, uncles, cousins; there were too many to mourn.

"Father!"

"Here." The soft word was spoken, not Sent.

The boy frantically scrabbled through the dead bodies until his hands touched warm flesh. He fell to his knees by the side of his father. Stef's face was covered with blood, blurring the familiar angular features. His eyes, normally dark and piercing, were clouded with pain and exhaustion, but they cleared when he felt the touch of a hand on his arm.

"I've come, Father."

"What, no other sons left?" asked Stef, his weak voice hoarse with anger.

"No, Father, just me."

"So be it. I will have more sons." With a gasping breath to

gather strength for movement, Stef drew back his cloak to reveal a small object nestled by his side. "Behold your birthright and your future: the king-maker, Ko N'ya!"

"This is what my brothers died for?" asked the boy. He had overheard Surrell and the others whispering in the dark when they had thought he was safely asleep; they had spun strange tales of a relic of great power that would bring immense wealth to the clan that possessed it. Yet this dull gray rock was not worth one day of Surrell's life.

"Death is a small price to pay for our place in history. My dynasty shall unite all Vulcan," said his father. He lifted up the stone and his voice grew louder. "We will live forever . . . rule forever."

The boy reached out to touch the rough surface of the Ko N'ya, but Stef pulled it away.

"Mine!" he hissed. "Do not be so eager to succeed me."

"No, Father, I never meant—"

Stef's cry of pain cut off the boy's apology. A spasm racked through the man's body, twisting his muscles into knots and robbing him of the strength to hold the stone. It slipped from his trembling fingers, and the boy lunged forward to catch it before it hit the ground.

Mine!

"Father?"

The soft flutter of Stef's Calling mind faded to silence.

The boy rocked back on his heels, the Ko N'ya in his hands. He was the only living being left on the plain of Ishaya.

Desert nights are chill on Vulcan. The borrowed warmth of the sun does not linger for very long in the dark. A young boy in a linen shirt and sleeveless vest would need to huddle close to the licking flames of a fire in order to survive until morning.

Not this boy.

He sat cross-legged on the cold ground, yet his limbs did not shiver and tremble. The stone rested in the palms of his hands where he held its weight all night without strain. Under moonlight it transformed into a crystalline gem, glittering and sparkling as if lit from within, but at dawn the spell was broken.

A hoarse shouting reverberated across the plain, and the boy looked up to see figures moving in the distance. At first he assumed the people of his village had finally arrived to seek out their dead, but as the group drew nearer he caught the foreign lilt to their voices. They spoke with the harsh bark of warriors, not healers. Another clan, probably the Ghe'Hara, he guessed once he could see the cut of their armor. He counted eight men scouring the field, darting here and there and rummaging among the dead as if in search of something.

More fierce shouting ensued when one of the men gestured toward the red flag of Stef's clan. The troop began to run across the field, heedless of the dead underfoot, and in their haste one of the warriors nearly trampled over the boy where he sat silent and unmoving.

"Th'a!" cursed the man, jumping back as if a serpent had crawled out of the grass. He took a wild shot with a phaser, and the boy felt the breath of the beam's passage a scant inch from his cheek. "Garamond, come see what I've found!"

One of the warriors veered aside to answer the call. He was tall and carried himself with a confident swagger. Where his companions wore the functional armor that would repel modern weapon fire, his suit was crafted along ancient design; and the decorative sword that swung from his belt was just as lethal as their phasers.

The sight of the boy, and what he possessed, brought a grunt of surprise to Garamond's lips. "You have something that belongs to me."

The boy looked up, but did not speak.

Garamond stepped back, instinctively brandishing his sword. A trick of the morning light had given the boy the face of an old man. One blink and the illusion was gone.

"Give it up to me, child."

"My name is Surak," said the boy quietly. "And I will not give you this stone. I will not give it to any living being."

"Are you so eager to die, young one?" Garamond

110

resheathed his weapon, more curious than kind in the face of this unexpected defiance.

"No, I don't wish to die," said Surak, "but I could not live with that deed on my conscience."

"Then you propose to keep this bauble to yourself?" The boisterous laughter that followed his question covered a growing uneasiness. Garamond's grip on the sword handle tightened again. If the stone held Powers, then this boy could be as dangerous as his elders and must be killed after all.

"No, I have no need for it now that the sun has risen." To Garamond's relief, the young boy bent forward and placed the stone on the ground.

"You have given it to me after all," the man crowed as his fist closed over the rough rock and hefted it high into the air.

Surak shook his head. "You have taken it of your own free will."

"A fine distinction, my young philosopher," said Garamond with a lifted brow. "But why do you disdain these Powers. It is rumored this dull gem you have tossed aside can fulfill all desires. The Ko N'ya could even raise the dead of your clan."

Surak surveyed the field of slaughter with a new dispassion. "They chose this fate, so restoring them to life would only prolong the battle."

His hands clenched, then eased again. Laying his open palms down upon his knees, he continued. "I don't seek the fulfillment of desires. I have chosen to end the desires themselves."

I have chosen to end the desires themselves.

The words were spoken in Ancient Vulcan, with the lilting cadence of a pre-Reform dialect. Picard shifted in his bed, and the movement pulled him closer to consciousness.

The phrase whispered again, but this time he could not fathom any meaning in the guttural sounds.

He slipped back into another dream.

* * *

The bedchamber walls were hung with intricately woven tapestries of panoramic views that rivaled nature, but the fabrics were muted by dust and heavy shadows. Rugs covered the flagstone floor, but their colors and patterns had been worn away by the scuffle and tread of five generations. Once the room had been filled with rich furnishings of dark wood: deep chairs that invited guests to linger and tables spread with trays of wine and bread to entice them to stay yet awhile longer. These were all gone now, removed one by one as the desire for fellowship dimmed, then guttered out like the cold torches set in their sconces.

A pall of age and decay draped like a discarded veil over the entire room, but it coiled most thickly around the bed and the single frail figure nestled deep in its embrace.

"I am old, J'ross. Our people die young on this new world, but even by our reckoning before The Crossing from Vulcan, I am old."

Garamond had uttered this petulant complaint so often that the woman at his side no longer tried to frame a soothing reply. Instead, she studied the blotchy, wrinkled skin of his face with new interest; his complexion had an ominous brown tinge that had not been there yesterday. His lean, bony features had turned gaunt. She wondered if either of the chamber's sentries had noticed the changes.

Her hand searched for the basket tucked under the bed. The contents were intact. She pulled out a small leather-bound book and turned to a marked page. "Shall I read to you this morning?"

"No, I am dying."

He had said this before as well, day after day for the last year, but she thought that today he might be right. There was a soft, dry rattle when he breathed that warned of lungs grown brittle overnight. Garamond had wakened only an hour before, yet there were dark smudges beneath his eyes and their puffy lids drooped down lower and lower.

His eyes closed. He drifted off to sleep.

Laying the book facedown, J'ross carefully shifted her weight off the bed so as not to wake the old man. With expert movements born of much practice, she straightened and tucked the tangled covers. He did not stir. She picked up the book and bent down. Her hands sought out the basket again.

"Who is there?" cried out Garamond, waking suddenly. His fingers clutched fitfully at his side. "Gone! It is gone!"

"Hush, my husband. It was only hidden by the covers." She guided his fumbling hands to the right place, then cast a glance over her shoulder to check the sentries' reactions.

Pymer had come to immediate attention with a drawn knife balanced in his palm; he took a hesitant step forward. Deemus was less alarmed, but his hand rested on the hilt of his sheathed sword. They craned their necks to see what was happening.

"I commend your diligence." She moved aside to give them a clear view of the bed where the old man cradled the stone in his arms. "But it was only another nightmare."

Pymer grunted, then slumped back against the wall and began idly picking at his teeth with the blade. Deemus sighed heavily.

They were, to the best of her knowledge, loyal to Garamond, but there was far less reason to trust their loyalty to her. J'ross feared that a dying king's young wife, no matter how beautiful, could hardly compete with Garamond's nephew. Taramuk's political sway was based in part on his bloodlines, but even more on his ambitions: he promised the Aegis a new purpose. Where Garamond had reduced the guard to a decorative, but essentially unnecessary, appendage to his House, Taramuk promised the soldiers global warfare, and ultimately, an empire.

All he needed was the Ko N'ya.

She moved back to Garamond's side, anxious to quiet his mewling. Pymer was bored, and bored soldiers were too curious for comfort's sake.

"Betrayed." Fortunately Garamond's voice had sunk to a whisper. "You have betrayed me."

"No, not so." She tucked a lock of straggling white hair back behind the elegant point of one ear. Despite his age, he had been a handsome man when they first met. "I have been true to you, Husband, in my own way."

He fell back against the pillows, exhausted by the outburst, and the stone tumbled out of the crook of his arm. When he made no move to recover it, J'ross tucked it against his side. Then she took a soft cloth and wiped the tears that streamed down his sunken cheeks, but there was nothing she could do to ease his labored breathing or still his feebly thrashing limbs.

An hour passed, then another. She waited patiently until Garamond exhaled deeply, then stirred no more. Her fingers pressed against his wrist, searching for a pulse. There was none; he was finally at rest.

J'ross pulled the basket out from under the bed to set about her next task.

"The king is sleeping. Do not disturb him," she commanded as she walked past the guards.

Deemus nodded; Pymer sheathed his knife and fell into step beside her. As the lady of the manor she had the right to an armed escort, but over the last year she had noted a subtle shift in the guard's demeanor, an increased vigilance and attention to her activities. As Garamond's health worsened, the privilege of Pymer's company had become more difficult to decline, and the few opportunities to slip away from his supervision had been hard won. Her guard was rapidly becoming her jailer.

They proceeded to the House kitchen in silence since her past attempts to make light conversation had only rendered Pymer more surly. This failure to charm confirmed her suspicions that the Aegis soldiers were ready to transfer their loyalty to Taramuk.

"Th'a! It's hot down here," cried Pymer as they descended the back steps. "This is no work for a soldier."

"The king's chamber is cool. You could have stayed there."

He only scowled.

No queen had set foot in the kitchens before J'ross, but then no other queen of the House had been a baker. Some of the servants admired her ascent into nobility, while others scorned her common origins; they all kept their distance when she entered their domain.

She threaded her way between bustling cooks and table servers with their trays, but the soldier was less nimble and earned several muttered curses when he blocked their path or tripped their feet. By the time he caught up with her, J'ross had pulled a ball of dough from her basket and was pinching shut the cracks in its surface. She then placed it on a wooden paddle and shoved it inside the nearest oven.

Pymer began to sweat. "How long is this going to take?"

"Not long," she said. "Spiced kahla doesn't need to rise."

His scowl etched deeper and deeper into his face as they waited, and his face had flushed a bright green from the radiant heat before she pronounced the crust to be properly browned.

"Anyone could do this," said Pymer as they retraced their path to the king's chamber. Irritation had loosened his tongue.

"It's not so easy as it looks," said J'ross. She swung the bread basket from one arm, but her free hand wiped a trickle of sweat from her brow.

Their entrance into the chamber caught the single sentry in the middle of a yawn. "The king is still sleeping."

"I hate to wake him, but he must eat to keep up his strength." She raised her voice as she approached the bed. "I've brought you fresh baked kahla, my lord. Your favorite delicacy."

She peered down at the old man's face. "My lord?"

She dropped the basket and fell to her knees by his bedside. "My lord! My lord is dead!"

Her cries turned to sobs as she threw herself over the still body. She could hear the pounding of the sentries' boots as they ran toward her.

"Move aside, woman!" commanded Deemus, shoving her away so that he could examine the king for himself. He touched the man's face, then snatched back his hand. "Th'a! He's already cold."

"Then he died on your watch," said Pymer quickly.

"Idiot, Taramuk won't care when the old king died." J'ross watched Deemus scrabble frantically through the bedcovers. "It's the rock that matters now. Where is—" He spun around, sword drawn clear of its sheath by the time he faced her.

Deemus, reflected J'ross ruefully, was much brighter than Pymer.

"Drop it, m'lady, or I shall be forced to kill you."

"Brave man, to attack the holder of the Ko N'ya." To her relief, the soldier froze in place. "With a single tap on this stone I could burn out your heart and twist your entrails into a knot. A wave of my hand and this castle will come crashing down over your heads, plague will kill any survivors, and monsters will grow in the womb of any woman who walks over this land for the next ten generations."

From the look of terror on his face, Pymer might have let her flee the room just to stop the stream of curses, but Deemus was almost grinning at her recitation. Almost. A sliver of uncertainty stayed his hand.

"Well said, my Queen, but I'll let my betters judge the weight of your threats." He edged backward toward the door. His eyes never left her or the stone she held. Pymer scurried after, and together they bolted shut the door.

She was left alone with the dead king.

J'ross calculated that a swift messenger could carry the news of Garamond's death to his nephew in just over an hour. It should take somewhat longer for Taramuk to make the return journey from his neighboring estate. If the Aegis was on his side, they would make short work of any token opposition to the joining of the two Houses.

Her fate would be settled by dusk.

Contemplation of her own death did not frighten J'ross. She had known the risks when she married old Garamond and then bore him a child that usurped Taramuk's position as heir; she had gambled that Garamond would live until her son was old enough to defend his reign, and she had lost. Death was the likely forfeit for her; however, if Rume had followed instructions, her child would survive. That was a victory of sorts.

The sun was still a finger's width from the horizon when she heard the sound of marching feet outside the chamber. There was a hasty scrape of metal against wood, then the doors burst open, shouldered apart by a force of Aegis soldiers.

As I expected.

To give him credit, Taramuk led the assault. Garamond's nephew was broad and carried his bulky armor with ease. Elaborate designs of beaten gold added luster to the metal breastplate. He was a warrior who planned to be an emperor.

J'ross raised the stone up above her head. "I have powers that are greater than those naked swords."

Taramuk merely laughed. "It takes more than a few hours to learn to wield those powers, J'ross. However, I expected some move for power on your part, so I've come prepared."

He clapped his hands and a soldier stepped forward. He was carrying a small squirming bundle. As the heavy cloth fell away, J'ross heard the crying of a child. Seconds later a naked boy tumbled out onto the flagstones.

"Did you really think you could hide him away? His wet nurse offered him to me for a single gold coin."

"Let him go!"

"Give the Ko N'ya to me," Taramuk said, "or the child dies."

J'ross shook her head ever so slightly. "Kill the king's son and rightful heir? Not even you would dare do that."

"Do you take me for a fool, J'ross? Garamond was nearly three hundred years old, too old by a century to sire a son." He prodded the trembling child with a boot. "You've been seen speaking to your village lover; this is the spawn of a potter, not the king's own flesh and blood."

"You're wrong. The child is blood of this House, Taramuk, which makes him kin to a butcher!"

Taramuk snapped two fingers.

"No!" she cried, but it was too late to forestall his order.

The guard's cutting slash brought forth a gout of blood from the boy's neck; waves of bright emerald green cascaded down his chest. The child's limp body collapsed into a crumpled heap onto the faded carpet; J'ross dropped to her knees as if felled by the same blow.

"You will be next," said Taramuk.

Even as he spoke, J'ross had let loose the stone. It tumbled from her slack hands, rolling across the floor toward his eager, grasping reach.

She remained silently in place, head bowed, as two guards stripped her of the gown she had been wearing, their rough hands tearing away the fabric until she was naked. Her jewelry was removed with equal force, raising welts and bruises about her neck and wrists; a trickle of blood marked where an ear-gem had been wrenched free of the lobe. Even her slippers were forfeit. They could not untangle the leather ties that bound her braided hair, so the braid itself was lopped off with the same knife that had slain the boy.

When the men had finished their task, she lifted her head high, as if in anticipation of a final killing blow.

Taramuk waved back the guards. "If you were less liked, and less beautiful, I would kill you myself. Instead, I will spare your life if you return to the mud village where my uncle found you."

"I won't beg for mercy from you," she said in a flat voice, "yet give me leave to take a cloak with which to cover myself and a loaf of bread to eat. To do less would shame your House. After all, I was its queen."

"You were a better baker," he said with a sneer, but he plucked a cloak from the back of one of his soldiers and threw it onto the floor. "Now go!"

With a clumsy bow of acquiescence, J'ross scooped up the cloak and wrapped the cloth tightly about her body and over her head. Then, taking up her bread basket, she walked past Taramuk with the same bearing and poise that once carried her across a throne room. The House guards hastily stepped back, eyes averted in acknowledgment of their betrayal. She left Garamond's bedchamber unhindered.

The estate appeared deserted by servants and Family alike, but she sensed eyes following her stately passage through the corridors and heard whispers coming from behind closed doors. Those who would have championed her cause were dead or in hiding.

She strode faster down the halls, through doorways, under arches, over steps and out into the courtyard. From high above her, a wailing of horns announced the king's death to the countryside. Impatient to escape the same air that Taramuk breathed, she ran over cobblestones until she reached a dirt road, one that led to the village of her birth.

J'ross waited until the looming towers of the House had faded into the distance before she loosed the laughter welling up inside her. Her feet had grown soft over the last few years of manor house living, and they pained her already, yet she danced barefooted over the rough pebbled surface. By the time the sun had set, she would be safely home.

"I am a better baker than you know, Taramuk the Mighty, Taramuk the Empire-Builder, Taramuk the Dead!"

The basket she carried was heavy, far heavier than a round loaf of kahla should weigh.

Tonight she and her family would feast on the thin crust of stale bread that covered the Ko N'ya baked inside. Taramuk might dine on fresh meats and wine, but it would be his last meal. The rock he carried into battle had been formed in the heat of a potter's kiln, and a lump of fired clay would offer little protection to him or his armies.

She and Rume would live to spit on Taramuk's grave. If even half the stories of the Ko N'ya's powers were true, her lover would spend the rest of his days making the statues he loved; and Garamond's infant son would grow tall and strong while the bones of that poor dead child—Taramuk's own whelp by a cast-off mistress—turned to dust.

J'ross stopped her dance for a moment, struck by an unsettling thought. If old Garamond was to be believed, she herself had a long life waiting to be filled. Regaining possession of the House would not occupy more than a few years of that span. What, then, was she to do for the next three hundred years? Unlike the king, she had no interest in idle pleasures of the flesh, neither did she intend to end her life alone in a dusty bedchamber.

After a moment's thought, she had her answer.

Taramuk was treacherous and cruel, but he was not entirely a fool; neither was she too proud to learn from her enemy. She had enjoyed being queen and had run the House with admirable skill; that same talent for organization could work as well for an empire.

Perhaps she could even return the Romulan people to the stars.

J'ross resumed her dance down the path.

CHAPTER 14

"**T**wenty . . . nineteen . . . eighteen . . ."

Chief O'Brien had started the final countdown, and most of the people gathered in Ten-Forward had quickly joined him.

Geordi La Forge was not one of them. "Look," he said to his table companion, "if just one more starship is diverted at the last minute, they won't meet the five-ship quorum for calling a championship match."

"Too late," said Worf, quaffing his prune juice in one gulp. "The USS *Venture* docked there an hour ago. That gives them six." He waved to Guinan for a refill.

"What!" cried Geordi. He had been too busy talking to take more than a few sips of his own drink. "But the *Venture* wasn't even scheduled for R and R at Luxor IV."

"Chief Engineer Logan reported a baffle plate malfunction yesterday."

"Yeah, right." Finally acknowledging defeat, Geordi slumped down into his chair. "And what do you bet he has it fixed by the time the game is over?"

Worf's glass was still empty. The Klingon raised his hand to signal again, but when he saw the number of people pressing up against the bar he decided the effort was futile.

"... fourteen ... thirteen ..."

William Riker sniffed at the colorful concoction that Guinan had dropped on the counter in front of him. His nose wrinkled at the burst of bubbles that rose to the surface.

"I ordered a Finnegan's Wake," he called out when the lounge host passed by again.

Guinan paused in mid-stride, a tray full of glasses balanced in her hands. "As far as I'm concerned, that *is* a Finnegan's Wake."

"Since when is a Finnegan's Wake purple?"

"Since half the starship crew decided to drop by Ten-Forward this morning," she said firmly and sped away.

"I hate bubbles." Riker pushed aside the drink and began to toy with several stacks of colored poker chips. Even seated, he towered over the woman who was perched on the stool beside him.

"I tried to get Beverly to join us, as a member of the team," said Deanna Troi as she dug her spoon into a mound of chocolate ice cream, "but she insisted she had too much work to do. I suspect our CMO is brooding instead; she seems to think that everyone blames her for our diversion from Luxor IV. I wish you would talk to her."

"I don't know, Deanna," said Riker with a shrug, "if it hadn't been for Beverly—"

"Will!"

"... seven ... six ... five ..."

Having spied the first officer from across the room, Ro Laren jostled her way through the milling crowd to reach the counter. The ensign was slim and muscular and used her sharp elbows to good advantage. "Are you ready to pay up, Commander?"

Riker shook his head. "Not until the game actually—"

"... one ... zero!"

The room echoed with a collective groan as somewhere on Luxor IV, the first hand of the Fleet poker championship was dealt out.

Riker heaved a sigh and shoved the stacks toward the

ensign. Red, blue, and green chips cascaded across the countertop. "Here's your hundred."

"Poker chips?"

"You never specified the exact form of payment," he said with a perfectly sober face, but there was an undercurrent of smugness in his voice. "So I've decided to pay up in chips."

Ro called out to Guinan as she swept by. "Can he do this?"

"What now?" asked the designated arbiter as she looked over her shoulder. Ro pointed to the chips on the countertop. "Yes, I'll allow it as legal tender."

"Fah!" said Ensign Ro as she scooped up the tokens, but the sight of Riker's amusement brought a wry smile to her own face. "You'll probably win every one of these back from me."

Riker's grin widened even more. "I certainly intend to try. Care to test your luck at tonight's game?"

"No, thanks," said the Bajoran. "I'd rather lose my money on Starbase 193."

The first officer shook his head. "Sorry, Ensign Ro, no shore leave privileges at this port."

"None?" Troi looked up from her dessert. "Not even for senior officers?"

"No one from this ship goes on that starbase," said Riker. "It seems the owner of a bar called the Due or Die is some kind of black market knowledge-broker, and the captain is concerned that she'll find a way to pump the crew for information on our current mission. Evidently, listening is her specialty."

"What did you say?" Guinan doubled back in her tracks to confront the first officer. "What's the name of this woman?"

"Something exotic," said Riker, searching his memory. "The captain said it was from Greek mythology . . ."

"Camenae?"

"Yes, that sounds right. How did—"

But Guinan had already slipped out from behind the bar and was halfway to the doors of Ten-Forward.

* * *

Picard's desk was cluttered with piles of books, yet her eyes were drawn immediately to a dull gray rock lurking amidst the disorder. It hunched half-hidden beneath the cover of an opened volume. "Am I disturbing you, Captain?"

Laying aside the thick textbook he had been reading, Picard said, "No, Guinan, come in." Yet she could see that his eyes were still clouded with thoughts far removed from her presence in the ready room. She remained silent and watched as his distracted gaze moved downward to the desk surface and his hand strayed out to stroke the rough surface of the rock.

Age emanated from it in waves. At times, after prolonged contact with short-lived races such as Humans, Guinan felt herself to be an old woman; this small object reminded her that she was still a child in the universe.

"That's a very unusual paperweight."

"What?" When Picard caught her meaning, his fist closed over the stone. Several seconds passed before he reached the decision to tell her more. "It's called the Devil's Heart."

Yes, the stone was very old indeed. "I've heard of it." She had heard other names for it as well, darker names that had laced through the mythology of her homeworld. That world was gone now, and so were her people's legends.

The stone had survived.

Picard was rubbing the bridge of his nose. She studied the cast of his shoulders, then said, "You look tired."

"Do I? Perhaps because I haven't been sleeping too well lately." He took a deep breath and recovered the sharp inquisitive look that usually resided on his face. "So, Guinan, has the wake in Ten-Forward driven you to the bridge?"

"According to Commander Riker, you don't know anything about that."

"The innocence of the young is frightening," said Picard with a smile. "As a newly promoted lieutenant, I lost a month's wages betting on my ship's crew at the same floating poker championship. All we needed were five starships in the same place, so as soon as I saw the docking roster at Luxor IV, I knew someone would call for a championship game."

"The crew were disappointed to miss the game."

"I knew they would be." The captain's expression of geniality evaporated. "But we were unavoidably delayed." His gaze flickered briefly to the Heart, but he offered no further details of their mission. "What can I do for you?"

"I'd like to visit Starbase 193."

He stared up at her for a moment, then said, "Surely you know that I've canceled all shore leave privileges for the crew?"

"Yes, but I'd like to go anyway."

Picard was not given to prying into her personal affairs. He grimaced before he asked, "For what purpose?"

"I'd like to see an old . . . acquaintance." Guinan had been about to say friend, but too much time had passed for her to make that assumption.

"I see." From the thoughtful expression on his face, she realized that he had made the connection very quickly. "Very well, Guinan. You have my permission for shore leave."

"Thank you, Captain."

Just as she reached the doorway of the ready room, Picard added, "When I first saw Camenae, I had the distinct feeling that we had met before. Now I realize that I was mistaken; instead, she reminded me of someone I already know."

She smiled and slipped quietly out of the room.

As soon as he was alone again, Picard picked up the book he had been reading and resumed his study of its contents.

Surak . . . Ishaya . . . Garamond . . . J'ross . . .

Familiar names and places met him at every turn of a page, yet the factual details of the pre-Reform era were difficult to separate from legend. Several dry accounts of Surak's life contradicted the possibility of his stark walk through the field of dead on the plain of Ishaya, and only one of his contemporaries had recounted a version that echoed Picard's dream of that pivotal moment in the philosopher's life.

The confusion only deepened after the exodus from Vulcan. T'Sara's foreword warned that her original sources for early Romulan history were impossible to confirm through other records. Those who had spurned the path of logic were the only witnesses to the taming of their new world and the building of new empires.

Picard snapped shut the book.

He had found the obvious root of his dreams. Even though some twenty years had passed since he had last read this history text, the names must have remained nestled in his memory. Finding the Ko N'ya had triggered his imagination to embroider an unusually elaborate tapestry around them.

Dreams . . . they were only dreams.

When Guinan walked into the Due or Die, the Andorian bartender pointed the way to the back of the establishment. Each step she took in that direction filled her with distaste. The lighting was dim, but not dim enough to hide the scruffy floor and battered furniture; the few customers scattered here and there at tables were bent over their drinks, gazing too intently upon an inner landscape to notice her. She expected a challenge from the stocky Norsican guard at the back, but he stepped aside without comment to let her pass through a doorway.

The shadowed interior of the next room was bleak and barren. It prepared her for Camenae's glacial expression. The woman sat motionless, with her hands folded together on the tabletop; only a flicker of Camenae's eyes betrayed any sign of recognition. She uttered no greeting to her visitor.

"I get the feeling I was expected," said Guinan in Federation Standard. She sat down in a chair that was uncomfortably hard, but then no one would choose to linger in this room.

"When the *Enterprise* docked at this starbase, I considered the possibility of your coming here."

"Then you knew I was working on a Federation starship?"

"You've been with them for several years," said Camenae. "Word gets around."

But you didn't call me. "I heard rumors you were off-planet when the Borg attacked, but I was never able to confirm that you were still alive. Or to find you."

"It's a large universe," Camenae said in a flat voice. "We were scattered apart by the solar winds." Then she dropped into the language of their race. "Leaves that have fallen from a tree do not attach themselves to a branch again."

There was a vestige of lyric poetry in her words, but her verse had never dealt with images of death or decay. The woman Guinan remembered had laughed often; now Camenae's face was carved in somber, unyielding lines.

Guinan shook her head, warding off the morbid spell cast her way. "I prefer to think of us as cuttings from a plant; we will grow tall in new soil."

Dropping back into Federation Standard, Camenae countered, "You won't grow at all if you continue working on a starship like the *Enterprise*. Wasn't one encounter with the Borg enough? Why must you persist in confronting them over and over again?"

"Danger comes with the job."

"And what of this visit? Is it also part of your job? Did Picard send you here to interrogate me?"

"No," said Guinan with a weary shake of her head. "I came because I wanted to see you again."

"How flattering." Camenae smiled, but it was not a pleasant expression. "I'm not sure that I believe you. Your captain was curious about the murder."

"Murder?" said Guinan. "I've heard about the deaths of the Vulcans on Atropos, but Picard already knows they were killed by Orion mercenaries."

"You must not be a very good Listener. One of my operatives on this starbase was killed as well."

Guinan shrugged away the insult. "That's not the type of information I seek out, and the ship's officers don't discuss classified matters with me, just personal ones."

"There's no profit in mending people's love lives."

"Is that what you do? Listen for profit?"

"Yes," said Camenae. "And what I hear is far more interesting than the petty problems of some homesick ensign."

"So you *do* know who murdered your—"

"Answering that question would betray a client confidence, a confidence I have been paid to keep."

"Let me get this straight," said Guinan incredulously. "You won't betray the murderers and thieves who are crawling over this starbase because they *paid* you?"

"My business ethics are the only principles I have left. I'm loathe to give them up."

Beneath the cynicism was a kernel of truth that saddened Guinan enough to bite back any more recriminations. Instead, she said, "Then I'd like to become one of your customers."

Camenae laughed with genuine amusement rather than scorn. "You can't afford me, Guinan. Not on a bartender's wages."

"My expenses are low; I can pay the debt off if you'll extend me credit."

Camenae shook her head. "Given your penchant for hazardous duty, you're a bad risk."

"Given how often I've survived, I'd say that luck is on my side, and that I'm a very sound investment."

"You're serious?"

"Dead serious," said Guinan.

Camenae frowned as she mulled over the request. "Very well," she said at last, "I will take you on." Then, with a swift and practiced motion she flipped three tokens onto the tabletop. "That's your credit stake. You can keep asking questions until I take all the coins back."

There were many questions Guinan wanted answered, but one above all others. "Tell me about the Heart."

"What do you know of its history?"

"Enough," said Guinan. "I'm more interested in current events."

After a pause to order her thoughts, Camenae recounted what she knew of T'Sara's ten-year quest on Atropos; then she described the Vulcan distress call that Grede had brought to her, the alterations to the message that had delayed the arrival of the *Enterprise,* and the frantic scramble among the Orions and Ferengi to take possession of T'Sara's discovery.

At the conclusion of her tale, Camenae reached out one hand and picked up the first token. "Vulcans can be such fools at times. They may lack the capacity for greed, but they should remember how many other races do not."

"Do you know who has the Heart now?" asked Guinan.

"As fact, no," said Camenae thoughtfully. "But I can offer a conjecture at a very reasonable price." Her hand hovered over the next token.

"I'll pay you to keep that conjecture to yourself." The second token disappeared. "And to keep any more information you hear about the Heart out of circulation."

"Exclusivity is hardly worth the expense at this point," said Camenae. "The news is beyond recall and spreading quickly."

"All I'm asking is that you don't fan the flames any further."

"Very well," sighed Camenae. She swept the last token from the table. "That concludes our business for today."

It was an abrupt dismissal, but Guinan had lost all desire to prolong their reunion. Gathering up the skirts of her robe, she rose from the table. She said good-bye in their old tongue and waited for some response from Camenae.

"I won't sell you information about my clients," said the woman. "But I will offer one piece of advice as a parting gift. Beware the race called the unDiWahn. They are more dangerous than I had judged."

After her warning, she fell silent again. Guinan left her sitting in the darkness.

By the time the end of Sendei's communiqué had scrolled across the screen of Picard's desk terminal, the captain was battling down a substantial tide of anger.

According to Sendei's instructions, the bodies of the archaeologists and the items salvaged from the encampment were to be shipped to the Science Academy. The director himself would then supervise the distribution of personal effects to the heirs; all of T'Sara's property, consisting of the research equipment and the excavated artifacts, had been willed to the Academy itself.

Sendei claimed the Heart as part of that bequest.

Yet the director did not acknowledge the discovery of the Ko N'ya. His brief reference implied the stone was merely a curiosity crafted by the original artisans of the Atropos colony.

"In the absence of medical validation by Vulcan physicians, I consider it prudent to accept Sorren's diagnosis of Bendii's syndrome. Unfortunately, the relic you recovered from the Ferengi provided T'Sara with a focus for her delusions."

With typical Vulcan condescension, that one paragraph summarily discounted Doctor Crusher's medical evaluations and Picard's scientific assessment of the stone's origins. Worse yet, Sendei dismissed T'Sara's achievement as the product of madness. Given that interpretation, he expected the Heart to be packed into a cargo container along with the rest of the shipment and shuttled from the *Enterprise* to any freighter on its way toward Vulcan.

Picard's every instinct argued against this prosaic conclusion to the starship's mission to Atropos and such a casual disposal of the Ko N'ya and T'Sara's remains.

No, I will not do this.

The captain cleared the screen of text and began to draft yet another communiqué to Admiral Matasu. Sendei's position at the Academy had gained him prominence in Starfleet circles; but Picard was not without influence of his own, and he intended to take full advantage of it now.

"No, I'm not much of a tea drinker," said Guinan, waving away the steaming cup.

"Take it anyway," said the captain. "I find that just the act of holding a cup of Earl Grey has great therapeutic value."

She couldn't help but smile.

Picard settled down beside her on the sofa, and they sipped the hot tea in silence. Guinan had never lingered in the ready room before; she had always thought of it as Picard's office, a place of business, but now she realized that it could also serve as a safe harbor from turmoil. The window behind the captain's desk offered a miniature version of the panoramic view in Ten-Forward, and for a while Guinan loosed her mind to wander idly from one star to another. The plush sofa eased the tension in her body, and Picard's undemanding companionship eased other deeper and less obvious aches.

"She's not the first to change so drastically from the person I knew before," said Guinan at last. "It affects some of my people that way. The loss of our families, our world, everything that we were, is simply too great a pain to bear. A part of them withers away, and they turn dry and bitter."

"You, however," said Picard softly, "chose to embrace life."

"That's my way of honoring the dead . . . perhaps even of mourning for them."

She had been born to a race of Listeners and had spent centuries honing her skills, but right now she needed someone to listen to her. Picard sat quietly as she recalled memories of Camenae as a girl, then as a young woman maturing into an accomplished poet, and of a friendship that had seemed strong enough to last a lifetime.

And then Guinan told him of Camenae's warning.

Picard set down his cup and moved to the ready room desk. Picking up the Heart, he said, "I welcome the information, but I don't think there is any need for concern about these unDiWahn. We'll be leaving Starbase 193, and this sector, very soon."

"You've received new mission orders?"

"No, I've requested permission to divert the *Enterprise* to Vulcan." He seemed to be speaking to the Heart when he said, "We're taking T'Sara home."

CHAPTER 15

DaiMon Tork twirled the heavy ring on the third finger of his left hand as he calculated its worth and what percentage of that figure he could actually obtain for it at the open bazaar.

Not enough.

A cut-rate sale of his entire payload had just managed to pay off his portion of the consortium debt, but he had been left without sufficient funds to continue docking his Marauder at Starbase 193. The last of his fuel had brought him to Smelter's Hold, only to find that the news of Maarc's debacle had preceded him. No one was willing to extend him credit to purchase new stock, for nothing scared away old associates so fast as financial failure.

Cursed be the day that Maarc had drawn him into that transaction with Camenae!

"You eat too much of my food," Tork said, lashing out at his first officer. Kazago was perched on a pile of boxes containing the last of their personal possessions and some items too worthless to be sold. He was crunching his way through one of the ration packets they had scrounged from the ship's emergency stores.

"It's not as if *I like* this food," said Kazago with sullen impertinence. "But you haven't paid me any wages for a month, DaiMon, so I can't afford to buy anything else to eat." He resumed his crunching.

"Enough of your complaints. I'll think of something; I always do."

Tork peered out the grimy window of the stockroom. Now he was in debt for a day's rental of this space, and the means of paying off even that pittance had eluded him so far; however, the bazaar down below was filled with customers spending money. There must be a way to siphon some of those funds back into his own coffers.

That was when he saw them: two Vulcans walking side by side down an aisle sporting used engineering parts. Traders by the look of them. Vulcans usually stayed within the boundaries of Federation space, but this pair probably had been detoured to the Hold by an engine malfunction. Even before Tork had formulated a plan, his instincts had centered on them as an essential element to recouping his fortune.

A scheme began to gel in his mind.

"Did we sell that universal text translator?" Tork asked his first officer.

"No, DaiMon."

The details clicked into place. It was, he concluded, a workable plan. Best of all, if it failed with the Vulcans, he could rework it to use on another alien race.

"If you ever hope to receive your wages, Kazago, keep those two Vulcans in sight and guard them from the crooks and thieves on this outpost. They're *our* prey."

Throwing aside his half-eaten food packet, Kazago raced out of the room; Tork pulled out the translator and a writing padd and began to compose a letter.

Ten minutes later, the DaiMon had finished constructing his first prop; the other he already had in inventory. He ripped the printout from the padd and scurried down the staircase to the bazaar. Kazago was hovering nearby and pointed Tork in the right direction. To his relief, the Vulcans had drifted even closer to his stall.

"You! Vulcans! I would speak with you."

"As you wish," said one, and they both came to a halt. Their unadorned tunics reeked of spice and grain.

"Vulcans are honorable, that is what I have always been told. So, like a fool, I believed this myth; I trusted a Vulcan when I wouldn't trust my own grandmother. But one of your kind has tried to dupe me! He owes me a king's ransom and paid for it with a worthless bauble."

"What is this to do with us?"

They had listened to his ranting with more patience and civility than he had dared hope, but it was time to present the bait and see if they were hungry.

"This note," he shook the printout in their faces, "supposedly explains his perfidy, but it is written in Vulcan!"

"I see," said the taller one with a solemn nod. "You have need of a translation."

"Brilliant deduction," exclaimed Tork with an acid sneer. "Your rapier mind should bring you much wealth and happiness." In his experience, sarcasm and verbal abuse disarmed suspicion by misdirection: watch my temper, not your purse.

He shoved the flimsy into the hands of Short Trader. "Tell me! What do those ridiculous squiggles mean?"

The two bent their heads together and scanned the text. After an exchange of veiled glances, Short Trader spoke.

"It is addressed to DaiMon Tork. 'I lack the funds to honor my debt at this time, so I have sent a family heirloom as a bond of my good faith. The item itself has little value, but my family holds it in great esteem.' It is signed by one named Suprell."

Got them! exulted Tork to himself. The message he had forged clearly stated that the debt was paid in full with the Ko N'ya. So, as he suspected, even Vulcans had their price; everyone did.

"What am I to do?" Tork stormed, presenting his marks with the opportunity to take advantage of him. "I need funds, not promises."

"You have not been misled, DaiMon," said Tall Trader. "We Vulcans are an honorable race, as I will prove to you.

Suprell's family is known to me, and I will redeem the heirloom and assume his debt."

"Excellent!" Tork beamed happily. For all their much vaunted intelligence, Vulcans were an absurdly naive race when it came to practical matters. He would have to pursue more business transactions with them in the future. "Come this way, come this way, so that we can arrange this matter in private."

He grabbed the sleeve of the nearest trader and led them both through the crowds and up the narrow staircase to the rented stockroom. The soft snick of the door closing behind them was like the teeth of a trap snapping shut.

After throwing off the boxes that covered a large chest, the DaiMon made a great show of fussing with the lock and then rummaging through the jumbled contents. His hands closed around a large round shape. "Ah, here it is!"

When Tork turned around with the synthetic gem in his hands, he immediately realized his mistake.

Vulcans did not smile, yet both of these men were smiling broadly. Then Tork saw the Romulan-issue disrupters they were slipping out from behind their cloaks.

Their trap, not mine.

The house in the Old Quarter was still standing after five centuries, proof of the skill of the architect who had designed its massive chambers and sprawling wings. In the beginning it had been grandly furnished, but each succeeding generation had stripped away its treasures room by room to slow the pace of their slide down into poverty. Eventually, all that remained of past glory and past wealth was the house itself.

Tonight a young warrior strode through the cold, empty halls. Despite the reversal of his family's fortune, he carried his wiry frame with a strutting arrogance that was the equal of any Klingon on the planet of Kronos. Passing by the foot of a wide spiraling staircase, he ducked down a shadowed corridor that led to the warmth and light of the servant's hall.

The last servant had left long ago; the old man who waited for him inside was the master of the house. Kruger sat hunched over a low trestle table, too absorbed in his dinner to look up at the sound of the opening door.

"She's dead," announced the warrior.

There could be only one "she."

The old man tore another mouthful of meat from the joint of beast. He chewed. He spat a piece of gristle onto the bare floor. "Fifty years ago I would have cared."

Kruger's grandson sat down at the table, but he did not pluck any food from the platter. There was little to spare, and he would eat better fare elsewhere at the expense of wealthy sycophants in awe of his ancient lineage. "According to security reports circulating in high Federation circles, she was killed by Orion smugglers."

"Did you learn this from your *cousin?*" Kruger spat out the last word with even greater distaste than he had the gristle.

"Grandfather, Ambassador Nedec has access to classified documents, and according to those documents—"

"Nedec is a toady to that upstart Gowron," shouted the old man. "Nedec throws you favors like scraps to a targ. You, who should be *his* emperor!" He threw the chewed bone onto the floor. "After my death, of course."

"According to those documents," persisted Kruger's heir, "the Ferengi were also involved with T'Sara's death."

"Meddlesome Vulcan crone! Your father was a fool to talk to her, revealing what should only be known to the Family."

The young man shouted back into his face. "You're the fool!" His impudence won a moment of silence and his grandfather's undivided attention. "Don't you see? She found something, something that both the Orions and the Ferengi wanted. Something that the *Enterprise* is carrying back to Vulcan."

"The Pagrashtak?"

"Yes, Grandfather. I think it must be."

Kruger took a swig from a tankard of ale. His close-set eyes were slitted in thought. "So, perhaps your father was not so much the fool as I believed."

"I think not. After all, she kept her word and did not publish the account of Kessec's disgrace in her texts. Instead, it seems she used the knowledge of his actions to trace the path of the Pagrashtak."

"*Our* Pagrashtak," said Kruger firmly.

"Yes, Grandfather. I will see to that personally."

Diat Manja wept at the news of T'Sara's death.

Nearly sixty years had passed since she had last set foot in this room, yet there were reminders of her presence everywhere he looked. Her textbooks and monographs were scattered throughout his bookshelves, along with bound volumes of their correspondence. She had sat for hours in this carved wood chair beside his desk, leafing through his translations; at other times she had nestled in the deep bay window to soak up the warmth of the sun as she read. He could open any of those manuscripts and find her scribbled notes in the margin of a page.

So few of the Iconian Dream texts had survived from ancient times; if there had been more, perhaps she would have stayed longer.

Most Dynasians on campus had been vaguely repulsed by the offworlder with an unadorned forehead and pale green skin, so young Diat had been the only scholar in his department who volunteered to help with her research. Unlike the others, he had been moved by her intensity of purpose and her complete disinterest in the opinion others held of her; both were qualities that he lacked.

His hands reached for the tails of the tattered scarf draped around his neck, and his fingers stroked the rough weave as if caressing the face of a lover. The scarf was made of a sturdy Vulcan fabric, and T'Sara had worn it throughout her visit because even during a heat wave the Dynasian summer was colder than Vulcan's winter. For years Manja had wondered if she left it behind by accident or by design. Vulcans were unsentimental by nature, yet she had fathomed the emotions of the beings in a multitude of cultures; and if she had suspected his love for her, then she had saved a poor young professor from humiliation by tactfully ignoring that fact.

After her departure from Dynasia, he had worshiped her

from afar and taken what comfort he could from the letters they exchanged. Some would consider that meager fare, yet this meeting of minds exceeded any pleasure he had ever found in the arms of his consort.

Now there would be no more letters.

Three days ago he had sent an urgent message to T'Sara telling her of a lost Iconian scroll that had been discovered in the archival vaults of the Flight Engineering library. The star map had been improperly cataloged as a technology-related text until one of Manja's former students stumbled upon it and recognized it as part of the Dream series he had studied in a literature class.

However, T'Sara had already died before the news reached her, and one of her colleagues had answered instead.

The professor reached for the crumbled communiqué that had arrived just an hour ago and smoothed out the creases. Through eyes still fogged by tears, Manja read the short message one more time. Like a typical Vulcan, Sendei had reported the tragedy in terse, dry language; yet, upon this second reading, Manja realized the double tragedy in the scientist's account of T'Sara's death.

The members of the Vulcan Science Academy did not even recognize T'Sara's greatest achievement! The director believed she had died in the first stages of madness.

"No!" cried out Diat Manja. "They must honor her success. After a century of searching, she found the Ko N'ya, the Gem of Ancient Iconia. I will see to it that the entire Federation learns the truth of her discovery!"

Then he slumped back into his chair, his skin flushing to an indigo hue from embarrassment at his outburst.

How could he possibly keep this vow? He was a tired, old man with no influence, even on Dynasia. Professors of ancient literature were held in low esteem on a world that hungered for technological sophistication. Besides, T'Sara herself would have cared little about her reputation.

Yet she had always championed the quest for truth.

Diat Manja took up a pen from his desktop. It was the only

weapon he could wield, so he would have to wage this campaign with words.

There was one person on Dynasia who might have the power to call attention to this issue, one who was in constant communication with members of the Federation Council; and while Manja had no influence with the warden, one of Manja's former students was now the man's secretary. Ganin would see to it that Warden Chandat read this letter, and then surely Chandat would see to it that justice was done.

Manja began to write.

CHAPTER 16

A cushioned sofa was positioned only a few steps away from his desk, but Picard had waited too long to seek out its comforts. Sleep, held at bay for hours, suddenly swept over him, robbing him of the strength or desire to move.

The book he had been reading fell from numbed fingers onto the desktop. Shoving the volume to one side, he dropped his head down into the cradle of his arms and released his hold on consciousness.

The sound of the captain's breathing could barely be heard, and his body moved imperceptibly with the steady rise and fall of his chest. The fingers of one hand twitched until they brushed against the rough surface of the Heart, then they stilled their movement.

As time passed, overhead lights dimmed automatically, tricked into quiescence by the still silence of the room. In the darkness, the gray rock came to life with an inner glow that dipped and flickered like the flame of a candle.

The man's lips began to move, framing alien words.

"This one is . . ."

* * *

". . . is dead," said Telev automatically, yet when he looked up there was no one to hear his pronouncement.

The nearest aide was at the far end of the ward passing out bowls of soup to those strong enough to feed themselves. If there was time, and food enough to go around, she would try to help the weaker ones eat. The woman stopped ladling for a moment, wracked by a chesty cough, and Telev suspected that before too long he would find her lying on one of the cots herself. He only hoped there would be someone left to bring *her* food by then.

The healer turned back to the dead man. A cursory search of the body confirmed that it carried no identification beyond a clan scarf. Telev studied the vaguely familiar pattern, but his mind was so numbed with fatigue that the answer was slow in coming.

Ah, yes, Assan.

There had been three family members attending an Assan in the ward just last week . . . weavers by trade . . . too poor to leave the city, but not too poor to pay for hospice treatment. Telev took a closer look at the puffy face of the man and recognized him as one of those three. So there were probably no Assan left alive or they would be here at this bedside.

Telev draped the scarf over the young man's throat. Eventually someone would come along and haul the body outside for the next passing death cart. They rumbled through the streets at all hours now, piled high with corpses, carrying their load to the funeral kilns that burned day and night to keep up with the victims of the Scourge.

Telev moved on to the next bed, where two sleeping children were huddled together as if for warmth. Chills and a creeping cold over the extremities were the first sign of the pestilence, but perhaps they only sought the comfort of each other's embrace. He listened to the steady sound of their intertwined breathing and was relieved that their lungs were still clear; their skin was still a pale blue, free of any mottled dark patches. By all rights, they were too well to merit space in the hospice, and the continued confinement put them at risk of contracting the Scourge, but as orphans he feared they would roam the streets of Andor until they starved or fell ill. There were more ways to die than from pestilence.

The condition of the last patient on the row was not so promising. The healer had known Evalla since childhood, had watched a quicksilver girl grow into a graceful young woman who had danced the *sissalya* cycles at the last fall solstice. Now, however, her white hair had turned as yellow as a grandmother's and her once agile frame was stiff and . bloated. Telev perched on the edge of her cot to examine her more closely. Air whistled in and out of her jointed antennae, an indication of their inflamed interior; her complexion had deepened to purple.

"She won't eat," said Shaav, the woman's consort. He held a half-eaten chunk of bread and carefully picked at the scattered crumbs that had fallen from her mouth onto the bed.

"It hurts to swallow," she said, gasping for breath. "I've gotten worse, haven't I?"

"Yes, quite a bit worse." Telev knew of several herbs that could at least ease her pain, but he had used up the last of them long ago, and there was no one left in the hospice who had time to search the countryside for more or even possessed the knowledge of where to find them.

"Am I dying?"

"Yes." In the beginning, Telev had offered hope to any who needed it. False hope. Most of the patients had died, as had those who mourned them. He had no strength left for telling untruths.

Evalla managed a weak smile. "I haven't paid my reckoning, Healer."

"You're in luck. Our collector is out sick today."

Shaav did not react to their words; he was too intent on salvaging crumbs. He had keened loudly when his mother died last month and railed at the death of his young sister soon after, then watched in silence as his father, two brothers, and a cousin were carried to the kilns in rapid succession. He

142

took meticulous care of his sworn consort, but he talked very little these days.

As Telev rose back to his feet, an old woman scurried down the central aisle of the ward. She spotted him immediately, the only standing figure in a sea of recumbent forms.

"I need a bed for my son," she demanded in a voice that was loud enough to rise above the moans and cries of the sick.

The healer pointed toward the dead Assan. True, there would be no time to change the laying cloths, but then Telev doubted there were any clean ones to be had. "If you dispose of the former occupant, that place is yours."

"Fair trade," she said with satisfaction, and scurried away to summon assistance in the chore.

A new patient.

And when he was done with this one, there would be another one, and yet another after that as the dead were carried away and the dying took their place. So much to be done but so little that he could do.

Telev fled the ward.

All available rooms, even those that had once served as studies and bedrooms for the healers, had been turned over to the care of the sick. Nonetheless, he had managed to keep one small closet reserved for his own use as a refuge. There was just enough space for a narrow cot, but he had given that up yesterday, along with the last of his extra shirts. All that remained was a hard pallet on the floor. The supplies that had been stored here were also gone.

Except for a canister of *talla* bark. It had no medicinal value and normally just was used to fill the stomach before a purge, nonetheless he still experienced a sharp pang of guilt for hoarding it away from others.

Telev opened the canister and measured out a small quantity of the dry flakes into the cup of steaming water he had snatched off a passing soup wagon. After a minute of steeping, too impatient to wait any longer, he eagerly sipped the hot brew.

Ah, that brings warmth back to my chilled . . .

Yes, his hands were cold and the air, so balmy for the last few weeks, seemed unusually biting tonight.

So be it. Even healers must die.

He took another gulp of the bark potion. It was a poor substitute for tea, but it was the only indulgence left to him. If only this were srjula that he held in his hands, but the wealthy merchants had fled the city at the first news of the spreading plague. If there was any tea left in Andor, it was locked in warehouses awaiting the return of owners and customers with the money to pay for their merchandise.

I'll probably never taste srjula again.

A small window in the outside wall of the closet afforded a view of the city below, bathed in the orange light of the setting sun. He leaned his forehead against the glass and searched for signs of life: people walking in the streets, lights springing up in houses, or even just the flutter of newly washed clothes hanging out to dry. Here and there he caught some reassuring indication that survivors endured, but they were very few in a city that once held a half million inhabitants.

He scanned the horizon as well, looking for the trails of smoke that had curled around the mountaintops for the past few days, but they seemed to have finally dissipated. Rumors of vast fires beyond the ridge were impossible to confirm.

Tap. Tap. Tap.

The rapping on the door was soft with apology.

Telev crossed the room in two steps and peered out into the corridor. "What is it, Sathev?" The aide had been a patient, one of the few to recover from the Scourge, but his face had been so badly scarred by his illness that he had chosen to stay in the hospice.

"There's someone at the south door asking to see the healer in charge of new admissions."

Telev laughed at the absurdity of such a formal request. Admissions procedures had collapsed when the healers themselves began to sicken and die.

"Well, I tried to explain how it is," said Sathev wearily. "But she was very insistent."

"Do not bother yourself further. I shall deal with it."

Some people, reflected Telev as he shuffled his way to the portal, had a remarkable ability to deny reality. The world they had all known was rotting away, yet they clung stubbornly to the old ways.

A woman and two men were waiting for him at the south entrance. At their feet lay a body wrapped in stained laying cloths; he would have mistaken the unmoving bundle for a corpse if not for the sound of a muffled groan.

"I am Viloff," said the woman, and lifted a lantern up to show her face. She was dressed in a nondescript tunic made from the sturdy cloth favored by the craft-trades, but her bearing was not that of a common worker; rather she held herself alert and erect, with one arm swung loosely by her side where it could reach up to her belt knife. "We need a room for our friend. He is very ill."

"We have no rooms, but in an hour or so we may have a cot."

"That will not do. He needs privacy. Now." He saw her weight shift ever so slightly as her hand fluttered upward toward the weapon.

"You can gut me here on the steps, but that will not gain you any space inside; it will simply make a mess."

"Enough!" she said. "Take me to your superior."

That placed her and her silent companions without question.

"What is your rank, Viloff?" asked the healer.

"You see too much, old man."

"And you are a foolish young woman, even if you are a soldier." Telev rubbed his hands to ease the stiffness in his finger joints. "There are no other healers. I am the last one."

"The last one . . ." she echoed. Her bravado collapsed like a leaking water-skin. "I *was* Subcommander Viloff last week, but for all I know now, I could be a battalion admiral. The plague hit the camps last month, and then there was an attack . . . we've traveled for two days without seeing another officer."

"Bring your friend into the wards," said Telev, impatient to escape the cold air. "I will care for him."

Viloff shook her head, danced a few steps of indecision, then grabbed his sleeve, dragging him over to the bundle. Bending down, she drew aside a fold of cloth.

Telev saw enough in the circle of lantern light to grant her demand.

"You can use my room," he said, beckoning them inside the hospice.

Viloff's two subordinates hoisted up the awkward bundle, ignoring a new spate of groans that issued forth, and followed the healer to the closet. There wasn't enough room for the entire group, but the men seemed eager to leave the matter to their commander; they stepped back into the corridor and stood like sentinels on either side of the door.

Viloff set the lamp on a high shelf.

Telev crouched down by the pallet and with a trembling hand pulled away the rough covers. He had taken the damp patches for blood until he saw their deep green color.

"Where did you find . . ." He had no words to describe what lay before him.

"We were attacked," said Viloff. "In flying ships that rival anything to be found on Andor. Our offensive weapons had no effect on them; in a matter of hours they laid waste to our forces in the western province. Then, as if by a miracle, their defensive shields seemed to collapse and one by one we were able to pick them off. I searched the wreckage, but this was the only survivor."

By now, the healer had completely unwrapped the alien creature. Even without a healthy specimen for comparison, it was obvious that its legs were broken; the skin covering its midsection was lacerated, the underlying muscles and organs torn and bleeding; scrapes and bruises covered the rest of its torso and arms.

"Ugly creatures, aren't they?" said Viloff. "The others, the dead ones, looked like this, too."

"I strive to find beauty in all living beings." Although in this case, Telev admitted to himself, he would have to try very hard. Even if one could overlook the peculiar dark hair and olive skin color, the alien's jutting forehead and atrophied auditory organs were quite disconcerting. Its naked body, when compared to that of an Andorian, was thick-framed and squat; and the sexual organs, if that was indeed their purpose, were in an absurdly vulnerable location.

"I am the Emperor Vitellius!"

Telev twitched and rotated his antennae away from the sound. The alien's voice was uncomfortably loud, and the strange language was hardened by a clipped accent and too many consonants.

"I shall lead the Romulan people to victory."

The alien's limbs trembled, but it was too weak to even raise itself. Telev noted that its eyes were not focused, and it had not reacted to their presence. In an Andorian, these symptoms would accompany eadiliac failure, but this species probably did not even possess an eadilium.

"You will surrender to me or die!" The raving and shouting were incomprehensible.

He guessed that the alien had lost a considerable quantity of the green liquid, but the healer couldn't replace the volume. The standard treatment of an infusion of water might kill rather than cure. "There's nothing I, or any healer, can do for this creature. It will die before I've learned enough about its biology to treat it."

"Too bad," said Viloff. "There is much we need to know about our new enemies."

Telev knelt closer to continue his examination. With a start, he realized that the creature was finally making eye contact.

"Let me go! I command you, let me go!"

Its hands were clutching at its side, digging in the rumpled laying cloth. Viloff explained the action with a rather apologetic sigh. "It carries some sort of talisman, a clan token perhaps, harmless. We tried to remove the thing when the alien was first found, but it held fast and wouldn't let go. Of course, it was stronger then."

"You must obey me, or the Ko N'ya will destroy you."

The alien suddenly lifted up a gray stone and shook it at them. It was an impressive display of strength for a being so near death.

"Surrender! I cannot be defeated."

The effort was short-lived; the creature collapsed back onto the bed as if drained of all strength.

"I am . . . the Emperor . . ."

The alien's voice dropped to a weak whisper, and it shut its peculiar dark eyes. Pressing a finger against the short neck, Telev monitored the fluttering pulse and wondered whether the rate was too high or too low, and what he could do about it even if he knew the answer.

The fluttering stopped altogether.

"It's dead," said Telev. All that remained of this strange being was the simple relic it had carried from its distant homeworld. Curious, Telev plucked the object from the alien's slack hands. "A superstitious race," mused the healer as he examined the rough stone. It was warm, apparently heated by the fevered body of its owner.

"We shall have to carry the body to the kilns ourselves," said Viloff. She stepped to the door and ordered the men to the task.

"Skae!" cursed one of the soldiers as they roughly bound up the corpse again. "I still reek of its gore."

"Forget what you've seen here tonight, Healer," said the commander. "Andor has enough worries of its own."

"Who would believe me?" He held up the stone. "What of this?"

But the soldiers were already gone, faded into the shadows of the night. The only proof of their brief visit was the ruined pallet on the floor.

And the stone.

It was still warm, easing the painful throbbing in his hands, and in the darkness its dull surface seemed to glitter and sparkle. So this and the cold cup of tea were his only remaining comforts, yet they were like a bounty of riches in the midst of devastation.

Tucking the alien talisman in the crook of his arm, Telev

148

carried the canister of *talla* with him to the wards. Sathev was able to steep five cups of weak tea from the contents and pass them around to the few patients who were still awake. A soft word, a gentle caress, these were the only weapons Telev had left to fight the ravages of plague, but he gave these away to all, even those who slept through his visitation.

By the time he had finished his rounds of the hospice, he was overcome with such a deep weariness that he could not go one step farther, but sank down onto the flagstone floor and curled around the fiery glow of the stone. He felt as if all his strength, all his life, was seeping away.

Must the knot untie so soon?"

As he waited for the final dissolution of his bond with the world, Telev heard the sound of laughter and the skipping steps of children running. He knew without seeing that all who had lain dying were now risen from their beds; that Evalla was dancing through the corridors, and Shaav was singing a triumphant ballad about her miraculous recovery; that Sathev was weeping at the feel of smooth skin on his face, and Avae had stopped coughing.

I seem to have borrowed a little luck from the stars.

If his life had blazed to its end that much sooner as a result of the talisman's powers, it was still a fair trade. He was a healer, after all.

Eager hands reached out to pull him into the circle of celebration, but he slipped away before they could touch him.

CHAPTER 17

The yellow DiWahn sun had not risen above the horizon, but King Akhanatos was already awake when a court aide sidled into his bedchamber.

"Your Highness, a visitor to the palace desires a private audience with you." Before Akhanatos could dismiss the request, the aide added, "He is unDiWahn."

The king quickly nodded assent, and the servant scurried out of the room. The curtains of the doorway had barely stopped swinging from his passage when a stranger stepped back through the entrance. The heavy cowl that covered his head cast a shadow on his face, but Akhanatos recognized the stately bearing of Master Kieradán.

The king rose from his couch to greet the robed emissary. Tradition reserved this gesture of respect for the landed nobility. As one of the stateless unDiWahn, this man owned no territories, but he was the leader of the Faithful and thus as powerful as any king.

"Well met, Akhanatos," said the unDiWahn. With the arrogance typical of his fellows, he did not bow, nor did he address Akhanatos by any of his honorifics.

"You honor me with your presence." The king was relieved

that they were alone so none of his other subjects would witness his meek acceptance of this disrespect. He owed the order too great a financial debt to act on his displeasure now, but he noted the incident for retribution at some later date.

"I bring you word from Admiral Jakat."

Upon hearing that name, Akhanatos felt his first tremor of suspicion. "What do you mean? My fleet admiral speaks directly to me."

"No longer." Kieradán spread wide his arms as if to welcome someone into his embrace. "Jakat's true name is Daramadán. He belongs to the Order of the Faithful and serves only the memory of our Iconian ancestors."

"Do not play games with me, unDiWahn!" Akhanatos was beyond hiding his alarm. "On this morning of all mornings, I have no patience for your mystic intrigues."

"Ah, yes. Today you were to launch your offensive against the Kingdom of Roshamel."

His impulse to deny the truth collided with his fear of having been discovered. Choked into silence, Akhanatos listened aghast as the unDiWahn outlined the assault plans that the king had delivered in person to Jakat three nights before.

"If you may remember," continued Kieradán, "your agreement with my order was that the ships would be used for peace, not war. The Iconian lore in our stewardship is preserved for the benefit of all of DiWahn, not the advancement of one of its petty fiefdoms. You have broken that covenant and betrayed our laws."

"You want peace?" said Akhanatos, recovering his pride and his tongue. "Only the unDiWahn can afford that dream. I paid a heavy price for your holy knowledge, and I paid even more for the construction of the fleet itself. Did you really think I would bankrupt my coffers to benefit my enemies?"

"No," the master said with an enigmatic smile, "you have acted just as we expected. Thus, as a penalty for your transgressions against the Faithful, we claim possession of the fruit which was born of our knowledge."

"So, you are turning my own troops against me."

Akhanatos finally fathomed the bitter depths of his gullibility. First they had led him into ruinous debt; now they were taking away the means for recouping his fortunes in war; and finally they would grind his kingdom into dust with his own weapons.

To the king's surprise, Kieradán shook his head. "Jakat is no traitor, and we have no interest in taking your territory from you. Instead, the admiral is preparing to pursue a mission of our choosing. If you are still here upon the fleet's return, we will meet again to discuss the terms of its future use."

"If I am still . . ." The question faded as Akhanatos answered it for himself.

Of course, once Roshamel learned of the fleet's departure, he would attack while Akhanatos was vulnerable. Both of their ground troops were roughly equivalent in strength, which meant any victory would be hard won. The surviving kingdom would be forced to deal with the unDiWahn from a position of weakness.

"I can still best you in this game." Akhanatos sneered in the master's face to show his disdain for the order's devious political strategies. "Be forewarned. If I make peace with Roshamel, both our kingdoms will thrive."

"We would applaud such a rational action, King Akhanatos," said Kieradán. "May your opponents always match you in wisdom."

After honoring the king with a low bow of respect, the unDiWahn emissary turned and swept out of the chamber.

To Kanda Jiak's relief, Davenport Terminal was smaller than Starbase 75 and far less crowded. After winding his way out of the docking bays, he found that a single dome contained all the passenger operations.

Stepping up to a ticket counter, the Iconian shoved his identity chip into a scan slot. "I'd like to purchase a one-way passage to DiWahn."

"DiWahn!" The Benzite clerk uttered a barking laugh. He ejected the chip and shoved it back at Jiak. "Out of the question. Even under the best of circumstances, DiWahn is off-limits to unauthorized Federation citizens. The entire planet is politically unstable."

"But I—"

"And the best of circumstances no longer exist," said the clerk. He sniffed loudly, inhaling the vapors of the atmospheric inhaler suspended under his chin.

"But I—"

"All traffic into and out of the system has been suspended indefinitely. If we had a diplomatic relationship with the planet, which we do not, it would have been severed this morning."

"This morning?" asked Jiak, dismayed to have missed his opportunity by such a slim margin. "What happened this morning?"

"That is none of your concern," snapped the Benzite. He waved aside the vapors from his face and peered at the young man's face. "According to your bio credentials, you are a resident of Redifer III . . . but you bear a passing resemblance to a DiWahn native."

"I do?" cried Jiak. In his excitement, he paid no attention to the figure that had moved up beside him.

"Yes, quite a resemblance," repeated the clerk, and Jiak belatedly recognized the man's suspicion.

"It's just a coincidence," said Del sternly. The freighter captain shoved herself between Jiak and the counter. "Come on, Kanda. You've overstayed your welcome. This clerk has other customers in need of his attention."

"Indeed I do!" said the Benzite. Like most of his race, he disliked having his bureaucratic routine disrupted.

Del clamped her hand around Jiak's upper arm and jerked him away.

"Let me go." She had no business trailing after him, thought Jiak angrily. He was not some orphaned child in need of a guardian angel. "I can take care of myself."

"Quiet down," the captain muttered under her breath, "or you'll end up in a detention cell."

Her warning stopped him from crying out again, but he still

struggled against her iron grip. Not that it did him any good. Del had dragged him to the other side of the Davenport terminal before Jiak managed to free himself.

"I'm still shorthanded on the *Haverford,*" said the captain. "I could use you on my next tour."

Jiak rubbed gingerly at the sore muscles of his arm. His disappointment at being shut out of DiWahn hurt much more. "This was just my first stop. I'm going to Dynasia next."

"What! That godforsaken place is a trillion light years away from here." Despite her exaggeration of the distance involved, Del jabbed her hand to a specific spot just to the left of his head. Jiak had no doubt that Dynasia could be found by traveling beyond the tip of her finger; the freighter captain had an uncanny memory for all the backroad planets in the galaxy.

"I don't care how far away it is," he said sullenly. "That's where I'm going next."

"Then you haven't got the brains of a Meegan glowworm." When he remained silent, she heaved a deep sigh. "The *Marshall* is docked in Bay 3. Find First Officer Conrad, and tell him I sent you. His freight run will get you to Hayhurst Junction, which is the closest Federation outpost to Dynasia. After that, you're on your own again."

Jiak's face flushed with shame at having resented her interference. "Thanks, Captain."

"Only members of my crew call me captain," said the woman. "My friends call me Del." She wrapped the boy in her arms, squeezed the air out of his lungs with the strength of her hug, then stalked away without a backward glance.

Thanks, Del.

He almost changed his mind and ran after her, but the impulse faded with the thought of setting foot on Dynasia. Eager to secure his next berth, Jiak settled his pack securely on his shoulders and headed back toward the docking bays.

CHAPTER **18**

"**E**ngage."

In Riker's mind, that simple word was inextricably inter-twined with the basso pulse of the starship engines and a dazzling starburst of warp light on the viewscreen. A feeling of suppressed excitement was underscored by Picard's crisp declamation; he never issued that order in an offhand manner.

"At current warp speed," announced Data, "our estimated arrival at Vulcan will be in three point six days."

Picard never even slouched when he occupied the captain's chair. At his most relaxed, he might cross his legs and lean back. Today, Riker noted, the captain had adopted his most regal carriage, with both feet planted firmly on the deck and his head held high as he studied the viewscreen. The very mention of Sarek and T'Sara's homeworld seemed to trigger this unconscious show of respect; Picard's only departure from a formal posture was the crooking of one arm to hold the Heart.

"I've been to Vulcan several times," said the first officer, "but I've never had a chance to actually visit the planet surface. I'm looking forward to that opportunity now."

When the silence that followed this comment lengthened uncomfortably, Troi leaned slightly forward from her position on the other side of Picard. "Yes, I'm also looking forward to shore leave there. It should prove to be very interesting, if rather warm." She spoke to Riker, but her eyes were on the captain.

Another silence.

"And I'm sure the Vulcan Science Academy will look forward to our arrival," said Riker, forging ahead despite a growing self-consciousness. He had started this damn conversation, but he couldn't seem to stop it as easily. "The Heart is a most unusual—"

"What did you say?" Picard turned to face his first officer. "What about the Heart?"

"Just that I'm sure the archaeologists at the Vulcan Science Academy must be very curious about it. As an historical relic, it should keep them occupied for quite some time."

Picard reacted to that admittedly banal statement with a frown. His one free hand tugged at the hem of his tunic. "Yes, I suppose it will."

"Isn't that the purpose of this trip?" asked Troi, and Riker wondered what emotion she sensed that made this request for clarification necessary. "To return the artifacts of T'Sara's excavation to Vulcan?"

"Of course, Counselor," said Picard with a grimace of impatience. "I was under the impression I had made that clear during our last briefing."

Troi nodded, but made no reply.

"In the meantime, it makes a dandy conversation piece," said Riker with a grin. No one laughed. "Although, I've noticed that it must be lighter than it looks. You don't seem to mind its weight." This was a rather blatant ploy for a chance to at least touch the stone; except for Data, the captain was the only one who had held the Heart.

"I hadn't given it much thought," said Picard. He did not proffer the stone to his curious first officer, and Riker wondered why Picard had bothered to bring the stone with him onto the bridge.

To Riker's relief, the next long silence finally signaled the death of this particular topic of conversation; but his trepidation returned when he saw Data swivel around in order to face the command center.

"Captain, I have completely reassembled and recalibrated all testing units in my laboratory, and I have certified that they are in excellent working order. If I could continue my examination of the Heart, we could provide the Academy scientists with valuable baseline information as to its nature."

"That's a very good point, Mr. Data."

"Thank you, Captain." The android swung aside the Ops console so that he could stand.

"Don't bother with it now," said Picard. "I'll deliver the Heart to the lab at the end of your duty shift."

Data sank back down into his chair.

"Until then," continued the captain, "I have some historical research of my own to attend to. Number One, the bridge is yours."

"Aye, Captain."

Riker was actually relieved by Picard's swift departure from the bridge to his ready room. This was a new feeling, and not one that the first officer welcomed.

"He's very tired, Will," said Deanna before he could even ask her to comment on the captain's state of mind. "I sense he hasn't been sleeping very well lately, and that makes him rather edgy."

"The Borg nightmares again?"

Troi paused, then shook her head. "No, I don't think so. He's not so . . . shaken. Just tired and somewhat distracted."

"Perhaps we should ask our chief medical officer to prescribe some warm milk at bedtime."

"Warm milk?" asked Data.

Riker hated having to explain his quips to the android since they always sounded so lame after a clinical analysis. "That was just a joking reference to an old remedy for insomnia."

"Ah. Then I might make a similar reference to using a wrench to regain possession of the Heart from the captain."

The android blinked in surprise when Riker laughed out loud. "Was that also funny?" he asked hopefully.

"Yes, it was, Data," said Riker, but his grin faded when he saw the look of concern on Troi's face. Apparently the ship's counselor was not so amused.

As the chief medical officer of the *Enterprise,* Beverly Crusher had more than a passing acquaintance with the methods the crew used to deal with stress. Some of the more exuberant attempts at tension-relief resulted in a visit to sickbay. Miles O'Brien, for instance, was fond of white-water rafting, and Deanna Troi tended to eat large quantities of chocolate; thus the former occasionally needed muscle and bone regeneration, and the latter a stern reminder on the importance of a balanced diet.

Crusher was more inclined to moderation and indulged herself by dancing in the holodeck with a succession of computer-generated partners. However, when she was feeling especially despondent, the doctor ended up in sickbay as well.

"Are you sure you don't mind updating these equipment inventories, Dr. Crusher?" asked the nurse as he held out his data padd. Lewis was a relatively new staff member, one who hadn't learned to take quick advantage of these rare moods.

"I don't mind at all." Crusher whisked the padd away from the man before he could change his mind. Two other nurses and a doctor had already cheerfully provided her with a full day's worth of mind-numbing busywork projects, the kind she usually avoided like the plague or foisted off on some hapless resident who had run out of patients.

"Well, I really appreciate this . . ." Despite his words, Lewis still looked as if he was waiting for the catch.

"Am I interrupting something important?" came a voice from the doorway to her office.

"Not at all, Geordi." She waved away the bewildered nurse and studied the chief engineer as he walked closer. La Forge showed no obvious signs of illness; except for an unusually somber expression, he appeared to be in good health. "What can I do for you?"

"This isn't a medical matter, Doctor. I just dropped by to see if you were coming to the poker game tonight."

Crusher winced with the sudden realization that this was the source of her bad mood. Odd how she had managed to avoid this self-knowledge all morning.

Geordi must have seen her reaction, because he sighed and said, "Look, I'm really sorry about the last few days. We all know it wasn't your fault we missed the championship, and I'd really feel bad if you stopped playing poker just because we've been acting like jerks."

"Thank you, Geordi," she said with a growing smile. "As it happens, I have plans for this evening, but it was very nice to be asked."

"Next time?"

"Definitely."

"Great." Her assurance seemed to ease his conscience, because he walked out of the office with a much lighter step.

As the last tatters of her melancholy evaporated, Crusher shoved aside the temptation to break her dinner date with the captain so she could attend the poker game after all. Her vindication could wait until another time. Besides, she hadn't seen much of Picard lately and . . .

She happened to glance down at her desk, a desk covered with the mountains of work that she had taken on, work she no longer had the slightest interest in doing.

Suddenly the pleasures of this evening lay too far in the future to even contemplate.

Data heard the sound of heavy footsteps marching down the curving bridge ramp. There was only one member of the crew who could overcome the shock-absorbent qualities of the deck carpet.

"Your duty shift is over . . . sir."

Data looked up from the captain's chair that he had occupied since Riker's departure from the bridge. The ship's security chief towered above him. "Thank you, Lieutenant Worf. I was just waiting for the captain."

Worf glanced over his shoulder at the closed doors of the ready room. "He is busy."

"Yes, it appears he is preoccupied and has forgotten our appointment. Perhaps I should remind—"

The Klingon's bony forehead gathered a new set of furrows. "One who holds the Pagrashtak should not be disturbed for trivial matters . . . sir." He shifted his broad body ever so slightly to block Data's view of the door. "The captain would be annoyed by an interruption."

"Then my concerns can wait," decided the android. Despite the belligerent delivery, Worf's assessment of the situation was probably quite accurate.

"As most senior officer present, do you wish to retain command of the bridge?"

"No." Data rose from the captain's chair. "I will be heavily involved in computer research on the aft deck. The conn is yours."

This answer seemed to mollify the Klingon—his glower softened into a frown—yet Data was aware that Worf was still watching him as he proceeded up the ramp to the back of the bridge. It occurred to the android that Worf could be a bit overzealous in the execution of his duties, especially where Captain Picard's welfare was concerned. No doubt these were admirable qualities in the chief of security, yet if Data were capable of emotion he would probably find them extremely irritating at times.

Taking a seat at an empty science console, Data changed its display option to a high-speed scan mode and quickly set to work.

During the last hour of his duty shift, he had prepared a contingency plan just in case he was delayed from working directly with the Heart. In the absence of new test results, he would proceed under the assumption that the anomalous data he had gathered was correct, and he would conduct a search for similar contradictory findings in both archaeological and geological data bases.

He began by requesting a listing of all instances in which variations in both dating and material composition were linked to one object. Cosmic space/time distortions were the first items to be ruled out; he narrowed the search field to objects less massive than black holes. Then he excluded artificially generated anomalies that were the result of esoteric physics experiments.

Then the screen froze.

A Human would not have noticed; however, given the rate at which Data processed information, the brief lag was quite obvious to him.

After a microsecond flash of a new file listing, the screen returned to the previous display of physics experiments.

"Search complete. No new matches on stated search parameters."

"That is not correct," said Data firmly. "Access Archaeology File TGOF-1284-678A."

"No such file is present in the data base."

The computer was in error. He had clearly seen that file listing added, then quickly deleted. "Repeat, access Archaeology File TGOF-1284-678A."

The screen went blank. *"Listing error: that file material has not been entered in the data base."*

Yet he had noted a considerable volume size in the file description. He considered a backdoor approach that might open a new access route. "Correlate data on the Devil's Heart with data in Archaeology File TGOF-1284-678A and—"

"Starfleet Command override . . . Attention Lieutenant Commander Data, USS Enterprise, *you have requested classified material. Your current security clearance is not sufficient to allow access to this file."*

"Intriguing." He tapped his comm insignia and began with, "Data to Commander Riker."

Less than ten minutes later, the first officer was standing by Data's side.

"Computer," said Riker sternly. "This is Commander William T. Riker. Show me Archaeology File TGOF-1284-678A."

The screen remained blank while the computer-generated voice repeated its refrain. *"Starfleet Command override . . .*

Attention Commander William T. Riker, USS Enterprise, *you have requested classified material. Your current security clearance is not sufficient to allow access to this file."*

"Damn." The first officer tapped his comm insignia. "Riker to Picard."

Less than two minutes later, the captain had joined them on the aft deck. He listened patiently to Data's recapitulation of the data base search. "And you think this file has material pertaining to the Heart?"

Data shook his head. "I cannot corroborate any connection until I have actually seen the file, but the request for a correlation triggered the security procedures."

"Then I agree this subject is worth pursuing," said Picard. "Computer, this is Captain Jean-Luc Picard. I require access to Archaeology File TGOF-1284-678A."

"Starfleet Command override . . . Attention Captain Jean-Luc Picard, USS Enterprise, *you have requested classified material. Submit your justification for access to Admiral Emm Wilkerson, Director of Starfleet Special Projects."*

"Well, I suppose that's progress of some sort," said Picard with a wry smile. "I'll send a priority request for an explanation to the admiral right away."

Given their distance from Command Headquarters, Data quickly calculated that the earliest possible response could not arrive for hours. In the meantime, however, he could conduct another round of laboratory tests.

"Mr. Data," continued Picard, "until we've received some clarification from Starfleet Command, I suggest we suspend any further attempts to analyze the Heart."

"As you wish, Captain."

"Why am I not surprised by that?" muttered Riker under his breath as he watched Picard return to his ready room.

This was a rhetorical question, decided Data; he was not required to respond. Nonetheless, he noted with interest that his own reaction matched that of the first officer.

Beverly Crusher had just started the last paragraph of the last page of a very dreary set of reports when she heard the sound of the outer doors to sickbay open and shut. Her fingers picked up their pace over the keyboard.

"I'm almost done, Jean-Lu—" Then she looked up. "Oh, Deanna."

"You were expecting the captain," said Troi.

"Yes, actually, I was. He invited me to join him for dinner tonight."

The counselor's eyebrows quirked in surprise. "A very late dinner."

Crusher cast a quick look at her desk chronometer and was amazed to see she had worked through most of the evening. "I've been rather absorbed in my work and lost track of time. He should have called me hours ago . . ." She could feel a slow burn of anger working its way up her neck. "In fact, I do believe the captain has stood up his chief medical officer . . . again."

"Oh," said Troi, her eyes bright with undisguised curiosity. "So this happened before?"

"Yes," said Crusher with a tight smile. "Last night we were supposed to have dinner to make up for a breakfast we missed. Only Jean-Luc didn't show up. This morning he apologized and explained that he had been distracted by an unexpected meeting with Guinan. To make amends, he promised to meet me for dinner tonight."

"Knowing Captain Picard, he's probably forgotten to eat entirely and is off somewhere studying the Heart."

"Probably." The doctor found scant consolation in this explanation. "He certainly is fascinated by it."

"Well, I just stopped by to see if you wanted to help me celebrate. I just won fifty credits from—"

"The poker game!" cried Crusher. "I forgot all about it. If the captain had bothered to cancel our dinner plans, I could have gone to the game instead."

"Beverly," said Troi in her most pedantic counselor voice, "it's still not too late to call *him.*"

"Oh, no!" she said, sweeping the work tapes off her desk into a drawer and slamming it shut. "After all, who am I to come between a man and his rock?"

He sat cross-legged on the bed, just as young Surak had sat on the cold ground of the desert, and the Heart rested in the cradle of his hands. The boy had been waiting for morning, but Picard was waiting for night.

It was so difficult to keep his eyes open, yet he fought to stay awake just a little while longer.

His cabin was dark, just as it had been that first night when he wakened from the dream of T'Sara's death and saw the stone transformed. He wanted to see the change again. Or had its glittering light been part of the dream as well?

Could he even tell the difference between waking and dreaming any more? For three nights in a row, he had been left with memories of other lands and other people that were too vivid to dismiss as fantasy, yet he had no other name for them.

Visions, perhaps.

Starship captains were not supposed to have visions. He knew he should tell someone, but he feared the telling would shatter the spell.

So tired. Too tired to watch the stone any longer. He slumped down onto the bed, curling himself around the warm, round shape.

Dreams were the voice of the Heart, and he would listen to what it had to say.

CHAPTER 19

Halaylah darted through the gathering crowd, skipping and twisting between the lumbering heavyset bodies that towered above her. News of the approaching bier had traveled quickly, outstripping even her nimble race to the doors of the Great Chamber. She wondered, in fact, if that knowledge had spread too quickly, whether there had been an air of veiled expectation when the cart lumbered up the causeway with its blood-sodden burden.

Three armor-clad admirals stood at the threshold of the throne room, planted like boulders in solemn and unperturbable authority, yet the guttural exchanges they whispered to each other betrayed their unease. As a rule, Klingons were not given to whispering; they bellowed and roared like wounded targs whether they were in a good humor or bad. She had been told they sounded much the same in battle or in lovemaking. After a decade of living on this planet, she still found the unleavened noise of its natives to be the most oppressive element of her captivity.

Skirting closer to the guarded entrance, Halaylah caught a whiff of the admirals' fear, incongruously sweet compared to the normal acrid smell of a Klingon adult. She listened to their awkward sibilant speech, then tucked a hidden smile inside her cheek. These mighty warriors, with the blood of a dozen space-faring races on their hands, feared facing the emperor. Each was desperately trying to escape the honor of announcing the processional that marched ever closer.

Skipping past the admirals, ducking under the crossed swords of the Imperial guards and under the arched entrance, she passed unchallenged into the interior chamber. This was the privilege of the mightiest monarch and the lowliest servant.

Dim red light obscured the bleakness of bare stone walls and a flagstone floor, but did nothing to warm the chill air. Even the warriors among her people had craved beauty, whereas Klingons seemed to disdain the cultivation of art and music. When she had ventured to question this lack of aesthetic development, Kessec had reminded her, not unkindly, that her elegant homeworld had been defeated in battle. Still, she wondered if she could have enjoyed victory over the Klingons if Tehalai had been as ugly as this planet. The loss of flower gardens and carved fountains saddened her more than the loss of her freedom.

Her slippered feet whisked softly over the hard tiles. At their sound, a deep voice cut through the murky air. "Approach and be recog—oh, it's you, child."

Kessec was unattended. More and more often she found him alone, yet he allowed her to enter and remain when all others had been sent away. Despite his seclusion, she always found him dressed in ceremonial robes and chain-link, sitting erect on the wide metal throne as if he were about to admonish his admirals and ministers. And always the Pagrashtak rested in the palms of his hands.

"Do they think I'm deaf?"

His hearing was sharper than hers, but even Halaylah could hear the muffled murmur of the crowd waiting outside.

"Your sons are bringing a bier to this chamber," she said.

"All my sons?"

"All that are left alive, my Emperor."

"Ah." He, alone of all the Klingons she had met, had the capacity to express himself with subtlety and restraint. He said nothing more until the death marchers arrived. The security guards moved aside to admit the emperor's sons and the burden they carried, but the procession stopped just over the threshold.

"Approach and be recognized!"

Halaylah, crouching in the shadows by the side of the throne, watched as Mohtr, the eldest son, stepped forward and saluted. He echoed his father's sturdy build, but his tangled mane was shot with white where Kessec's hair remained black.

"Durall, son of Kessec, has brought honor to his family!"

She glanced quickly upward to study Kessec's face. He betrayed no sign of emotion, yet she knew young Durall had been a favorite of his. She drew a deep breath and learned the smell of grief.

"How many shared that honor with him?" asked Kessec.

Mohtr hesitated, emitting the same sweet scent that had glistened on the skin of the admirals outside. "None. His death was an accident, Father."

"A very small honor, then," said Kessec. "There have been many of these accidents of late among my sons: bruises, wounds, broken bones. Now death."

"We are warriors!"

Leaning forward, Kessec curled back his lips. "Warriors die in battle, not in accidents; they kill their enemies, not their brothers."

"You have left us precious few battles to fight, my Emperor," said Mohtr, baring his teeth in return.

"Yes, that is one of the unexpected disappointments of overwhelming victory against our enemies." Kessec sank back against the unyielding throne. "So is watching my sons squabble like scavengers over the right to succeed me."

"*If* we succeed you. Unlike you, sire, we grow old. Better to die like Durall than to reach our dotage still yearning for our right to succession!"

"Enough, Mohtr." Kessec dismissed him with an abrupt wave of his arm and called out, "Bring me Durall's body."

Even in the murky light, Halaylah could discern the sullen looks on the faces of the five bier-bearers as they shuffled forward and laid the pallet at the foot of the emperor's dais. Durall's body, once possessed of a wiry vitality, was limp and drained of color; his tunic was stiff with crusted blood where his chest had been crushed inward. She wrinkled her nose at the whiff of decomposition. Death smelled the same here as it did on Tehalai.

"I see there was no hurry to bring me this honor," said Kessec as he rose from his throne. The Pagrashtak was cradled in the crook of one arm.

"We were far from home, Father," muttered Tagre, Fourth-born. "Travel was difficult."

"No doubt." Kessec stepped down from the circular base. Several of his sons were taller and broader of frame, yet to Halaylah they lacked his presence and gravity. She wondered if he had been born with that quality or whether it was another gift of the stone.

With one hand Kessec brushed aside a lock of Durall's hair. The gentle gesture seemed to bring Kessec pain, a physical pain that stiffened his body; it lacked the aroma of grief. His fingers sought out the young man's throat. Time passed, but the emperor's ragged breathing was the only sound in the chamber. Halaylah had never mastered the Klingon Discipline of Waiting, but she was too frightened to move. She could smell the changes in the body before she saw its skin darken with the warmth of flowing blood.

When Durall finally stirred, Kessec dropped his hand away.

"Is there anything the Pagrashtak can't do?" cried Gistad, Second-born. Alone among his brothers, he met the restoration of life with a smile of wonder and joy. A politic reaction, noted Halaylah, for a man who might be the next to die.

She also noted the slump in Kessec's broad shoulders, the effort with which he kept his head raised. The arm holding the Pagrashtak was drooping by his side.

"You are tired, Father," said Mohtr, taking a step closer to the emperor. He averted his gaze from the stone, but his body twitched ever so slightly when Kessec shifted the talisman to his other hand.

"I will be fit enough by morning, as will Durall. And then we shall hear his account of this accident that befell him."

"Hearing him speak again will be a miracle, but miracles are taxing; you must keep up your strength through eating." Mohtr bellowed out for food. His call had barely stopped echoing before servants came running into the chamber with brimming bowls of meat, steaming pies, and jugs of ale.

"Such concern for my welfare is touching, Mohtr."

His hand signal was weak, lightly sketched in air, but Halaylah had been waiting for the emperor to summon her. She scrambled out of the shadows to Kessec's side.

"I'm partial to the *rougath,*" he said, scooping out a ball.

She leaned forward and sniffed his choice. The smell of the food itself was pure, but the tart glutinous paste had been handled by someone who had smeared his fear like icing over the top. Halaylah glanced up to the emperor and blinked her eyes in a gesture of rejection. Better not.

Kessec sighed. "Perhaps I will eat later."

"You let this slave's whelp run your life?"

"An eccentricity of mine. You, on the other hand, are welcome to ignore her warning." He profferred the morsel to his First-born.

"I'm not hungry."

"No, of course not." Kessec dropped the food back onto a tray and carefully wiped his fingers on the rough fabric of his robe. "Leave me. All of you."

The words were softly uttered, but even an emperor's whisper had to be obeyed. The servants fled, dropping the tainted bowl, and everything else they had carried, onto the flagstones. His sons were less quick to abandon their dignity, but they too edged away without protest.

As they retreated from the chamber, Kessec called out to Mohtr one last time.

"Take a deep breath, First-born. Deeper! That tightness you feel in your chest is from a bout of Gorault's fever that you contracted as a boy. Few children survive that illness."

"My survival is a sign of my strength!" Mohtr cried in defiance, then marched out of the chamber.

"Ah. Of course."

Halaylah stayed. She knew when Kessec did not want her with him, and this was not one of those times.

"Come closer, child." In the early days of her service to the emperor, Kessec had tried to wrap his thick Klingon tongue around the delicate syllables of her name, then joined in her laughter at the clumsy result; but he had not laughed for over a year now, and there was no one else to speak her name aloud, no matter how mangled.

"I have another story to tell you," he said, and she settled herself at his feet to listen.

"In a time before this one, there lived two brothers who had been born of the same mother and on the same day. Kessec and Batahr, for those were their names, were so alike in appearance that it was as if they were a single man and his still-water reflection walking together on land. Their hearts were equally mirrored; within each burned the bloodlust of a warrior, and when they fought together in battle, their enemies fled before them like dry straw on a high wind rather than face their raging fire.

"They shared the honor of their victory, just as they shared their weapons, their house, and their lovers. In time, they even shared the reign of all the territory within a two week's march of their birthplace."

His deep, rasping voice fell silent.

"Then it came to pass," prompted Halaylah when the pause in the story grew too long. The form of the telling was familiar, but she had not heard this tale of Kessec's life before and was curious to hear more.

"Ah, yes, then it came to pass that the brothers defeated their greatest enemy, a neighboring warrior-king, and in their victory found the one thing which they could not share. The

first brother to touch the Pagrashtak felt its warmth and heard
its whispers; the other held a cold, silent stone. Soon, the first
brother was loathe to loosen his grip on the prize. Instead, he
swore an oath to share the fruits of its powers. Despite this
generous offer, the second brother brooded and grew sour
with jealousy and suspicion, until he forgot all honor and slew
his twin while he slept."

Halaylah sniffed cautiously at the lip of a mug of ale, then
passed it over to Kessec. He took a deep draft of the hot
liquid before continuing.

"The traitor grasped the stone and felt its powers, but he
also repented of his murderous deed, so he used the stolen
Pagrashtak to bring his dead brother back to life."

"You saved him just like you saved Durall!" cried Halaylah
with a joyful stamp of her feet. Klingon tales rarely had such a
satisfying ending.

"No, child," said Kessec. "Batahr raised *me* from the dead.
And for that deed, I quickly slew him in turn. Then I burned
his body and scattered the ashes so I could never be tempted
to resurrect him."

Not such a happy ending after all, she sighed to herself.

"All this happened long ago," said Kessec, reciting the
formulaic ending of a historic narrative. He studied the face
of his youngest son, the one who looked the most like him and
who, she realized, must also look like his dead brother. "Or so
I thought."

Durall's breathing was still labored and his limbs trembled
with the pain of his wounds. Kessec laid a palm flat against
his son's heaving chest and kept it there until the boy sighed
and slipped into an untroubled sleep.

The effort left the emperor so weak that he lost his grip on
the Pagrashtak. Halaylah cried out in distress when the stone
rolled away from him.

Her dismay deepened when she heard his next command.
"Take it, quickly, before I recover my strength. And my
greed."

"Sire?"

"Take it!"

She took the Pagrashtak in her hands. It was warm to the touch and not as heavy as she had expected.

"Go," whispered Kessec. "Go as far from here as you can, child. Found your own empire if you must, but take this curse away from me and mine."

Slipping the stone into her shapeless tunic where it nestled like a curled beast against her stomach, Halaylah ran from the throne chamber for the last time.

Those light footsteps were still echoing in T'Sara's mind when her eyes opened. She breathed deeply of the cool air of the Collector's chamber. The desert night encircling the tower would be even colder.

"So that is what you were once," said the Vulcan woman to the mummified body. "And look at what you have become now."

When had the generous young slave girl turned into the miserly, grasping, and selfish fanatic that T'Sara had met in other dreams?

Ten years of excavation had shown that Halaylah used the powers of the Pagrashtak to found an artist's colony on Atropos, but it had flourished for only a century. Over time, her desire for creating beauty had narrowed into a rapacious hunger for possession.

T'Sara had tried to explain to Sorren what had happened, to teach him to feel how the self-entombment of their founder would horrify Halaylah's followers. While he acknowledged the physical evidence of the disbanding of the colony, he would not allow himself to fathom their motivation. Young Vulcans were like that; too unsure of their emotional control to risk the dangers of empathy.

"But I am old enough to contemplate what I will not emulate: you wanted to keep the Ko N'ya to yourself for all eternity. If not for me, you would have succeeded, but I have taken it from you."

T'Sara stroked the glittering stone. "Did none of them ever wonder what *you* wanted, Ko N'ya? I have seen much of your journey, but I keep searching the dreams for a clue as to where you are going."

Her head fell back against the chamber wall.

But I am old . . . and so tired . . . I may not have the strength to find your answer.

Her eyes closed . . .

. . . and the outermost shell of nested dreams shattered when Picard opened his eyes. He felt as old and tired as T'Sara until he drew a shuddering breath and revived his own strength.

"A journey?" he asked the glowing Heart that hugged his side. "Is that what this is all about?"

Its inner fire seemed to flare more brightly than before.

CHAPTER 20

Estrella Miyakawa had reached the rank of lieutenant commander of the USS *Brande* through sheer hard work, but by that point in her career it was obvious that her promotions were lagging farther and farther behind those of her Academy classmates. Then Starfleet Command had made it clear that a transfer off a starship would be her only route to becoming a full commander; affronted by the mandate, she finally had agreed to an administrative post rather than remain at that lower rank forever.

She had expected a prestigious but routine desk job at any one of a dozen major starbases. To her dismay, however, she found herself in charge of an isolated docking base on the fringes of Federation space. Insult had been added to injury.

So for the first year of her assignment at Starbase 193, Miyakawa had nursed a bitter grudge against Starfleet and the character assessment tests that had robbed her of the command of a starship. Then, by the second year, her innate sense of honesty had reasserted itself, and her resentments had eased in the face of self-knowledge: while she possessed the independence of mind that all good captains needed, she had

174

never learned to moderate that trait. Blunt to a fault and impatient with subordinates, she had earned a reputation for being difficult and creating unnecessary tension among the crew of every ship on which she had served.

By her third year of duty, Miyakawa knew she had found her proper niche in life. As the sole officer on the base, she had no one to answer to but herself. On a starship her brusque manner and snap decisions had ruffled feathers; here they had earned her the respect of the hardened locals and a rapid promotion to captain. Over the course of five years, Starbase 193 became her home, and Miyakawa lost the desire to walk any deck other than this one.

Still, there were times when she would have welcomed the presence of another Fleet officer.

Now was one of those times.

The commander scanned the page in her hand once again. Despite its dry tone, the Starfleet security communiqué troubled her. During his brief visit, Picard had teased her about the tendency of administrators to exaggerate the magnitude of their problems. She had bristled at the implied criticism of her judgment, but today she yearned to hear his opinion on this matter.

Lifting her gaze to the curving windows of her office, Miyakawa studied the tranquil scene of exterior base activity with growing unease. An Andorian passenger ship floated through space in search of the orbit coordinates dictated by the station dockmaster; maintenance droids swarmed over the hull of a Tellarite freighter; a shuttlecraft ferried a salvage crew to the remains of a Ferengi Marauder. To all appearances, this was the start of another routine, uneventful day.

Yet, if there *was* a Romulan warbird out there, it would be cloaked and invisible to her eyes.

She shook her head and returned her attention to the communiqué. Really, the very notion that there might be Romulans headed for this sector was absurd. Even if Starfleet intelligence was accurate and a warbird had indeed crossed the Neutral Zone, there was nothing of value at Starbase 193 to attract the attention of any enemy of the Federation. Six other sectors had received this routine warning and any one of them was a more likely target.

Tapping her comm insignia, Miyakawa said, "Miyakawa to dockmaster."

"Ramsey here."

"Initiate Security One shutdown procedures for all docking operations."

She was accustomed to immediate obedience from her staff, but Ramsey's brief silence was understandable under the circumstances.

"What's going on, Commander?"

"I'm feeling bored today." She wasn't ready to explain her decision to anyone yet, not even herself.

"Right. Well, this should liven up everyone's life. Security One shutdown now in effect."

Within seconds, the Andorian passenger ship came to a dead stop; maintenance droids scurried away from the freighter, then dove through the closing doors of a cargo bay; and the repair shuttle executed a sharp turn on its hasty return to the station. There would be no more dockings or departures without her express permission, and every crewmember or passenger on shore leave would be automatically recalled to his ship.

The decision to suspend service operations would outrage every captain in the sector; it would disrupt tight flight schedules and inconvenience thousands of passengers and merchants. So before the first wave of irate calls could flood through her office, Miyakawa made a second announcement.

"Attention all starbase personnel. Security One alert procedures are now in effect. This is not a drill. Repeat, this is not a drill."

The scramble to close down shops and return to quarters would keep everyone quiet for at least fifteen minutes. She had that much time to think of an excuse for her actions.

Someone tell me I'm overreacting.

Camenae was just the person for the job, thought

Miyakawa ruefully when the bar owner swept into the Starfleet office. Of course, Miyakawa's open-door policy was not in effect during a security alert, but Camenae was not known for her adherence to station regulations.

"I need to talk to you, Commander."

If this had been a normal alert, Miyakawa would have had no patience for interruptions, but this time there was no discernible emergency, no further demands on her authority, so there seemed little point in turning Camenae away. "I imagine you're here to register a complaint from the trade community."

"No. I was already on my way here." The woman sat down, leaned her elbows on the desk, and said, "Four twenty-three mark seventy-six mark three sixty-seven."

Miyakawa puzzled over the sequence. "Those coordinates are in this sector." She punched the numbers into her viewer padd, then studied the screen image. "However, according to Federation star charts, there's nothing but a few asteroids at that intersection."

Camenae shook her head. "One of those asteroids is three kilometers in diameter, large enough to hide Smelter's Hold in its hollow core."

"What! Starfleet has been trying to confirm the location of the Hold for years; now you walk in here and *give* me its coordinates. Why?"

"Because I suspect the outpost no longer exists."

The commander's sense of approaching danger grew stronger. "Explain."

"I had an operative working at the Hold," Camenae hesitated, then continued with an uncharacteristic revelation, "who was tracking after Reyjadán."

"The DiWahn who killed Grede?" It was Miyakawa's best guess, but she knew better than to expect any confirmation. When Camenae nodded agreement, the commander's alarm deepened yet again.

Camenae began to talk faster, as if rushing against time. "The Squib witnessed a curious scene at the Hold bazaar.

DaiMon Tork was pulling a scam on two traders . . . two Vulcans. He left the bazaar in their company and did not return."

The commander's fist clenched, crumpling the communiqué into a tight ball. "What are the odds of any Vulcan trader knowing about the Hold?"

"That was my first thought, but I didn't have the chance to ask any more questions. Our communications were cut. All contact with the Hold has been lost."

With her heart racing from a sudden surge of adrenalin, Miyakawa asked, "Camenae, do you know of any reason why a Romulan warbird would be headed to this starbase?"

"I think they are after T'Sara's Ko N'ya."

"I find that hard to believe." Yet that very suspicion had been at the root of her apprehension. "Would the Romulans risk an interstellar war with the Federation and its allies for so little?"

"If the Romulans gain possession of the Ko N'ya," said Camenae, "they could probably win that war."

Miyakawa reached for her comm insignia one more time. "Attention all starbase personnel. Initiate evacuation procedures. This is not a drill. Repeat, this is not a drill."

Finally, she knew what to do next.

"Dispose of him," said Commander Taris, stepping away from the limp body.

She waited, seemingly impassive, as two security guards rushed forward to remove the Ferengi from the chair. In truth, she had to clench her jaw to keep from snapping at them to hurry as they fumbled with the bindings that held the subject in place.

Subcommander Vedoc was less self-disciplined; she could hear his boot tapping impatiently on the ship's metal deck. "So, this wretched Ferengi was telling the truth after all, and he hid nothing from us."

"I could have done with far less revelation," Taris said dryly. The clever trickster had dissolved into a babbling fountain of information even before he was attached to the mind-sifter; she wondered if all of his species were equally weak-willed.

The last of the restraints were unfastened, and one of the guards easily lifted the small alien into the air. Both of the subject's eyes were still open, darting this way and that in independent directions. The highest setting of the mind-sifter seemed to sever the brain's ability to coordinate muscle movement; it severed many other connections as well. The DaiMon was still alive in a technical sense, but this vegetative state would not persist for long as the body's nervous system functions continued to fail.

When the guards had carried the body away, Taris could speak more freely. "The *Enterprise!* I might have known it would be involved with these tales of the Ko N'ya's reappearance."

"But Commander, most of what he told us was speculation rather than fact."

"Learn to trust your instincts, Vedoc." She suspected that instinct was another of the leadership qualities that he lacked; worse yet, he apparently lacked a comprehensive knowledge of their enemies. "The captain of the *Enterprise* has a fondness for ancient cultures, and this would not be the first time he has meddled in our affairs."

"Then it will be his last!"

"Your enthusiasm is noted," said Taris.

The young man jerked to attention, chest puffed out; he had mistaken her sarcasm for praise. What a shame that his finely chiseled features were not accompanied by an equally impressive intellect.

With a weary sigh, the commander turned on her heel and marched swiftly out of the interrogation chamber. Vedoc scuttled after her.

When they stepped into the circular bridge, the quiet air of efficiency restored her temper. Unlike the subcommander, the soldiers hunched over their work stations had served on the *Haakona* for years. Taris had weeded out the weak and the stupid, leaving her with a leaner crew than most warbirds possessed, but one that was more competent.

She stepped up onto the dais of the captain's chair. Each of the crew cast her a quick side-glance that signaled their ready status; a simple nod on her part would have elicited a verbal report; a series of hand signals could relay her own orders. The subtlety of this silent communication usually unnerved Vedoc, who preferred to bark out his commands.

A flash of orange light warned of a sudden change in the ship's status.

"Third-stage perimeter alert, Commander," explained the weapons officer. "Vessel one approaching on a direct intercept vector, seven minutes; Vessel two approaching on a direct intercept vector, eleven minutes; Vessel three will pass within firing distance in five minutes."

The viewscreen was clouded by the dampening effect of the *Haakona*'s cloaking field, but she could see three globular shapes growing in size as they drew nearer.

"We'll be surrounded," whispered Vedoc. Even in the subdued light of the command pit, Taris could see him tremble at the thought.

"Surrounded by two freighters and a passenger ship," explained the weapons officer without any trace of amusement. Seemus was too well trained to reveal contempt for a superior officer, even one who had not learned the difference between an alert and a warning.

"Full power to the cloaking device," ordered Taris. Her voice carried easily across the still bridge. "Evasive maneuvers to avoid collision."

The first of the approaching vessels filled the viewscreen, then veered off to one side. Her helmsman had steered the *Haakona* out of harm's way with an economy of motion. He ducked under the second trade ship, then returned the warbird to its previous course heading.

"Estimated arrival at the starbase in twelve minutes."

If fortune favored this mission, the *Enterprise* and her captain would soon rue their theft of Romulan property.

A new shape took form on the viewscreen, the triangular profile of an orbital docking station. Even with the compromised resolution of the image, Taris could see that the space surrounding the station, an area normally cluttered with stationary vessels, was empty.

She looked to her navigator for an explanation.

"Commander," said Etrajan, "sensors reveal there are no life-signs on the starbase."

"Your instruments must be in error!" Vedoc stepped behind the man and peered over his shoulder to double-check the instrument readout. "Life support functions are still operating . . . energy collectors near maximum . . ." He scowled fiercely, then said, "no life-signs."

"And no *Enterprise.*" Little else mattered to Taris, but Vedoc kept prattling on about the station.

"Somehow they must have been warned! A full-scale evacuation explains the ships we passed earlier. We could still catch one—"

"No," Taris snapped, growing weary of his inflexibility; a good soldier learned to adjust to the fluctuations of war. "Let them pass on. We have larger game to track."

"Yes, Commander." He ducked his head, visibly chastened by her reprimand, another sign that he was too easily swayed even from a bad opinion. At the conclusion of this mission, she would recommend that his highly placed uncle find another post for his nephew; Vedoc would not serve on her ship again.

"What is our next course of action?" he asked.

"Destroy the base as planned."

His large brown eyes blinked rapidly in confusion. "But there's no one even on the station."

"It doesn't matter, Subcommander." Perhaps, if she was exceptionally clever, he could die honorably in battle; his uncle would probably thank her. "Upon hearing of the destruction of a Federation starbase, the nearest starship will proceed immediately to this sector."

"And that starship will be the *Enterprise,*" said Vedoc, finally comprehending the obvious.

"Photon torpedoes locked on target," announced Seemus.

"Fire."

A cluster of dark shapes shot out from beneath the

warbird's curving hull. She lost sight of them as they sped through the void toward their target, but the weapons officer tracked their progress.

". . . three . . . two . . . one . . ."

Commander Taris smiled as she watched the starbase explode into a cloud of molten metal.

Its fires flared like a beacon in the cold night of space.

CHAPTER 21

Having reached the limits of his own understanding, Data swiveled his Ops station around to face the occupant of the captain's chair.

"Commander Riker, I have been reviewing your evocation of 'Lady Luck' during the course of the game last night. Despite your repeated requests for intervention from that entity, in actual fact, your poker performance fell below your usual standards."

The first officer sighed. "Luck is fickle, Data."

"And do you believe that explains why Counselor Troi won?"

"No," said the first officer. "Deanna cheats."

"Intriguing." Data had not expected that explanation. "However, I saw no evidence of—"

"That was a *joke.*"

"Yes, of course." A very small one, Data decided; he would forgo a laughter response. Besides, according to Geordi, the chuckle he had developed was still in need of refinement.

The android was about to resume a forward position when a soft beep from the aft deck caught his attention.

"Incoming message from Starfleet Command," announced Worf as he scanned the communications console. "A Priority One, security-coded communiqué from the Department of Special Projects."

"That is probably the answer to our inquiry on the Heart," said Data. The response time was three hours and thirteen minutes shorter than his estimate, which implied a greater urgency than he had assigned to the matter.

"Pipe it to the captain's ready room, Lieutenant," ordered Riker, as he rose from his chair.

Data slipped out from under the console to accompany the first officer.

"You are not included, Mr. Data," said Worf firmly. "According to my security instructions, only Captain Picard and Commander Riker have been granted clearance to view this message."

The android sat back down.

"Sorry, Data," said Riker. "You know how the Brass loves to guard its secrets; but I'll bet that by the end of this mission, we can fill you in on the details."

"Thank you, Commander. Nevertheless, I suspect this is one conundrum I will never be allowed to solve. Fortunately, I have no—"

"—no emotions." Riker completed the sentence for him.

"Correct. So I am not disturbed by the lack of resolution in this matter."

The first officer shrugged. "If you say so, Data."

"Yes, Commander, I do say so." However, this clarification only seemed to amuse Riker; he was still smiling when he walked into the ready room. Data had encountered this same veiled skepticism among members of the crew on other occasions; Dr. Crusher and the captain often made similar asides to his declarations.

Data addressed the security chief. "I do not possess the capacity for emotion."

Worf grunted. "I do not care . . . sir."

* * *

"What exactly is Special Projects?" asked Riker as he sat down across from the captain.

"Few people below the rank of admiral seem to know." Picard plucked the Heart off a stack of books and shoved them to one side. When he had cleared the area around the small viewscreen, he said, "I've heard it called the 'black hole' department because information goes in, but it rarely comes back out."

"Well, then, this should be very interesting."

A figure suddenly appeared on the screen. Admiral Wilkerson was a spare, elderly woman with a tight bun of fading coral-red hair and a brisk but congenial manner.

"Captain Picard, if I played this by the book, neither you nor Commander Riker would be allowed to hear anything I'm about to say. Fortunately, Special Projects is given some latitude in its affairs, and it is my judgment that you need to know the scope of the situation."

Her expression grew more somber.

"The analysis anomalies which you reported are not unique. They have been detected emanating from a . . . structure, perhaps even a being, of immense age. We call it the Guardian of Forever, and there is a strong possibility that the relic you possess is a fragment broken from the Guardian."

Out of the corner of one eye, Riker could see the captain's hands close protectively around the stone.

"If this is so," continued the admiral, "the legends of the Heart's powers may not be exaggerated. The Guardian itself is beyond our comprehension; we haven't even confirmed whether or not it is sentient . . . and it has other properties that are best not talked about."

Like what? wondered Riker with growing unease.

"A team of researchers from Special Projects will be waiting for you on Vulcan; they can take the Heart to more secure quarters. However, be very careful on your journey here, Captain Picard. At all costs, the Heart must be kept out of the hands of the Federation's enemies."

Admiral Wilkerson blinked away, and once again the screen went dark.

"The Guardian of Forever," said Picard, but he was looking down at the Heart as he spoke. "Is that where you belong?"

"Captain?"

Picard looked up as if startled that he was not alone. "Yes?"

"Up until now, we've assumed this rock was a harmless archaeological relic." Riker shook his head in disbelief at Starfleet's revelations. "But if what the admiral said is true, you'd be safer holding a photon torpedo in your hands. Shouldn't we keep the Heart in a guarded security vault?"

The captain frowned at the suggestion. "I don't think deep storage will be necessary. If anything, it will simply draw extra attention to the Heart. However, to be on the safe side, I'll order an end to any more of Data's attempts at laboratory analysis."

This wasn't the result Riker had intended, but before he could marshal an argument, Picard added, "That will be all, Number One."

"Aye, sir." Riker rose and walked swiftly out of the room and onto the bridge.

Data looked up from his Ops console, his gold eyes gleaming with unasked questions.

"Don't hold your breath, Data."

"Sir?"

Riker kept walking.

He passed through the command area and was halfway up the side ramp when he tapped his comm link and said, "Riker to Counselor Troi. Meet me in the main conference room."

The captain's chair of a starship was comfortable—Worf knew this from personal experience—but until such time as he earned the right to assume command authority, the Klingon preferred his position on the aft deck. From this lofty perch, he could observe every action on the bridge and overhear almost all conversations. He had little personal interest in most of the information he gathered, but as the chief of security, Worf felt it was his duty to be aware of the petty concerns of the crew and the weightier matters that involved the senior officers.

So Worf did not miss the anxious look on Commander Riker's face as he strode off the bridge toward the conference room; his call to the ship's counselor was duly noted as well.

"There appears to be a problem," said Data. The android had a comment for every event, no matter how minor; he would not have lasted very long on a Klingon warship.

"Messy Human problems." Unfortunately, Troi's involvement was usually a warning of an imminent disruption to order and discipline on board the ship.

"In theory, the counselor's early involvement can forestall the development of greater difficulties."

"Bad theory." Worf had little faith in the android's understanding of such matters. "Klingon ships have no counselors, and they have fewer problems."

Before Data could prolong this exchange, Worf turned away to a more concrete task, one that did not involve speculation about Human frailties.

Flickering green lights on his console indicated the presence of a faint communications broadcast in the sector surrounding Starbase 193. The steady pulse of a blue light indicated that the signal was an automated message, sent out at regular intervals but without sufficient power to reach a starship traveling at warp speed.

The security chief made a slight adjustment to the alignment of the ship's antenna array. Then another.

By the time Riker had returned to the bridge, with Counselor Troi following in his wake, Worf had established that the call was spread across all the frequencies used by commercial freighters and passenger liners, and that it was broadcast in a scattershot pattern that would saturate the sector. Since only a starbase had the energy resources for that effort, the implication was that Commander Miyakawa was transmitting information of importance to local ship traffic.

Worf rechanneled more auxiliary power to the amplifiers of the subspace transceivers.

* * *

Deanna Troi rang the chime to the ready room. As she waited for a response from within, she could feel Riker watching her. The first officer's concern hovered like a cloud over the bridge, but during their meeting in the conference room he had fumbled for words to explain his unease. In the end, Riker simply shrugged and asked her to see for herself if she sensed any changes in the captain.

"Come."

The counselor stepped forward through the opening doors, then paused on the other side of the threshold until the sliding panels had closed behind her; she needed the barrier to help her block out Riker's anxiety. Taking a deep breath, Troi cleared her mind of expectations, then approached the captain's desk.

She had planned to begin this session with a casual conversation, thus constructing an oblique approach to probe Picard's mood. As soon as she drew near, however, the empath sensed an intensity of emotion that would not yield to such subtle methods. Although the captain was looking straight at her, his mind was focused on the book he held and on the Heart, which rested near his right hand.

"You've been very absorbed of late," remarked Troi.

"I've been following a hunch," said Picard. She read an excitement, almost an exultation, in that statement. Her timing was fortunate; he was in need of an audience. "I believe that T'Sara saw a pattern in the Heart's travels to different worlds, and that is how she tracked the stone to Atropos in the first place. Although any record of her conclusions was destroyed in the attack of the campsite, many of the original pieces of the puzzle are still here in her writings."

"Tell me more," said Troi. She was mildly curious about the Heart, but even more curious about the captain's reaction to it.

"For instance," Picard said, "the Heart appears in both Andorian mythology and early Klingon history. But how could it possibly have traveled from the healers of Andor to the emperor Kessec? The key lies in the records of the first Andorian/Ferengi contact: the Ferengi threatened wholesale slaughter of the populace if they were not provided with 'trade' merchandise."

"How charming." She noticed that the lines of his face were more pronounced than usual. Had he lost weight in the last few days?

"Among the items of tribute may have been the Heart. However, unaware of its true value, the Ferengi merely loaded it into the hold of a freighter and carried it away." Picard opened the book to a marked place near the back. "T'Sara's appendix includes the ship's manifest; it lists 'assorted baubles and trinkets' which were later traded to the barbaric natives of a technologically primitive world known as Kronos."

"This is all very fascinating, but what is its significance to our current mission?"

"Deanna, you must see that the Heart is going somewhere. It also has a mission."

"Really?" she said. "I'm not sure that I would have drawn that conclusion." But Picard did not appear to hear her doubt.

He swiveled around his desk viewer so she could see the star map on its screen. His enthusiasm flaring like an aura around him. "If I can chart where the Heart has been, perhaps I can determine where it is going, its final destination . . . and its motivation."

"You make it sound alive." She reached down and picked up the Heart. She sensed nothing from the stone, but Picard's shifting emotions were obvious. "You resent my holding it. Why?"

"Not at all, Counselor. I'm simply concerned that—"

"Riker to Captain Picard. We've picked up a distress call from Starbase 193."

How ironic, Troi observed, that it was Riker himself who was interrupting the session, one that he had specifically requested.

"On my way, Number One," called out Picard, quickly rising to his feet.

Troi stepped aside to let the captain pass, but he stopped

just long enough to pull the Heart from her hands. With a frosty smile, he said, "We shall have to continue this discussion some other time."

Instead of putting the Heart back on the desk, Picard carried the stone away with him.

Like every member of the bridge crew, Lieutenant Worf held himself to high standards of performance. Fulfilling one's duty was no cause for congratulations; competence was expected, not rewarded. Nevertheless, he felt a measure of satisfaction in having captured the transmission from Starbase 193 just before the *Enterprise* had traveled beyond the range of the signal. He had undertaken the effort as an exercise in long-distance communications recovery, but the result had proved to be of far greater importance than he had expected.

"Status report, Number One," demanded the captain as he strode out of the ready room.

To the Klingon's gratification, Picard carried the Pagrashtak with a care and dignity that showed the proper respect for its powers.

Riker rose to his feet, vacating the captain's chair. "Lieutenant Worf has picked up an automated distress call from Starbase 193."

At a nod from the first officer, Worf touched his console to release the message. Commander Miyakawa's voice was coldly factual, but emphatic.

"*. . . is not a drill. Repeat, this is not a drill. Starbase 193 has been evacuated; do not approach the base; do not attempt to dock. I strongly advise all vessels to leave the sector. This is not a drill. Repeat . . .*"

Worf cut off the repeating loop.

"Why have they evacuated?" demanded Picard.

"No explanation," said Riker with a shrug of frustration.

After checking another panel of the console, the Klingon shook his head. "Channels are open, but there is still no answer to our hails."

"Continue contact efforts, Lieutenant." The captain took his place in the command center and addressed his next spate of orders to the helm. "Set course for a return to Starbase 193."

Even though he concentrated his visual attention on the tactical station, Worf still listened to the general activity on the bridge: Data laid in the new course, Geordi confirmed sufficient power for a sustained warp eight, and Picard sent the *Enterprise* back toward the starbase.

The deck throbbed beneath Worf's feet as the high warp speed strained the propulsion engines to near maximum capacity. Within seconds, the faded distress call from Starbase 193 reappeared on the communications console.

"Estimated arrival in four hours and seven minutes," said Data.

Just under Worf's tactical station, Picard and Riker were discussing reasons for the unexpected diversion. Their muted voices drifted upward.

"The likeliest explanation is that the station suffered some kind of equipment malfunction," said Riker.

"But why weren't we notified? Miyakawa knew our course headings; she could have sent a distress call directly to us if—"

A flurry of crimson alarms suddenly tripped across the tactical consoles on the aft deck. From where he stood, Worf could see identical patterns washing over Data's Ops controls as well.

"Captain," called out Worf. "Long-range sensor scans have detected an explosion in the sector."

The android confirmed the announcement with a sharp nod of his head. "Magnitude of the energy release would be consistent with the detonation of a starbase's generators."

"And the base distress call has stopped," added Worf. All signs of the strengthening signal had disappeared.

"Damn!" exclaimed Riker, jumping to his feet. "We'll need survival rescue teams, paramedics—"

"Hold on that," said Picard. His order froze the first officer in place. "Lieutenant Worf, are there any other Federation vessels within this quadrant?"

Worf quickly checked the latest position reports from Starfleet Command. "At warp nine, the *Portsmouth* could reach Starbase 193 in six point five hours; the *Plath* would take seven hours."

"Captain!" protested Riker. "Those extra hours could mean the difference between life and death to any people who were on that station."

"We will have to trust to Commander Miyakawa's efficiency and assume there was sufficient time for a complete evacuation. If she had wanted the *Enterprise* to provide assistance, she would have signaled us directly; she intended for us to stay away."

"But why would—"

"I suspect someone destroyed the starbase while in pursuit of the Heart," said Picard. "We have become a magnet for trouble, Number One, and our best course of action is to draw that trouble away from innocent bystanders."

"Deliberately make ourselves a target?"

"Exactly."

Picard rose to his feet, moving to the center of the bridge. As he turned toward the aft deck, Worf could see that the captain gripped the Pagrashtak in both hands, just as a warrior might hold fast to the pommel of his sword.

"Lieutenant Worf, transmit a message to the *Portsmouth* on an uncoded channel: '*Enterprise* has urgent business elsewhere, request you proceed immediately to Starbase 193 to aid survivors.' And for good measure, send the same message to whatever may be left of Starbase 193. Be sure to include our current coordinates."

Next, Picard turned to face the helm. "Mr. Data, set course for . . . one twenty-three mark twelve. Reduce speed to warp six."

Their path was obviously picked at random, and this arbitrary choice seemed to disturb the first officer; his face creased with worry. Unlike Riker, however, Lieutenant Worf knew their final destination, and he faced it with courage and eager anticipation.

Since the days of Emperor Kessec, no other Klingon had been honored with the opportunity to serve a commander who wielded the powers of the Pagrashtak. This journey would soon become legend, and all Klingon legends ended in death.

CHAPTER 22

"**H**ere it comes—brace yourself!" cried Miyakawa as she pressed herself deeper into the cushions of the acceleration seat.

The cubical lifeboat bucked wildly, buffeted by the explosive force of expanding vapors and a deadly hail of disintegrating fragments, all that remained of Starbase 193. Force fields protected the pod's hull, but she knew that each muffled impact sapped just a little more energy from a finite supply.

Seconds later, the wave of flying debris had passed and the jarring collisions stopped just as abruptly as they had begun. The lifeboat's reaction control system hissed on and off in short bursts until the craft slowed its tumbling motion, then stabilized with a constant horizon line.

"Down to sixty-five percent of power reserves," she said after scanning the control panel.

"Is that good or bad?"

Miyakawa turned to her companion; the commander could just make out Camenae's broad face in the faint glow of light from the illuminated console. "It means we have about fifty-six person-days of life support left, which means the two of us can survive in here for twenty-eight days."

The dark wing of a Romulan warbird swooped across the view screen, blocking out the vista of stars.

Miyakawa quickly reached for the pod's manual override switch; even the smallest puff of the accelerators could give away their existence. She held her breath until the uncloaked ship had receded into the distance.

"Of course, power reserves are immaterial if the Romulans detect us first," said Miyakawa in a low whisper. According to the pod's rudimentary sensors, the warbird was traveling through space in a wide arc, tracing a lazy circle around the guttering fires of her dead starbase.

They would be back.

"But we'll have to risk using impulse engines soon," said Camenae. "If we're still in this area when the *Enterprise* arrives, this lifeboat could get caught in some very nasty cross fire."

"The *Enterprise* won't be coming back to this sector," said Miyakawa. "In fact, there may not be a rescue effort for quite some time."

"What!"

"I didn't notify Starfleet about the evacuation; instead, I restricted the broadcast to this sector's traffic channels. The Romulans are using my starbase as bait, and I wasn't about to help them set the trap."

"I see," said Camenae. She shifted uncomfortably in the narrow confines of her chair. "This isn't going to be pleasant. I've seen packing crates with more room to move."

Miyakawa couldn't argue the point. The escape pod's truncated cube shape provided storage compartments for generous quantities of survival supplies, but the four crew seats took up most of the remaining space of the interior.

"I'm sorry, Camenae, but I assumed you would leave the station on a freighter or a liner like everyone else. If you had followed my orders, you would have been safely away by now."

"And *you* would have been vaporized. Like some melodramatic sea captain who refuses to abandon a sinking ship."

After a long silence, Miyakawa said, "I lost track of time."

The other woman snorted. "There wasn't that much time to keep track of."

Miyakawa shrugged, then realized that her companion could not see the gesture in the dark. She hadn't made a conscious decision to stay on the starbase, but she hadn't scrambled for the lifeboat until she found Camenae wandering through the deserted docking bay. "Wait a minute. Why were you still on board the station?"

Camenae's silence lasted so long that it seemed she was not going to answer at all. There was a quaver in her voice when she finally spoke. "I've been through this before . . . and I'm tired of being a survivor."

So, they had rescued each other, reluctant heroes sacrificing their own death so that the other might live.

"I'll see to it that you survive again this time, whether you like it or not," said Miyakawa with a fierce conviction that welled up from inside of her. "A starbase can be rebuilt. Our lives can be rebuilt."

"That's a job for the young." Camenae uttered a weary sigh. "And I'm much older than I look."

"Not too old to feel sorry for yourself."

"Thank you, Commander," said Camenae dryly. "Your sympathy is appreciated."

Miyakawa laughed. "My charming personality is well-known throughout Starfleet. Think how fortunate you are to be cooped up with me for—"

A flashing light signaled the activation of the pod's transceiver. "Incoming message."

She released the sound into the cabin.

"*Attention USS* Portsmouth: *Priority distress call . . . Starbase 193 has been destroyed . . .* Enterprise *has urgent business elsewhere . . . request you proceed immediately to aid survivors.*"

"I don't get it." Miyakawa shook her head in disbelief. "That was an uncoded broadcast. Everyone in the sector probably heard that message."

"Look!" Camenae pointed to the viewscreen.

In the distance, they could see the Romulan warbird changing course. Its curved path flattened out into a straight line. As it gathered speed, the ship's image rippled and shimmered, then faded out of existence. The cloaking device had been activated.

"Dammit!" cried Miyakawa. "I risked my life to protect the *Enterprise,* but they've fallen prey to the Romulans anyway!"

"Don't underestimate Captain Picard." Camenae's smile flashed in the shadowed interior of the pod. "I think he's constructing a trap of his own."

If this was so, Picard's ploy was a dangerous one.

"Good luck, Jean-Luc," whispered Miyakawa.

"Forward thrust . . ." ordered Commander Taris, ". . . now."

Vedoc staggered back against a metal bulkhead, unbalanced by the *Haakona*'s jolting acceleration to high warp speed. For a moment, before the dampening field could counteract the pressure of inertial forces against his chest, he could hardly breathe.

Others among the bridge crew seemed to be fighting for breath as well, but none of them betrayed any surprise at the painful effect, so this was no ship malfunction. Vedoc was familiar enough with the warbird class to know that Taris must have reset the inertial dampening field below standard specifications; undoubtedly this was another small shaving of energy to funnel toward the weapons system.

The crush of g-forces finally eased. With a wheezing gasp of relief, Vedoc lurched back to his position by the side of the commander's throne.

Taris met his return with a condescending smile and said, "Of course, it's a trap."

Vedoc assumed a feigned look of surprise just a second too late, and then feared she would begin to suspect his deceit. To his relief, however, the sneer on the commander's face showed she had mistaken his bad timing for stupidity.

"A trap, Commander?" he asked with exaggerated bewilderment. Evidently she was convinced that he was an idiot and would continue to interpret all his reactions accordingly.

"Your gullibility is touching, Vedoc." Taris seemed to enjoy displaying her contempt for her subcommander; if she had any weakness as an officer, it was this intractable arrogance. "Picard has given away his position on purpose. The Federation is very protective of its civilian population, and they will often undertake such risks to shift combat to a more isolated area of space. All the better; we are more than a match for the *Enterprise.*"

Vedoc nodded obsequiously, too distracted to contrive a suitably inane response for his idiot persona. If the commander's custom modifications to the operating systems of the *Haakona* were any indication, her boast was founded on fact rather than vanity. This knowledge sharpened the young man's sense of urgency, but over the past few days he had found no way to change the course of the events surrounding him.

Would Surak have waited passively for opportunity, or would the ancient Vulcan have made his own opportunities? Vedoc longed to ask his teacher this question, but the catacombs of Romulus were light-years away.

"Commander Taris." He assumed the manner of an eager pup desperate to please its master. "Give me more to do than stand by your side. Let me take even a small part in this kill."

She snorted under her breath, but managed to contain any more blatant expression of her amusement at this offer.

With fear lodged at the base of his throat, he pushed harder. "I'm newly posted to this warbird, but I have served with distinction on other ships. If nothing else, let me assist at the auxiliary weapons station."

"Oh, very well," said Taris. "But if Etrajan has any cause for complaint, you will return to the bridge."

"It shall be as you order, Commander!" he proclaimed with a flourishing salute. This archaic and melodramatic response wrung an explosion of laughter from the normally impassive crew. As if mortally embarrassed by their disdain, Vedoc fled the bridge.

His boots rang loudly on the metal decks as he raced through the main corridor of the ship's spine. The auxiliary bay next to engineering remained unmanned until battle was imminent; if he stayed far enough ahead of Etrajan, Vedoc would have a few minutes of unsupervised time in which to act. Despite lungs that were still sore from the launch, Vedoc pushed himself to keep running. He swallowed the bitter taste of blood, yet still he did not slow his pace. An extra second could mean the difference between success and failure.

By the time the subcommander skidded into the empty alcove, he had selected his target. With a quick look to make sure he was not observed and that no stray engineering operative was in the vicinity, Vedoc grabbed a sonic wrench from a recessed shelf, then fell to his knees by the side of a forward shield generator.

A quick inspection confirmed his suspicion that Taris had implemented a number of unorthodox modifications to the deflector system as well; but for every gain there was an equivalent loss, so some other aspect of the ship's performance must have been sacrificed for this advantage. What basic crew comfort had she deemed an expendable luxury?

Disabling the diagnostic sensors in the unit was a straightforward exercise in sabotage. As an easily bored ensign, he had repeatedly assembled and disassembled similar components while his ship patrolled the borders of the Neutral Zone. Perhaps it was those same long duty shifts that had given him time to reflect on history and philosophy.

The next step was even less complicated, but far more decisive. The power coupling leading to any shield generator was a weak link that was rarely broken; it lay too far inside the warbird's hull to be vulnerable to enemy attack. Setting the proper frequency on the wrench, he loosened the electron-bonded connections on the cable's casing.

All he had to do now was pull.

Is this the right path?

He had not followed the teachings of Spock long enough to know if this scheme was true to the philosophy of Surak, but Vedoc did not have years in which to master the dictates of logic. He had only a matter of minutes in which to act.

His hand hovered over the conduit.

Assuming that he had the courage to forfeit his own life for his beliefs, could logic grant him the right to kill his unwilling shipmates with the same gesture? Surak had urged peace and an end to killing, yet if Vedoc assumed a strict pacifist stand, the *Haakona* would obtain the means to subjugate the Federation, and millions of people on both sides of the conflict would die.

In the end, he chose according to the dictates of his own conscience, however flawed.

This is best for all my people.

Vedoc jerked on the conduit, pulling it out just far enough to loosen the connection without actually severing the current. Repeated power surges to the activated forward shield would eventually blow the two sections apart.

Springing to his feet, Vedoc reshelved the wrench. Then, with three long strides he covered the distance to the photon torpedo console. That was where Etrajan found him a few moments later.

"Don't touch anything," said the crewman with a dour scowl.

"I am yours to command," replied Vedoc with a sweeping bow that hid the sweat beading on his face.

As he took his place by Etrajan's side, Vedoc allowed himself to briefly reflect over what he had just done.

The Ko N'ya would remain with the *Enterprise*. From what he had read of the blood-drenched lore of the stone, the Federation would have little cause to thank him for that bequest.

Keyda Chandat searched the night sky for a glimpse of the starship that circled high above his planet. Starfleet might consider the Miranda-class USS *Sullivan* to be little more than a scoutship, but the warp-powered saucer was far more impressive than any spacecraft known to the inhabitants of Dynasia.

"There, Warden," said the Federation ambassador, pointing a finger to direct him.

"Yes, I see it." But that was a lie; all Chandat could see were stars. He pulled his gaze back to the ground before one of his aides returned and caught him with his face upturned like a foolish child dreaming of the lost grandeurs of Iconia.

As they continued their stroll through the garden, he stared fixedly at the plants bordering the path they followed. Perhaps the beauty of the flowering aurelia would ward off the temptation of another glance upward. "Like all my people, I was expected to master some aspect of the ancient texts. My specialty was Flight Engineering, and I yearned to someday touch the wonders my Iconian ancestors had designed. When I finally faced the impossibility of that desire, the schematics of their starships flattened into mere lines on a page . . . and I decided to become a bureaucrat instead of a scientist." His fingers brushed against the metallic disk dangling from a thick-linked gold chain around his neck. "Of course, I never expected the yoke of this office would become so heavy as it has this year."

"If the Dynasian Faculty chooses to pursue admission, your children will walk the decks of our starships. They may even command them." Ambassador Tommas was quite adept at promoting the Federation agenda.

"A more likely scenario is that my children will die in civil war first," said Chandat. His legs were cramped after hours of sitting in council, and though he was tired, it felt good to finally move freely. "Regardless of what decision the Faculty government reaches, there will be an opposing faction enraged by the outcome. If conservative forces prevail, we must resort to mass executions to repress the native insurgents; if the admission factions win, our central authority will disintegrate and anarchy will reign in its place. You have unleashed a storm that will tear my world to pieces, yet you will not commit military forces—"

"Warden, our Prime Directive—"

"Yes, I know all about your Prime Directive of noninterference," he said bitterly. "Having shattered our political unity, you will step back and watch us writhe in our death throes."

"That is unfair." A dark color flooded over the ambassador's pale cheeks; Chandat wondered what Human emotion that signified. "Dean Shagret's request for admission to the Federation constituted a formal invitation to open negotiations."

"He did not have the authority to issue that request!"

"Just the means," sighed Tommas. "You can hardly blame us for his duplicity."

"No, Ambassador, I do not. My weariness is speaking louder than my reason."

In truth, Shagret's treason had been cleverly executed. A lifetime of exemplary administrative service had gained the man the coveted post of Dean of Communications and thus the means to send a message directly to the Federation Council. Who would have suspected that a highly placed conservative professor harbored radical insurgent sympathies?

Chandat twirled around, alarmed by the sound of someone running up behind them. In the last week, native partisans had gained access to halls and libraries, areas once thought beyond their reach, but surely not to the Faculty garden as well? To his relief, the boy who approached was a trusted aide. Or could anyone be trusted in these dark times?

"Warden," called out the boy. "The Faculty Council is ready to resume the debate."

Having delivered this message, he darted back down the path. So, fear of terrorist attacks had spread to the students as well.

"May I meet with you again after this session?" the ambassador asked as they strolled back toward the flying buttresses of the Athenaeum.

"No," said Chandat, though he longed to say otherwise. "Not until the Faculty has reached a consensus." He had enjoyed these audiences with Tommas too much; his longing to touch lost wonders was resurfacing, clouding his judgment and his objectivity.

Or am I gaining new perspectives?

The warden mused upon this conflict of interests as he pushed his way through the crowd of professors and students that were milling by the entrance to the council chamber.

Inside, he found that the debate had resumed without him.

"Traitors! Admission to the Federation will completely undermine our authority and our financial base on this planet."

The last of the straggling Faculty members rushed into the room to hear the Dean of Architecture berate her opponents. As warden, Chandat was responsible for maintaining order, but he decided the attempt to exercise control would only inflame tempers further. He would let Thorina rave a while longer.

"All that the Dynasian natives possess, we have given them. They were scrabbling in the dirt when we arrived, and they would be scrabbling there still if not for our superior technological knowledge."

"That 'scrabbling' populace has taken care of us for a millennia," retorted Shagret with the smug demeanor of a self-righteous zealot. His forehead bore the intricate ridges of a noble family, but he affected the accent of a native. "They have grown our food, built our libraries, even bathed our very bodies; in return, we have doled out scraps of technology to them like sweet favors to an obedient child. Then we execute those who would use it without tithing our coffers."

Thorina dismissed this defense with a contemptuous wave. "Unfettered development would have destroyed their culture."

"We have strangled any true development centuries ago," said Shagret. The warden noticed with some unease that several more professors had grouped around him to show support. "We play games of the mind in soaring towers but have forgotten how to turn thought into action. The master plan of the Ancients has fallen into disuse because it called for the eventual participation of the planet's natives; the ideals of our Iconian ancestors have been corrupted into self-serving exploitation."

"Admission is inevitable," cried out a junior Faculty member in Physics and the leader of a growing Pragmatist faction. "If we vote in favor of joining the Federation, we can then control the population's access to new sources of knowledge."

"Your naïveté is stunning," sniped Thorina. "And very dangerous."

The one native professor on the Faculty, little more than a token until now, stood up to speak. Oomalo's scales glistened with the iridescence of anger. "If you deny us this opportunity for advancement, my people have vowed to return to 'scrabbling in the dirt,' only this time you will have to scrabble along with us for your living. Without our labor, your fine libraries will rot and your stomachs will go empty."

The hall erupted into chaos. Chandat's calls for order were drowned out as the cries of outrage from those who feared the natives mixed with the cries of indignation from those who championed their cause. What warden in the history of the Dynasians could forge a consensus from such divergent convictions? He fell silent rather than add his own voice to the tumult.

As the uproar continued unabated, a hand fell on his shoulder, and Chandat looked up to find his secretary bending down to whisper in his ear.

"Warden," said the man as he pushed a document into Chandat's hand. "I bring an urgent memo from Professor Manja."

"Manja? By the Three Gates, not now!" scolded Chandat. Under the circumstances, the doddering scholar's plaintive requests for increased funding were especially ill-timed; Iconian Literature was not a priority for this Faculty at the best of times.

"Read it, Warden!" said Ganin with an urgency that startled Chandat into compliance.

He read the message. Then he read it again.

As a man of science, the warden had never believed in miracles, but the words before him were like the answers to a prayer. There was no time to confirm the veracity of such an outrageous claim, but true or not, it would serve his immediate purpose.

Rising from his seat, the warden waved for silence. When he finally had gained the unruly Faculty's attention, he read them a judiciously edited version of Manja's report.

It was met with stunned silence. For once, the assembly of professors had nothing to say.

Chandat took shameless advantage of their confusion.

"This Ko N'ya is the very Gem which Kanda Jiak used to operate the Gateway from Iconia to our world—we must act now to seize it from those who do not suspect its powers. With the Gem in our possession once again, we can regain the heights scaled by our Iconian forebearers; the planets of the Federation will come begging to us for a superior technology beyond their understanding; and *all* the people of Dynasia will share in wealth beyond imagining."

Every face in the hall was turned toward him with eyes that burned with patriotic fervor.

Warden Chandat rejoiced. He had restored unity to his world after all.

CHAPTER 23

"T'Sara."

No . . . do not wake me anymore . . . I am so tired.

"T'Sara."

She opened her eyes, but the man who had called her out of the healing trance was not Sorren. Of course he was not Sorren; Sorren was dead.

And I am dying even now.

The cool air of the Collector's chamber made her shiver for the first time. She rubbed her hands together for warmth, then stopped suddenly and looked down at her palms.

Her hands were empty.

"I have it now," said the stranger kneeling before her, and she saw that the stone was sheltered in his large, muscular hands.

"If I no longer hold the Ko N'ya," said T'Sara, "then this must be *your* dream, young man."

He had the lean, sharp look of a Vulcan until he smiled at her words. "It has been many years since I've been called a young man."

"Your hair may have turned white, but you will never grow so old as I am now," she said simply, and he met her

206

statement with a gentle nod of acceptance. Humans were short-lived compared to her own people, but this one seemed to have made more of his brief moment than others of his race. "Why do you call me?"

"I am trying to unravel the path of the Ko N'ya, T'Sara. It began at the Guardian of Forever, but I don't know how it left there or where it is going. Or even why it travels."

"Greedy Human," she sighed. "Not even I could live long enough to answer all of those questions . . . but I almost touched the truth of Where."

"Almost?"

"In one of my last visions I saw the next step in its journey; not the end of its quest, but possibly the end of its dealings with our affairs."

"Tell me, T'Sara!" he pleaded with an urgency that saddened her.

She pointed to the wizened body of the Collector, who crouched above them. "Halaylah learned the ways of the stone better than anyone, but when she saw that same vision, she walled herself up alive rather than let the Ko N'ya fulfill its destiny."

"I am not the Collector; I wish to find a way to continue what you—"

"No!" she cried out. Her waning strength was not sufficient to suppress her anguish. "Do not lay the burden of your actions on me. I have too much to answer for already."

"'I will not give it to any living being,'" he recited slowly. "I remember, those were your words."

"And Surak's. As a child he was far wiser than I could ever hope to be. He released the stone before it could tempt him beyond the limits of self-control; I thought I could do the same, but I waited too long. You have waited too long as well."

The man shook his head as if angered by what he heard. "It is not evil, T'Sara."

"No, not evil. Just dangerous." There was not much time left to her, she realized. On the other side of this dream, death was waiting. "The Ko N'ya is not of our world; its powers were meant for other purposes. It constantly struggles to free itself from the tangle of our grasping hands."

Overcome by weakness, her head fell back against the wall. *Must the knot untie so soon?*

"No, T'Sara!" he cried. "I need to know where!"

She extended an arm up toward his head, her fingers searching for the contact points on his temple. The man stiffened but did not resist her; he had mind-melded before.

She reached inward.

When their thoughts were one, she showed him the place: the constellation of stars and the speeding messenger that waited for the Ko N'ya.

There!

Her arm dropped down, breaking the link. The fingers of her hand flexed, then clenched like steel clamps around the cloth of his shirt. With the last of her strength, she pulled him so close he could feel her dry breath on his face as she whispered, "Remember this about the Ko N'ya . . . the blood never stops flowing."

Picard stumbled out of the shadows of the Collector's chamber into the ruined plaza surrounding the fallen tower.

Staring up into the night sky, he tried to make sense of the stars. They were all wrong, and it was so very important that they be right. He reached out his hands to move them into their proper positions, to arrange them according to the image T'Sara had revealed to him . . .

. . . but his fingers hit against the transparent barrier of an angled ceiling window.

He was standing in the middle of his cabin.

Despite this abrupt awakening, his sense of urgency remained: somehow he must fix the stars in their place. Stepping over to his desk, Picard snatched up a data padd and stylus and began to sketch a series of small circles. Even as the meaning of what he drew faded out of his understanding, he fought to preserve the image that lingered in his mind's eye.

His hand finally stopped, but he knew he was not quite

finished. There was still something missing, an element that had given this scene a distinctive configuration.

Not another star . . .

. . . a comet.

He drew a flurry of lines to mark the comet's streaming tail, and the sketch was complete.

With the padd gripped tightly in one hand, Picard walked back to the threshold of his bedroom. If the Heart had come to life during the night, he had missed its shimmering display. He could barely make out its rounded silhouette on a low table by his bed.

Picard whispered into the shadows, "If I am to take you to this place, I must know why."

CHAPTER 24

The bridge was always quiet during the night shift.

Too quiet, as far as Riker was concerned. Although a full crew complement was posted at all the duty stations, the men and women talked in low voices and went about their work with a more subdued manner than their day-shift counterparts. The hushed atmosphere made Riker feel uncomfortably self-conscious. He was a large man who was accustomed to moving freely and taking up space; any attempt to rein in his body robbed him of composure.

During the day, Riker would have sprawled in the captain's chair and called out for any information he wanted, and he would have conducted discussions across the length of the bridge. During the night, however, he felt constrained by the lull around him and chose to walk from station to station to gather reports.

The first officer even shortened his stride as he walked up a side ramp to the tactical station on the aft deck, but his boots still thumped too heavily.

"Status, Lieutenant?" Riker asked in a voice that was too loud.

"Shields raised; energy reserves holding steady at ninety-five percent," said Worf. His voice was deeper than Riker's, yet it seemed to travel less far. "Sensor scans do not reveal pursuit by any kind of vessel."

"So the captain's decoy plan doesn't appear to be working. That's assuming someone really did attack Starbase 193."

To Riker's consternation, Worf's eyes narrowed to baleful slits. By nature, Klingons were fiercely loyal to their commanding officer, but Worf was especially sensitive to any implied criticism of Captain Picard. "Do not forget the report of Romulan incursion into Federation space."

"An unconfirmed sighting of a warbird, with no indication of where it might be headed . . ." The first officer shrugged. "Well, I suppose it's possible."

"We must remain vigilant."

"Absolutely," said Riker. Fortunately, this display of enthusiasm seemed to appease Worf sufficiently to ease the belligerent expression off his face. "Carry on, Lieutenant."

Riker had just turned away to continue his tour around the bridge when he heard the telltale trill of an incoming message registering on the communications console. He waited for the security chief's explanation before taking another step.

"Commander, we are receiving a scrambled transmission . . ." Worf scanned the signal packet information, ". . . from Commander Miyakawa, currently aboard the *Portsmouth.*"

"Well it's about time!" All across the bridge, heads snapped around at the sound of Riker's cry, but he no longer cared whether he was conspicuous or not.

"Unscrambling in progress."

Moving to Worf's side, Riker eagerly read the text as it scrolled across a small window.

Even before he had finished reading all of Miyakawa's account, the first officer reached for his comm link. "Captain Picard to the bridge." Then Riker turned to the security chief and, taking a deep breath, said, "Raise shields . . . and go to yellow alert."

The tranquillity of the night shift was shattered as amber panels of light throbbed on and off and sirens whooped to life. Complacent crewmembers jumped to attention or scurried to secure their stations, and Riker knew that a thousand sleeping people throughout the decks of the starship had just been rudely awakened.

We have become a magnet for trouble.

The captain's ominous words echoed in Riker's mind. With hands gripping the aft deck rail, he leaned forward to stare at the main viewscreen.

One cubic meter of space looked very much like another, but somewhere in that tenuous soup of interstellar gases was a cloaked Romulan warbird, an invisible raptor in search of an all too visible prey.

Deanna Troi struggled to stifle a yawn, but fortunately the ensign sitting across from her was too absorbed in his own misery to notice her momentary lapse of attention. He was hunched forward on the edge of the sofa, staring down at the carpet as he spilled out the details of a failed romance.

"How can I continue living when I've lost the one person that gave my existence meaning?"

His roommate had been sufficiently alarmed by this sentiment to roust the empath out of her bed in the middle of the night for a counseling session. However, Troi had quickly sensed that Asadourian was not truly suicidal, merely histrionic. Perhaps she would pass his name on to Beverly Crusher so he could indulge his flair for melodrama on the stage of the ship's theater.

Certain that the ensign had unburdened himself of the worst of his grievances against his former true love, the counselor gently urged him to return to his cabin.

"You'll feel better in the morning," she assured him as they walked out of her office. She could tell that he didn't believe her, but then lovesick young men never did.

As Troi strolled down the quiet corridors of the ship, she admitted to a slightly wistful envy of Asadourian's passion; it was incredibly disruptive, yet so much fun, to fall madly in love. Many years ago, she herself had experienced a considerable amount of emotional turmoil in connection with a certain tall, dark Starfleet officer.

"And stay out of trouble until that heals!"

Picking up her pace at the sound of the familiar voice, Troi turned a corner in time to catch a fleeting glimpse of red and blue as Beverly Crusher ducked back into sickbay. Ensign Brengle, the recipient of the doctor's commandment, was limping away down the corridor.

On the spur of the moment, Troi decided to take a short detour. After all, as long as she was awake, she could attend to certain frictions between the captain and his chief medical officer.

The outer ward of sickbay was empty of patients, but several nurses were clearing the area of used medical supplies, and Crusher was standing in the middle of the room frowning at the data padd in her hand.

"Busy night?" asked Troi.

"You could say that," said Crusher, with a weary sigh. "No major emergencies, just a steady stream of minor injuries from freak accidents. For instance, did you know there's a holodeck scenario for riding dinosaurs?"

"That sounds like one of Wesley's ideas."

"Probably," said the doctor.

"But surely he wouldn't construct a dangerous program?"

With a shake of her head, Crusher said. "Oh, not even Marte blamed the computer for her accident. The fail-safe parameters can protect you from being trampled on by an allosaurus, but they can't stop you from tripping over a Jurassic vine and twisting your ankle."

"Interesting setting, but I think I'll stick to more modern sports." Troi assumed her best pretense of nonchalance to ask, "When is your shift over?"

Crusher scratched a quick note on the tablet, then handed it to one of the departing nurses. "Right now."

They were finally alone, which gave Troi the opportunity to

ask her next question. "So are you going to have breakfast with the captain this morning?"

"No," said Crusher emphatically. "In fact, I have no intention of meeting the captain for any meal whatsoever in the foreseeable future."

"I see," said Troi. "He hasn't apologized for your broken dinner engagement."

"He hasn't even remembered that we made plans."

"Even so, I wish you would make a point to meet with him soon." Troi held up a hand to forestall an indignant protest. "He doesn't seem to be sleeping well lately."

"Maybe he has a guilty conscience."

"Actually, Beverly," said the counselor. "I'm getting a little worried about him, and so is Will. The captain's interest in the Heart has become so intense that I'm inclined to term it an obsession."

"Are you serious?" Crusher folded her arms over her chest in an unconscious gesture of distrust.

"I am very serious." Fortunately, she was able to say this with complete sincerity. "I'm not ready to request a formal medical exam, but I'd like your professional opinion on his condition."

"Off the record?"

"Yes."

"All right, Deanna." Crusher unlocked her arms and shoved her hands deep into her coat pockets. "You win. I'll stop by the captain's cabin this—"

Her last words were drowned out by the intrusive wail of yellow alert sirens.

So much for that clever plan, thought Deanna ruefully. And so much for any more rest that night.

The fact that Data did not sleep was well-known throughout the ship, so it was not unusual for the android to have visitors at any time of day or night. Both Geordi La Forge and Miles O'Brien were in the habit of stopping by Data's cabin if they had worked late and were in the mood for company.

Captain Picard, however, was not known for making impromptu visits; yet, there he stood in the hall just outside the android's quarters, fingers rapping impatiently on the back of a data padd.

"Come in, sir," said Data, stepping back from the threshold to let his commanding officer enter.

Picard advanced a few feet into the room, just enough to allow the doors to close behind his back. "I need your assistance, Data."

"Certainly, Captain. I—" The android stopped in mid-sentence to peer down at the tablet that Picard had thrust into his hands. After a brief study of the crude graphic on the screen, Data ventured a hypothesis. "These circles represent stars?"

"Yes, of course they're stars. This is a map of a particular location that . . . well, that is important for me to identify. So, I need you to ascertain the coordinates of this site."

Data slowly rotated the padd. "A two-dimensional representation of three-dimensional spatial arrangements is insufficient for this task. I will need a reference point of some kind."

"There isn't one," said the captain with an impatient shake of his head. "Except for the comet."

"Captain, comets are extremely common. To date, the Federation registry lists approximately—"

"I'm well aware of the difficulties, Mr. Data. However, it is imperative that you establish just where this spot," Picard tapped emphatically in the center of the map, "can be found."

"I will do my best." The placement of the circles formed a distinctive pattern. Data blinked in an involuntary reaction to the activation of his neural subprocessors and confirmed that the arrangement of stars was not a constellation that he could immediately match with any images stored in his memory. "But this could take a very long time. On the order of several weeks, if not months."

Picard frowned his disapproval of the estimate. Snatching

the padd out of Data's grasp, the captain stared down at the sketch. "If only I could remember . . ." His eyes closed. His fingers traced over the figures he had drawn.

Data waited patiently.

"We were with the Collector . . . the vision was given to her . . ." Picard's eyes flew open. "Presume that this is a constellation that can be seen from the surface of Atropos if you were standing in the plaza where you found T'Sara's body."

"Thank you," said Data. "That specification should provide adequate information to narrow my search parameters."

"Fine, fine, just let me know as soon—"

"Captain Picard to the bridge."

Before Picard could answer Riker's hail, yellow alert sirens signaled a significant change in the ship's status.

"Our adversary has surfaced," said Picard, and Data noted the look of triumph that lit his face, if only for a moment. Flinging aside the data padd that had absorbed his attention until now, Picard spun on his heel and marched out of the cabin.

Data advanced through the doorway in the captain's wake, then came to a sudden halt just in time to avoid a collision. Picard had stopped in the middle of the corridor; he was poised for movement, yet hesitated as if unsure of which direction he should take.

"Captain?"

"I left something in my cabin . . ." said Picard, looking back over his shoulder. The flashing alert lights seemed to highlight the hollows beneath his eyes. ". . . but it will have to wait until later. There really isn't time."

Despite the declarative form, Data sensed an implied question in the captain's statement. "No, it does not appear that there is any margin for delay."

Picard bolted into motion again. "Then what are you waiting for?" he called out as he raced down the corridor.

Data scrambled to catch up.

* * *

216

Mission briefings were usually held in the sequestered comfort of the observation lounge, but by unspoken agreement, Riker conducted this session in the command center of the bridge. Tonight, the time to move from one room of the ship to another was a luxury they could not afford.

The first officer leaned forward, hands planted on his knees, as he related his knowledge of the approaching danger to the captain and Data; Worf loomed above the seated group from his aerie on the aft deck.

"According to Commander Miyakawa's account," said Riker, "the warbird was still circling Starbase 193 when we broadcast the distress message to the *Portsmouth.* The Romulans cloaked moments later, and presumably departed the area on an intercept course with the *Enterprise.*"

Data canted his head to one side as his positronic brain incorporated time and distance into his calculations. "If that is the case, I estimate that the warbird could approach firing range of the *Enterprise* within seventeen minutes."

"That's too close for comfort," said Riker with an involuntary glance at the main viewscreen.

"Bear in mind, Commander, that this conjecture is based on a theoretical performance rate of one hundred percent. Depending on the degree of efficiency of the ship and its crew, actual values will fall short of that figure."

"For safety's sake," said Picard, "let us presume they are very efficient. Helm, increase speed to warp nine."

"Aye, sir." The android swiveled his console chair back into a forward position as he implemented the captain's directive. Somewhere down in engineering, Geordi had anticipated this demand because the warp engines immediately purred into high speed.

Picard called up to the aft deck next. "Lieutenant Worf, reduce power expenditures throughout the ship and channel all available energy to the deflector shields."

Pitching his voice low, so only the captain could hear him, Riker asked, "Do you think we can outrun them, sir?"

"Probably not," said Picard. "They have too great a lead already. However, cloaking devices are a heavy drain on a warbird's resources, so we can make them pay a high price for this pursuit. If they stay invisible, they will drain their weaponry system."

"And if they drop the cloaking field, we have a target we can see."

"Exactly, Number One." Picard rubbed a hand over his face, as if to wipe away fatigue, then fixed his gaze on the viewscreen. "The rest is a waiting game."

At close quarters, Riker could hear a faint rasp in the captain's voice. Picard's eyes were rimmed with red, another sign that he hadn't gotten much rest tonight; but then, if he had been asleep in his cabin when yellow alert sounded, his arrival to the bridge would have been delayed by at least a few more minutes. No, Riker suspected the captain had already been awake when he received the call to duty.

"Captain," rumbled Worf. "Long-range sensors detect an approaching vessel . . . intercept in fifteen seconds."

"Go to red alert, Lieutenant," said Picard grimly, and in an instant the bridge was bathed in red light.

Riker shook his head in disbelief. "If it's the Romulans, they're well ahead of schedule."

"It appears I was in error," said Data, looking back over his shoulder. Riker hadn't intended to slight his estimate, but the android evidently felt the need to justify his miscalculation. "Apparently they have sacrificed the stealth afforded by a cloaking device for speed and strength of arms."

"Closing at five hundred thousand kilometers . . ." warned Worf.

Riker saw Picard nod to himself, a sign he had chosen his strategy for the coming conflict.

"On my signal," said the captain, "go to quarter-impulse speed. With luck, they'll overshoot us by a decade."

"Four hundred thousand kilometers . . . three hundred thousand . . ."

"Now!" said Picard.

The *Enterprise*'s sudden drop out of high warp drive sent a shudder rippling through the saucer hull. On the main viewscreen, Riker could see the warbird flashing past, but too slowly for warp speed. "Dammit! They've second-guessed us."

"But at full-impulse speed, they still overshot," said Picard. They watched the Romulan ship as it circled back to confront them. "It gives us a few extra seconds."

"Phasers locking on target," announced Worf.

"Fire at will, Lieutenant."

Riker gripped the arms of his command chair in anticipation of the coming assault.

The Klingon unleashed a barrage from the phasers, but the warbird charged straight through the curtain of fire. Then, as the ships closed, the space between them burned with a dazzling crisscross of energy beams. The bridge rocked as the starship's shields absorbed a series of blows.

"Evasive maneuvers," ordered Picard.

The *Enterprise* responded with quicksilver movements under the helm's control, yet the Romulan pilot was equally adept. The two ships twirled through space, paired like dancers who never pulled too far apart. Warbirds were not known for their grace, but this ship was different, realized Riker, and the difference could be deadly.

"Deflector power down to fifty-seven percent," called out Ensign Taylor from the aft deck.

Again and again, Riker was tossed and shaken as the Romulan phasers pounded against the starship's shields. Worf scored as many hits on the warbird, but only a scattered few actually touched the warbird's hull.

"Minor damage to their starboard wing," said the Klingon.

However, his announcement was quickly followed by another damage report from the ensign. "Shield failure imminent in Engineering, Sector 52."

"Auxiliary power supplies are almost depleted." Geordi's intercom voice barely cut through the battle's thunder. *"We can't increase shield strength without compromising life support."*

"Shields gone on Primary Hull, Sector 36."

As the damage reports flooded in from all decks, Riker saw a pattern emerge. The ship was being attacked in noncritical areas where the deflector shielding was most vulnerable to strong blows.

"What are they doing?" cried Riker. "Taking us apart bolt by bolt?"

"They're trying to cripple us," said Picard, "so they can recover the Heart intact."

The *Enterprise* was rocked by yet another hit. Worf's counter charge hit the attacker broadside, but its main shields were still holding. Although warbirds were the most formidable vessels of their class, built solely for combat, the *Enterprise* should have proved to be a strong opponent. However, this particular Romulan ship was tougher than most.

"Hull breach on Deck 38!"

"Shield failure imminent in Engineering, Sector 59."

"We could use a miracle right about now," said Riker through gritted teeth.

"If we cannot win this battle," said Picard, "then we must lose it completely; the Romulans must never be allowed to gain possession of the Heart." Drawing a deep breath, he said, "Number One, prepare for initiation of a self-destruct—"

"Captain," called out Data. "Sensors detect a gap in their deflectors . . . a forward shield has collapsed."

Riker jumped to his feet. "Worf! Aim for that—"

But the Klingon needed no urging. With the swift instincts of a born warrior, he had already seized the advantage.

A single arrow of phaser fire flew straight through the chink in the Romulan ship's defenses and drilled a white hot hole through its hull to the center of the warp drive engines.

"Got them!" exclaimed the security chief with an intimidating display of pointed teeth.

The warbird shuddered, then bucked, as a chain reaction of internal explosions ripped through the length of its frame. A spidery web of cracks radiated across its hull and licking flames laced with roiling black smoke streamed from the breaches.

"You were saying, Captain?" asked Riker.

"I can't recall." Picard rose to stand beside his first officer.

As they stared at the ruined carcass of their defeated enemy, he said, "You're the one who asked for a miracle, Number One."

"I'll just have to remember to ask sooner, next time." And yet Riker couldn't help wondering if any of the dead soldiers that once walked the decks of the warbird had also prayed, in vain, for a miracle.

CHAPTER 25

Beverly Crusher was the last of the senior officers to slip into place around the conference table but the first to be fixed with Picard's intense questioning gaze.

"Doctor?"

Although she had brought a medical padd with her, the report it contained was still fresh in her mind. She recited the statistics to a somber audience.

"Reports of minor injuries are still filtering in from all decks, but the current count of notable casualties is thirty-five. Intensive care has two crewmen who are in critical condition and another five in serious condition; twelve patients are in the general sickbay ward; the rest have been released after treatment." Fighting against a feeling of defeat, she finished with, "There were three fatalities."

This last statement keyed the tension in the captain's shoulders even tighter, but he made no comment beyond a curt nod of acknowledgment. Picard turned to Geordi La Forge next.

"Maintenance teams have repaired the hull breach," said the engineer, "and Deck 38 is already repressurized, but

we've uncovered serious damage to several starboard deflector shield amplifiers and at least two gravity field generators."

Crusher half-listened to Geordi's unfolding report, but her
attention was focused mainly on Picard. Troi's concern had
been well-founded; it was difficult to assess the captain's
condition from across the length of the conference table, but
what she could see from here was disturbing.

At first glance, even as she had entered the room, Crusher
had been struck by the haggard look of his face. Picard was a
lean man at the best of times, but now the bones of his skull
were far too prominent, and the skin that covered them was
pale and stretched taut. From previous experience, the doctor
knew that prolonged stress had a tendency to melt flesh off his
frame, but she had never seen him develop a nervous tic
before. Yet she noted that Picard's hands were in constant
subtle motion, with fingers twitching or tracing patterns on
the surface of the table.

Crusher waited until the round of reports had concluded
and the other officers were filing out of the room before she
approached the captain. Picard was still sitting at the head of
the table, fingers drumming a repetitive rhythm, but he had
turned to face the window. His eyes were flitting from side to
side as he scanned the vista of stars. She wondered what he
was looking for.

"Captain."

His head jerked up, as if pulled against his will. "Yes,
Doctor?" His query was clipped with impatience.

One look at the stubborn set of his jaw, and Crusher
realized that gentle persuasion would only waste her breath.
"You look like death warmed over. My medical recommendation is that you get some rest, immediately."

As she expected, he shook his head. "In light of Mr. La
Forge's damage reports, Doctor, I don't have the luxury of
abandoning my duties to satisfy your whims. Please direct
your excess medical passion to the patients in intensive care."

Crusher drew a sharp breath, stung by the cutting remark.
Yet she also recognized that Picard's bristling anger was

probably just another symptom of his exhaustion. Before she could frame a tactful reply, the doctor felt someone brush against her arm; Riker had stepped back from the doorway to stand beside her.

"Captain," said the first officer with an affable grin. "I don't think a quick nap could be construed as abandoning your duties. In fact, this would be a good opportunity to take a break so you'll be refreshed by the time Geordi has a new status report."

Crusher rushed in before Picard could debate this point. "And if you've been having trouble sleeping, I can prescribe appropriate medication." This was the obvious recommendation under the circumstances, yet she knew that Picard would perceive this suggestion as a veiled threat.

The captain shifted his glance from her over to Riker, then back again to her. Rising from his chair, Picard said, "No drugs will be necessary, Doctor. I will go to my cabin without further protest."

"Very sensible," she said, with what she hoped was a lighter tone, but Picard's stoic reserve did not soften. He stalked from the room without uttering another word.

Crusher turned to the first officer. The grin on his face had faded away. "How long has he been this way, Will?"

"He's grown noticeably worse in the last day," said Riker. "But I think the trouble started when he took possession of the Heart."

Crusher sighed. "I was afraid you'd say that. Unfortunately, this is one condition I don't know how to treat."

Picard stripped off his uniform jacket and tossed it aside. This would be his one concession to comfort for tonight. Doctor Crusher could order him to his cabin, but now that he was in the privacy of his own quarters, he had no intention of following her instructions any further.

Sleep was out of the question. Even closing his eyes was asking too much when reminders of disaster continued to mock him at every turn. After leaving the conference room, he had walked through smoke-filled corridors and listened to the crackling exchanges of repair crews on the intercom; the deck had lurched several times as a gravity stabilizer weakened, then failed; and now, Picard could see the blackened hulk of the Romulan warbird drifting in space just outside his cabin window.

Perhaps Counselor Troi would argue that it was symbolic of his success in defeating an enemy. She would remind him that not all conflicts could be resolved peacefully and that sometimes even the right decisions could not lead to triumph against overwhelming odds. To him, however, the wreckage was a reminder of his failure to protect his own ship.

The *Enterprise* was crippled, stranded far outside Federation territory, and he alone was responsible for this situation.

His glance dropped down to the Heart, a crude centerpiece for the elegant glass-topped table that held it.

What if this quest for the Heart's destination was a fantasy created within his own mind? If that was the case, the entire starship crew would pay the price for his self-delusion. On the other hand, what if the Heart could help pull the *Enterprise* out of this predicament?

You have waited too long . . .

T'Sara had advised him to give up the stone, or at least to stop making use of its powers. Yet, so far he had only taken part in the dreams. Surely there was no harm in that? And perhaps the dreams could show him the way to safety.

He stooped to pick up the Heart, his hands eagerly closing around its familiar shape. If there was even a chance of that being true, he must take the risk.

With measured steps and grim determination, Picard carried the stone into his bedroom. He placed it at the head of his bed, then slipped beneath the covers without bothering to undress.

Closing his eyes, he waited impatiently for that night's dream to claim him . . .

The morning sun was still low in the Delula sky, but he could feel sweat beading on the back of his neck. He shivered, chilled by a cool breeze brushing over damp skin, and rubbed his hands dry on the front of his thin shirt. There was nothing he could do to quell the fluttering emptiness in his stomach. He told himself the ache was hunger, but the very thought of food brought a rush of bile up his throat. He swallowed it down and fought against the impulse to gag.

"Nervous, Picard?" Chiang's inquiry sounded sympathetic, but his mouth curled ever so slightly at one corner. His body was solid, thicker than Picard's wiry form; his blue shorts and shirt were crisp and dry.

"No, I'm not nervous." The hoarseness of his reply betrayed the raw burn in the back of his throat.

"No, of course not. After all, you're going to win this race." Chiang's smile deepened into a sneer as he tossed a white towel into the air. "Here, before you flood the field."

Picard lunged forward to catch the towel before it could fall to the ground, a certain offense for a lowly first-year cadet. By the time he straightened up again, Chiang was walking back to a tight knot of upperclassmen gathered by the field house.

"Damn you," Picard muttered softly under his breath, but he took no pleasure in the curse. He cast a furtive glance at the cadets around him, wondering how many had noticed the exchange and understood its significance. They seemed intent on their own business: Drager and T'Soron were on the grass, arms and legs waving gracefully back and forth as they stretched hamstrings and triceps; Miyakawa was knotting her hair into an intricate braid that would keep her long black tresses out of her face; and Gareth was fastening and refastening his shoes for the perfect fit that always eluded him.

"Too tight this time?"

The young Andorian looked up from his task. "Too loose," he corrected and cast his gaze quickly downward again. It was the shortest conversation they had ever had; usually Gareth was tediously chatty.

Picard felt himself flush with shame, and the wave of warmth drove more beads of sweat out of his skin. So, Gareth had heard.

Everyone at the Academy had probably heard.

He mopped his face and neck with Chiang's towel and

226

raked back a wayward curl of hair. Well, there was no help for it now. The boast had been made and was beyond recall.

He heard the crunching tread of boots on grass coming up behind him, and his muscles tensed and tightened, counteracting the effects of his recent warm-up.

"Jean-Luc."

"Oh, hello, Walker." He continued to dry himself off, rubbing first at one arm then another, careful not to turn and look his friend in the face. Walker Keel lacked flair, some cadets even implied he lacked the fire necessary for command, but at this moment Picard would gladly trade all of his own brash bravado for just an ounce of Walker's quiet dignity.

"We'll be waiting for you at the finish line."

His hands clenched and twisted the soft cloth into a knot. "Jack's here, too?"

He caught Walker's nod out of the corner of his eye. "The crowd is already pretty thick, so we're taking turns holding our space."

"Actually, I'd rather . . . it would be easier . . ." Picard couldn't finish, couldn't find the words to tell them both to go away. Neither of them had reproached him for his arrogance, for the absolute lunacy of his drunken outburst, yet facing them at the end of this race would be as great a trial as suffering the scorn of the entire Academy for the remainder of the term. "You know something, Walker? I talk too much."

"Yes, I've noticed that," said Walker with a slow smile. He thumped Picard's back with an open hand, a gesture of both exasperation and affection, then strolled away, melting into the stream of spectators rushing to take their places along the path.

"Starters up!"

Blue-clad figures all across the field froze in mid-motion at the announcement, then responded to the call with a leisurely approach to the broad white line that marked the beginning of the 40k marathon. Picard mimicked their nonchalance, but his gait felt stiff and unnatural. He longed for another stretching session, but there was no time left.

As fifty-three pairs of feet stepped up to the starting line, he had one last stabbing thought: What if Boothby had heard?

The sharp crack of the starting gun caught him unprepared. He pushed off last, almost immediately trailing behind the throng of runners who jostled for position and pace. He was a front-runner—he'd always been a front-runner—but his concentration had flagged during that critical instant when reflexes triggered muscles into a first burst of speed. Faced with an unexpected wall of pumping legs and flailing arms, he faltered again, then braced himself for a collision with any runners moving up behind him. He risked a darting backward glance.

There were no other runners. He was last.

No freshman has ever won the Academy Marathon . . . until now!

Those echoing words—his own foolish words—set fire to his lagging feet. Enough of this self-pitying indulgence; he had a long race to run. Shoving aside despair, he narrowed his mind to the demands of the moment. The track surface beneath his thin-soled shoes was firm with a slight texture that provided traction without gripping for too long. He barely registered the towering forest trees that lined the first portion of the winding path, but he welcomed their cool shade as exertion warmed his body.

For the first two kilometers he worked at loosening his tight muscles and setting a rhythm to his breathing. In the process, he passed six runners out of the fifty-three, counting them off one by one. By the fifth kilometer he was sufficiently centered to ignore such petty distractions and his weaving progress around slower runners was unconscious, the automatic avoidance of obstacles.

When he broke out of the forest into bright sunlight and baking heat, he spied the quarter-marker of the Delula course. The air was filled with the sounds of cheers from the waiting crowds, and he had only to reach out his arm to have a cup of cool water eagerly thrust into his hand. He drank greedily of the first offering and reached out again for some more. A fresh burst of cheers, then another, signaled the appearance of more runners from the forest track.

At least I'm not last.

The memory of his late start propelled him ahead even faster, but his breathing remained steady. Another cup was thrust into his hand, and he poured its contents over his head before he succumbed to the temptation to drink too much.

He began to run for the sheer joy of it.

By the time Picard reached the halfway marker, he had finally passed Gareth and seen Miyakawa crumple to the ground with a cramp in her calf. All the other freshmen cadets were running behind him on the course.

At the three-quarter mark, he approached a tight knot of five upperclassmen that blocked his way. He could hear the sound of their breathing, ragged with the effort of keeping pace with each other. They were all pushing themselves a little too hard and a little too fast by their determination to break free from the pack. Picard swung left and drove himself forward through a narrow gap on the edge of the path. He caught a glimpse of faces twisted with annoyance at the sudden increase in congestion. An elbow knocked against his side as one of the less generous runners moved to keep him back in place. The unwarranted jostling fueled his next burst of speed.

He was running alone now.

The level path gave way to the rise and swell of gentle hills. In his training runs he had fought to keep a steady pace as he worked the slopes, but now he used the pull of gravity to gather another sliver of speed as he sped downward, then pushed to maintain the new pace on his climb up the next rise. Sweat poured off him, stinging his eyes with its salty flavor; the soft cloth of his clothes chafed against damp skin. The slight tingle in his thigh and calf muscles would turn to a tremble if he misjudged his endurance and pushed too hard. He tossed his head, slinging back the hair plastered to his forehead, and then threw off the intrusion of physical discomfort with an equivalent mental shrug. It was important to feel his body at work, and that included the pain, but that knowledge must not distract him from the run.

He crested another hill and spotted a string of four runners just ahead. Chiang was leading them, but even as Picard watched, the others were challenging his position. Telegar, the fastest of the Andorians, must be the woman in second place. The other two cadets were probably Dorgath and Stemon, both favored to win the race and both pushing the front-runners to exhaust themselves on the final stretch.

As he sped steadily onward, driving one foot after the next, his breath heaving in and out of his chest, a dull background roar sorted itself into the sound of a cheering crowd, and he realized that there were throngs of people lining the path up the next slope.

No, not just the next slope. He was approaching Mount Bonnell, the last hill of the marathon.

No freshman has ever won the Academy Marathon . . . until now!

Perhaps it hadn't been such an empty boast after all. Reaching deep inside himself for the last of his reserves, Picard propelled himself faster down the slope. The ground leveled beneath his pumping feet. He passed Dorgath just as the ground began to rise again. Chiang was ahead, having fallen back to third place.

Momentum carried him up the first few meters of the hill without effort. When the weight of the climb finally hit him, he expected to slow down, but he was locked into a rhythm and grace of movement that remained steady and controlled.

Then the terror struck.

It happens here, soon.

It was as if his mind were detaching from his body, pulling back to observe and comment on the scene.

I've done this before. This run, this dream.

Chiang had been flagging for the past few minutes. He was easily overtaken.

Oh, god, it's a very bad dream.

Telegar and Stemon remained ahead. As Picard pulled even with the Andorian, the dread deepened and clarified.

I stumble. Any step now, I stumble.

He willed himself to wake up, to stop from reliving the humiliation of that one false step. The last few minutes of the race stretched out before him like a rack. How many times had he tortured himself with these memories?

All the false sympathy, all the pity. But they were relieved to see me fail. I came too close to winning.

Now only Stemon remained. He had a Vulcan's superior muscular strength and stamina, but the humidity of the Delula atmosphere clogged his lungs and reduced their efficiency. If his keen hearing picked up the sound of Picard's approach, he was still unable to summon more speed. The gap between them narrowed.

Now? Two steps from now?

Picard tried to brace himself for the sharp jolt that would signal his loss of footing, but he could no longer control his body, could hardly even feel it, and thus he could not avert the disaster about to happen.

The scenario varied. Sometimes the jarring fall landed him at Chiang's feet, at other times he actually took the lead before dropping to the ground, breath knocked out of his air-starved lungs, as the four upperclassmen thundered past him. The countless variations had plagued his sleep so many times and for so many years that he couldn't remember when the real fall had actually taken place. Doubtless any number of his classmates at the Academy would remember the true accounting of events.

Even fifth place would have been a cause for celebration . . . if not for my boast.

That was the true misstep. Perhaps his subconscious had searched for a metaphor to frame his arrogance. Certainly this was no less plausible an explanation for tripping on a smooth path than the imaginary pebble he had conjured afterward to explain his sudden failure.

His body passed Stemon.

Now. It must come now. I've never gone beyond this point.

But he crested over the hill and began the descent at a breakneck speed that would have tangled his feet if this hadn't been a dream. Physical sensation returned, and the rush of air against his outstretched arms felt like the lift of wind on the wings of a hawk flying through the sky.

The cheering that had sent him up Mount Bonnell to overtake the other runners was nothing compared to what met him on this side. He was buffeted by the clamoring sound of massed voices.

The white ribbon over the finish line rippled and waved a greeting to him, waiting for his embrace.

He closed his eyes, too sick with dread to watch any longer.

No. This is more than I can bear. To lose when I'm this close . . .

Then the ribbon cut across his chest.

Picard woke screaming in the dark. He threw himself forward to a sitting position, his chest heaving. His undershirt and pants were drenched with sweat, as were the sheets wrapped around him like the torn tails of the ribbon at the finish line.

I won.

He gulped for breath and mopped his face with the sleeve of his tunic. Sweat was still trickling down into his eyes; he rubbed his hand over the smooth scalp of his head.

Of course I won. I only lose the race in my dreams . . . or is it the other way around?

The two memories battled for predominance in his mind, shimmering back and forth from one reality to the other, each remembered with a clarity that was unsettling.

"Computer . . ."

His hoarse whisper was too garbled to activate the system. Picard cleared his throat and tried again. "Computer, who won the Starfleet Academy marathon at Delula II in the year 2324?"

The whir of access links was followed by the answer.

"The Academy Marathon of Delula II was won by Freshman Cadet Jean-Luc Picard."

Yes. Of course. Had he actually doubted it?

Throwing back the damp covers, Picard scrambled out of

bed to search for some clean, dry clothing. His walk through
the cabin brought back another flood of memories. He had
collapsed two steps beyond the finish line, only to be lifted
high into the air by Jack Crusher and Walker Keel and
seemingly every other cadet in the freshman class. Even
Commander Hansen had been in the crowd that day, taking
note, though it would be years later before the newly promoted Admiral Hansen would reveal that fact to his protégé.

In under two hours, a freshman's arrogant boast had been
miraculously transformed into a confident prediction, adding
another achievement to his growing reputation as a cadet to
be reckoned with.

Picard opened the top drawer of his dresser and plunged his
hands deep inside, but instead of pulling out clothes, he
removed a small, flat case. He hadn't opened it in years,
hadn't felt the need. A flick of his thumb triggered the lid.

The medal was shinier than he had remembered, and
smaller. His fingers traced over the etched words. It was cold,
too.

Yes, of course I won.

Yet he had never taken any pleasure in this prize, only
relief. The close escape from public humiliation had sharpened his recognition of the easy arrogance that courted such
disasters. He had always been grateful that this lesson in
humility had remained a private one. The empty boast
wouldn't haunt him for four solid years, tucked into the sly
sneers and whispered insults of fellow cadets. Chiang had
turned the remainder of that term into a living hell . . .

Stop it! I won. The rest was only a nightmare.

The false memories that followed that fall were surprisingly
sharp. He took a deep shuddering breath, and they began to
fade.

His fingers closed tightly over the metal disk, its thin edges
cutting into his skin. The medal was real. It was proof.

*I won. I must have won. The Heart had nothing to do with
this.*

CHAPTER 26

Keyda Chandat was robbed of breath as he contemplated the beauty of Dynasia as seen from space. Roiling white clouds ran like liquid glaze over the polished emerald gem that was his planet. He had been awed by images of Iconia in the ancient texts, but he had never dreamed that this new world was Iconia's equal in splendor.

"Do you ever grow tired of this sight, Captain Mycelli?" the warden asked. "Is it now so commonplace that your people are not moved by such wonders?"

"No," said the dapper Federation officer. His eyes were fixed on the bridge's viewscreen as well. "And I shall resign my commission if it ever fails to thrill me."

Ambassador Tommas was too clever a diplomat to miss an opening. "Perhaps continued visits to this starship will demonstrate some of the benefits of Federation membership to the Faculty."

"And I would be delighted to personally conduct a tour of the USS *Sullivan* before the council convenes," said Mycelli, graciously following her lead.

The warden accepted the offer with a bow. "If anything can melt the stony hearts of our conservatives, Captain, it would be your vessel." The sentiment Chandat had just uttered was sincere, and therefore doubly disarming. They suspected nothing.

"Captain," said First Officer Dier, approaching the trio that stood on the elevated aft deck. "The Dynasian delegation reports it is ready for transport."

"If you will excuse me, Warden," said Mycelli. "I must go greet our other guests."

As soon as the captain and his first officer had departed for the transporter room, Chandat wrenched his attention away from the viewscreen and turned to face Tommas. He could not afford to let his attention wander away from the demands of the unfolding conspiracy.

"Ambassador, I very much appreciate the use of this starship's conference facilities. The entire Faculty recognizes the need for neutral territory, not to mention that the safety of these accommodations will ease any tensions raised by the specter of insurgent attacks."

"So, you are making some progress."

"Of a sort," sighed Chandat. "There is still no movement toward an agreement over the issue of admission to the Federation, but I have managed to reduce the size of the quarrel. By restricting each Faculty faction to one deputy, the noise level of our debates has been substantially reduced."

The ambassador laughed in recognition of the value of even this small achievement, and Chandat regretted that their flowering friendship would soon come to an abrupt end. They continued to chat about less weighty matters, and if Tommas noticed the warden's mounting apprehension, she must have attributed it to the pressures of an impending council session.

A parting of doors announced the arrival of the Faculty deputies. As Mycelli escorted one troupe of Dynasians onto the aft deck of the *Sullivan,* a turbolift at the forward end of the bridge discharged Dier and her charges onto the command deck.

Chandat waited patiently for his colleagues to finish gaping at the sight on the main viewscreen; if nothing else, this reminder of their common origins would reinforce a spirit of unity. Then, one by one as they recovered their composure, each of the professors surreptitiously moved into place next to a member of the bridge crew.

Spreading wide his arms in a gesture of welcome, Chandat said, "Now!"

To his relief, the Dynasians actually obeyed.

Oomalo and Shagret, the most muscular of the academics, had been chosen to subdue the captain and his first officer. Given her Starfleet training, Dier was more than a match for the dean, but she stopped fighting him the instant she saw the native Dynasian professor put a choke-hold on Mycelli and lift him off his feet. Oomalo's thick reptilian body was impervious to his kicking boots.

The ambassador easily threw off Dean Thorina's fumbling grasp, but ever the diplomat, Tommas called out, "Don't fight them!"

Fortunately for everyone involved, the Federation crew obeyed her order, and Oomalo lowered the choking, red-faced captain back down to the deck.

"I appreciate your cooperation, Ambassador," said Chandat. "It is not our wish to hurt anyone."

"Then what is the purpose of this assault?" Anger at his betrayal of trust had wiped away all traces of her former amiability.

"We have need of the *Sullivan.*"

"Are you mad?" demanded the first officer. Her captain was still gasping and incapable of speech. "How long do you think your people can retain control of this starship?"

"Long enough for our purposes, Commander Dier. You see, certain rare Iconian artifacts in our possession are still in working order." Chandat reached for the medallion at the end of his chain of office. "This one, for instance."

Pressing his finger against a depression in the center of the disk, he waited to see what would happen.

The effect of the sonic waveform generator was dramatic and instantaneous. The ship's first officer crumpled to the deck too quickly to even groan, as did the ambassador and all the other Humans.

I got it right! Chandat was astounded that his estimate of the proper stun frequency for this alien race had been correct. Perhaps he had missed his calling as a scientist after all.

"It worked," cried Shagret, equally startled by their success. A foolish smile spread across the dean's face as he surveyed the sea of fallen bodies. Then he stooped down to check on Dier. "She's still breathing."

"But of course," said Chandat, although privately he had feared the high-frequency sonic wave might be fatal. "And they will all remain unconscious for hours, long enough for us to immobilize them." This was another prediction based on ancient lore, but he was suddenly confident that the technology of his Iconian ancestors could be trusted to perform as described.

"But what about the others?" demanded Oomalo, with the pragmatic attitude of a native.

Chandat stepped over Tommas's prone form in order to move down to the command deck. "Fortunately, the crew complement of a Miranda-class starship is small, so the remainder of the crew will be conquered with even greater ease."

Some leaders might have chosen to sit in the captain's chair, but Warden Chandat walked eagerly to the helm of the *Sullivan.* As he settled down behind the controls of the starship, he called out for Diat Manja.

The old man had lingered on the periphery of the bridge, taking no part in the action. Upon hearing his name, however, he shuffled forward. He clutched a parchment scroll close to his sunken chest.

"But Warden," said Manja in a bewildered voice. "How can all this violence help forward T'Sara's cause?"

"Please, Professor, do not worry yourself with the petty details of interplanetary diplomacy; that is my job." Chandat studied the flight control console with growing delight. He would gladly forfeit his life for these next few days of space travel. "Now, if you will, the coordinates for this Appointed Place you mentioned."

With a heavy sigh, Manja unrolled the parchment scroll to display an ancient star map.

Asao Matasu had just closed his eyes when the trill of an intercom hail shattered the serene silence in his cabin.

"My apologies for interrupting your meditation, Admiral," said his aide's voice a second later, *"but Lieutenant Commander Kiley-Smith said it was urgent; something about a starship that has dropped out of sight and is not responding to any subspace radio hails."*

"Thank you, Lieutenant," he replied, unfolding his lanky body from the lotus position. "Please meet me at Communications."

The commander of Starbase 75 walked with a slightly bowed head through the halls of the station. He appeared to be in constant meditation, but the posture was more practical than philosophical; Matasu was a very tall man whose head would brush the ceiling otherwise.

Lieutenant Abell was already waiting for him outside the entrance to the communications complex. She smiled a greeting, and said, "This way, Admiral," then turned so as to trigger the doors to open.

Matasu ducked his head to follow her over the threshold. His last aide had given up even the pretense of eye contact and had addressed all his comments to the admiral's stomach. Matasu appreciated Abell's greater show of courtesy, but hoped she did not suffer unduly from the effort. Perhaps he would recommend yoga exercises to keep her neck muscles supple, just as he did to counteract the constant strain of looking down.

Once inside, however, the admiral was able to straighten up to his full height. The control room of the communications center was a spacious dome whose curving walls were alight with colorful data displays. Dozens of maps, charts, and graphs tracked the streams of information that moved in and out of Starbase 75 from every point in the sector and many places beyond.

"Still no word from the *Enterprise?*" asked Matasu.

"No, sir," said Kiley-Smith as he stepped away from the base-to-ship tracking console. "But now we've lost contact with the *Plath,* a Klingon bird-of-prey, crew complement of twelve."

The console operator continued the specifics of the briefing, "The starship's navigator transmitted a coordinate check just after the *Enterprise* reported the destruction of Starbase 193. Captain Duregh volunteered to assist the *Portsmouth* with the rescue effort, but then the *Plath* never arrived."

Starbase 193 had covered an area that was far beyond the reach of Matasu's current resources, and the loss of the station blinded him as to what was happening in that sector; he needed eyes to see through the darkness. "Are there any other starships in the area that could investigate this matter?"

Kiley-Smith shook his head. "The *Portsmouth* and the *Clarke* are still docked at Luxor IV, but currently both are committed to other missions."

"I shall see to uncommitting one of them," said Matasu firmly, but he knew that the diversion would take time to arrange and that even the fastest vessel would require considerable time to cover the distances involved. "Meanwhile, issue an alert to all Starfleet facilities in this quadrant; tell them to be on the lookout for both the *Enterprise* and the *Plath* . . . and their attackers. I will prepare a report for Starfleet Command advising them of the situation."

"Aye, sir."

As the admiral headed toward his office, head bowed once again to facilitate his passage through the corridors, Lieutenant Abell echoed his own worried thoughts.

"What's going on out there, Admiral? Exploding starbases, missing starships . . . Could the Romulans be planning a new offensive for the Empire?"

He shook his head. "A warbird is powerful, but I don't think it could take down two Federation starships in a row."

Abell accepted the admiral's assessment with a puzzled frown. "Then what could?"

"I don't know, Lieutenant," said Matasu, "but I hope whoever, or whatever, is responsible stays the hell away from *my* starbase."

And may the gods help Jean-Luc Picard, wherever he may be.

Kanda Jiak shivered when he stepped into the cold air of the detention cell. He longed for the thick knit sweater tucked into his backpack, a farewell present from First Officer Conrad, but all his belongings had been confiscated when he entered the security complex.

Turning to his armed escort, Jiak protested one last time. "But I'm not a Dynasian!"

"Right," said the guard with a weary sigh. "You just happen to look like one." Her finger tapped out a rapid sequence on a wall panel.

The young man jumped back as the high humming sound of a force field snapped into place along the frame of the portal. The immigration official of Hayhurst Junction had described this detention as a bureaucratic formality, so Jiak had expected to spend a few hours in a passenger lounge; instead, he had been taken to a security chamber for interrogation. The references to ambassadors and starships and insurgents had been completely bewildering, but there was no mistaking the consternation of the Starfleet officers. Somehow, the Dynasians had angered the Federation even more thoroughly than the DiWahns.

Jiak gingerly approached the entrance of his cell. Careful not to touch the field itself, he craned his neck to look up and down the outside corridor. The guard was gone.

I'm a political prisoner.

That realization was almost as comical as it was frightening. In either event, it was a reality that could not be wished away or cried away, so he blinked back tears and turned to greet his companion in confinement.

Jiak had caught only a brief impression of a robed figure huddled on one of the narrow cots. Upon a closer look, however, the young Iconian made out the features shadowed by the heavy cowl. The man's forehead was ridged in a fan-shaped pattern that arched over his purple eyes, and his skin was a delicate shade of violet. This was no mirror image of Jiak's own face, but they both clearly bore the stamp of a shared genetic heritage.

When he could breathe again, Jiak stammered, "Are you . . . a Dynasian?"

"That is what my identity papers maintain," said the man. His lips curled into a sly smile.

"I've never seen another Iconian before . . . at least, not since I was a small child." Jiak struggled for composure, restrained by his cellmate's apparent indifference to this statement. "My name is Kanda Jiak."

"The Gem-Bearer's namesake!" The Dynasian's richly colored eyes took on a gleam of excitement. "How did you come by such an illustrious name?"

Buoyed by this welcome, Jiak settled cross-legged on the floor by the man's feet and spilled out the story of the last days of Ikkabar and his own flight from Redifer. "Before I reached Hayhurst Junction, I tried to visit DiWahn, but—"

"DiWahn!" The man darted forward and grabbed a fistful of Jiak's shirt. "What do you know of the planet DiWahn?"

"Nothing . . . all travel to the system was suspended." The intensity of the man's demand was unnerving. "Conrad said the trouble had something to do with an armada and the threat of armed aggression against the Federation."

"Ah, so the fleet of the Faithful was launched!" Releasing his hold on Jiak, the man fell back against the cell wall. He gazed into the distance, as if witnessing a vision shimmering in the air. "After generations of waiting, our time to enter the Dreaming has arrived."

T'Sara's writings on the diaspora had recorded the beliefs of the DiWahn: they were obsessed with the dreams of the Gem-Bearers. "But you said you were a Dynasian!"

"I have said many things in my life." The Iconian uttered a throaty chuckle. "The consulate is checking my identity papers, just as they are checking yours. Who knows what they will find in their search? If they find the truth, I will remain in this cell, or one very much like it, for the rest of my life."

"I'm sorry," said Jiak, yet he wondered uneasily what crime the fugitive DiWahn had committed. Life imprisonment was usually reserved for murder.

"Save your pity for yourself. I have fulfilled my life's quest, whereas you have just begun yours."

"What was your quest?"

The DiWahn was still staring into space with a rapt expression. "Like you, I spent my childhood among the races of the Federation. I have never even set foot on my homeworld, but my father showed me the path of the Faithful. My sworn duty was to follow after T'Sara."

"You know T'Sara?" cried Jiak. Hearing her name was like meeting a friend in an unfamiliar place. "Please, tell me about her."

The DiWahn was too absorbed in his own memories to attend to the interruption. "My only regret is that I could not return home in time to join the armada. In order to elude capture by unbelievers, I bought forged papers listing me as a Dynasian. That choice was my undoing." He shrugged his resignation. "Imprisonment is a small price to pay for recovering the Gem."

"The Gem?" Jiak's eyes widened at the mention of the powerful icon. "You mean the Dream Gem is not just a legend?"

The DiWahn hesitated, his reply forestalled by the distant sound of doors parting, followed by the tread of boots echoing down the corridor.

"No, not a myth, Kanda Jiak, Gem-Bearer," he whispered. "See for yourself. Join our order and hear the Telling."

"But how can I find—"

"Ask a woman named Camenae on Starbase 193. If you're willing to meet her price, she will answer all your questions. Find the Gem, and you will find the Faithful."

The footsteps stopped outside the cell.

"Hey, I don't have all day," said a voice edged with irritation.

Jiak looked up to see that the force field had been deactivated. The guard standing by the entrance was holding his backpack in her hands.

She beckoned him with a jerk of her head. "The Federation consulate has confirmed your residency on Redifer III. You're permitted to leave the Junction so long as you stay away from Dynasia."

"Go!" urged the DiWahn softly.

Jiak scrambled to his feet, his mind still reeling from the man's revelations.

Thousands of years ago, the Dream Gem had opened the Three Gates that saved the Iconian people from annihilation. If the first Kanda Jiak had walked through the Gate to Ikkabar, the powers of his Gem could have tamed the planet. Without his assistance, the third branch of the Iconian race had withered away.

However, if Kanda Jiak's namesake gained possession of the Gem, perhaps that tragic history could be revised.

Grabbing his pack from the guard, the last survivor of Ikkabar raced down the corridor. He was headed toward freedom and a new destination.

CHAPTER 27

Main engineering was rarely quiet. Most often the rumble that permeated the area came from the steady pulse of the matter/antimatter reaction chamber. Today, however, the warp propulsion system was shut down and the ship's engines were cold; instead, the noisy bustle of Humans filled the air as a constant stream of engineering personnel moved from one work station to another, then dashed away.

Yet there was an island of stability in this whirlwind of motion. The master situation monitor covered most of the forward wall section in engineering, and for the past five hours Geordi La Forge had returned again and again to the cutaway schematic of the *Enterprise* that was on display. When he had first assessed the damage to the starship, broad sections of the diagram had been highlighted in red. Now, as the chief engineer continued to track the progress of repairs, yet another of the system indicators blinked from red to green.

After checking the value of a number on the board, Geordi turned to face the ship's first officer. "Well, the good news is that the deflector shields are working again."

"So what's the bad news?" asked Riker dutifully.

"They're only at about forty-six percent efficiency, and they're going to stay at that level until we replace at least five conformal transmission ████████ the primary hull and then realign the entire a██████

"Let's do it."

With a warning shake of his head, Geordi said, "Yeah, but to work on the grids we have to take the graviton polarity source generators off-line, which leaves us without *any* deflector shields for over four hours. Usually that's a procedure performed only in spacedock, because if we disassociate our shield generators in space . . ."

"The *Enterprise* would be a sitting duck," finished Riker. "Anybody with a peashooter could take us on."

"Exactly," said the chief engineer. "Not only that, without operational deflector shields, we couldn't travel above impulse speed without turning to Swiss cheese. Even full impulse for a sustained length of time would risk serious micro-meteoroid degradation of the hull's duranium substrate."

"You haven't left us with many options, Geordi."

La Forge shrugged. "I thought miracles were your department, Commander."

"It looks like I've used up my quota for now." The first officer glanced over at the schematic and frowned. "Captain Picard will have to make this decision. I'll get back to you after we've had a chance to talk it over."

"No problem, Commander," said Geordi with an amiable grin. "I'll be right here."

The engineer turned back to the master display just as another red light turned green. Slowly but surely, piece by piece, the ship was returning to normal.

The broad, curving windows of Ten-Forward provided the best view of space on the *Enterprise,* and it was a view that Deanna Troi usually enjoyed. Today, however, she found the scene outside the lounge to be a disquieting reminder of their present danger. The damaged starship was adrift in the midst of desolate space with the skeletal remains of a warbird as its only companion. Perhaps others among the crew were filled with dread at the sight, because only a few of the tables in the room were occupied, and the people sitting there were all facing away from the windows.

The counselor settled herself at the bar and tried to think of something to order. Out of the corner of one eye, she watched Guinan set two glasses in front of a couple at the far end of the counter, then drift back in her direction.

"What can I get for you?" asked the hostess. She was dressed in an embroidered robe of forest green; a wide square-brimmed hat of the same color, only darker in shade, covered her head.

"I haven't made up my mind," said Troi. "What would you suggest?"

"Well, that depends. Are you more in an eating or a drinking mood?"

"I'm not really hungry," Troi decided. She wasn't really thirsty either, but she would feel less awkward about her visit to Ten-Forward if she adopted some token excuse for her presence.

Guinan picked up a conical glass. "A drink it is. What about a Venusian fruit cider?"

"Yes, that's exactly what I'm in the mood for." Troi's enthusiasm sounded forced to her own ear, and it must have appeared equally insincere to Guinan, because she made no move to fill the glass.

"I get the feeling there's something troubling you, Deanna."

Troi sighed, and with a guilty smile, said, "I'm supposed to be the counselor around here, remember."

Guinan chuckled with a throaty voice that almost purred. "Even counselors need a sympathetic listener now and then." She turned to pour the drink, giving Troi time to collect her thoughts.

The cider was delicious, and somehow talking seemed easier after a few sips of its delicate flavor. "Will Riker is worried about the captain's fascination with the Devil's

Heart. He fears that it has become an obsession . . . and so do I."

"What makes you think so?"

"Well, the course change which brought us out here," Troi inclined her head in the direction of the windows, "was very troublesome. Captain Picard says it was to draw our pursuers away from vulnerable Federation colonies, but I can't help wondering if there was another motivation at work, if he wasn't actually searching for an excuse to delay giving up the Heart."

The hostess dipped her head for a moment, and the flat rim of her hat obscured her expression. When she looked up again, the concern she had tried to erase from her face could still be found in her dark eyes, yet she said, "I don't believe Picard would let his command judgment be seriously compromised by the Heart."

"You sound very sure of that. Why?"

"Because," said Guinan, "all the stories I've heard speak of temptation rather than coercion. The Heart can turn your own desires against you, but it can't make you do anything against your true nature."

"And Captain Picard would never choose to hurt the *Enterprise* or the people on it." Guinan nodded, and Deanna toyed with letting the whole matter end on this comforting note, yet she knew Riker would not be so easily reassured. "Could I have another one of these drinks?"

"I'm glad you liked it." Guinan whisked away the empty glass, and plucked up a clean one from beneath the counter.

"Guinan, the captain trusts you more than any other person on board the *Enterprise*. If you could persuade him to give the Heart to you for safe—"

The glass the hostess had been holding slipped from her fingers and crashed to the floor.

"What's wrong?" Troi was surprised that her request could rattle the imperturbable Guinan. "Are you afraid that he won't hand it over to you?"

"No, Counselor, I'm afraid that he might."

"But it would be for only a short time," said Troi, "long enough to carry the Heart to a storage vault where Will could secure it for the remainder of our journey."

Guinan shook her head back and forth as Troi talked, then said, "One of the advantages of growing old is learning your own limitations, and this is definitely a risk I'm not qualified to take. I trust Jean-Luc Picard with the Heart far more than I trust myself."

"But why?" Troi's alarm concerning the stone's powers returned in full force.

"Among my people the Heart was known as the Master of All Stories, and for a race of Listeners, that can result in a fatal enchantment."

"Enchantment? You make it sound like a fairy tale, and the captain is the unlucky prince who has fallen under an evil spell." Troi laughed at the analogy, but then she asked, "Guinan, do you think the Heart is evil?"

"Only living things have the capacity for good or evil. So, do you think the Heart is alive?"

"I sense nothing from it . . . yet more and more the captain speaks of it as a sentient being." The empath thought for a moment, then shook her head. "I just don't know."

"Neither do I, Counselor," said Guinan softly. "Neither do I."

As the doors to the ready room opened, Data regarded the interior scene with dispassion. The android was an impartial observer, and as such the presence of the Heart on Picard's desk did not arouse any emotion in him. However, the stone did trigger a complex set of associations with recent disruptive events. On purely intellectual grounds, therefore, Data would have preferred that the Heart had never been brought aboard the *Enterprise.*

"Did you enjoy your rest, Captain?" asked Data as he walked across the room.

"What?" Picard looked up from his desk viewer. "Oh, my rest. Yes, I did, thank you."

Data had often observed that Humans used certain phrases

for their iconic value in expressing a sense of connection with community members, rather than in a literal sense of providing accurate information. He concluded that this must be one of those occasions because the captain's physical condition did not appear to have substantially improved since the conference in the observation lounge.

Picard glanced back at the computer, then over at the padd in Data's hands. "Didn't I just receive your Ops report?"

"This is not a status update," said Data. "Rather, I have identified the pertinent coordinates of the location in which you were interested."

"Let me see." Leaning forward over his desk, Picard reached out eagerly for the padd, then sighed with relief at the sight of the Federation star map that had matched his sketch. "Yes, that's the place exactly! But it certainly took you long enough to find it."

"My apologies for the delay," said Data. "However, my search was complicated by a rather curious aspect of the scene you drew. That particular juxtaposition of the comet against the designated constellation of stars has not occurred yet; in fact, it will not occur for at least forty-eight hours."

"In the future . . ." murmured Picard. His brow furrowed with the intensity of his thoughts, and one of his hands dropped down onto the Heart. "Yes . . . yes, of course. That means there is still time to act."

"Intriguing. What particular action does this call for?"

"Thank you for your help, Mr. Data." The captain did not remove his gaze from the map. "That will be all for now."

Data's positronic brain forged a new connection, one between the star map and the Devil's Heart. As he left the ready room, the android began to calculate the probability that another catastrophic event would occur soon.

Troi felt unusually conspicuous walking onto the *Enterprise* bridge, and the empath quickly determined the focus for that unease: Lieutenant Worf was tracking her progress from the aft turbolift to the command center. She sensed in him the usual uneasiness that always seemed to underlie their interactions, especially those involving Worf's son, Alexander; but this was overshadowed by a new set of emotions that were more difficult to untangle. For some reason she could not fathom, the Klingon was wary of her.

Riker and Picard were engaged in a somber discussion involving shield repairs, so she quietly slipped into place beside the captain.

". . . no question that we must improve our shield strength," continued Picard. "This mission isn't over yet, and we dare not continue without maximum protection."

"Agreed," said Riker, although Troi could easily sense his apprehension about this decision.

She could also read the question in his eyes when he stole a quick glance in her direction. A subtle shake of her head was all it took to indicate that Guinan could not help them, but Worf must have seen the gesture from his perch above because the Klingon's suspicions broadened to include the first officer.

The captain cast his voice upward to engage the intercom system. "Picard to La Forge. Let's proceed with the deflector shield repairs before we attract any more company out here."

"Acknowledged, Captain."

While the captain and the chief engineer exchanged technical information about the repair procedure, Troi surreptitiously evaluated Picard's physical and emotional condition. His fatigue was even more pronounced than before; he seemed to hoard his strength by moving only when absolutely necessary. On the other hand, the growing mental agitation she had sensed in the conference room was gone now. The counselor wondered if Picard's composure had been restored by the Heart, which was tucked securely into the crook of his arm.

"Conformal grids on the primary hull have been deactivated," continued Geordi. *"Graviton generators are going off-line . . . now."*

Troi shivered in response to the feeling of vulnerability that suddenly radiated from the entire bridge crew. She strengthened her empathic shields to block against the projected emotions, yet she was still left with her own feelings of helplessness.

As the first few minutes of the repair project dragged by, the thought of four hours stretched into an eternity . . .

. . . that was shattered by yellow alert.

"Captain," called out Data. "Sensors detect an object two hundred thousand kilometers dead ahead."

"There!" Riker pointed to the main viewscreen, and Troi looked up to see that the placid vista of distant stars had begun to shimmer and ripple with distortion waves. A ship was uncloaking before them.

"Phasers locking on target," announced Worf tersely.

"Hold fire until my signal, Lieutenant," said Picard as he rose to his feet.

Troi could sense that the captain was straining against the desire to shoot first without waiting to see the face of their enemy, but Picard's Starfleet training repressed the urge to provoke a battle they could not hope to win. Even a lightly shielded vessel would withstand a phaser attack long enough to retaliate against the unshielded *Enterprise*.

The phantom form took solid shape. Angled wings stretched wide on either side of a narrow-necked forward hull.

"It's a bird-of-prey," said Riker, his chest heaving with a sigh of relief.

"Captain." There was a hint of elation in Worf's voice when he said, "We are being hailed by Captain Duregh of the *Plath*."

"On screen, Lieutenant." Picard appeared too drained by the sudden emergency to share in the general rejoicing.

Stars gave way to a close shot of Duregh's face. Troi thought him young to be commanding his own warship, but Duregh had the lean, feral look of an ambitious Klingon warrior.

"Greetings, Captain Picard." The dim red lighting of the *Plath*'s command pit washed down over the furrows of Duregh's brow; his deep-set eyes were lost in shadow. "We heard of your plight from the *Portsmouth* and have followed your trail in hopes of joining in combat against the

Romulans. Obviously, we have arrived too late to share that honor."

"Not so, Captain," said Picard. "We welcome your assistance while we effect certain repairs to our ship."

"Ah, yes. My weapons officer informed me you are without shields." Despite his smile, Duregh's facial muscles were stiff with repressed tension. The empath thinned her emotional barriers to read him more fully. "So our journey was not in vain."

Something is wrong.

Troi leapt up from her chair. "Captain, wait, I sense—"

Her warning came too late.

The Klingon ship discharged its phasers and seconds later an explosion somewhere in the primary hull rocked the bridge, throwing the counselor off-balance. As she grabbed at a bridge railing for support, the Klingon warship fired a second time on the *Enterprise,* scoring a hit to the engineering hull. Red alert sirens overlapped the babble of damage reports from all decks.

Picard had managed to keep his footing on the deck without releasing his grip on the Heart. "Fire phasers!"

"Phasers inoperative," replied Worf.

Duregh laughed loudly at the result of his treachery. "Our next assault will destroy your ship, Captain Picard."

"Why are you doing this?"

Eyes drawn to the stone in the captain's hands, Duregh said, "Because the Pagrashtak is mine. Transport Kessec's jewel over to me, and I will spare your life."

"No!" cried Picard. "Such an action will only perpetuate the chaos which has surrounded this relic. I will not give it up to you or to anyone who would abuse its powers for violent ends."

"Then prepare to die. I can rake the Pagrashtak from out of the rubble of your blasted ship and the corpses of your dead crew."

"Traitor!" stormed Worf from the aft deck. "You have no honor!"

"Fool," said the Klingon commander with a snarl. "You

speak of matters that are beyond your understanding. I do this to *recover* my honor. I am a direct descendant of Durall, son of Kessec. The Pagrashtak was stolen from him, and thus stolen from me; it is my birthright."

The captain shook his head. "No, you are wrong. Emperor Kessec willingly gave up the Heart . . ."

"Silence!"

". . . to a slave," declared Picard, "not to his sons."

"And for that disgrace he died by their hands!" screamed Kessec's descendant, his face contorted by rage. "You have only a few seconds of life remaining, Captain Picard, and I no longer care whether you surrender or not."

He stretched out an arm to signal his crew.

"Duregh!" Raising the Heart before him like a shield, Picard shouted, "I'll see you burn in hell for this!"

The arm dropped. "Fire!"

A phaser beam lanced out from the underside of the *Plath* . . .

. . . then suddenly blossomed into a fireball that burned back along its own path until it enveloped the bird-of-prey.

With a cry of pain, Troi threw up her hands to ward off the blinding light of the explosion that stabbed her eyes. When she finally dared look again, the blazing remains of the *Plath* still crackled and flickered on the viewscreen.

"Captain?"

Picard stood transfixed in the center of the bridge; he was staring down in horror at the Heart clutched in his hands.

CHAPTER 28

A constant cold wind droned through the abandoned city, lifting clouds of fine-grained dust into the air. Dusky blue light, stripped of heat, fought its way down through the haze to illuminate the ground on which Picard walked. He could still make out faint traces of a pathway, but most of the paved surface had been scoured away. The weight of eons had tumbled all the buildings down and chipped away at their foundations. At first he had thought he was on Atropos, then he realized that this place was much older.

Age frosted the entire planet, but the pulsing glow of the Heart warmed his hands. Whenever his foot strayed off the path, the stone shifted in his palms, gently pushing him to one side or the other until he recovered his way. Picard let the Heart guide him over the pitted terrain until they reached a line of broken columns. There he stopped to gaze in wonder at the sculpted form just ahead.

The thick slab of rock was set on edge. Its original shape may have been oval, but now its outer rim was broken and irregular; the opening in its center appeared to be part of the ancient design, but it was eroded as well.

Picard was buffeted by waves of an invisible but palpable force emanating from the structure. Or was it a being?

"The Guardian of Forever," he whispered in awe.

At the sound of his voice, the crystalline stone of its ring-shaped body flickered and glowed from within, suffused with the same quality of light that fired the Heart.

The reaction was a reply of sorts, and Picard wondered if he could communicate with the being. There were so many questions he wanted answered, but one above all others.

Picard held up the Heart. "Guardian, what is this stone I carry?"

"It is a seed," said a deep thrumming voice. The light flickered in rhythm with its words. "One meant to grow in a better soil than this dead planet."

"How did it become enmeshed in our history?"

"Those who created me, created the seed; but the Architects were mortal, and after their passing there was no one to guide it on its true path. The seed went astray."

Mist pooled in the center of the slab, then cleared away to reveal a stream of images framed inside the stone border.

Picard moved closer, mesmerized by the clarity of the visions. He saw the Heart fall like a blazing meteor through a purple sky, then plunge deep into a grassy plain. Alien hands scrabbled through the dirt of the crater until they uncovered the stone. To Picard's horror, he saw the simple hunting culture of a race known as the T'Kon erupt outward into a far-flung stellar empire, then wither away and die.

New hands seized the stone, starting yet another undulating wave of murder and war. Fiefdoms burst into imperial splendor, then toppled as greed-driven betrayals weakened their foundations. He caught a brief flash of Garamond and Kessec in the timeslip, but the rest who had held the Heart went by in a blur.

As Time flowed on, the ripples of disruption spread wider and wider, all part of an unceasing pattern of struggle for possession of the Heart.

"Guardian, can this damage be undone?"

"Yes," said the voice, "but if you take back the seed early in the affairs of these beings, you also unravel all the greatness built with its powers. The universe you know will be torn from its roots, and the river will flow through different channels."

Picard shook his head; this was no solution. The consequences of the Heart's presence had gathered too much weight to be dislodged from the past. "I must remove the Heart from my own time before it causes any more upheaval. Show me how to return it to the path you spoke of."

The mist gathered again, then cleared to reveal a new scene: the blackness of deep space, a scattering of stars and a comet with its tail stretched out behind it like a banner.

"I know this place," said Picard. "It was in the vision given to me by T'Sara."

"Planting time draws near again," said the Guardian. "The seed must be sown here."

As if called by those words, the Heart stirred in Picard's hands. He edged to the very lip of the portal and gazed raptly at the image of the comet. The seed's yearning to continue its journey almost drove him to step through the opening. His fingers closed tightly on the rough texture of the stone's surface. He knew what it wanted, but letting go was difficult.

Taking a deep breath, he loosened his grip and steeled himself to toss the stone into the well.

"No!" A spidery hand pawed at the captain's arm before he could move. "Do not be so hasty."

Picard twirled around to face the gaunt figure of the Collector. The spare flesh of her body had not dried yet, but her ravaged face was that of a being near death. On the other side of her own dream, Halaylah was sealed in her chamber.

"Let go of me," he said, shuddering away from her bony fingers. The sight of her filled him with revulsion. "You died trying to keep the Heart to yourself, but it has passed on to me. I'll decide its fate now."

Her shriveled lips contorted into a leer. "You do not comprehend what you are about to throw away. In order to act wisely, you must fully understand its powers, Captain . . ."

". . . Captain." He could feel the touch of a hand on the sleeve of his uniform. "Captain?"

Picard opened his eyes and found himself slumped over his desk, head cradled in his arms, with the Heart resting by his elbow. There was a stranger, oddly familiar, leaning over him.

As the dream-induced confusion began to clear, Picard belatedly recognized his first officer. Struggling to pull himself free of the vapors that clouded his mind, the captain sat up in his chair. "What is it, Number One?"

"We have company." The first officer pulled away from the desk and assumed a more formal stance while delivering his report. "A long-range sensor scan has detected the presence of a fleet of warp-driven craft at the periphery of our detection range. The total number of vessels is still difficult to determine at this distance, but Data confirmed there are at least twenty ships."

Picard longed for solitude in which to recall the details of his dreaming, but he forced himself to attend to Jack's words. "Do you have any idea who they are?"

"All we have so far is a name," said Crusher. "According to some stray bits of their ship-to-ship communications, the fleet belongs to a race who call themselves the unDiWahn."

"The unDiWahn!"

"You know them?"

"Yes, I was warned about them by . . ." Picard reached out for a name, but it wasn't in place. There was a gap in his memory where a person belonged.

"Warned by a dream?" asked Crusher. There was a bitter edge to the question. His resentment of the Heart's influence over his captain was growing stronger each day.

"Jack . . ." It was a signal between them, worked out over the years, that Picard needed to talk to him as a friend, rather than as a commanding officer.

Nodding his understanding, the first officer pulled a chair up to the desk and sat down across from Picard. In the decades since they had left Starfleet Academy, Jack Crusher's boyish face and lanky frame had filled out and grown more rugged; gray had roughened the texture of his hair, and adversity had hardened the look in his eyes; but his smile was still as welcoming now as it had been when they were fellow cadets.

"I'm worried about you, Jean-Luc. So is Beverly, both as a doctor and as a friend."

"The Heart is not a danger to me," said Picard. It was so difficult to explain with fatigue dragging him back toward sleep and the intoxication of more dreams. He reached out to touch the stone, drawing strength from its warmth. "It is sentient, Jack, a being in trouble that needs our help, and I intend to hold fast until the Heart has reached its destination."

He had been so close to understanding before the Collector interfered. Perhaps the Guardian could complete the instructions in his next dream.

Crusher dropped his head down, burying his face in his hands. When he looked up again, his brow was furrowed as if in pain.

"Jean-Luc, if you look out the window behind you, you'll see the charred wreckage of two warships. We haven't even finished patching the *Enterprise* back together again from our battle with the *Plath,* yet if we so much as sneeze we could suddenly be facing an entire fleet of these unDiWahn. The longer we stay out here, the less chance there is that we'll ever make it back home alive."

"I intend to do everything in my power to succeed without that sacrifice. However," said Picard with a fervor solidified by his dream of the Heart's origins, "I believe that this mission is of overwhelming importance, and that its completion is so crucial that it demands our continued efforts no matter what the risk."

Crusher was silent for a long while. At last he said, "What

you ask is difficult, Jean-Luc, but I've trusted you with my life, and with the life of my wife and children, for over twenty years now. So I guess I'm not about to stop now . . . Captain."

Captain . . . That last word echoed in the air, only the second overlapping voice Picard heard was not Jack's, and it was muffled as if by fog and the distance of many years.

"No," whispered Picard, fighting back a sudden panic born of some terrible knowledge that lurked in the shadows of his mind. "I won't let this be taken from me."

"What's wrong, Jean-Luc?" Alarm jerked Crusher back onto his feet.

"Nothing, Jack. I'm just tired." Picard felt the touch of a ghostly hand on his shoulder. Its fingers gripped him with a disconcerting solidity.

No! Don't do this!

"Captain?"

Picard opened his eyes to find that he was slumped over his desk once again. He looked up. The man who had called him out of the dream was taller than Jack, and he sported a closely cropped dark beard.

Will Riker . . . my first officer is Will Riker.

Grief churned through Picard's stomach, and he swallowed down an upsurge of bile. This was reality; the other scene had been nothing but a dream. He was awake now.

Awake, yet still tantalized by the fading memories of a past spent with other people and other endings to the stories of his life. If he had finished his dream without interruption, could he have continued walking along that alternate path or would it have faded away? Surely, if he had wanted that reality strongly enough, the Heart could have kept Commander Jack Crusher alive.

I did want it, Jack. You must believe that!

Then Picard realized that the dream had been directed by the Collector. His only failing was in matching her control over the Heart. If Jack's resurrection was truly within the scope of its powers, then Picard could also learn how to conduct such miracles. It would take time, but eventually he could change the circumstances that had led to his friend's death, and the alternate reality could be recovered.

However, if he gave up the stone, Jack Crusher would be lost to him forever; Beverly would remain a widow; and their other children would remain unborn.

"Captain?"

"Yes, what is it Number One?" asked Picard, automatically walking through the lines of his role as this man's captain.

Riker stepped back from the desk to deliver his report. "Lieutenant Worf has just intercepted some subspace radio transmissions coming from the periphery of our sensor range. Some race called—"

"—called the unDiWahn," said Picard as one last lingering tendril of his dream coiled tightly around his chest.

CHAPTER 29

The engineering schematic of the *Enterprise* was covered with red highlights once again. These tags were deceptively neat and orderly, but Riker could envision the messy damage they symbolized: a starship becalmed in space with its hull scorched and pitted. This haunting image darkened his thoughts as he and Data listened to Geordi's updated status report.

"Repairs to the weapons system should be finished within two hours," said the chief engineer, pointing to a forward section of the saucer where the first barrage from the *Plath* had drilled straight through the dorsal phaser array.

"So much for our offense," sighed Riker. "What about defense?"

Geordi's hand shifted to another area of the situation monitor that was still livid with contrasting colors; the second blow from the *Plath* had landed in the engineering hull. "We've almost completed the original repairs to navigational shields—"

The ones that got us into this mess in the first place. The decision to proceed with repairs had seemed like a sound one at the time, but it was difficult for the first officer to remember that as he stared straight at the consequences of that action.

"However," continued La Forge, "the new damage to the deflector shields has compromised tactical defense. There's a limit to the repairs we can conduct out of spacedock, but I should know what percentage of our performance capacity has been restored in about four hours."

Riker would have found the information reassuring if not for the recent sighting of the unDiWahn. "Geordi, a rather large space fleet just wandered through this area. They appear to be gone for now, but there's always the possibility they could circle back and find us. Without weapons and without defensive shields, our only recourse is to tuck tail and hope we can outrun them."

"Fortunately," said Data, "our sensor scans indicate the fleet is moving slowly. The unDiWahn may lack the capacity for high warp speeds."

"At the moment, so do we." La Forge waved at the diagram of patchwork repairs in progress. "The warp reactor core has been off-line for the last hour while we replaced the starboard nacelle generator coils. As a result, we'll have to ease into warp drive as we align the matter/antimatter injectors."

"Swell," said Riker. "At the first sign of trouble, we'll limp out of here."

"Yeah, but if we'd taken one more hit from the *Plath,* we wouldn't be able to *crawl* out of here, so I'd say we're pretty lucky."

The engineer's comment brought a puzzled frown to Data's face. "Geordi, I am most curious about the *Plath*'s destruction."

Riker had no way to cut off the discussion without drawing undue attention to the subject; instead, he listened as La Forge answered the android's question.

"I can't explain it, Data. There's an outside chance it was some freak weapons malfunction, but I just can't imagine what could make a warship's phasers detonate like that." Geordi glanced back toward the schematic. "And frankly, I haven't got time to worry about the *Plath* right now."

"Then we'll leave you to carry on more important work," said Riker, relieved that the engineer had dismissed the matter so quickly.

A few minutes later, when he and the android were walking down an empty passageway, Riker broached the subject himself. "Data, I would prefer an end to any more speculation about the explosion on the *Plath*. If anyone asks, we can attribute it to a faulty detonation control."

"You wish me to lie?"

"Well, as a matter of fact . . ." Then Riker sighed, and said, "Let's just say that I'd rather not concentrate too much attention on the incident."

"Because it would corroborate certain powers attributed to the Heart?"

The first officer shook his head. "I can't answer that." The only person who had the authorization, or the knowledge, to deal with that question was the captain; and Riker wasn't entirely sure that he wanted to hear Picard's explanation.

Data was still silently pondering the implication of Riker's evasion, when an intercom hail echoed through the corridor.

"Crusher to Commander Riker."

"Riker here."

"I'm ready to make that house call we discussed."

"Proceed, Doctor," said the first officer, coming to a sudden stop. "I'll wait for you in Counselor Troi's office."

He turned to walk in a new direction, then realized that Data had overheard the entire exchange and might refer to it at some inopportune moment. Riker tried to think of a plausible excuse for this covert arrangement with the chief medical officer, but the strain of a last-minute invention must have showed because Data took the initiative.

"Commander," said the android. "Would you prefer that I did not concentrate too much attention on this event as well?"

"Yes, Data," said Riker with a sigh of relief. "Your inattention would be most appreciated."

For now, at least. However, if Beverly Crusher's effort was

not successful, then the circle of involved officers would have to widen to include Data.

The lights of the ready room were dimmed to their lowest level. Taking a cautious step over the threshold, Crusher peered toward the star window. There was no one sitting at the desk, yet she had heard Picard call out permission for her to enter.

The doors shut behind her, cutting the doctor off from the bridge and throwing the room into even greater darkness. "Captain?"

"Have you come to order me to my cabin, Doctor?" His words were faintly slurred with fatigue.

"No," said Crusher, turning in the direction of Picard's voice. She could barely make out a shadowy form hunched on the sofa. "After all, it doesn't seem to have done much good last time."

"Sleep doesn't refresh me . . . too many dreams . . . I was on the verge of a dream when you came in."

The doctor noted that Picard's response time was significantly slower than usual, as if he was still working his way back to consciousness. "I'm sorry I disturbed you."

"No, don't apologize," he said. "I'm not sure I want to dream again."

As her eyes grew more accustomed to the dark, Crusher could see that the captain was bent over the Heart. For a moment, a trick of the subdued lighting made her think the stone in his hands was glowing, but when she stepped closer the doctor realized its surface was the same dull gray she had seen before. "I'd like to run a few tests on you."

"What?" Irritation roused Picard out of his lethargy. "Go to sickbay? I haven't time for that now."

"I knew you'd say that." Crusher patted the medical tricorder hanging by her side. "So I came prepared to do a scan right here in your office."

"Very well," he said, slumping back over the Heart. "Do as you like."

Moving quickly, before Picard could change his mind, she

pulled the peripheral scanner off the tricorder. After a few passes of the whirring instrument, she had a preliminary result that confirmed the exhaustion she had already observed and also indicated some minor evidence of general neglect. "According to my readings, you're somewhat anemic and your blood sugar levels are depressed. When was the last time you ate a decent meal?"

But Picard was lost in his own thoughts and didn't hear her. "If I had understood its powers better, I could have saved the *Enterprise* without killing the crew of the *Plath.*"

A flick of Crusher's thumb abruptly ended the scan; his mental state was of more interest to her after that statement. "Captain, do you really believe the Heart was responsible for the explosion?"

"I've tried to find some other explanation, but there is none. I regret . . ." He shook his head as if to dislodge the memory of the Klingon ship engulfed in flames. "The Heart obeyed my anger rather than my reason, yet over time I could learn how to wield its powers more directly."

"Learn? How?"

"It speaks to me, Beverly," whispered Picard, and she knelt down by his side to hear him more clearly. "In dreams I see wonders you can hardly imagine: unseen vistas of the cosmos, times long past and yet just within reach. The Heart is as old as the stars and has powers beyond imagining. Why, the destruction of the *Plath* was mere child's play. I could—"

"Jean-Luc! What if you're not the one in control?"

"You don't understand," he said. "The Heart doesn't compel action, it merely offers the means to gain one's ends. With this small stone in my possession, the *Enterprise* could be proof against all enemies and their betrayals, free to explore the entire universe without danger . . . I could never fail."

"Failure is human," said Crusher. "We learn from our mistakes."

"Some mistakes serve no purpose; some defeats only bring pain and humiliation." He looked into her face, meeting her gaze directly for the first time. "If I were the only one involved, Beverly, perhaps I could accept my mistakes; but the consequences of my actions have affected so many other people. I've even hurt you and Wesley, and if it is in my power to make amends . . ."

"No, don't torture yourself with those memories." Crusher laid a hand on his arm, trying to reach through the sorrow that clouded his eyes. She had made her peace with Jack's death, but evidently Picard had not. "You can't change the past, Jean-Luc."

"But what if I could?" He leaned so close that she could feel his breath on her cheeks; his voice took on a deeper, more ominous tone. "Given the opportunity for study, I suspect I could learn to hold the flow of time itself in my hands. Do I have the right to refuse those powers? Would you, as a doctor, throw away the ability to restore health, save lives, or even . . . raise the dead?"

Mesmerized by Picard's words, Crusher saw the Heart as if for the first time. How could she have missed the aura of strangeness that surrounded its rough form?

She reached out to touch the stone.

The captain pulled away with a possessive gesture. Mine! he seemed to say as he clutched the Heart to his chest. "Are you finished with your medical exam, Doctor?"

"Yes, Captain." Crusher rose to her feet and backed away. Just those few steps broke the Heart's uncanny spell. Once more, the captain was holding just a rock.

Picard leaned back against the cushions of the sofa and crossed one leg over the other. In an amiable, conversational tone, he said, "I promise to take better care of myself from now on."

"That's all I ask," said Crusher with a smile that was stretched thin over her apprehension.

She left the captain sitting alone in the shadows of the ready room.

Troi had suggested her counseling room as the most comfortable and convenient meeting place, but the unspoken understanding among the three senior officers was that it also offered more privacy than the CMO's office. Unfortunately, this need for privacy imbued their actions with an unpleasantly furtive nature, and the empath could sense a general discomfiture when they gathered. Although the cushioned furniture was designed to encourage relaxation, Will was perched on the edge of his chair, and Beverly was pacing back and forth as she described her encounter with the captain.

"There was no opportunity to take the Heart from him"— Crusher shuddered at some unpleasant aspect of the memory —"and I'm just as glad I didn't even touch it."

"Why not?" asked Troi curiously.

Beverly shrugged away the question as if not really sure herself. "One moment he seemed himself, then the next he was like a man possessed."

"Are you qualified to perform an exorcism, Doctor?" asked Riker. The grim expression on his face robbed the question of any humor.

"I don't believe an outside agent is the problem, Commander," said Troi. After her talk with Guinan, the counselor had reached a new understanding of the captain's behavior. "Even if the Heart is sentient, I don't sense that it has taken control of Captain Picard. It acts more like an amplifier of all his emotions, and it has transformed his fascination with the stone's legend into an obsession."

"There's more to it than that, Deanna," said Crusher. "It's no secret that our captain strives for perfection, that he dislikes making mistakes or losing. And after his abduction by the Borg . . ."

"Ah, yes," said the counselor, pleased by the additional insight Beverly provided. "After his abduction he felt very vulnerable. So now he has what he believes to be the key to preventing failure of any sort."

Riker frowned at the exchange. "You mean the Heart has made him an offer he can't refuse?"

"Yes," said Troi. "Yes, perhaps it has."

"Engineering to Captain Picard."
Picard woke with a start to find he was still sitting upright

on the ready room sofa, and he wondered if he had been pulled out of sleep or into a dream.

"Engineering to Captain Picard," repeated La Forge patiently.

"Picard here."

"The engine core is back on-line, Captain. We'll have warp speed in ten minutes."

"Acknowledged, Lieutenant."

Geordi's voice was familiar, and there was no sense of the disorientation that had accompanied Jack Crusher's presence, so Picard decided he was truly awake.

Tapping his comm insignia, he said, "Picard to Riker. Prepare for an immediate departure from this sector."

"Aye, Captain!" came the first officer's enthusiastic response. Riker was obviously eager for a return to Federation territory; the demand for yet another diversion would be difficult for him to accept.

Tucking the Heart securely into the crook of his arm, Picard whispered, "You have shown me where you need to go, but I still don't know what to do when we get there."

If only there had been time for one more dream . . . but despite his need for further guidance, Picard had fought against sleep. The encounter with Jack Crusher had shaken him too deeply to slip willingly into unconsciousness. So now, even though the past history of the Heart had been illuminated in exquisite detail, the future remained cloaked in mystery.

Unfortunately, the stakes were too high to delay action. He would have to proceed anyway, blindly trusting that the Heart would eventually reveal the last of its secrets.

The bridge was alive with the sound and movement of a ship restored to good health. Every console was fully powered and brightly lit; crew members marched briskly back and forth across the deck from one duty station to another; and minute by minute, the air Riker breathed was growing sweeter and warmer.

"All systems are operational," called out La Forge from the

aft deck engineering station. From his post at tactical, Worf echoed the engineer's words; and Data looked over his shoulder and nodded to confirm the helm's ready status.

To Riker's mind, however, the return to normalcy would not be complete until the vacant captain's chair was filled. Picard's absences from the bridge were growing noticeably longer. The first officer was not given to undue flights of fancy, yet he imagined that the Heart could sense the crew's antagonism to its presence, and like an animal under siege, it constantly urged a return to the safety of its den.

Rising to his feet at the sound of parting doors, Riker studied Picard as he emerged from the shadowed recesses of the ready room. The bright, even lighting of the bridge emphasized the captain's drawn face and pale complexion; the impression of a live animal crouched on his arm was strengthened by his protective embrace of the Heart.

While the captain walked toward the command center, Riker continued with the routine preparations for the ship's departure. "Mr. Data, lay in a course for Starbase 75."

"Belay that order, Mr. Data," said Picard. "Set a new course heading."

The string of destination coordinates the captain called out next meant nothing to Riker, but he was appalled by the direction Picard had chosen. This sense of shock was universal; the entire bridge crew had frozen, arrested in mid-motion by the unexpected command.

"Captain," said Riker. "That course is on a direct line *away* from Federation territory."

"I'm aware of that, Number One," said Picard. "Helm?"

Data's hands immediately blurred into motion to make up for his momentary hesitation. "Course laid in, sir."

"Warp one." The captain stabbed his hand in the air as if to point the way through space. "Engage."

On the viewscreen, pinpoint stars transformed into streaks of light as the *Enterprise* slipped into warp speed. Heavy vibrations shuddered through the primary hull as La Forge adjusted the injection settings, but within seconds the trembling eased away. Working in tandem with the chief engineer,

Picard ordered incremental increases in speed until the starship was cruising smoothly at warp four.

"The bridge is yours, Number One," announced Picard without warning. He turned sharply on his heel and strode back to his ready room.

Riker was the first to speak in the wake of the captain's abrupt departure. "Data, where are we going?"

"I can find no significant aspect to the designated location," said the android. "However, the coordinates for the site came from a star map the captain has in his possession."

"A star map? Where did he get this map?"

"That I cannot say, but I suspect it is somehow involved with the Heart."

The association was not surprising, but it was definitely alarming. "Data, we've got to get that . . . thing away from the captain."

The android adopted a dubious expression. "He has been most reluctant to release it from his possession."

"Enough!" said Worf.

Riker looked up in surprise to find the Klingon leaning over the deck rail, his face glowering with suspicion.

"The Pagrashtak is best left in the hands of Captain Picard. As his security chief, I will not allow it to be taken by force."

"No, of course not, Lieutenant," said the first officer, compelled into a hasty retraction by this unexpected opposition. "It's entirely the captain's decision when to give up the Heart."

Yet Riker seriously questioned whether Picard would ever reach that decision on his own.

And just what am I going to do about that? he wondered as they all sped farther and farther toward nowhere.

CHAPTER 30

"**C**ome," called out Picard, and waited to see who would enter the ready room.

He had known there would be repercussions from his last set of orders. His involvement with the Heart was gathering momentum, and he was pulling his crew faster and faster along with him toward a murky climax that was beyond their understanding. It was beyond his, as well, or he would have tried harder to explain his actions. Their loyalty to him ran deep, but for how long could he take advantage of that faith?

"Do you ever put it down, Captain?"

Picard glanced up from his contemplation of the Heart to find that Counselor Troi had fixed him with a speculative look. It was a familiar expression, and one he had learned to distrust in the past.

"What are you talking about?" asked Picard, although he knew quite well what she meant.

Troi only smiled at his clumsy evasion. "Its very presence seems to comfort you, physically as well as emotionally."

Her observation was uncomfortably perceptive. His ready room must have cooled by at least five degrees when life support services were reduced to conserve power, but Picard had barely felt the cold as long as he was in contact with the stone; and its weight, cupped in his hands or tucked in the crook of his arm, was a constant reminder of the protection it offered.

"So," Troi persisted, "I couldn't help wondering if setting the Heart aside distresses you. How long can you go without it?"

"Counselor," said Picard with a forced smile, "you make it sound like an addiction."

"Do I? That's very interesting."

"Oh, no," he said with a shake of his head. "I have no intention of getting drawn into a discussion about addiction and obsession. I can end this matter right here and now."

Rising up from the sofa, the captain walked over to the far side of his office and tucked the stone on a high shelf. Stepping away from the wall unit, he said, "There, Counselor. Are you satisfied?"

"This is not something you must do to please me," said the empath. Her dark eyes flitted up and down, measuring the distance from the floor to the shelf, a height that was well beyond her reach. "I only ask you to reflect on how the stone has affected you. How do you feel about putting it away?"

"I feel nothing other than the desire to get a good night's sleep."

"Yes, you seem to spend much of your time alone these days."

Really, there was no pleasing the woman. "Would you prefer that I drop by Ten-Forward instead?"

"It's not *my* preferences that are the issue, Captain. You should do what *you* wish."

He uttered a mock groan. "And regardless of what I do, you'll take notes and look pensive."

"Probably," said Troi with a good-natured laugh. "Goodnight, Captain."

The counselor walked out of the ready room, but her challenge concerning the Heart remained behind, taunting him. Even worse, the exchange with Troi revived memories of another warning.

It is not too late for me, T'Sara. I can still maintain control.

Picard shivered in the cool air and without thinking reached out for the Heart's warmth.

He stopped himself before his fingers touched the rough surface of the stone, but the arrested motion seemed to rob him of an alternate purpose and direction. His original intention had been to resume his wait for a new dream to guide his next steps, but now the ready room seemed a bleak and uninviting place to sleep. Yet the thought of walking out onto the bridge filled him with a vague anxiety.

What should I do now?

Guinan looked out from under the broad brim of a burgundy bonnet. "Tea?" she asked of her new customer.

Picard nodded. "Tea."

"One Earl Grey coming up."

"No," he said on impulse. "Not Earl Grey. I'll have Srjula instead."

"Srjula? An Andorian tea?" The hostess turned to a tidy row of canisters on a shelf behind her. Common teas could be requested from the food replicators, but the molecular patterns of the more exotic brands were rarely available, and the drink had to be made from real leaves. Guinan pried open the lid of one of the jars and peered at the contents. "We don't get much call for this on the *Enterprise.*"

"I'm in the mood for something different."

"Srjula is certainly different," she said, setting a clear teacup and saucer on the bar. The crumpled leaves that she sprinkled into the cup were orange, but when hot water was poured over them, they turned bright yellow, then dissolved. She sniffed experimentally at the pungent aroma, then grimaced. "I've never actually tasted it, myself."

Picard picked up the saucer and took a tentative sip from the cup. His mouth pursed involuntarily. He took another sip. "Yes, that's perfect."

"It is?" said Guinan.

He nodded emphatically. Srjula. The memory of its tart, bitter taste was borrowed from a dream, yet he knew that it was just as it should be.

Guinan shrugged and moved on to her next customer, yet Picard felt her gaze following him as he walked across the deck. He wound his way to a table where Beverly Crusher was finishing off a slice of pie. She hastily licked a smear of whipped cream off her upper lip.

"You came alone tonight, Captain."

"Alone?" he said as he sat down across from her. A backdrop of deep space framed her body.

Crusher pointed to his hands, which were wrapped tightly around his teacup. "No rock."

"Oh, that." Picard loosened his grip; the warm, round shape between the palms of his hands had been familiar and reassuring. "I left it in my cabin. It's not as if I can't do without it."

"No, of course not." She made a token effort to hide her amusement by eating the last bite of her dessert, but he detected the ends of her smile curling up around the spoon.

"Let's not talk about the Heart," he said.

"That's an excellent idea." She shoved aside the empty plate and leaned forward. Her voice dropped to a conspiratorial whisper. "Instead, why don't we—" She stopped. Her nose wrinkled ever so slightly. "What on earth is that smell?"

"Tea," said Picard, lifting the cup up to his lips.

"You're *drinking* that?"

"Yes, of course." He took a sip, but had to fight an impulse to spit out the liquid. His craving for the astringent brew had faded. He swallowed anyway. "It's delicious."

As he set down the cup, he caught a flash of movement outside the Ten-Forward window.

"If you say so." Crusher pulled back slightly and began again. "As I was saying, why don't we—" She stopped again, obviously alarmed by the sudden change in his expression and the silence that had fallen over the entire room. "Captain? What's wrong, Jean-Luc?"

He tried to answer, but his throat had closed too tightly to let the words escape.

They're back.

The doctor checked back over her shoulder; she was the last to see it. A simple cubic shape hung in space, its baroque metallic structures gleaming softly in reflected starlight.

"Oh my god," she cried. "It's the Borg."

As her words echoed through the room, flashing red lights began their staccato pulse and alert sirens sprang to life. Picard scrambled to his feet, overturning the table and chair in his haste, knowing only that he must get away quickly.

"Captain to the bridge! Captain to—"

Riker's intercom voice was drowned out by the high whine of a Borg transporter beam. Picard froze in his tracks; the sound brought forth a memory of pain, a pain so fierce that he would do anything to escape it again.

Five Borg materialized in the center of the room, back-to-back in a tight formation like a satanic pentagram. Each took a step forward and began to fire straight ahead.

No! Not again. Please not again.

Another step, another round of fire. Screams. People were screaming; people were falling to the deck; people were dying.

I should do something. I must do something. I'm the captain. But the terror that gripped him was so strong that he couldn't move. If he moved, they would see him.

He watched instead.

He watched as Guinan pulled a phaser out from behind the counter. She was hit before she could even pull the trigger. Her body went up in flames.

The Borg took another step and five more people crumpled to the floor. A few writhed and groaned, the others lay still.

He watched as Beverly Crusher brushed past him, rushing to the aid of one of the dying crewmen. A sweep of a Borg arm sent her flying through the air. Her body landed at

Picard's feet, her back oddly twisted and her face slack and wooden.

One last step. A Borg was standing right in front of him.

Picard watched as it raised an arm and extruded a whirring metal rotor from the tip. The twirling blades shredded the cloth of his uniform, the skin beneath, and then bored a hole straight through to his heart . . .

Picard woke with a burning sensation deep in his chest; there were other pains, needle-sharp and throbbing, embedded in his muscles and bones. Two years after their removal, his body still remembered exactly where the Borg implants had been placed. He clutched the front of his uniform and nearly retched at the feel of the damp, sticky cloth.

It's only sweat.

He took a deep, shuddering breath. Not so bad. After all, this nightmare hadn't wrenched tears and screams from him. He was beyond the need to drag Deanna Troi out of her bed to hear him babble about terror and cowardice and loss of control. This was just a predictable reaction to the presence of a captured Borg on board the *Enterprise* last month; Picard's brief impersonation of Locutus had triggered uncomfortable memories . . .

. . . or the dream was a warning.

No, dammit, this has nothing to do with the Heart.

His fingers curled, cold and stiff, as if they yearned to wrap themselves around the stone's fire. His chest was still aching. Had he experienced a routine nightmare or another vision? If the Heart could show him the past, could it also show him the future?

"Picard to bridge," he called out as he swung his legs over the edge of the couch.

"Data here, Captain."

He rose and moved across the room to his bookshelves. "Lieutenant, increase speed to warp six and initiate evasive maneuvers."

"Sir?"

276

"You heard me. Maintain our previous destination coordinates, just get us there a different way than originally planned."

"Yes, sir."

The captain reached up to the shelf and closed his hands around the Heart. Its warmth flooded through him, washing away the tension in his muscles.

The pain in his chest began to fade.

CHAPTER 31

Warden Chandat was accustomed to spending long hours sitting in place while maintaining an air of dignity and supreme authority over tedious proceedings. He had developed this skill presiding over countless Faculty meetings, but he was somewhat disillusioned to discover that the demands on a starship commander were not so very different from his own administrative duties. The bridge chair was more comfortable than the one in the council chamber, Chandat conceded, but the view was less interesting. Over the last two days, the novelty of staring forward at nothing but stars on a flat screen had worn off.

"Estimated time of arrival is one hour and five minutes," announced Dean Shagret from the helm. He, unlike the warden, could constantly entertain himself by scanning the console readouts and playing with the controls.

"Maintain course and speed." The phrase felt less foreign on Chandat's tongue after several repetitions. Without such squelching directives, the dean had an annoying tendency to practice new flight maneuvers that sent the ship careening in unexpected directions.

"Initiating long-range sensor scans," announced Thorina. This would be her third scan within the last hour, but whenever Shagret issued one of his status reports, she was spurred to activate her console again.

Their rivalry had started soon after the *Sullivan*'s departure from Dynasia when the two deans began squabbling over who among the Faculty had sufficient seniority to sit in the command area. Recognizing the importance of this symbolic center of authority, Chandat had reluctantly given up his place at navigation to secure his position as leader of the expedition. Then his first official act as the ship's commander had been to order the two deans to posts at opposite ends of the bridge.

A muffled sound drew Chandat's attention to the old man seated by his side. The professor had remained silent until now.

"So near . . ." whispered Manja. His voice was husky with sorrow. "If only T'Sara could have lived long enough to share this moment with me."

Chandat would have preferred to keep the historian out of sight; Diat was a constant reminder that the basis for this venture was taken from a hoary myth in the Dream literature. However, banishing the professor from the bridge would have been too cruel. Manja thought this mission had been mounted on his behalf, as a champion of T'Sara, and he would have been hurt by any attempt at exclusion. As it was, the old man would be hurt eventually, but Chandat tried not to cast his thoughts that far ahead.

Fortunately, the demands of operating a starship had fully occupied the attention of the other professors and prevented them from asking too many questions about their destination. However, the *Sullivan* would arrive at the Appointed Place soon, and then the folly of this quixotic search for the Gem would be all too apparent to all the Dynasians.

"Chandat!" Thorina's cry of alarm jerked the warden out of his reverie. "I've got something on the scanners!"

"Could you be more specific?" asked Chandat. Since she

had issued several false alarms during the voyage, he had quickly learned not to attach too much significance to such outbursts.

"There's a Federation starship dead ahead, registry number NCC-1701D."

The warden started up out of his chair and twirled around to face the dean. "Are you sure?"

"Confirmed," said Oomalo, peering down over the dean's shoulder at the tactical screen. "Their trajectory matches ours. It appears that we will not be the first to arrive at the Appointed Place."

This news was most unsettling; the warden had never thought to factor another starship into any of his contingency plans. Chandat wracked his memory for an appropriate command response. "Open hailing frequencies."

"Do what?" asked Thorina, who was still flustered by the unexpected success of her scan. "Oh, yes, the radio."

With a dubious frown, she jabbed her finger at the midsection of the communications console. A high-pitched squeal of static burst over the bridge speakers. Thorina jabbed again and the noise turned into a stream of chattering voices.

As Chandat listened to the oddly familiar, yet incomprehensible language, Shagret called out with disdain, "That's not Federation Standard."

"The incoming transmission is not from the starship," said Oomalo. The native professor edged in beside Dean Thorina, and with a refreshing display of competence, rapidly tapped a sequence over the console surface. "Activating the universal translator."

"I would have done that next," snapped Thorina, but she moved aside to give Oomalo better access to the controls.

The abstract sounds suddenly turned into words.

"... *must rely on sheer numbers to maintain our advantage. The Federation's weapons technology is superior to that of any one of our vessels.*"

Oomalo glanced over at the tactical monitor. "We appear to have intercepted intership communications from a group of vessels just entering the sector. They also are headed for the Appointed Place."

An answering transmission crackled over the subspace radio channel. *"The unDiWahn captains are united as one mighty fist, Admiral. We shall crush the* Enterprise *and reclaim the Gem."*

"DiWahn?" cried out Manja. "Did they really say DiWahn?"

"By the Three Gates," said Chandat in amazement. "I heard it, too."

"Ancient history is coming alive, Warden!" Excitement at the discovery wiped away the old man's grief. He was a Dynasian after all, and knowledge was the first love of all their race.

Chandat's respect for T'Sara's scholarship overwhelmed his own concerns for just a moment. Thanks to the Vulcan, two branches of the scattered Iconian peoples were finally reunited on the other side of the Gate.

Oomalo, unmoved by legends that were alien to her own people, was more practical in her reaction to the revelation. "We had better make a friendly overture to these DiWahns before they mistake us for a Federation faction. If we offer to combine forces, then the starship will be easily overpowered."

"How very inconvenient," muttered Chandat to himself. Fortunately, his heretical comment was drowned out by the ragged victory cheers of the Faculty.

The ancient engineers of Iconia had obviously respected the need for introspection. On each of their starships they had reserved space for a small niche that would shelter a body in meditation. After boarding the flagship of the unDiWahn fleet, Master Kieradán had retreated inside just such a niche and spent the duration of the journey through space in consultation with himself.

Traditionally, the reciting of the Dream Lore was done in a circle of the Faithful, but Kieradán was conducting a private Telling. In the circle of his own mind, he was both dream-teller and listener as he reviewed the accumulated knowledge of his order and searched for new insights. The men and women of the Faithful had spent their lives exploring the lessons laced in the dreams of the Gem-Bearers, and now Kieradán had five short days in which to judge this wisdom for the last time.

"Master."

The unDiWahn was pulled out of his thoughts by a low voice from outside the enclosure. Admiral Jakat would not have interrupted this meditation without good cause, but Kieradán resented the intrusion anyway. He had so little time left.

Drawing aside the curtain that closed off the niche from the outer room, he said, "Yes, Daramadán?"

The admiral stepped closer to the high shelf where Kieradán sat. He moved with an unusually stiff gait. "We have established communications with a lone starship of Federation registry; however, the crew claims to be Iconian. Warden Chandat of Dynasia asserts that they, too, are on course for the Appointed Place."

This news explained the tension locked in the muscles of the admiral's body. Kieradán felt his own frame stiffen in reaction to this unexpected company.

"So, the Dynasians have survived on the other side of their Gate."

This was no cause for rejoicing. Another contingent of Iconians could complicate his plans for the Gem. Despite this risk, Kieradán decided he would allow the strangers to continue . . . for now. After all, they might have a place in the Dreaming, too.

"Propose an alliance to the Dynasians," said Kieradán, "but make it clear that they must follow our lead and let me negotiate for the Gem. If they agree to these terms, let them live."

"As you wish, Master." The admiral withdrew without asking for further instruction. He was a capable leader in his own right and required little direction.

Closing the curtain, Kieradán resumed his meditation on the future of the Dream Gem.

Over the past century, those who held the title of master had reached a consensus of opinion as to the role of the Faithful in the Gem's affairs. Upon his investment as leader of the order, Kieradán had pledged to honor that agreement when he reached the Appointed Place, yet the autonomy of his position encompassed the authority to change his mind. It was that freedom that troubled him now. His sworn duty had seemed much easier to contemplate on DiWahn than it did here in space, drawing ever nearer to the Gem. With each hour that slipped away, he discovered new arguments with which to counter the decision of his elders.

Even if he affirmed the conclusion reached by his predecessors, Master Kieradán wondered if he had the strength of will to keep his feet on the true path they had outlined. The title he bore was for mastery over oneself, not over others, but he was the first of the unDiWahn to actually face the Gem and test his convictions.

Kanda Jiak, the last Iconian to be called master, had failed. He had paid for that failure with his life.

CHAPTER **32**

Like a gull skimming the still surface of an ocean, the USS *Enterprise* dropped out of warp speed and coasted into a leisurely orbit around a cooling star.

The white dwarf had no name, just a number assigned by astronomers as they charted the desolate reaches of space beyond the Federation. The star had burned in isolation for nearly five thousand years; but now, at the end of that long wait, the dwarf's single companion was drawing near again.

The heat of their meeting had transformed the speeding ball of rock and ice into a streak of luminous vapor; thus, for a few short months along the course of its elliptical orbit, the comet flared into prominence. Later, once it passed perihelion and fell farther and farther away into cold fringes of the system, the tail would fade, and the comet would continue in anonymous invisibility for another five thousand years.

Riker knew that comets were nothing more than stray pebbles adrift in space, kicked into motion by tidal waves of gravity. Over the years of his Starfleet service, he had seen wonders of far greater beauty and mystery than this lonely traveler in its brief flash of glory, but perhaps it was precisely that ephemeral quality that moved him with a mixture of sadness and joy.

When he entered the ready room, Riker found the captain staring out his window at the same bleak tableau of the white dwarf and its consort. With a softly uttered sigh of irritation, Picard turned away from the scene to hear his first officer's status report.

"Engineering has managed to restore our deflector shield capacity to fifty-seven percent," said Riker, "and Geordi expects another ten percent improvement in the next few hours, but for now we're extremely vulnerable."

Picard's gaze kept flicking away from his first officer; he seemed to constantly fight against the impulse to look over his shoulder. His hands were equally restless, reaching for the Heart, then darting back to the data tablet on his desk. "Do the best you can with what we have, Number One."

One role that Riker often played with the captain was devil's advocate; Picard had always encouraged him to present any opposing arguments that would offer a different perspective to critical issues. Rarely, however, had Riker felt that the stakes were so high as now. "The best we can do, Captain, is to leave this area before we're attacked."

This statement secured Picard's undivided attention and sharpened his voice. "Are you questioning my present command decisions?"

"No, sir, I'm not, but our orders—"

"My orders," said Picard with icy reserve, "were to keep the Heart out of the hands of the enemies of the Federation. I intend to do just that."

Riker's intuition led him toward a disturbing corollary. "But you're not going to take it back into Federation space, are you?"

"No." Picard lifted the stone up off the desk as if to include the Heart in the discussion of its fate. "Self-determination is one of the basic tenets of Starfleet's philosophy; as a sentient being, this entity must be accorded control over its own destiny. Just as important, in my judgment the interests of the Federation are best served by removing the Heart from our affairs. Captain Duregh's betrayal convinced me that its continuing presence would eventually destabilize our current political alliances."

"Can you tell me how you plan to remove it?" asked Riker. He had hoped for just such an opening to discuss the captain's plans for the Heart.

"This place is essential. We must stay here until . . ." As he groped for words, Picard unwittingly revealed the depth of his uncertainty. ". . . until the Heart's mission has completely unfolded."

"The longer we remain here, the greater the chance that the unDiWahn—"

"The unDiWahn are not a danger, Number One." With the Heart still clutched in his hands like a talisman warding off evil, Picard said, "You've seen what it can do with your own eyes. As long as I hold the Heart, they can't even touch us."

Even before his return to the bridge, Troi could sense the rising intensity of Riker's emotions. When he finally stepped out of the ready room, however, she was relieved to see that Riker had successfully masked his frustration and anxiety behind an expression of vague geniality.

She watched as the first officer sauntered across the command deck. His carefree air would convince anyone but an empath that he had just enjoyed a casual exchange with the captain. A quick sidelong glance toward the aft deck nearly gave Riker away, but Lieutenant Worf was too absorbed with his tactical sensor readings to catch the telltale sign of wariness.

Once Riker settled down beside her, however, he shook his head. No success.

"Now what?" asked Troi in a low voice.

He shrugged. "Your turn again."

"No, I can feel his emotional reserve heighten whenever I approach him. If he won't even listen to me, he certainly won't relinquish the Heart to my care."

"Well, then . . ."

In perfect accord, she and Riker both turned and fixed a speculative look on the android working quietly at the helm.

Since Picard appeared entranced by the view outside his window, Data stood patiently in front of the ready room desk, waiting for the captain to break out of his reverie. While he waited, the android considered how he might best attempt to fulfill Riker's directive.

Persuading Captain Picard to give up the Heart would prove an interesting challenge in interpersonal dynamics, but it was an area in which Data judged himself to be somewhat inadequate. Considering the strong emotions that were involved, Data doubted that he would be able to succeed where Doctor Crusher and Counselor Troi had failed.

Then, catching sight of one of the books on the office desk, he was reminded of the captain's deep respect for T'Sara and Ambassador Sarek. Vulcans did not appeal to emotions, yet Picard was often persuaded by these writings. Perhaps logic could provide a more promising approach.

Under his breath, Picard muttered, "How long must I wait for an answer?"

Data determined the captain was addressing the Heart resting in his hands. Apparently he received no response from the stone, because Picard then swiveled his chair around to face the android.

"What is it, Mr. Data? Am I to be subjected to a visit by each of my senior officers in turn? How can I think straight with these continual interruptions?"

Without any preamble to soften his intent, Data said, "We are concerned about the extent to which your actions are being governed by the Heart."

"Then you need worry yourself no longer. I am acting of my own volition." Evidently Picard regretted the overly curt nature of this response, because he stopped to take a deep breath and then said, "Data, there is something the Heart needs, a place it must reach, for reasons I don't entirely understand, that I may be incapable of understanding, yet its urgency is unmistakable."

"Does this mean you will relinquish the stone so that it can reach that destination, Captain?"

"Yes . . . of course." Picard's eyes widened ever so slightly as he contemplated that scenario. "But not until the time is right."

"Intriguing. When exactly will that time occur?"

"Not yet," said the captain. "I'll know when the time comes."

"I admire your certainty. However, my analysis of the Heart's history indicates that if you delay too long, the stone will ensure its own release by leaving us vulnerable to attack."

"No! The Heart offers us protection."

"Does it?" asked Data. "On this journey you speak of, the Heart has left a trail of death and devastation in its wake. This is not legend or myth, but fact. We have seen the evidence ourselves in the destruction of the Orions and the Ferengi."

"The Heart is not to blame for those deaths," said Picard with a vehement shake of his head. "The Orions died due to their own greed, as did the Ferengi; they courted their own downfall."

"And what of the Vulcans? Did T'Sara deserve her fate?"

A spasm of grief, akin to pain, creased the captain's face. This time he shook his head more gently.

"From what I have observed," said Data, "the protection it offers has a tendency to fail if the Heart can secure a more useful host. When will it tire of your custody?"

Picard fell silent for a moment as his thoughts turned inward. "You aren't the first one to warn me that I've held on too long." In a voice tinged with a Vulcan accent, he recited, "It constantly struggles to free itself from the tangle of our grasping hands."

Encouraged by this admission of doubt, the android pressed his argument even harder. "In the years that we have served together, you have stressed how much you value my unique perspective. Captain, trust to my objectivity, to my lack of emotion, when I tell you that the Heart is more of a danger to us than any alien fleet. Give it up now, while you still can. If you rely on its powers to shield us from harm, we will be destroyed."

He held out his hands, palms upturned, to accept the stone.

"Data," said Picard, "neither Surak or T'Sara would lay this burden on another living being. I don't have that right either."

"Remember that I have held the stone before with complete immunity. As an android, I cannot be seduced by its powers."

Picard's hands trembled when he lifted up the Heart, as if this slight effort required a concentration of all of his strength and will. "Then take—"

"Bridge to Captain Picard," boomed Worf's voice over the intercom. *"The unDiWahn fleet has reentered the perimeter of our sensor field . . . the ships have been dispersed in a surround pattern and are drawing in toward us."*

"Surrounded . . ." Picard froze in mid-gesture. "Data, I won't leave the *Enterprise* vulnerable to attack!"

This was as much a plea for help as it was a declaration of defiance. Data urged the obvious solution. "Then we must leave this place while there is still time to break through their formation. At our fastest warp speed we can outpace the entire unDiWahn fleet."

"Leave?" Despite his reluctance to accept this suggestion, the captain was unable to marshal a counter argument. "Yes . . . I suppose we must."

Data reached out to take hold of the Heart.

"Captain," said Worf again. *"Sensors have detected a Federation starship approaching the sector."*

The android's finger brushed against air.

Picard had pulled the stone back a few inches. "The cavalry has reached us just in time, Data."

"The registry number is that of the Miranda-class USS Sullivan," continued the security chief. *"However, they are not answering our hails, and Starfleet records indicate the vessel was last assigned to diplomatic duty in another quadrant."*

"Yet another betrayal," said Data, quick to underscore

their growing danger. "All the more reason for us to depart this sector."

"On the contrary," said Picard unexpectedly. "This proves the futility of retreat. Enemies follow in our wake wherever we go. Even if we escape these forces, new enemies and new betrayals will be waiting for us at every port. We carry violence with us like a plague. The chase must end here."

A calmness seemed to settle over the captain, smoothing away the furrows of confusion and doubt that had etched themselves into his face. Cradling the stone to his chest, Picard said, "I will need the Heart for just a while longer."

CHAPTER 33

"**M**ake it so."

The huddle of officers around the captain flew apart. Like players aiming for their marks on a stage, they all moved briskly to their bridge stations.

Picard took a step forward to center himself in the command area, and Riker planted himself by the captain's side; Worf assumed his background role at the tactical console; and in the foreground, Data took the helm. Transporter Chief O'Brien, the one foreign element in this familiar tableau, marched through the turbolift's opening doors and disappeared.

"Status report, Mr. Worf?"

"Sensors show the unDiWahn fleet is still closing at six hundred thousand kilometers . . ."

Images began to form on the viewscreen. From a distance, the unDiWahn ships appeared surprisingly delicate. Their colorful hulls were curled in spirals and waves, like autumn leaves twisting in the wind. The thick saucer section of the lone Miranda-class starship was stiff and ungainly in the midst of these undulating shapes.

". . . five hundred thousand . . . four hundred thousand kilometers."

A hush fell over the bridge as the alien ships drifted closer and closer until their fluting edges nearly touched. The assembled fleet formed the thin shell of a sphere with the *Enterprise* captured in the hollow center. For all its beauty, the pattern was also an overwhelming display of military strength.

"Captain," said Worf in a low voice. "We are being hailed by the unDiWahn flagship."

"Establish visual communications, Lieutenant."

Squaring his shoulders, Picard mentally prepared himself for the raising of the curtain that would reveal him to an audience. His hands tightened their hold on the Heart, the key element in the unfolding drama.

The chase would end now; the last blood to be spilled would be here, on the bridge of the *Enterprise.*

To the uninitiated, the gray rock was an unremarkable object, but Kieradán knew that its plain cover masked a crystalline structure that sparkled in the dark. What could not be seen, what could only be felt, was the heat that radiated from it. If only he could warm his hands on the Dream Gem for just a few moments . . .

With the greatest of difficulty, the master raised his eyes to meet the Gem-Bearer's gaze. "I am Kieradán, leader of the Faithful."

"I am Jean-Luc Picard, captain of the *Enterprise.*" While the captain introduced his senior officers, Kieradán noted that fatigue had left its marks on Picard's face, bleaching his skin of color and sharpening the planes of his skull. His fingers were rigid with tension, gripping the Gem in a vise of bone and muscle.

As soon as the tedious formalities were concluded, Kieradán spoke. "Captain, I request that you return the Gem to the keeping of the unDiWahn. We are its Guardians and have charge of its future."

Picard shook his head. "With all due respect, Kieradán, I

don't recognize your claim of ownership. The Gem remains with me."

"Brave words for the commander of a starship far from the safety of Federation space."

Picard's first officer strutted forward, filling more of the oval viewscreen. "Our safety is of less importance than the security of the Federation. This crew has pledged to destroy the stone rather than let it fall into the wrong hands."

"I do not believe you," said Kieradán. "No bearer would willingly give up possession of the Gem."

"We're going to prove you wrong." Riker then looked back to Picard as if expecting the older man to echo this challenge. When the Gem-Bearer was silent, Riker prompted him by saying, "Captain, we agreed we must put an end to—"

"No," said Picard, sidling away from the first officer. "No, I've changed my mind. Such an extreme measure won't be necessary after all."

Riker's arrogance gave way to dismay. "Captain!"

"Number One, with the Heart in my possession I can defeat anyone who tries to take it away from me." Picard's threat was directed at his first officer, rather than the unDiWahn.

"As you can see," said Kieradán to the young officer, "this matter is between myself and your captain."

"I wouldn't be so sure about that," said Riker. He slapped at a metal insignia on his chest. "Now!"

All the doors to the bridge snapped open at once. As security guards stormed through the portals, the officer at the helm slid out from behind his console and lunged toward the captain.

"Data, no!" cried out Picard.

The pale-skinned helmsman had wrapped his hands around the Gem in an attempt to displace Picard's hold. The Klingon on the aft deck tried to rush to the captain's aid, but armed guards immediately dragged him away from the bridge railing. It took five of them to keep the warrior's arms pinned behind his back.

Kieradán had expected trouble; it was an inevitable companion to the Gem's travels. "Daramadán," the master whispered, "prepare to fire at my next command."

In the frame of the viewscreen, the two men were still grappling for dominance. The Gem-Bearer's face was contorted by a fierce possessive rage that would have intimidated most assailants. However, with a display of unusual strength, Data wrenched the stone out of the captain's grasp.

While two guards wrestled Picard facedown onto the deck, Data raised the stone up into the air like the head of a vanquished enemy. "The Gem is mine!"

Kieradán's clenched fist held the admiral at his side in check. Negotiation was still in everyone's best interests. "You have only weakened your position, *Enterprise*. It takes time to learn how to use those powers."

"I do not need any time at all," said Data, "because I plan to destroy the Gem now."

Alarmed by the man's resoluteness, Kieradán opened his fist and said, "Daramadán, fire!"

The *Enterprise* bridge rocked and swayed as the Iconian weapons salvo collided against its defense shields. This sudden assault threw the crew off-balance. Cries and shouts rang out as they confronted the deadly consequences of their resistance. From his vantage point as a spectator, Kieradán also saw Picard take clever advantage of this widespread distraction.

"Worf!" screamed the captain as he twisted out of his guard's choke-hold. "Stop Data!"

With a mighty heave, the Klingon threw off the men holding him. One swipe of his muscular arm ripped a phaser from a guard's belt. Roaring like a wounded animal, he took aim at the android and fired.

A narrow red beam lanced out across the bridge. With reflexes faster than Kieradán would have believed possible, Data spun around and blocked the force of the phaser blast with the Gem itself.

The stone absorbed the energy like a sponge. For a moment, the master thought it would survive the blast, but then the soft glow at its crystal center ignited.

The Gem and its new bearer disappeared in a fiery bloom of light.

"Don't move!"

The security guard planted his knee in the small of Picard's back and shoved the captain flat against the deck. The air was knocked out of his lungs by the impact, and a raw scrape on his cheek burned hotly as his face was ground into the short fibers of the carpet. Picard battled for breath against the crushing weight of the body pinning him down.

"The unDiWahn have severed the communication link . . ." Riker's voice came from a direction behind and above where Picard lay, so the first officer must have taken over the tactical console. ". . . and the fleet appears to be retreating."

Pinpoints of colored light were forming on the captain's retinas when Riker finally said, "We did it!"

The guard released his hold.

With a soft groan of relief, Picard rolled over onto his back and sucked in a lungful of air. When the dancing spots had faded away, he made a weak attempt to sit up and discovered that his ribs were painfully bruised. Two security guards grabbed hold of his arms and pulled him up to a standing position.

"Sorry, sir," said a third guard as she hastily brushed off the front of the captain's tunic. "I guess we got a little carried away."

Picard mustered a wan smile to allay their anxiety, but his first words were directed to the ship's intercom. "Bridge to transporter room. Good job, Chief."

"*Thank you, Captain,*" replied O'Brien. A flash of white light exploded in front of the helm for a second time. "*I enjoy a spot of fancy work now and then.*"

The entire crew erupted into laughter, shattering the tension that had gripped them all during the confrontation with the unDiWahn. Picard led a round of appreciative applause, but even after the clapping ended, high spirits persisted. Worf sauntered back to his tactical station, the security squads jostled their way off the bridge, and Riker vaulted over the aft deck railing to land with a heavy thud in front of the captain.

"Your bluff worked!" exulted Riker. "They really believe Worf destroyed Data and the Heart."

Picard tugged at his rumpled tunic. "Yes, Number One, it seems that—"

"Captain," cut in Worf. "The unDiWahn fleet has halted its retreat. All vessels are holding position at five hundred thousand kilometers, just outside of phaser range."

This statement hit Picard with greater force than any physical blow. Robbed of speech by bitter disappointment, the captain whirled around to stare at the viewscreen. The unDiWahn ships sparkled like metallic sequins scattered through space.

"At least we've bought some time, Captain," said Riker in a subdued whisper.

But time to do what? wondered Picard. Only minutes had passed since the Heart had been taken from him, yet he could already feel his empty hands aching to hold the stone again. *What if I must destroy it after all?*

Master Kieradán stared out the port window of his cabin, studying the Appointed Place. He had no interest in the star, just its single orbiting satellite. The comet was a cosmic hourglass, and the length of its tail indicated that valuable time had been lost.

"Do they take us for fools, Master?" The sound of Daramadán's heavy tread traced the admiral's progress back and forth from one end of the room to the other. "That was a trick, a show of lights meant to dazzle and confuse the simpleminded. The Gem has not been destroyed!"

"No," said Kieradán softly. "I don't sense that it has left the Dreaming in that manner."

Yet he wondered if this conviction was based on hope rather than on truth. His mind was spinning from the attempt to make sense of the scene he had just witnessed. Picard was the last of the Gem-Bearers to appear in the Dreaming; yet even though he had just given up the stone to another being, his action had not affected the Telling.

"Let us attack and take—"

"No!" The temptation to agree with Daramadán was strong, but there was so little time left in which to act. Recovering the Gem by force might take too long, and the consequences of such a miscalculation would reverberate for five thousand years. "There is something different about the one they call Data. He holds the Gem without being touched by it."

Could I do the same? Do I dare take the place of someone who has already passed that test. Kieradán looked deep inside himself and did not like what he saw.

Forsaking intellect, trusting to his instincts, the master said, "Do not attack, Admiral. Instead, your fleet must remain in position to ensure that the *Enterprise* does not leave before the Appointed Time."

"But I thought our mission was to take possession of the Gem!"

I thought so, too. "We must trust that Picard will aid the Gem to fulfill its destiny." If the captain failed in his task, the Gem would have to wait yet again to complete its journey.

"You speak in riddles, Master."

Kieradán gestured to the port window. "Watch. You will understand soon enough."

When Picard stepped inside his ready room, his gaze was drawn unerringly to the Heart. His fears that it might have been damaged by the intraship transport were eased by the sight of the stone nestled in the crook of Data's arm.

"We're at a stalemate with the unDiWahn," explained Picard when Data looked up from his examination of the wall aquarium. Evidently the android considered the Heart an object of less interest than a fish swimming idly in place. "However, visual communications have been severed, so it's safe for you to return to the bridge."

Data acknowledged the news with an impassive nod. "Thank you, Captain."

I chose to give it up.

That knowledge did not lessen Picard's sharp pangs of jealousy as he watched Data carry the Heart across the room. Each step brought the two of them closer and closer. When the android passed near enough to touch, Picard lashed out with one arm. The fingers of his hand wrapped around Data's wrist, just inches away from the Heart.

Picard worked to keep his voice steady. "I still haven't discovered the reason for the Heart's journey to this place. If only I could dream one more time . . ."

"Captain, we agreed that it would be best if I retain possession of the Heart. I do not think we should change that arrangement."

"Yes, I suppose you're right." Picard forced himself to release his hold on the android's arm and walk away.

Heedless of direction, the captain ended up at the ready room window. Picard studied the scene outside the starship to distract himself from regrets.

According to Worf's calculations, the comet was approaching perihelion, its closest distance to the white dwarf, and thus the height of brilliance for its gaseous tail.

Catching a glimpse of the Heart's reflection in the window, Picard's thoughts rocketed back to the events of the last hour. On the bridge, when the time came to actually let go of the stone, he had tried to fend off Data. Only the android's superior strength had ensured that the staged event was resolved according to plan.

"Data, you'd better leave—"

"Bridge to Captain Picard," called out Riker. *"Sensors have detected an ion disturbance off the port bow."*

Somewhere beyond the comet, Picard spotted a pinprick of gleaming light. It was surrounded by a shimmering aura of radiant energy.

"Indications are that a wormhole is forming out there."

"A wormhole?" whispered Picard to himself.

A split second later, the pinprick expanded into a glowing sphere, then exploded outward. He found himself staring into the gaping maw of a tunnel that had bored its way through light-years of space.

"Data, that's it!" Picard marveled at the ingenuity of those who had built the Guardian of Forever. "The comet is merely a herald for the wormhole's appearance. If the Heart passes through that cosmic gate, it will be sown in some far distant galaxy."

"That is an interesting hypothesis, Captain."

"No, Data, this is more than just a theory; it is the fulfillment of a dream." Tapping his comm insignia, the captain said, "Picard to transporter chief. Mr. O'Brien, I have one last miracle for you to perform."

Moments later, Picard listened to the high whine of the transporter beam at his back. Without looking, he knew, he could feel in his very bones, that Data's hands were now empty.

Pressing his palms flat against the window's cold surface, the captain searched in vain for some glimpse of the Heart's reappearance. The stone was too small and too dark for him to trace its passage through the vast tunnel.

As the comet passed perihelion and began its long fall toward night, the ring of the wormhole rippled and quavered, then collapsed. This fleeting channel into another galaxy was gone, and it would not return for another five thousand years.

With the shuddering breath of a man waking from a long sleep, Picard pulled away from the window.

"Our part in this story has ended now, Data."

CHAPTER 34

"We are being hailed by the unDiWahn," said Worf. Picard nodded and turned toward the main viewscreen.

With one word, Kieradán could order his forces to advance and destroy the *Enterprise* in a storm of fire. Picard had accepted his own death as the price for the Heart's escape, but the loss of his ship and crew filled him with bitter regret.

The master appeared. His face bore a serene smile.

"Good-bye, Gem-Bearer," said Kieradán. "Our guardianship is over, so it is time for us to leave this place."

Before the captain could reply, the leader of the Faithful had faded off the bridge viewscreen, displaced by an image of deep space.

"Do you think he means it?" asked Riker. "Are they really leaving?"

The captain nodded. Somehow the unDiWahn had sensed the stone's passage through the wormhole. He would have expected knowledge of its loss to trigger a violent retaliation against the *Enterprise,* yet Kieradán had addressed him with respect. Gem-Bearer. It seemed a hollow title to Picard now that the Heart was gone.

A patch of color flashed across the screen, then another. One by one, the unDiWahn ships were breaking away from their spherical formation to gather around their flagship. When the last vessel had reached the tail end of the swarm, they all took flight. Soon distance worked its magic, and the deadly fleet was transformed into a cloud of butterflies fluttering away on a summer breeze.

In their wake, however, the Faithful had left behind a lumbering stepchild.

"We are being hailed by the USS *Sullivan*," announced Worf.

"On screen, Lieutenant."

The view shifted once again, this time to the bridge of a starship. Picard winced when he took a close look at the man sitting in the captain's chair. He had a greenish-purple bruise on his forehead and a jagged scratch down one cheek. "You look like hell, Richard."

"Oh, these are old wounds, Jean-Luc," said Captain Mycelli, shrugging off his injuries. "As soon as the unDiWahn fleet cut loose, the Dynasians surrendered peacefully. I'm back in command of the *Sullivan*."

"Do you need additional security?" asked Riker.

"No, the ringleader is in custody, and . . ." Mycelli was rendered speechless by the sight of Data returning to his place at the helm. He stared at the android for several seconds, then looked back to Picard. "I look forward to reading your mission report, Captain."

"I'm sure you're not the only one, Captain," said Picard with a wry smile. To his relief, however, Mycelli did not ask for details, and the exchange of further amenities was brief.

"Number One," said Picard when contact with the *Sullivan* had ended, "it's time for us to leave as well."

Lowering himself into the captain's chair, Picard let his first officer arrange the details of their departure. Orders and confirmations echoed across the bridge until Data said, "Course laid in for Vulcan."

The crew fell silent.

Picard had tested their loyalty to the limit on this mission, so he could hardly resent their anxiety as they waited for him to utter one crucial word.

"Engage."

Anger was not a useful emotion for a diplomat, reflected Ambassador Tommas as she entered the security complex of the *Sullivan.* Allowing such a simplistic emotion to overwhelm her thoughts would only hinder her analysis of the Dynasian situation.

Damn him!

The hijacking of the starship was essentially a political act, yet she had been personally betrayed by Warden Chandat's actions. Trust was an integral component of forging ties between the member planets of the Federation, and that link began between individuals. How could she reconcile her deep respect for Keyda Chandat with the unpleasant fact that he had taken advantage of her overtures of friendship?

Steeling herself for the coming confrontation, Tommas stepped up to the portal of a security cell. On the other side of the glowing frame, the warden was seated on a narrow cot. Some prisoners might slump or lounge in captivity, but he held himself erect, as if overseeing an invisible council. Even in detention the man appeared to be in complete control of his surroundings; however, his followers were not so self-assured. After Chandat's surrender, any effective resistance from the other academics had collapsed entirely.

"Good evening, Ambassador," said Chandat with a gracious nod of his head.

Tommas could not bring herself to echo the warden's civility. "For the Faculty's crime against Starfleet, our Council has ruled that Dynasia will be barred from admission to the Federation for at least a century."

"A century?" He appeared curiously unruffled by this lengthy sentence of punishment. If anything, the corners of his mouth turned upward with smug satisfaction.

"Warden, I don't believe you comprehend the severity of your offenses."

"Of course, I do, Ambassador." Uttering a sigh of exasperation, the Dynasian leaned forward and spoke in the didactic tone of a professor instructing an especially dim student. "A century of grace will ease the pressures that have splintered the Faculty into warring factions. With time, when the conservative members have all died off, a new generation of Dynasians may choose to reapply for admission to the Federation . . . and deserve it."

For the first time, Tommas realized how seriously she had underestimated the warden's commitment to his people. "You planned this outcome from the beginning."

Chandat's smile broadened. "My scheme was nearly undone by the appearance of the unDiWahn, but fortunately Captain Picard's clever ruse convinced them to retreat, and it gave me an excuse to surrender the *Sullivan*. Historians may record this foiled grab for the Gem as my greatest failure, yet the stone has granted me my heart's desire: I have restored peace to my planet."

As a counterpoint to inner reflection, the ancient Iconian engineers had also designed an observation chamber for looking outward. The room was missing any flight controls, so the curving transparent walls served no functional purpose beyond fostering contemplation of the universe. Kieradán was deeply grateful for the change of scenery after the prolonged examination of his own soul. Over the days of their return journey to DiWahn, he would have the freedom to enjoy this expansive vista of stars.

The admiral of the fleet was less inclined to philosophical musings. After a cursory glance to check the formation of the armada trailing behind the flagship, Daramadán continued his argument against their retreat. "But Master, the powers of the Gem could have carried our people back to the grandeur of our Iconian ancestors."

"We fell from that height because Jiak held on to the Gem too long. Our duty as Guardians was to make atonement for his misjudgment, not to repeat past mistakes."

This had been the consensus of a long line of masters, and

Kieradán had adhered to the spirit, if not the letter, of their directive. He had forsaken the honor of personally sending the Gem on its way through the wormhole, but then he had also avoided the temptation to keep it for another five thousand years.

A heavy sigh from Daramadán signaled an acceptance, if not an understanding, of his leader's wisdom. "Having left this battlefield empty-handed, must the Order of the Faithful disband?"

"No, Admiral, there is a great deal of work still to be done. A new era has begun for the descendants of dead Iconia. You and I will return to a country that is at peace with its neighbors for the first time in centuries; your fleet will serve the needs of our planet, not a war-mongering king. Our store of knowledge will be shared with all who seek it."

Iconia's scattered children had spent too many centuries resisting their fate. With some sadness, but even greater pride, Master Kieradán announced, "The unDiWahn are now the DiWahn."

Ten-Forward provided one of the best scenic views aboard the *Enterprise,* but tonight Picard had been unsettled by a sense of vulnerability when he entered the lounge. Halfway through dinner, he angled his chair to avoid looking out the spacious windows. After that, his sense of dread gradually dissipated.

"Earl Grey?" asked Guinan as she passed by the table.

"Yes, please," said Picard. "Most definitely Earl Grey."

For some reason the mention of tea touched off the memory of a sharp, bitter taste. The basis of this odd association hovered just out of reach.

"Jean-Luc?"

He blinked, then realized that he had been staring at his dinner companion without truly seeing her. At least Beverly was smiling at his distraction. It was a generous reaction considering he had invited the doctor to join him, then proceeded to lapse into longer and longer silences.

"Jean-Luc, why don't we—"

"Here you are." Guinan set a steaming cup of tea down in front of the captain, then rushed away before he could thank her. She had been especially attentive this evening, which was her way of expressing affection.

Picard wrapped his hands around the warm, round cup. "You were saying?"

"Hmm? I don't remember."

"Why don't we . . ." he prompted.

"Oh, yes. Why don't we call it a night. You're obviously exhausted."

He fought against the sudden urge to yawn, but lost. When his mouth had stopped its convulsive gaping, he said, "I suppose you're right. I have quite a bit of sleep to catch up on."

This admission of weariness seemed to sap away the last of his strength. He tried to sip his tea, but the weight of the cup was too much for him to lift more than a few inches off the table.

"Come on, Captain," said Beverly, rising from her chair. "I'll see you to your cabin."

"According to ancient etiquette," muttered Picard, "that's supposed to be *my* line." Despite this half-hearted protest, he let the doctor take hold of his arm and guide him out of Ten-Forward.

By the time they had threaded their way through the ship's corridors to the door of his cabin, Picard could barely lift his feet. Beverly propelled him through the open threshold with a gentle push, and he stumbled to the bedroom with his eyes already half-closed in anticipation of sleep.

He threw himself down on the bed without bothering to undress, but even though his body was spent, his mind clung tenaciously to consciousness.

For the first time since he had touched the Heart, he was alone in the darkened cabin.

No more dreams . . .

After its long fight to reach the wormhole, the seed was

working its way toward another world. Someday it would land on alien soil, and a new Guardian would grow to maturity, crystal by crystal.

Picard's hands clenched, then relaxed. The aching hunger to touch the Heart's rough surface was fading away.

His sharply etched memories of other hands that had cupped its weight—of Kessec and Halaylah, of a dying Andorian healer and an exultant Romulan queen—all these were dimming as well. He could recall the shriveled face of the Collector in her chamber, but he had lost the image of her in life; and there had been a young Vulcan scrambling through a field of fallen soldiers, but Picard no longer remembered where the boy was going or why.

Ko N'ya. One bearer lingered long enough in his mind to whisper its name for the last time.

"It's gone, T'Sara," said Picard softly. "The blood has finally stopped flowing."

Then he fell into a dreamless sleep.

Epilogue

Camenae snapped the towel into the air to shake off any dust, then plucked a tumbler out of the shipping carton and wiped away the packing foam. When the glass sparkled once again, she tucked it into a low shelf beneath the bar.

Guinan had donated the glassware to the new venture; Anlew-Is had imported the counter from Orion in payment of his past debts; and the two tables and five chairs in the middle of the lounge were on temporary loan from the Starfleet office. Miyakawa had cheerfully acknowledged that she wouldn't have time to sit down for at least the next two years.

Camenae snapped the towel again, then picked up a long-stemmed wineglass. Although the commander was driving the base reconstruction effort with a manic zeal that probably would win her a promotion to commodore before the year was out, a few amenities were still lacking. Sonic dishwashers, for instance.

The doors to the room slid open, and a young man peered inside. He hesitated for a moment, taken aback by the sparsely furnished interior, then evidently took courage from the presence of other customers and crossed the threshold.

The Do or Die was not officially open for business, but a

few people had already drifted inside this morning, content just to sit and talk. There was only one familiar face in the group of Rigelians who had settled at one table. Some of the old customers had been killed when Smelter's Hold was destroyed; others, like the bartender, had left during the evacuation and never bothered to come back. Camenae could have used some extra help with setting up the new establishment, but unfortunately Miyakawa paid better wages.

The newcomer sidled up to the bar. At close quarters, he looked even younger than she had first thought. Beneath the furrows of his brow, his round face wore the anxious, earnest look of a child trying to act like an adult.

He tossed a credit chip onto the counter with an awkward imitation of nonchalance.

Camenae glanced down at the payment, then smiled. "My drinks aren't that expensive."

"I didn't come here for a drink. I heard you could give me some information." He shoved the credit chip closer to her.

"What kind of information do you want?" she asked.

"I'm trying to find a Vulcan named T'Sara."

With a sigh, Camenae said, "I can't take your money for that information. Everyone on this starbase has heard of T'Sara's death."

The boy's violet skin flushed a deep indigo, and he bowed his head as if in sorrow.

"I'm sorry," she said, with a frown of discomfort at his reaction. "I didn't realize you knew her."

"I didn't." Yet when he lifted his head, his eyes were filled with pain. "I read that she once visited my homeworld, and I had hoped to talk to her about her trip."

Camenae expected the boy to take back the credit chip and leave, but he swallowed hard and dropped his voice to a conspiratorial whisper. "So tell me about the Dream Gem instead. I need to know where it is."

Camenae finished polishing the wineglass, then she slid the chip back across the counter. "You're in luck. Someone else has already paid that bill, and she gave me permission to answer your question free of charge."

His eyes brightened with anticipation.

"The Gem is gone," said Camenae. "Gone beyond the reach of any being in this galaxy."

He shook his head angrily, refusing to believe. She shrugged and picked up yet another glass to clean.

"You don't understand—I must find it!" said the young man.

"And if you don't?"

"I must! The Gem is a part of my heritage. It once belonged to my people, and I would give my life for the chance to get it back."

"You're too late to make that sacrifice." Camenae stopped in mid-motion. "Why does this mean so much to you?"

At first it seemed the boy would not answer, but at last he said, "T'Sara would have understood . . . I'm the last of the Ikkabar and . . ." Some strong emotion choked off his next words.

"No, don't stop now," said Camenae softly. "Tell me more. Perhaps I can help."

She set aside the glass, leaned her elbows on the bar counter, and began to listen.